The Living Room

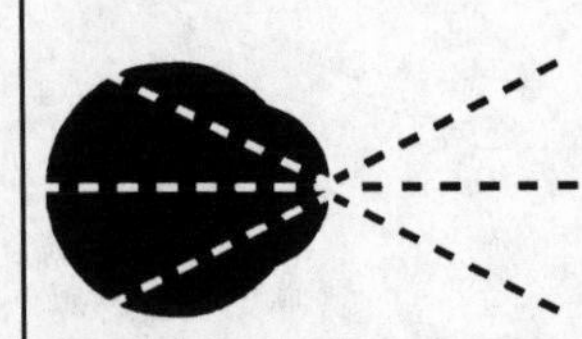

This Large Print Book carries the Seal of Approval of N.A.V.H.

The Living Room

Robert Whitlow

THORNDIKE PRESS
A part of Gale, Cengage Learning

GALE
CENGAGE Learning

Detroit • New York • San Francisco • New Haven, Conn • Waterville, Maine • London

Thorndike Press, a part of Gale, Cengage Learning.

Thorndike Press® Large Print Christian Mystery.
The text of this Large Print edition is unabridged.
Other aspects of the book may vary from the original edition.
Set in 16 pt. Plantin.

LIBRARY OF CONGRESS CATALOGING-IN-PUBLICATION DATA

Whitlow, Robert, 1954–
The living room / by Robert Whitlow. — Large print edition.
pages ; cm. — (Thorndike Press large print Christian mystery)
ISBN 978-1-4104-6071-4 (hardcover) — ISBN 1-4104-6071-1 (hardcover)
1. Large type books. I. Title.
PS3573.H49837L58 2013b
813'.54—dc23 2013026225

Published in 2013 by arrangement with Thomas Nelson, Inc.

Printed in Mexico
1 2 3 4 5 6 7 17 16 15 14 13

To creative people. You are made in the image of your Creator.
May your dreams become reality.

When you send your Spirit, they are created, and you renew the face of the earth.

— PSALM 104:30

One

Amy couldn't resist visiting the final scene of the novel one last time. Repositioning her long legs on the leather ottoman, she pushed her straight brown hair behind her ears and adjusted her brown-framed glasses. She shifted her laptop so the sunlight streaming through the window didn't wash out the words on the screen:

> For a few anxious moments I couldn't find Rick among the crowd of passengers making their way across the tarmac.
>
> Then I saw him.
>
> He was walking slowly, his right leg dragging slightly behind him, his left arm immobilized in a sling and strapped close to his body. As always, his khaki uniform was neatly ironed and creased. He was staring intently toward the terminal building. I knew he was looking for me.
>
> Tears, a mixture of joy that he was alive and sorrow at the pain he'd endured,

streamed down my cheeks. I bowed my head in thankfulness and leaned my forehead against the window glass for a second. I glanced up as he reached the terminal and quickly dried my eyes. Rick's first sight of my face should be filled with nothing but welcoming love. He held the door open with his good arm to let an elderly woman pass through ahead of him, then followed her into the baggage claim area. I cried out in a loud voice that couldn't hide the anguished longing of my heart.

"Rick!"

He turned his head. And in that instant everyone and everything else in the airport vanished. Rick was home. The sleepless nights and lonely days were over. The fretful hours sitting at the computer waiting for an e-mail had ended. Ten thousand prayers that he would come home to me were answered.

We met at the end of the baggage carousel. A red light flashed as the carousel noisily started to turn, but nothing existed in my world except Rick. He held out his right arm and wrapped it around me as I buried my face in his shoulder. Now my tears could flow without spoiling the moment. I raised my head, and our lips met.

"It's you," I said softly when our lips parted.

"I came home, just as I promised," he said.

"Yes."

"Thank you for waiting, Kelli."

"Wait," I repeated, shaking my head. "That's a word I don't want to think about or hear for a long time."

Rick smiled.

"Our new word is 'now,' " he said.

I gently touched his left arm.

"How is it?"

"Not much use to me yet," he said with a shrug. "The doctors say the shrapnel severed a nerve. Other nerves will try to take up the slack, but it will take a long time to see how much strength and mobility I get back."

"I'm sorry. I wish it could have been me."

"No!" Rick's face grew serious. "I went over there to keep something like this from happening to you. Knowing I was protecting you kept me strong."

There was more strength in Rick's little finger than most men had in their entire being.

"Do you know what I thought about when I was lying on the ground waiting for the helicopter to rescue me?" he continued.

He reached into the front pocket of his uniform and took out a worn sheet of paper. It had been opened and closed so many times that there were tiny rips at the crease lines. Instantly, I knew what it was. He handed it to me, and I cradled the sheet as gently as I would an ancient parchment.

Penned in my best handwriting were the words of the verse I'd given him the night before he left. One corner of the paper was stained dark brown. I stared at the corner.

"Is this —" I stopped.

"Yes, but that's not what I want you to see. Read the words. I want to hear them in your voice."

I took a deep breath. " 'The eternal God is your refuge, and underneath are the everlasting arms. Deuteronomy 33:27.' "

"My arm may be weak," Rick said, touching his left shoulder, "but his arms stayed strong."

"I needed them too," I said softly.

We kissed again. I tucked my hands beneath Rick's right elbow.

"And now his arms are going to keep us together," I said. "Forever."

The voice of Ian, Amy's ten-year-old son, shattered the moment.

"Mom!"

Amy lowered the screen of the laptop.

"I'm in the writing room!" she called out.

Ian's feet pounded up the steep, ladder-like steps. Amy's husband, Jeff, had converted a corner of the attic into a private place for Amy to read, work, and pray.

"We're out of milk," Ian panted when his freckled face came into view. "And there is only one cookie left in the jar. Me and Bobby are hungry."

"Bobby and I are hungry," Amy corrected him.

"Bobby and I are hungry," he responded dutifully, "but that doesn't make there be any more cookies in the jar."

"I baked two dozen oatmeal raisin cookies on Wednesday. What happened to them?"

"Ask Megan." Ian looked down at his scuffed sneakers. "She was in the kitchen with a bunch of her friends yesterday while you were up here. Maybe they ate them."

Amy set her computer aside and got up from the chair. She knew she'd neglected her family. The final edits of her second novel had consumed every spare moment during the past three weeks. She'd challenged adverbs, mercilessly shortened narrative paragraphs, and made countless changes designed to increase microtension on every page. Finally, she spent two whole days on the last chapter. An emotional payoff at the end of a contemporary romance novel is crucial. She hoped the scene in the airport was a satisfying cherry on top of the fictional sundae.

"My book is done," she said, getting up from the chair. "From now on I'll have the time to make sure we have plenty of milk and cookies in this house."

"Yeah!" Ian responded.

"And fresh fruit," Amy added. "Why don't you eat a banana? I know there are bananas on the rack next to the microwave."

"Bobby doesn't eat bananas. He likes apples."

"Okay. I'll come to the kitchen in a minute and help you find a snack."

Ian bounded down the steps and out of sight. Amy followed, keeping a tight grip on the handrail. Ian had the nimble balance of a gazelle. Jeff was convinced their son's combination of strength and agility would translate into high school football stardom with a possible college scholarship. Amy didn't like the thought of eleven muscular brutes trying to slam her baby violently to the ground. She could casually allow the male lead in her novel to be seriously wounded by a rocket-propelled grenade, but when it came to her son being tackled in real life on a grassy gridiron, she was as protective as a mother bear.

The second floor of the narrow house contained three bedrooms. The master suite was beneath the writing room. Two other bedrooms were down a narrow hallway. Ian's bedroom was next to his parents' room. Megan, age fourteen, had turned the third bedroom into a private world she preferred to keep off-limits to the rest of the family. When guests from out of town came for a visit, Ian gave up his room and slept on a trundle bed.

The stairway from the second floor ended

at one end of the large, rectangular family room. To the left of the family room was the eat-in kitchen. Except for Megan, the Clarke family spent most of their waking hours in the kitchen and the family room.

Ian was balancing on the arm of a dining room chair trying to open the door of one of the top row of cabinets. Bobby stood beside the chair, holding it steady.

"Ian, what are you doing?" Amy asked. "Get down before you fall! There's nothing you need up there."

"That's where Daddy hides those chocolate peanut things he eats after I go to bed," Ian replied from his perch above her head.

"And he's all out until I go to the grocery store."

Ian jumped from the arm of the chair and landed cat-like on the floor. Bobby, who idolized Ian, watched in awe. Amy rubbed the top of Bobby's closely trimmed brown hair.

"Let me see if I can find an apple."

There was a solitary apple in the vegetable keeper of the refrigerator. Amy pressed the skin. The flesh was still firm.

"I'll cut this into pieces," she said.

"Can we share the last cookie?" Ian asked.

"After you eat the apple."

Standing at the sink, Amy looked across the front yard toward Canterbury Lane, the neighborhood street that ran in front of their house. Ninety miles southeast of Raleigh,

Cross Plains, North Carolina, was in the middle of the sandhills region of the state. With its slender pine trees and loamy soil, the town bore no similarity to the English countryside, but that didn't keep the subdivision's developer from borrowing street names from famous English locations. Amy's best friend, Natalie Graham, lived a few blocks to the east on Devonshire Way. Amy cut the apple into four identical slices and handed two to each boy.

"My mom just finished writing her new book," Ian said to Bobby as he munched on one of his pieces of apple.

"My folks keep the one you signed for my mama on the table in the living room," Bobby said in his slow drawl.

Amy smiled. A trade paper novel, even if autographed by the author, wasn't exactly display material for a formal living room.

"That's very sweet of her."

"My daddy started to read it," Bobby continued as he took a bite of apple, "but he didn't finish it. He has a big stack of hunting and fishing magazines that he looks at all the time."

"Because he likes to hunt and fish," Amy replied. "People read what interests them. If I ever write about a man who loves the outdoors, I'll be sure to talk to your daddy about it."

"Did Mr. Clarke read your book?" Bobby asked.

"Of course." Amy winced.

Jeff had enough husband sense not to complain when Amy asked him to read the manuscript of her first novel. The occasional sighs that came from his chair while he turned the pages communicated all she needed to know. For him, reading a romance novel was in the same category as going to the dentist for a root canal.

"Is Dad going to read the new one?" Ian asked as he popped the last piece of apple into his mouth.

"That's up to him. One of the main characters is in the army, and I used information he told me to make the story more realistic. A writer has to do research to make sure a book is accurate."

Amy broke the cookie in two and handed a piece to each boy. Ian gave her a puzzled look.

"I thought you got your ideas when you were dreaming?" he asked.

Amy caught Ian's eye and quickly shook her head. Bobby didn't seem to notice.

"You boys go outside," she said. "It's not going to be this warm in a couple of weeks."

There was a scuffed-up football on the floor in the corner of the kitchen. Ian picked it up and twirled it around a few times on the tip of his index finger. It was a trick he'd seen an NFL quarterback perform on TV, and he'd practiced until he could do it, too.

"You can be quarterback first, and I'll be the wide receiver," Ian said to Bobby. "I've figured out a new pass play we can use during recess at school."

The boys ran out of the kitchen. Amy took the broom from the closet and swept the kitchen floor. It needed to be mopped, but there was no use doing it now. The boys would return shortly with bits of dirt stuck to their sneakers.

Completing the novel was bittersweet. Amy would miss the daily interaction with her fictional friends. Much of her life, even before she became a novelist, had been spent in her imagination, and it was the place where she felt most comfortable. During the months it took to write a book, the characters she created were her closest companions. They ate together, lived through trials and hardships, laughed, cried, and interacted with the Lord. Although not strictly autobiographical, the main character in both her novels reflected Amy's personality — a veiled public expression of her private self. And like a woman giving birth to a child, Amy sacrificed a part of herself to bring forth the book to a waiting world.

Writing had also opened the door for a shy, reserved person like Amy to interact from a safe distance with a multitude of people she didn't know and communicate with them at the intimate level reserved for the readers' own minds. The end result was a tremendous opportunity to bless people. She could influence total strangers for good without having to leave the security of her attic writing room.

Amy thought again about the airport reunion between Kelli and Rick as she used the broom to dislodge a few bits of food from the corner of the room. Her cell phone on the counter vibrated, and a picture of her agent, Bernie Masters, came up on the screen. In the photo, the balding, overweight man was holding an advance copy of *A Great and Precious Promise,* Amy's first novel.

"Hey, Bernie," Amy said. "Good timing. I finished the final line edit of the new novel about fifteen minutes ago, and I'm ready to send it to the publisher. I'll pop off an e-mail to Cecilia thanking her for the editorial help and letting her know the manuscript is coming."

"Great. Have you been to your mailbox?"

"No. Why?"

"The royalty check paid this quarter for *A Great and Precious Promise* isn't going to overwhelm you."

Amy glanced at the calendar on the wall of the kitchen. She'd not realized it was time for a sales update.

"I haven't gotten the statement," she said.

"Mine landed on my desk ten minutes

before I called. I didn't want you to be shocked."

"Shocked?"

"Yeah. The total paid for the quarter was $843. After deducting my fifteen percent, your check will be $716.55."

Amy leaned against the kitchen counter. "I brought home more than that working two weeks for the law firm."

"Which is why most writers don't quit their day jobs. But it's not your fault. Listen, I know you don't want to make the publisher mad by complaining, but it's my job to speak up for you. Just because a novel has cleared advance isn't an excuse to drop the ball on marketing. If you give me the green light, I'll go straight to Dave and find out what's going on."

Dave Coley, the head of the publishing company, was a dour-faced man who rarely smiled.

"I don't want to risk having them decide not to exercise the option for a third book," Amy said.

"Don't let fear dictate what we do. We have to hold the publisher's feet to the marketing fire. *A Great and Precious Promise* earned back the advance in a little over twelve months. Less than half the novels in this market ever dig out of that hole. My beef is with the lack of ongoing publicity and marketing efforts. You're a fresh talent that deserves a chance to shine."

Amy appreciated Bernie's zeal, especially considering that his part of the royalty check was only slightly more than a hundred dollars.

"And *The Everlasting Arms* is going to solidify your brand and enable you to go to a much higher sales level," he added.

"You haven't read it yet."

"I looked at the synopsis and first three chapters. There's an immediate hook with the conflict between Kelli, Rick, and the old boyfriend with cancer who comes back into her life. A snappy beginning is the key to any story. After a reader swallows the hook, you can drag them anyplace you want."

Bernie's use of clichés and disconnected metaphors was his trademark.

"The ending is important, too," Amy said. "And the spiritual message."

"Sure, so long as the couple lives happily ever after."

"Rick has permanent nerve damage from his battle wounds. Will that spoil the happy ending?"

"No way. That gives Kelli an excuse to baby him. Women readers love a strong man with just enough weakness to need the feminine touch. Believe me, your new book is going to hit a huge, fat sweet spot in the market."

"I don't exactly say that Kelli is going to baby Rick," Amy replied, still stuck on

Bernie's previous comment.

"It's implied. And if I got the message from the synopsis, don't you think your intuitive female readers will, too?"

"I'll ask Cecilia about it when we talk about the manuscript. Her insights and suggestions about both novels have been so helpful. I don't know where I'd be without her."

"Do whatever you want, but don't slow down the printing press with more revisions. We need to get this book into the stores as soon as possible." Bernie paused. "When are you going to start book number three?"

Amy almost dropped the phone.

"I thought I'd bake a batch of cookies first," she managed.

"Buck up. You're a professional now with two books under your belt. Remember, a writer isn't a writer except on the days she turns on the computer and cranks out at least a few decent paragraphs."

"I know, but I don't have an idea for the next novel. I haven't given it any thought because I didn't want to be distracted."

"And the ability to focus is one of your strengths. Don't take me wrong. I'm just doing my job. Most cheerleaders have hair on their heads, not their legs, but I'm going to do my best to keep you moving forward."

An image of Bernie Masters in a cheerleading uniform flashed before Amy's eyes. She smiled.

"Thanks, Bernie. I promise I'll start praying about my next novel. You should pray, too."

"My skills lie elsewhere. And hear me on this. I'm not going to let the publisher lie down like a camel in the middle of the road. You did your part delivering a good, solid book. Their job is to make sure it's on the bookstore shelves and has a strong presence in the e-book market. As soon as Cecilia accepts the manuscript for the new novel, I'll give Dave a call."

"And be nice."

"I won't yell. And get back to me as soon as you have an idea for the next novel. You've primed the pump and need to keep the water flowing."

The call ended, and Amy placed her phone on the counter. Bernie didn't know it, but the theme and title for each of Amy's novels weren't the result of brainstorming in the writing room, searching the Internet for something that jump-started her creative juices, or flipping through the Bible until a verse caught her eye. Amy was a gifted person with a fertile imagination, but the genesis for her writing came from another source.

If Amy was going to start writing another book, the first thing she needed to do was fall asleep.

Two

For most of her life, Amy had known the difference between the chaotic activity that takes place in a regular dream and the serene order of a spiritual one. Regular dreams could be the result of too much pepperoni on a pizza, the unconscious release of pent-up stress, an attempt to work through a real-life problem, or any one of countless other possibilities. Amy rarely remembered the details of regular dreams. Spiritual dreams were less common and much more memorable.

As a small child, Amy had a series of almost identical dreams in which she found herself in an empty, windowless room with shimmering walls. The best way she could describe the setting to her mother was that the walls seemed to be breathing. And with a child's literalism, Amy started calling the place "the living room."

Just being there was so wonderful that Amy did nothing except bask in the moment. It was a place with fragrant air, clear light, and a presence that permeated her being. No matter how long the dream lasted or what happened during it, Amy never wanted to leave, and she treasured the lingering influence that remained after she awoke.

When she learned about heaven in Sunday school, Amy had no problem believing Christians could be completely satisfied in a place God had prepared for them. The story of Adam and Eve in the Garden of Eden made perfect sense to her. Human beings were made to be with their Creator. Only in constant communion and fellowship with him could people be fully alive and totally fulfilled.

Her mother warned her not to talk openly about her dreams, but in childlike enthusiasm Amy mentioned her dreams to a friendly Sunday school teacher. The teacher passed along the information to the church pastor. Soon thereafter, the pastor pulled Amy and her parents aside after a Sunday morning service. Amy couldn't hear what the grown-ups discussed, but her mother sat her down when they got home and sternly told her to keep quiet about her dream life.

The other times Amy said something to friends or relatives about her dreams, she received strange looks or comments about her vivid imagination. Eventually, she stopped trying to share what was so intensely private and precious. Words couldn't adequately describe the supernatural. The human mind isn't naturally programmed to comprehend spiritual experiences.

When she was twelve, Amy had her first spiritual dream that was both visual and auditory. A tall, skinny, introverted girl with a mild acne problem, Amy was going through the intense insecurity common to preteen girls who don't have a perfect body shape and bubbly personality. One night, as she was leaving the living room, she heard a penetrating voice say, *He brought me to the banqueting house, and his banner over me was love.* The words from the dream wrapped themselves around her like an affirming blanket. Amy found the passage in her Bible, wrote down the verse on an index card, and carried it with her for more than a year. The message reminded her that no matter how her peers treated her, there was a loving Father who accepted her, and he had prepared a place for her to be with him.

During her teenage years, the number of living room dreams decreased and eventually stopped. Amy was deeply disappointed, but her mother received the news with relief. She told Amy the nighttime experiences had probably been a unique form of the imaginary friend phenomenon common among little girls. Amy, who had two imaginary friends, listened but didn't agree. She knew the difference between make-believe and reality.

The summer before her senior year in high school, Amy landed a job as a counselor at a Christian camp for girls in the mountains of North Carolina. It was the first time she had been away from home for an extended period of time. Homesickness hit her as hard as it did some of the young campers.

Each night of the week there was a program held in an open-air pavilion. A speaker at the end of the first week challenged the girls whether their relationship with Christ was their own or something passed down from their parents. Amy's heart was touched. Pushing away her shyness and swallowing her pride, she joined a number of campers at the front of the meeting. The speaker prayed with her.

That night Amy had a living room dream. She found herself in the familiar place, yet she saw it through maturer eyes that could better appreciate the life it contained. Divine refreshment filled her soul like a cool drink on a hot day.

She awoke to tears of joy rolling down the sides of her face. She no longer felt homesick; she'd come home.

Jeff and Megan walked into the house as Amy put a potato casserole in the oven. Jeff gave Amy a quick peck on the lips that bore little resemblance to the passionate reunion between Kelli and Rick at the airport. Amy patted her husband's broad shoulders. His first name was printed on the shirt issued by the window installation company where he worked as a foreman.

"The book is done," she said. "I sent it to Cecilia Davidson about an hour ago."

"Congrats."

Rick flipped through the stack of mail on the kitchen counter.

"Speaking of books, isn't it time for a royalty check?" he asked.

"I put it in the bill drawer beside the computer in the family room," Amy said, turning away from him toward the oven.

"How much was it?"

"Later," she replied cryptically.

Megan was standing in front of the open refrigerator door. Tall, slender, and graceful, Megan's hair stretched down her back.

"Tell me about dance class," Amy said to her. "How is Ms. Carlton's ankle?"

"Okay."

Jeff handed Amy an envelope. "Ms. Carlton gave this to me while Megan was changing out of her leotards. There's going to be a big price increase at the studio beginning in January."

Megan had been taking dance lessons for five years. The cost of the classes was manageable when Amy worked as a secretary for a local law firm. Now, with her annual income cut by half, whether to continue the classes was a bimonthly discussion.

"Don't talk about money in front of me," Megan said, still peering into the open refrigerator. "We're out of cranberry juice. When are you going to the grocery store?"

"Tomorrow." Amy worked to keep her voice calm. She was determined not to let Megan bait her into an argument. "Put anything you need on the grocery list by the toaster."

Megan let the refrigerator door close on its own and left the room without adding anything to the list. Amy opened the notice from the dance studio and inhaled sharply.

"That's a twenty-five percent increase. Does Megan know?"

"Yes" — Jeff shrugged — "which was a mistake. She told me that dance is her life, and she's not going to give it up."

"Did you tell her she might have to stop?"

"No."

Amy ran her fingers through her hair. "But she assumed the worst and blames me because quitting my job has put us in a worse financial bind."

"That didn't come up. She said the studio is the only place where she feels good about herself. Then she clammed up."

Amy tensed. "That makes me wonder what's going on at school. If the kids were still at Broad Street Christian —"

"We'd be stuck in a duplex on the south side of town flushing rent money down the drain every month."

Jeff was right. It had taken three years to scrape together a down payment large enough to get them into the house. And that had been with Amy working full-time for the law firm. Private school tuition simply wasn't possible.

"Bernie is going to pressure the publisher to be more aggressive in marketing my books," Amy said hopefully. "He says my popularity should increase with the release of *The Everlasting Arms.*"

"I hope he's right. We blew through the money you got when you signed the contract because we thought you were going to be the next Karen what's her name."

"Kingsbury. And that's not true. She's in a different publishing universe than I am."

"Whatever. This time I'm going to include every penny of the book money in our budget."

Financial discussions upset Amy, but unlike Megan, she couldn't brush Jeff off. He worked hard at his hourly job, and to earn extra money bid on home remodeling jobs he performed on the weekends with a friend who was a contractor. She wanted him to know she was standing with him.

"How much was the royalty check?" he asked. "You may as well tell me."

"Over seven hundred dollars," Amy replied, trying to make the news sound positive.

"For three months?" Jeff opened his eyes wider. "Bernie said it would be several times that much."

"I know. That's probably one reason he called. He wanted to soften the blow."

Jeff dropped his head as if he'd been punched.

"I know I haven't had a lot of financial success yet," Amy said, determined to stay strong. "But I believe the most important thing is that people's lives are being changed. I got two e-mails today from women who were blessed and encouraged by *A Great and Precious Promise.*"

"Yeah, but it would be nice if you could be blessed in the here and now, not just later when you get to heaven." Jeff glanced through the opening between the kitchen and the family room. "But I have much worse news than an increase in the cost of dance lessons."

"You didn't lose your job, did you?" Amy's face turned pale.

"No, no, but Mr. Crouch had a meeting with all the employees when we got back to the shop. Beginning in January, we have to pay one hundred percent of our dependent health coverage. The company is only going to provide benefits for employees."

"How much will that cost us?"

"About five hundred dollars a month to insure you and the kids."

Amy didn't know what to say. The publisher

would pay a small advance for *The Everlasting Arms,* but she and Jeff had planned on using that money to pay year-end bills and buy Christmas gifts.

"Most companies quit underwriting family coverage years ago," Jeff continued. "I know Mr. Crouch didn't want to make a change, but he doesn't have a choice. The costs are going through the roof. He spoke to the foremen afterward and told us he was going to authorize as much overtime as the projects can support. That will help a little bit."

Amy stepped forward and put her arms around Jeff's neck.

"You work so hard," she said. "And I appreciate it. I'm trying to do my part, too."

Amy waited for Jeff to speak, but he didn't. If their dilemma had taken place in one of her books, they would have engaged in a heartfelt discussion about their unwavering love for each other and trust in God's faithfulness. But life doesn't always imitate art.

"I'd better get back to supper," she said, turning away.

"Yeah, I'm hungry. We were behind schedule today, and I only had fifteen minutes for lunch. Where's Ian?"

"I'm not sure. He's been in and out of the house all afternoon. Bobby was here for a couple of hours."

"I'll check the backyard," Jeff said.

He left Amy alone in the kitchen. Interacting with Ian was the only uncomplicated relationship in Jeff's life, and Amy knew it was both a joy and an escape for him. As she cut up tomatoes and cucumbers for a salad, she concentrated on the sharp knife. Jeff respected her dream to be a novelist and almost never complained about her time away from the family in the writing room, but above all else he was practical. He viewed her writing as a home-based job that needed to show a profit.

The incredible excitement she'd felt when Bernie called and told her a publishing company wanted to offer her a two-book contract had validated the lonely hours she'd devoted to creating a spec novel. Working full-time at the law firm, running a household, and trying to be a godly wife and mother while writing a book had been tough. Amy had turned down so many requests to volunteer at the church that the head of the women's council rarely talked to her.

She'd been surprised by the small size of the advance Bernie negotiated but accepted it as part of getting her foot in the door. Thousands of writers never even got an offer from a bona fide company. Then reality hit harder when Amy was told the initial print run would be thirty-five hundred copies. Where was Dave Coley's faith in her ability? Bernie stepped in and assured her that publishing companies kept their inventories low because books could be printed rapidly as demand increased. Also, the number of physical books shipped to brick-and-mortar bookstores was shrinking. With the explosive growth of the e-book market, a sale was only a mouse click away.

As she worked on *The Everlasting Arms,* Amy tried to keep her simmering frustration with the business aspects of writing from affecting the creative process. However, a seven-hundred-dollar royalty check and the disappointment in Jeff's face couldn't be ignored. She put down the knife and rested her hands on the kitchen counter.

"What am I doing?" she asked herself.

"Cutting up stuff for a salad," Megan responded in a puzzled voice.

Amy glanced over her shoulder. "And talking to myself. How was school?"

"Okay." Megan came into the kitchen and sat at the round table where the family ate most of their meals. "Mrs. Baumgartner is moving to Jacksonville. It has something to do with her husband getting a new job."

The history teacher's husband had been out of work for nine months.

"I'm glad he found a job but sorry she won't be your teacher."

"The new teacher was in class today. Bethany and I think he's going to be cool."

"A man?"

"Yeah, he's from somewhere out west,

maybe California or Colorado. I'm not sure. After class I heard him talking to a couple of the guys about surfing and snowboarding. He has gorgeous blond hair and blue eyes to die for."

"What's his name?"

"Mr. Ryan. Bethany and I are going to get to class early tomorrow and grab seats up front."

"I just hope he can teach world history." Amy scraped the tomatoes and cucumbers onto the top of the lettuce in a large white salad bowl. "Do you want a hard-boiled egg in your salad? Your dad and Ian won't eat any, but I'll be glad to —"

"Are you really going to make me quit dance lessons?" Megan interrupted.

Amy placed the salad bowl on the counter and gave Megan her full attention.

"You're a talented dancer, and I know how important dance is to you. The solo jazz routine you did last spring was fantastic. You received the only standing ovation in the entire program. But we're going to have to discuss what to do about the future."

Amy braced herself for an explosion that didn't come. Instead, Megan spoke slowly and calmly.

"How would you feel if Dad told you that you had to quit writing books and go back to work because you're not making as much money as you used to?"

"Uh, we'd have to discuss that, too."

"Are you going to?"

"We talk about everything."

Megan sniffed. Amy knew she wasn't buying the claim that her parents had a perfect marriage communication model. It's hard to bluff a fourteen-year-old girl.

"You have your talent. I have mine," Megan continued. "Is it fair for you to get to do what you want and I can't?"

Hurt welled up inside Amy. She'd sacrificed so much for her children that it stung to have her commitment questioned. The small amount of the recent royalty check made her feel especially vulnerable. But it wasn't a time to show personal insecurity or wounded feelings.

"I hear what you're saying," Amy replied, hoping her voice didn't shake. "And I appreciate how much you've thought it out."

Ian came running into the kitchen.

"Is supper ready?" he asked.

Amy glanced at the timer on the oven.

"Ten minutes. Where's your dad?"

"With I. He sent me in here to find out."

"With me," Amy corrected.

"I didn't think it sounded right, but that's not what you told me this afternoon."

Ian ran out, and Megan stood up.

"I hate it when we talk in circles," Megan said. "It makes me not want to come out of my room to try and have a conversation."

"I want to hear what you think," Amy said. "And if we don't talk, I'll have to guess how you're feeling. Let's pray together before you go to sleep tonight."

Megan gave Amy a look that let her know she doubted God would take time out of his busy schedule to devote his attention to dance class. The nights when Amy and Megan would kneel beside Megan's bed and pray were a fading memory. Now Amy wasn't sure what her daughter believed.

"Nothing will be done about dance until after Christmas," Amy said quickly. "That's when the price increase kicks in."

"Is that a promise?" Megan shot back.

"Yes."

"Then tell Grandma and Grandpa Clarke and Granny Edwards all I want for Christmas is money for dance lessons." Megan paused. "And from Uncle Bob and Aunt Pat, too. No gift cards to stores where I don't shop or lame presents I have to pretend to like."

Megan left the kitchen with a lightness in her step. Amy leaned against the counter and tried to figure out how her daughter had so quickly outflanked her.

THREE

Later that night Amy and Jeff sat on the green-plaid couch in the family room. Spread out on a low table in front of them was the royalty check from the publishing company, a printout of their recurring monthly expenses, and several envelopes containing bills. Jeff picked up the statement for the credit card Amy used for household expenses like groceries.

"What is this charge at Ricardo's Restaurant three weeks ago?" he asked. "It's over a hundred dollars."

"Natalie, Jodie Walker, and I went out to eat on Natalie's birthday. It was the Friday night you were doing the job with Butch at the house on the lake."

"And you paid for everyone's meal?"

"Yes. Jodie forgot her purse when we picked her up. She promised to repay me for her meal and half of Natalie's food but never did."

"Did you ask her for it?"

Amy swallowed. "I started to bring it up the other day when I ran into her at the pharmacy, but I didn't have the heart to ask her when she started telling me about her mother-in-law. She has cancer, and the local oncologist is sending her to a specialist at Duke."

"I'm sorry about Jodie's mother-in-law, but we can't pretend to have enough money to plop down a hundred dollars for a meal without thinking about it."

"I thought about it," Amy said defensively, "but Natalie is my best friend, and I wanted to do something nice for her. You know how much she loves the tiramisu at Ricardo's."

"You ordered dessert?"

"Yes," Amy replied with increasing defiance in her voice. "And I don't think I should have to justify every penny I spend. What do you want me to do? Go back to work at the law firm? That's not possible. Mr. Phillips gave my job to Emily Ashburn, who'd been scheming to get it for five years. I could try to find a cashiering job, but they don't pay anything, and I wouldn't be here when Ian comes home from school. Also, if I get a job, we'd have to find after-school care for him."

"Ian is ten years old," Jeff said, seemingly unaffected by Amy's tirade. "He can unlock the door and turn on the TV."

"And I would go crazy worrying what he might get into when he gets bored or has a buddy come over to play. He'd climb onto the roof of the house if the urge hit him."

"You could look for something part-time while the kids are in school. Maybe you could clean houses. That's what Denny's wife is doing. She printed up business cards a few months ago and is already working four mornings a week. She averages over fifteen dollars an hour."

Amy's mouth dropped open. She couldn't believe what she was hearing. Did Jeff really want her canvassing the neighborhood trying to drum up business as a domestic worker? And her shock wasn't because the job was demeaning. Cleaning toilets was honest labor. But Amy never volunteered to go door-to-door for charitable projects and barely knew their neighbors on either side of the house. The thought of approaching total strangers to ask for work and then going to their houses on a regular basis made her hands sweat.

"The mornings are my best writing times," she said, grabbing the credit card statement from Jeff's hand. "Why don't we count the dinner with Natalie and Jodie as my Christmas present? You don't have to buy me anything else. You spent over two hundred dollars on the necklace you gave me last year. This way you can save a hundred dollars, and I won't feel guilty for spending an evening with my friends."

Jeff stared at her for a few seconds. "Don't

you like the necklace?"

"Of course I like it. I wore it on —" Amy stopped. "I wore it Mother's Day when we went to church. It looked perfect with my light blue dress."

"That was five months ago."

Amy dropped the credit card statement on the table.

"Okay, Jeff," she said. "Where are we going with this discussion? I know our finances have been tight, and I know it's going to get worse."

Jeff didn't respond but picked up the statement instead.

"The rest of the charges make sense," he said after a few moments of additional review. "But didn't we agree this card was to be used for household expenses only?"

"Yes, and I handed it to the waiter at the restaurant without thinking."

"Then why did you get so defensive when I asked you a simple question?"

"Because it came across as an attack," Amy sighed. "And like I told you, I already don't feel like I'm doing my part to help pay the bills. Your news today about having to pay for our health insurance and the increased charges for Megan's dance lessons made it worse."

"Nothing will change about her dance lessons until after Christmas," Jeff said.

"Are you sure?"

"Yes. We couldn't do anything else after you promised her she could continue."

"How did you know —" Amy began.

"She thanked me while you were cleaning up after supper."

"I'm sorry. We should have talked it over —"

"And I would have agreed to do the same thing. The issue is what to do when everything changes in January."

"I want to find a way to let her keep going," Amy sighed. "But do you really think cleaning houses is the way to do it?"

A half hour later Amy knocked on Megan's door. Megan didn't answer, so Amy knocked louder.

"What is it?" Megan called out.

"May I come in?"

"Yeah."

Megan's room was a mixture of little-girl holdovers and early teen paraphernalia. Dolls on a shelf and a well-loved teddy bear on the bed shared the room with schoolbooks, scattered clothes, and music posters. Megan was propped up in her bed with earbuds in place and a pink MP3 player in her right hand. Her head was bobbing up and down. Amy had given up trying to regulate what Megan downloaded on the device. There was a large pile of shirts and pants on the floor. Amy knew the clothes were clean.

"I'll pick them up," Megan said, following her mother's gaze. "I was trying to decide what to wear tomorrow. Bethany and I almost matched today, which would have been a disaster. We're friends, not twins."

"I like the purple top with your dark jeans," Amy offered, picking up the shirt from the pile.

"Yeah, I might wear that. Bethany is going to wear a yellow top."

"Your dad said you thanked him for the dance lessons. We agreed that you can continue through Christmas."

"Cool. Ms. Carlton is going to bump me up to the advanced contemporary class next week."

"Congratulations. That's great."

"Yeah. Good night."

Megan reinserted the loose earpiece and resumed her bobblehead-doll imitation. Praying obviously wasn't on Megan's playlist, and at the end of a long day, Amy wasn't willing to force something that only had meaning when done voluntarily.

"Lights out in thirty minutes," she said in a loud voice.

Megan nodded more vigorously, and Amy backed out of the room.

Jeff was asleep by the time Amy brushed her teeth. Her husband could lose consciousness faster than a newborn infant with a stomach full of milk. Amy crawled under the covers and stared at the ceiling. At least Jeff didn't snore. Natalie had confided that her husband, Luke, snored so loudly it sounded like someone trying to break into the house.

Amy pulled the sheet up to her chin. One solution to their financial pressures would be speedy completion of another novel. The advance for a third book, if the publisher decided to exercise the option contained in the contract, would add enough money to the family budget to take some of the stress off Jeff. And it would help Amy feel like a contributing member of the family.

Amy calculated how quickly she could complete the first draft of a book. She didn't write as fast as some novelists who could crank out several thousand words in a single writing session. A productive day for her was a thousand words, and her contract required a book of at least 90,000 words. *A Great and Precious Promise* and *The Everlasting Arms* were each around 110,000 words. Amy liked longer novels and believed if readers enjoyed the world of the story and the characters who lived there, they would appreciate a few extra chapters. Multiple e-mails from women who raved about *A Great and Precious Promise* and begged for a sequel confirmed Amy's opinion. But she knew she couldn't average a thousand words each and every day. There were plenty of weekends when family activities kept her from turning on her computer at all. Other days she might write for several hours and then review what she'd written and realize it had no chance of ending up in the final version of the story. Cecilia had suggested she cut several long scenes from her first two novels because the passages didn't advance the main plot and would be skimmed by most readers. The possibility that readers might not bother to slow down and consider the words Amy had slaved over for hours, if not days, made her sick to her stomach.

Jeff grunted and rolled onto his back. In the best-case scenario, it would take at least five months for Amy to complete the first draft of a new book. That would be two months faster than it took her to finish *The Everlasting Arms.* However, turning in the first draft was just the initial step. The editorial process would take another three or four months. Only after the final version was approved would a check be issued. And that could happen only if Dave Coley decided the book was worth publishing at all.

Amy shut her eyes and commanded her mind to slow down. Being a writer wasn't supposed to be a grinding job. When she'd worked for the law firm she never lay in bed at night worrying about job security or fretting over whether she'd be paid on Friday. Becoming a novelist was supposed to be the path to freedom. She loved the solitude of the attic, but if her writing career was chained to the financial demands of life, it would be a deathblow to creativity.

All Amy's calculations about how long it would take to write another novel were meaningless if she didn't have an idea for a story in the first place. Cecilia had nixed the possibility for a sequel to *A Great and Precious Promise,* and *The Everlasting Arms* didn't lend itself to another book with the same characters. Rick and Kelli had suffered enough. They deserved to live out their fictional lives in peace and quiet and raise healthy, happy babies.

Amy slipped out of bed, knelt down, and prayed that God would give her the idea for a new book. And do it soon.

Four

Amy sipped a cappuccino. She loved the complex smells of different coffees brewing and the relaxed atmosphere of the local coffee shop, but she allowed herself only one or two visits a week. It was hard to justify paying as much for a single cup of coffee as a pound cost at the grocery store.

While waiting for Natalie, she glanced down at a copy of the local newspaper an earlier customer had abandoned. A headline at the bottom of the first page caught her eye: "Local World War II Hero Dies."

Before she read the first line of the article, Amy guessed whom it was about. Sure enough, Sanford "Sonny" Dominick had passed away at the age of eighty-four from complications associated with pneumonia. The reporter summarized the basic facts about the son of a textile worker who worked as a crop duster before volunteering for the US Air Force during World War II. Dominick survived in the jungles of Burma for two weeks after the airplane he piloted developed mechanical problems and had to make an emergency crash landing in a dry riverbed. He and one other crew member, who'd suffered a broken arm, were alone deep in enemy territory. Dominick set the man's bone, and they followed the riverbed for four days before going cross-country for eleven more days. In the process they avoided numerous Japanese patrols and survived by eating insects, tree roots, and raw fish Dominick caught in a trap made from twigs and baited with grubworms. Megan saw a model of the fish trap when she was in elementary school and told Amy all about it.

Upon returning home to Cross Plains, the war hero went into business and became a multimillionaire who went through almost as many wives as he had millions. Mr. Phillips was Mr. Dominick's lawyer, and Amy had met the tall, white-haired man with the colorful personality on several occasions. Even though he was very charming and garrulous, there was always an underlying pathos that touched Amy enough that she started praying for him. She finished the article and placed the paper on an empty chair. Sonny Dominick's medals and millions wouldn't be relevant wherever he was today.

While she watched people come into the shop and order drinks, Amy thought again about a visit she'd made the previous night to the living room. It had been a time of needed encouragement after the stress related to Jeff's job and the family finances. Nothing came out of the dream about another book; however, the experience ended with an unusual twist. As Amy felt herself being pulled away from the room, a quick series of images raced past her eyes. It happened so fast that she couldn't remember the pictures, and that left Amy puzzled. As she took a drink of coffee, she tried to revisit the scene and slow down the slide show, but it remained a blur. Amy lowered her cup as her petite friend with short black hair and sparkling dark eyes came into the store and rushed over to the table.

"Sorry I'm late," Natalie said in her Midwestern accent. "I'm driving car pool this week and had to wait on Braxton Green. It's a good thing being tardy won't get you kicked out of kindergarten."

"That's okay. I've enjoyed relaxing and watching the people. I've been busy this morning, too. I mopped the kitchen floor after Megan and Ian left for the bus stop."

"Already? I'm impressed."

Natalie slipped off her coat and draped it over a chair. She had two sons. Ben was a second grader at Broad Street Christian School, and Noah was in kindergarten. There was no bus service to the private school.

"I went through the same thing when Ian

and Dallas were in kindergarten together at Broad Street," Amy said. "Being on time is tough for Kim and her kids."

"Yeah, but Braxton is the cutest little guy. Every time I hear that lisp in his voice, it makes me want to give him a hug and pinch his cheeks."

"Is Kim still putting product on his hair?"

"Oh yeah. It was spiked up a couple of inches when he got in the car. Noah wanted to touch it, but I wouldn't let him unbuckle his seat belt."

Natalie went to the counter to order. Amy drank either a cappuccino or a morning blend of regular coffee if she needed an unflavored jolt of caffeine, but Natalie experimented with different drinks. In a couple of minutes she returned with a clear glass mug filled with light brown liquid topped with foam and unidentifiable sprinkles.

"What is it today?" Amy asked.

"Cinnamon dolce latte."

"A coffee candy bar."

Natalie took a sip. "Yep. No afternoon chocolate for me."

Amy and Natalie were sitting at a table for two in the back corner. They sipped their drinks and watched an older couple enter. The man was wearing a black beret and had a thin mustache. The woman's gray hair was covered with a colorful scarf.

"You should put that couple in your next

novel," Natalie said in a low voice. "I'm sure they have a story to tell. I mean, how did a man who wears a beret and sports a French mustache end up in a town in eastern North Carolina? And his wife looks like she has a lot of flair."

"She sure does." Amy stared at the couple for a moment. "Natalie, how do you know they're married? They could be reuniting forty years after first falling in love. They met years ago at a French coffee shop a lot like this place. He was working in Marseilles, and she was an American college student traveling across Europe with a friend. They both ordered a latte and an apricot pastry and realized they had something in common. A halting conversation began. She was limited by two semesters of college French, and he spoke broken English, but they communicated in the way that mattered most — the affairs of the heart. Their first conversation led to long, romantic walks along the Mediterranean. Then an emergency call from home forced the girl to leave without telling him good-bye. They eventually married other people, but now those spouses are dead, and they've found each other again. The question is — can the flame of love that burned brightly so long ago be brought back to life?"

The torrent of Amy's words suddenly stopped.

"Keep going," Natalie said, leaning forward

on her elbows. "I'd read that book."

"You know how it works with me." Amy smiled and shook her head. "I can get a running start with ideas like that, but they always hit a wall."

"It's still a cool beginning."

Amy touched her heart. "I need something that starts in here. Otherwise I know I'd be wasting my time."

Both women took a sip of their drinks.

"Yeah," Natalie said. "*A Great and Precious Promise* wasn't just a story. It was like a testimony. I thought about Ann Marie and Landon for weeks after I finished the book, and not just because we're friends. Most people would have placed all the blame for their problems on Landon, which makes sense, but the scene between them was so much more powerful because Ann Marie realized the speck in her eye could be just as blinding as the log in his. It made me think about my relationship with Luke. There are so many self-righteous women who need to —" Natalie suddenly paused. "I'd better quit preaching."

"I like your preaching," Amy said with a smile. "And what you're saying means the world to me. Even though the characters are made up, their stories can still help real people. That's why I write."

"Oh, and I'll never read the word 'covenant' again without thinking about the book. It gave me chills when you explained what it meant in the Old Testament." Natalie leaned in closer. "And I can't wait to get a signed copy of *The Everlasting Arms.* It was cruel to only let me take a peek at a couple of chapters."

"I wasn't trying to be mean," Amy apologized. "I wanted to make sure that I wasn't getting off track with the part about the old boyfriend —"

"I'm kidding," Natalie interrupted. "It's just neat for me to sit here and realize that my best friend is a published author."

"Who's making about half as much writing books as she did typing pleadings at Jones, Barrington, and Phillips." Amy sighed.

She told Natalie about the paltry royalty check and the possibility that Megan might have to stop taking dance lessons in January. She didn't feel comfortable mentioning the health insurance crisis without Jeff's permission. Natalie listened sympathetically.

"And I feel like I'm slowly losing contact with Megan," Amy said. "I know part of it has to do with her age, but that doesn't make it any easier."

"You and Megan are both so talented. I'd think seeing you follow your dream would encourage her to believe that the same thing is possible for her."

"It hasn't worked that way. Last night she wanted to know why it's more important for the family to sacrifice so I can write than it is for her to dance."

"Wow." Natalie's eyes widened. "I never could have cooked up such a sophisticated argument to use with my mom. But Megan is so smart that she intimidates me. She's just like you. I mean, she makes straight A's without trying."

"Maybe, but she's much more outgoing. And I don't have any personal experience from my teenage years to draw on in relating to her. I was the quiet, obedient second child trying to make up for the trouble my older brother gave my parents."

"I can't help you out there. I was the spoiled only child."

"No you weren't."

"Until Jesus changed me."

Amy looked at her friend and felt her emotions rise to the surface. There was such genuine sweetness in Natalie that it nourished Amy's soul every time the two women got together.

"Did I say something wrong?" Natalie asked.

"No." Amy shook her head. "You always help me remember what's really important."

They stayed at their table and lingered after their coffee cups were empty.

"Noah was so excited this morning," Natalie said, reaching for her purse. "His class is going on a field trip to the fire station this afternoon."

Natalie's words banished the pleasant feelings Amy was enjoying. A terrifying image that seemed vaguely familiar flashed across her mind.

"Are you one of the chaperones?" Amy asked sharply.

"No, they have plenty of volunteers. I was going to get a manicure. My nails are in terrible shape."

"I think you should go on the field trip."

"Why?" Natalie gave her a puzzled look.

Amy shut her eyes for a second, which made the picture in her mind even more vivid.

"To keep a close watch on Noah," she said, trying to speak calmly.

"Amy, what's going on?" Natalie asked with concern. "Why are you worried about the field trip?"

Amy took a deep breath.

"I know it sounds crazy, but when you mentioned the field trip, I remembered something I dreamed last night." She paused. "I think it involved Noah. He was lying on white pavement beside a big red truck. His eyes were closed and his head was tilted to the side at an odd angle. I'm not one hundred percent sure, but it could have been a fire truck."

"And you think this is going to happen?"

"I don't know. Maybe." Amy hid her face

in her hands for a moment. "I'm sorry."

The two women sat in silence. Then Natalie spoke. "I'm going to go on the trip," she said in a matter-of-fact tone of voice.

Amy looked up. "What about your manicure?"

"That can wait. And I'm going to hold Noah's hand the whole time."

Amy's stomach was in knots as she drove home. Natalie knew Amy had dreams, but she didn't know about the living room. Each time Amy had considered sharing her secret with Natalie, she hesitated and the moment passed. Now she had impulsively dragged Natalie into her unconscious world. Amy wished she'd kept her mouth shut, but that thought made her feel even more uncomfortable.

Whether true or false, real or imagined, she'd sounded an alarm.

Amy spent the rest of the morning in an emotional upheaval. She ate a piece of fruit for lunch. Several times she picked up the phone to call Natalie but never completed the call. What would she say? Had anything changed since they'd parted outside the coffee shop?

At 2:30 p.m., her cell phone rang, and a photo of Natalie appeared. Amy fumbled with the phone and almost dropped it.

"Hey," she said as quickly as she could accept the call. "Is everything okay?"

"Yes," Natalie responded. "I went on the field trip, and Noah had a great time."

Amy leaned against the counter and closed her eyes for a moment in thankfulness. When she opened them, she felt embarrassed.

"I'm terribly sorry I upset you this morning," she said. "I guess my imagination got away from me. It was so unnecessary and —"

"I wouldn't be so quick to jump to conclusions," Natalie interrupted. "While we were at the station an alarm came in and two trucks had to leave in a hurry. We herded all the kids away from the entrance, but there were a few moments of confusion. If I hadn't been right beside Noah, he could have turned the wrong way and put himself in danger."

Amy wasn't sure how to respond.

"Did you hear what I said?" Natalie asked.

"Yes."

"That means I'm glad I was there with Noah. What if something horrible had happened and you hadn't said anything to me?"

"I'd want to die," Amy answered truthfully.

"Right. Instead, I had a nice field trip with him. He can't wait for Luke to get home so he can tell him all about it. I'm sure he'll want to be a fireman now when he grows up."

"I still feel weird about the whole situation."

"I can't control your feelings, but I'd rather be warned about a danger that can be avoided than have to pray for a miracle when disaster

strikes. Are you listening to me?"
"Yes."
"Good."
Amy thought for a moment. "Are you going to say anything to Luke about this?"
"Not if you don't want me to."
"Please don't. He might think I'm a nut."
"Okay. But thanks again. Even though it was a hard thing to do, it showed me how much you care for me and my family."
After the call ended Amy felt as if a big weight had lifted from her shoulders. However, her relief was short-lived. A few minutes later, while folding the laundry, the realization hit her that she might have more dreams rooted in reality.
"No, no, no!" she spoke loudly as she shook the wrinkles from one of Jeff's shirts.

FIVE

The following afternoon Megan burst into the kitchen shortly after she and Ian got off the school bus. Amy was sitting at the table looking at recipes on her laptop.

"What are you doing home so early?" Amy asked. "I thought you were going to the pep rally for the football game tomorrow against Loudon County."

"I skipped the pep rally," Megan said with a dismissive wave of her hand. "Mr. Ryan asked me to come by his classroom instead. I made the highest grade in the class on a quiz, and he wanted to get to know me better."

"Get to know you better? What did he ask you?"

"Oh, what I'm interested in. Do I like to read? What are my favorite subjects in school?"

"Did you tell him you loved Ms. Sweeney's American Literature class?"

"No way. I told him World History was my favorite subject."

"That's not true."

"It is now. Oh, here's the coolest thing. When I mentioned that I've been dancing for five years, he wanted to know everything about it. He had a student in California who went to the Debbie Allen Academy in Los Angeles."

Megan's enthusiasm for the new teacher made Amy uneasy.

"Is Mr. Ryan married?" she asked.

"Uh, I'm not sure, but I didn't see a wedding ring on his finger."

"That's a sign he isn't. It's not smart for you to spend time alone after school with a male teacher."

Megan rolled her eyes. "Mom, I'm not dumb and don't you be stupid."

"Watch your words," Amy shot back.

"I'm a freshman in high school," Megan responded without any hint of remorse. "Teachers have meetings with students. You ought to be happy that Mr. Ryan cares about us."

"I don't have any problem with a teacher who supports his students, but I don't want you to meet with him alone after school."

"We were in the classroom."

"Was the door open?"

Megan glared at Amy for a moment, then stormed out of the kitchen without answering. Amy watched her go with a sinking heart. She heard Megan's bedroom door slam shut.

Amy was still brooding about the conversation when Jeff came home from work and gave her a quick peck on the lips.

"I worked on a new project today," he said. "It's a renovation of a large two-story brick home on McDonald Street. Do you remember the house with big holly bushes out front and a white gazebo in the side yard?"

Amy knew the house. It was one of a handful of hundred-year-old homes that hadn't been swallowed up by the expanding downtown area. Most of the historic estate houses that hadn't been torn down were now offices. Jones, Barrington, and Phillips had its office in one of the survivors, a mansion formerly occupied by one of the richest families in town.

"Yes."

"Mildred Burris lives there. She must be at least eighty years old. We ordered custom windows that are a match to those already in the house but are much more energy efficient."

"She was one of Mr. Phillips's clients," Amy said, her mind still on the argument with Megan. "I met her a few times at the office."

"Nice lady. Never married. Her father was in the textile business years ago and must have made a lot of money. She and I talked when I was on my lunch break, and she mentioned that she needs someone to clean the house and help her with things she can't manage on her own. The woman who was working for her moved away, and she hasn't found a replacement."

"What?" Amy suddenly bristled. "Did you tell her I was looking for a domestic job?"

"Not exactly, but I found out as much as I could about what she needs done. There would probably be times when you wouldn't have anything to do and could set up your laptop in a spare room and write. There must be at least six bedrooms, and she's the only person living there."

Amy stared at Jeff. She took a deep breath.

"I can't think about that right now. I had another argument with Megan."

"What happened?"

Amy told him about Megan's unsupervised conference with the new World History teacher. Jeff furrowed his forehead.

"What did the teacher say to her?"

"Nothing, but she shouldn't meet in private with a male teacher after school."

"We've never told her that."

"I know, and when I tried to suggest it, she blew up and left the kitchen. That's been two hours ago, and she's not left her bedroom since."

"I'll talk to her," Jeff said.

"Should we do it together?"

"That might set her off again."

Jeff was right, which made Amy's opinion of herself as a mother drop another notch. If it went much lower, she'd have to cut a hole in the floor.

"Okay," she said. "Can you do it before supper? I hate sitting at the table when the tension is so thick that it's hard to swallow my food. And please don't bring up your part-time job idea tonight. I don't want to think about it."

"Sure, but it's not like you'd have to wear a maid uniform —"

Something about the look in Amy's eyes stopped Jeff short.

"I'm on my way upstairs right now," he said. "Where's Ian?"

"He's been at Bobby's house all afternoon. I'll call Nancy and ask her to send him home."

Amy hated to come across as a complaining wife. While putting the finishing touches on supper, she resolved to make things right between herself and Jeff before they went to bed. Ian popped through the door.

"Is Dad in the backyard?"

"No, he's upstairs talking to Megan."

"Is she in trouble?"

"No."

"Then why is he talking to her?"

Before Amy answered she heard Jeff's heavy footsteps on the stairs. He entered the kitchen with Megan trailing along behind him.

"Hi, Dad!" Ian cried out with enthusiasm.

Father and son faced each other across the

kitchen. Their eyes locked and they both crouched down. Suddenly, Jeff leaped forward, grabbed Ian by the ankles, lifted him upside down, flipped him right side up, caught him with his right arm, and deposited him on the floor. Ian laughed.

"What would you like to drink?" Amy asked Megan.

"I'll get it," Megan replied, her voice less icy than Amy expected. "Dad and I had a good talk. I understand what you meant about Mr. Ryan."

"Who's Mr. Ryan?" Ian asked as he vainly pulled on his father's right ankle and tried to get him off balance.

"Megan's new World History teacher," Amy replied.

"I can't wait to go to high school," Ian said. "I've never had a man teacher."

Supper passed without any further problems. Afterward Megan returned to her room. Ian finished his homework and sat on the couch between Jeff and Amy while they watched a nature show about crocodiles on TV. Partway through the show, Ian inched closer to Amy and snuggled up to her. Amy's heart melted.

"That was a good show," she said when it ended.

"I liked it, too," Ian said, bounding up from the couch.

"I didn't know you loved crocodiles so

much," Jeff said to Amy with a twinkle in his eye.

"Can I have a snack before getting ready for bed?" Ian asked.

"Yes," Amy immediately answered.

Ian left the room.

"Eat a cookie for me," Jeff called after him.

After Amy tucked Ian into bed, she thought about going directly to the writing room so she could read in private. But to avoid Jeff would be an act of cowardice. She returned downstairs to the family room and curled up on the couch with a book while Jeff was on the computer adjusting his roster for a fantasy football league he'd joined with some friends from church. Amy took a break and fixed a cup of hot tea. Jeff joined her at the kitchen table, and she braced herself for a fresh volley of reasons why she needed to get a job as a domestic worker.

"Don't be too hard on yourself about Megan," Jeff said. "She wants to please us, but she also feels the need to show that she's an independent person."

"I know that's part of growing up, but the growing pains are real."

"For both of you. And I don't always pick up on what's going on between you. Let me know when you need reinforcements."

"I will."

"Promise?"

"Yes."

Amy felt herself relax. Knowing Jeff cared and wanted to be there for her with Megan helped a lot. He reached out and touched her on the arm in a simple gesture of reassurance. She picked up his hand and kissed it.

Before going to bed that night, Amy and Jeff prayed together. One of Jeff's best qualities was honesty when he talked to God, and he never tried to manipulate Amy in his prayers. He honored her earlier request and didn't mention working for Ms. Burris. The simple integrity of Jeff's prayer life was an attribute Amy knew she would incorporate into a book character someday.

Toward the end of the prayer, Jeff placed his right hand over Amy's left hand and asked God to bless her and give her strength. When they finished praying, Amy knew she'd rather have Jeff with his real flaws and strengths than the more perfect yet imaginary men who lived in her stories. She closed her eyes and drifted into a peaceful sleep.

In the middle of the night, she found herself in the heavenly living room.

Most mornings Jeff got up before Amy and went downstairs to brew a pot of coffee. Amy joined him as the last bit of water seeped through the grounds.

"Did you knock on Megan's door?" she asked. "It's been taking her longer to get ready the past week."

"No. Do you want me to go upstairs and do it?"

"Drink the first cup of coffee," Amy said with a wave of her hand. "I'll let her know it's time to get going."

Megan groaned in response to Amy's gentle nudge of her shoulders.

"How does my hair look?" she asked, her eyes still closed.

Amy surveyed the silky dark strands that covered her daughter's pillow.

"Like something from the cover of a women's magazine at the grocery store. Your hair is always beautiful. All you'll need to do is brush it out."

Megan rubbed her eyes. "Thanks for giving me straight hair."

"You're welcome. What do you want for breakfast?"

"Is Dad cooking?"

"I'm not sure."

"Tell him a bowl of oatmeal with raisins and brown sugar would be nice."

When Amy returned to the kitchen, Jeff was cooking oatmeal the old-fashioned way on top of the stove.

"How did you know Megan wanted oatmeal?" she asked.

"She mentioned it last night before she went to bed. I'm glad she didn't change her mind in her sleep."

"I had an interesting night," Amy said as she took her favorite mug from the cupboard. "I went to the living room."

"Did you get an idea for a new book?"

Amy put a spoonful of sugar and a dash of creamer into the mug, which was decorated with pictures of hummingbirds from all over the world. She added coffee until the dark brown liquid reached the top. She stirred it slowly as she debated whether to repeat the words she'd heard in the night.

"I'm not sure, but I don't think so," she said.

"Uh-oh," Jeff said, glancing down at the stovetop. "Hey, get me some water, please. This oatmeal is getting too thick."

Amy filled a measuring cup with water and handed it to him. Jeff never asked about her dreams. After they were engaged, she told him about them and emphasized how personal they were. Jeff wasn't curious about supernatural things and didn't challenge her desire to keep her dreams private.

When Amy received the biblical foundation for her first novel in a dream, Jeff perked up because it might have a practical impact on their lives, but he continued to honor the barrier Amy had established. If she wanted to tell him something, she would.

Breakfast wasn't a family meal. Jeff ate his oatmeal while Amy made sure Ian was awake. Ian liked to eat before he got dressed, and he had returned to his bedroom by the time Megan appeared and sprinkled brown sugar over a scoop of raisins in her bowl. Jeff came through the kitchen on his way out of the house to work.

"Thanks for remembering, Dad," Megan said. "It looks yummy."

Jeff patted her on the head and gave Amy a quick kiss.

"We'll be working at the Burris house all day," he said. "Would it mess you up if I put in an hour of overtime?"

"Go ahead. I'll save supper for you. And don't forget the football game. Ian wants to go."

"Sure."

"Anything you want me to ask Ms. Burris?"

"No," Amy said more sharply than she'd intended.

"Okay." Jeff held up his hands.

"Please, not yet," Amy responded. "I need to think about it some more."

After Jeff left, Amy put a small serving of oatmeal into a bowl. She might delay the conversation, but working as a housemaid for Ms. Burris would be a topic for future discussion with Jeff. She poked at her oatmeal. Amy's mother had never perfected the art of cooking oatmeal and usually produced a gelatinous mess. Jeff's version was much more appetizing, but fifteen years of marriage hadn't reprogrammed her attitude toward the dish.

"Are you going to the football game tonight?" Megan asked her.

"No. I'll stay home."

"Bethany's mom is going to take us."

"Okay. Then you can come home with Dad and Ian."

Megan looked up from her bowl. "Some of us want to go out for pizza after the game."

"Who?"

"Bethany, Crystal, Alecia, and Sadie."

"Where?"

"Pizza Palace."

The locally owned restaurant was large, well lit, and crowded on Friday and Saturday nights. There weren't any dark booths or secluded corners. It was as safe a place as existed in Cross Plains for fourteen-year-old girls to go in a group.

"Is Bethany's mom going to stay with you?"

"No, but she's going to come back and get us after about an hour or so. Can I go? I really want to. Alecia has to be home by eleven, so we won't be out late, and I have my own money for pizza. Crystal and I are going to share a small one with spinach and mushrooms on it."

"You've thought about this a lot, haven't you?"

"I really, really want to go," Megan responded with a plaintive look.

"All right."

"Thanks," Megan said.

Megan returned to her oatmeal. Amy took a few sips of coffee.

"How did Bethany talk her mother into doing all the driving around?" she asked.

"Oh, she's nice," Megan said without glancing up.

Megan finished breakfast and went upstairs, leaving Amy to mull over the difference between nice and not-so-nice mothers. She hoped Megan's memories of her would be more pleasant than Amy's childhood recollections of oatmeal.

Amy spent the morning performing maid duties in her own house. She cleaned the upstairs bathrooms, a job that included fishing Megan's hair from the bathtub drain. Long strands of her daughter's hair didn't look so beautiful covered with soap scum. Then she organized the items under the cabinets and scrubbed the floors. When she finished, Amy inspected her work with satisfaction but knew no member of the family would notice or thank her. A follow-up thought stopped her. What if Jeff noticed and used it as a reason to push the possibility of a part-time housecleaning job?

After taking a shower, Amy dressed for lunch. It was a five-minute walk to Natalie's house. It was a clear, cool day, so she pulled on a burgundy sweater on her way out the door. The air was crisp, and Amy was glad the stifling humidity of summer was gone.

The developer of their neighborhood had installed narrow concrete sidewalks on one side of the street. The two hundred cookie-cutter houses in the subdivision were built close together. The total population of Cross Plains was around thirty thousand people, so the neighborhood was one of the biggest residential areas in town. Owners of the homes ran the gamut from retirees wanting to downsize, to young professional couples just starting out, to families like Amy's with the primary wage earner employed in a high-paying hourly job.

An older woman walked slowly down her driveway to retrieve a rolling trash container from the curb. The woman looked familiar, but Amy couldn't remember her name. There wasn't time for Amy to make a quick detour to the other side of the street.

"Good morning," Amy said as she came closer.

The older woman squinted at her through her glasses.

"Oh, it's the author," she replied. "What are you doing out on a walk? You should be home writing another book. I loved your novel and bought a copy to send to my sister in Phoenix. She liked it, too."

Amy desperately tried to recall the woman's name.

"Thanks, Mrs. Brewster," Amy said with relief.

"Would you have time to meet her for a few minutes when she comes for a visit at Christmas? I don't want to be a nuisance, but it would mean a lot to her."

"Uh, sure. Just let me know. You can stop by my house or I can come to you."

"That's wonderful. She'll be excited. She goes to a huge church and has loaned her copy of the book to all her friends."

Cecilia had told Amy that each book was read by an average of 2.3 readers. Extensive loaning hurt sales, but it also meant the message was getting out to a larger audience. That figure mattered the most to Amy.

"Let her know I finished a new novel last week. It will be available early next year."

"I can't wait to find out what happens to Ann Marie."

"It's not a sequel. It's a fresh story with new characters."

"But I really liked Ann Marie," Mrs. Brewster said with obvious disappointment. "Her trust in God even when her husband was unfaithful to her was so inspirational. And when he asked for her forgiveness, I cried like a baby."

This was familiar territory for Amy. Series were popular, especially with female readers, but both of Amy's books were stand-alone novels. She often had to respond to similar comments forwarded to her website.

"Me, too," she answered. "But I think you're going to enjoy the new novel. It's called *The Everlasting Arms.* The title is taken from the first part of Deuteronomy 33:27: 'The eternal God is your refuge, and underneath are the everlasting arms.' "

"Oh, I like that already," Mrs. Brewster said, brightening up.

"Maybe I can give you and your sister a sneak peek and share a page with you when she visits."

"That would be wonderful! But I'm not going to tell her. It'll be a Christmas surprise."

Amy said good-bye and continued her walk. What a writing career lacked in financial stability, it made up for in personal satisfaction.

Natalie's house had a brick facing, which made it slightly different from Amy's house on the outside, but the two houses had identical floor plans. It was odd walking into the same house and seeing it decorated so differently.

Natalie's husband worked as a professional photographer. Amy knew that their income fluctuated; however, Natalie had received a sizable inheritance when her parents died, and her house was beautifully furnished.

She'd turned the master bedroom into a fantasy suite complete with a whirlpool tub, and the backyard was filled with top-of-the-line playground equipment for the boys. The kitchen had granite countertops and a beautiful ceramic-tile floor. On the walls throughout the house were original watercolor paintings. Natalie was a talented artist who specialized in beach and nature scenes. She'd given Amy two paintings as gifts. Amy hung one in her kitchen and the other in the master bedroom.

Jeff believed it would be hard for Luke and Natalie to recoup what they'd invested in the house when they sold it, but Amy knew Natalie didn't think that way. She feathered her nest the best she could, then opened it up for others to enjoy. An invitation to one of her holiday parties or summer cookouts was highly prized in the neighborhood.

Amy rang the door chime that played the first few notes of Beethoven's Ninth Symphony. In a few seconds Natalie opened the door. She was wearing an apron that made her look like a busy housewife from the 1960s.

"What have you been doing?" Amy asked.

"Cooking something messy. I'd like to give you a hug, but I don't want to get anything on you. Come into the kitchen."

Amy could see splotches of brown, green, and yellow on the apron.

"Where did you get the apron?" she asked

as she followed Natalie through the family room with its large flat-screen TV and fancy speaker system. A separate part of the family room was arranged for people to sit and talk.

"It belonged to my grandmother. I found it when I was cleaning out my mother's house and couldn't bear the thought of throwing it away. When I was a little girl, my grandmother would wear it when we made sugar cookies or brownies."

"What are you making today?"

"I hoped it would be a treat for our lunch, but it's turned into a science experiment."

They entered the kitchen.

"Walk softly," Natalie whispered.

"Why?"

"I don't want the soufflé to fall."

Amy glanced at the wall-mounted oven.

"What kind of soufflé?"

"Herb. It's got basil, rosemary, thyme, nutmeg, fresh mustard, Monterey Jack cheese, and more eggs than a doctor would recommend for a lumberjack to eat in a month. I bought a bunch of fresh stuff at the new organic market."

"Sounds like fun."

A buzzer went off.

"That's it," Natalie said.

Natalie gingerly took a pair of oven mitts from a drawer and cautiously opened the oven door. She raised one of the mitts to her mouth.

"Uh-oh," she said.

She reached into the oven and took out the soufflé and held it so Amy could see it. The dish was golden brown with generous green sprinkles, but it was as lopsided as a ski slope. One side towered over the other, which had completely collapsed.

"It looks like a volcano erupted and blew off half the mountain," Natalie said with a frown as she set the casserole dish on a blue trivet. She pointed at the collapsed side. "And the people who lived on this side were buried alive under a molten egg-and-cheese mixture."

Amy laughed. "I bet it tastes scrumptious."

Natalie took off the apron and hung it on a hook beside the stove.

"I wonder why it does that?" she said, inspecting the soufflé from another angle. "The one on the cooking show was as flat as an airport runway."

"You're inspiring me," Amy responded.

"What do you mean?"

"The way you describe your soufflé is more entertaining than some of the scenes I write in my books."

"You're just trying to make me feel better. At least it's you. I'd hate to serve something like this to a group of women from the church."

There was a small antique cherry table against one wall of the kitchen with a vase of fresh flowers in the middle. Natalie scooped out a serving of soufflé from the fluffy side for Amy and another for herself. It was steaming hot.

"It'll cool in a jiffy," Natalie said. "Let's eat."

Amy put a tiny bite in her mouth. The hot soufflé instantly melted, leaving a marvelous combination of flavors on her tongue.

"This is amazing," she said.

Natalie looked skeptical but sampled a bite herself. Her eyes lit up.

"Yeah, it's pretty good."

Nibbling the soufflé occupied the next few minutes. Amy didn't want conversation to distract her from savoring the dish.

"I won't forget this lunch," she said, placing her fork beside her plate. "I expected a nice salad. This is so much more fun."

"If I can't experiment on you, who would be my guinea pig?" Natalie asked.

"I ate like a pig. Are you going to feed this to Luke for supper? I think it would taste good warmed up. The boys might even try it."

"I'll fix a plate for Luke so he won't see how lopsided it is, but I can't count on the boys. They'll need a backup dish, something I know they love, like ravioli from a can. Do you want some hot tea?"

"Sure."

Natalie filled a kettle with water and put it

on the stove before returning to the table.

"I haven't been able to get your warning about Noah's field trip out of my mind," she said.

Amy flinched. She'd hoped they'd get through their time together without the subject coming up.

"Tell me more about the dream that made you believe he might be in danger."

Amy took a deep breath. "Like I said, it was a quick image that came back to me when you mentioned the fire station."

"So, if I hadn't said anything, you wouldn't have brought it up on your own?"

Amy hadn't thought about that aspect of the experience.

"Yeah, I guess that's true. Your words triggered it."

"Then I'm glad I mentioned it," Natalie said. "Is that the first time that's happened to you? You know, seeing something that might happen in the future and warning someone about it?"

"Like that, yes."

"But you've had other dreams?"

"A lot," Amy admitted. "Ever since I was a little girl."

"I knew it." Natalie clapped her hands together. "I've always thought you were hiding a big piece of your heart from me. I didn't want to be nosy, but there was something going on with you I couldn't quite put my finger on."

The teapot whistled, and Natalie left the table to make the tea. She had her back to Amy, who looked at her friend and debated whether to open up to her about the living room. Natalie returned to the table with tea bags steeping in two cups.

"The titles and themes for both of my books came to me in dreams," Amy said.

Natalie's eyes widened. And throwing caution to the wind, Amy told her about the living room. There was a surprising sense of freedom in baring her soul. Natalie listened in silence until Amy reached the part about the dreams returning after she committed her heart to the Lord at the summer camp during high school. A tear rolled down Natalie's cheek.

"What's wrong?" Amy stopped, fearing she'd overstepped her bounds.

"Nothing. It's so beautiful. The way God has shown his love to you is unbelievable."

"Which is one reason I've kept it to myself. Jeff knows about the dreams but doesn't bug me about them, and my mother never brings them up. I'm sure she secretly hopes they've stopped."

"I'm sorry." Natalie shook her head.

"Why?"

"That you've been hurt over something wonderful that you couldn't control. You were an innocent child who received a great gift from a loving heavenly Father."

Now it was Amy's turn to become teary. She grabbed a soft paper napkin from a holder in the center of the table and touched it to her right eye. The two women sat in silence for a few moments.

"Tell me about the books," Natalie said.

It took several minutes for Amy to tell her about the role the dreams had in creating her books.

"That gives me chill bumps," Natalie said, rubbing her arms. "To know that your books are based on Bible verses you heard directly from God is awesome."

"Don't get too carried away. My novels aren't written in red letters."

"I know, but it's the closest to that sort of thing I've ever known. It makes sense now why what you've written could touch me so deeply. It came from a secret place in your heart and can go to the same place inside a reader."

"That's exactly my prayer." Amy smiled. "And you've given me more encouragement sitting at this table than I've received in my whole life."

"It's about time!" Natalie exclaimed. She paused and took a sip of tea. "How often do you go to the living room now?"

"I had a God dream the night before we met at the coffee shop and another last night."

Amy suddenly stopped and stared at a vase of flowers in the center of the table. It was a colorful arrangement of irises and dahlias surrounded by greenery.

"What?" Natalie asked.

Amy spoke slowly. "Last night I saw a vase of flowers that looked exactly like those and heard the words from 1 Peter 1:24–25: 'All people are like grass, and all their glory is like the flowers of the field; the grass withers and the flowers fall, but the word of the Lord endures forever.' "

Natalie rubbed her arms again. "Quit giving me goose bumps."

"Were those flowers here when I came by last weekend to drop off the hand-me-down clothes from Ian for Ben?" Amy asked. "Maybe what I saw in the dream was a snapshot memory."

"That's impossible. I bought them yesterday. Why do you think you would hear that verse and see a vase of flowers from my house?"

Amy shrugged her shoulders. "I've been asking the Lord to give me the idea for a new novel. A story with flowers in it would be —"

"One with a wedding," Natalie interjected immediately.

"I like that." Amy nodded, then paused as her face became serious. "Or a funeral. The verse mentions how the grass withers and the flowers fall. That speaks more about death than life."

Natalie wiggled in her chair. "That sent the wrong kind of chills down my arms."

"Sorry."

"No, it's okay. I understand a story has to be sad before it can be happy. That's why people keep reading — to find out how problems are solved, people changed, and dangers overcome. What would the title be?"

Amy thought for a moment. "*Fading Flowers* might work. Or *The Flowers of the Field.* That sounds less ominous."

"I like the second one better."

"Whether it's a wedding, a funeral, or both, there has to be more to it," Amy said. "If these verses have anything to do with my next book, I'm going to need a lot of insight before I start writing."

"What if the verse and vase don't have anything to do with a new novel?" Natalie asked.

"Of course, that's possible," Amy replied. "Most of the dreams aren't related to my writing."

"Exactly." Natalie leaned forward. "You dreamed about the vase of flowers and then saw it the next day. What if the Lord starts showing you what is about to happen even more clearly than the warning about Noah's field trip? It's an interesting thought, isn't it?"

Amy felt like the air had been sucked out

of the room.

"Natalie, I wouldn't want the responsibility that would come with that kind of information."

"Which is why God could trust you with it. A person who's curious might misuse —"

"Stop!" Amy said with more force than she intended. "Don't say another word!"

Natalie shut her mouth and gave Amy a wounded look.

"Sorry, I shouldn't have cut you off," Amy said.

"It was just a thought that popped into my head," Natalie said quietly. "Don't take me too seriously."

"And I didn't mean to hurt your feelings," Amy said, "but even the possibility of some kind of window into the future terrifies me."

A somber mood descended on the two women as they finished their tea. The conversation lagged.

"I ruined the soufflé and our lunch," Natalie said glumly when Amy got up to leave.

Amy stepped forward and gave her a hug.

"No. The soufflé was delicious, and what kind of friends would we be if all we talked about was silly girl stuff? It helped a lot to be able to tell you about the dreams. It was healthy for me to share with someone I trust." Amy paused. "But please don't say anything to Luke, okay?"

Natalie crossed her heart with her finger. "I

promise. And if you like, the next time we get together the only topic for discussion will be nail polish."

Six

As she loaded the dishwasher after supper, Amy looked forward to an evening alone while the rest of the family went to the football game. She put Jeff's plate of food in the microwave. Megan, who spent a long time in the bathroom after the meal, came downstairs to the kitchen. Upon seeing her, Amy's immediate reaction was to send her back upstairs to wash her face and start over.

"Why all the makeup?"

"I want to look nice."

"Don't you think you overdid it with the green eye shadow and extra eyeliner? I've never seen you lay it on so thick."

"No. I talked to the other girls. We agreed that we don't want to look like eighth graders."

Amy couldn't prevent the transition from middle school to high school, but she didn't want Megan to rush the process.

"You know how eye shadow fades," Megan continued. "And it won't show up when it gets dark."

"The lights at the football field are bright as day." Amy paused. "Unless you go behind the stands where it's dark."

"Please, Mom. Don't hassle me. I'm not going behind the stands, and I'm not committing some big sin by wanting to look my best."

Jeff came into the kitchen from work. His clothes were covered with fine white dust.

"Don't hug me," he said to Amy, holding out his right hand. "And will you bring my robe to the laundry room? I don't want any of this plaster dust in our bedroom. We had to do extensive wall repair in an upstairs bedroom at the Burris house before we could install the window units." He glanced at Megan. "What's with all the sparkly green eye shadow?"

Megan spun around and left the kitchen.

"You came in on the end of our conversation." Amy pointed at the spot their daughter had vacated. "Megan and her friends are ganging up on us about getting all dolled up, and she played the 'We're all doing it card.' I was trying to decide if fighting excessive makeup was a hill I wanted to die on or not."

"It's not worth dying. And I have a surprise of my own. I'm going to take Ian to the Pizza Palace after the game. That way I can see what kind of group Megan and her pals hang out with."

"She'll be furious."

Jeff shrugged. "I have a right to be there with my son. We'll make sure to sit as far away as we can."

"She'll think I put you up to it."

"And I'll set her straight if that comes up. It's important for Megan to know that her father cares about what she does, where she goes, and who she's with."

"I wish you weren't covered with plaster dust," Amy said.

"Why?"

"Because I'd give you the best hug you've had in weeks."

"Can I save it for after I clean up and change clothes?"

"Yes."

When Bethany's mother arrived, Amy and Megan walked outside in silence. The side door of the blue minivan opened so Megan could get in. Amy could see that Bethany was wearing more makeup than Megan, and Crystal, a slender, blond-haired girl with a very pale complexion, had slathered such a mismatched variety of colors on her face that she looked clownish. A stifling cloud of perfume hung heavy inside the vehicle. Amy couldn't tell if the fragrance was coming from Bethany or Crystal or both. She moved to the driver's-side window.

"Hey, Barb," she said to Bethany's mother.

"Thanks so much for taking the girls to the game and out for pizza."

"You're welcome," Barb responded. "I'll have Megan home around eleven thirty. I'm going to drop the other girls off first."

"Okay." Amy lowered her voice to a whisper. "Keep the window cracked. I don't want you to suffocate."

Barb rolled her eyes, and Amy glanced in the rear seat one last time. Crystal was turned sideways talking to Megan. An image of Crystal crying and alone with her makeup a mess flashed across Amy's mind. Barb started to back out of the driveway. Amy took a few steps to keep up with the car.

"Be safe, girls," she called out. "And stay together!"

Megan gave Amy an exasperated look. Crystal didn't seem to notice.

After Jeff and Ian left for the game, Amy went upstairs to the writing room. The attic space doubled as her reading and writing spot and private place of prayer. The house was quiet. Amy sat in her chair and watched the Canterbury Lane streetlights wink on. She wanted to relax.

But she couldn't get her mind off Crystal.

Amy thought about calling the girl's parents, but what would she tell them? That she had dreams? About the vase of flowers at Natalie's house? About Noah and the fire truck? She'd never had anything more than a brief conversation with Crystal's mother and knew nothing about her father. She tried to imagine herself on the phone attempting to explain to Crystal's mother about the living room.

Amy got up and paced back and forth. Her footsteps caused the thin subfloor to creak and pop. She stared out the window at the darkness descending upon the neighborhood. Leaning her head against the wall, she offered up a silent prayer for help but received no guiding answer. Finally, she sat down and turned on her computer. Opening a private file where she kept a journal, she typed out a brief prayer for Crystal's safety. Staring at the words, she doubted their efficacy. But it was all she had the courage to do.

Amy went downstairs, ate a snack, and tried to lose herself in a romantic comedy on TV.

Jeff and Ian were the first to arrive home from the football game. Ian bounded into the house, his cheeks red. Jeff trailed behind him.

"Mom, I caught a real football!"

"Tell me about it."

"It happened when the other team kicked an extra point after a touchdown. Bobby and me were playing behind the goalposts and stopped to watch. The ball came over the fence, and I caught it. I threw it to one of the men in the white-and-black shirts. He told me I had a nice spiral."

Jeff nodded. "I was in the stands and saw the whole thing. It was a dandy over-the-shoulder catch. Everybody in the stands was giving me a high five and talking about how good Ian is going to be in the future."

"How was the Pizza Palace?" Amy asked.

"There were a bunch of people there," Ian said. "Megan was with her friends, but Dad wouldn't let me go over to where they were sitting."

"There must have been twenty kids crowded around a table for ten," Jeff said.

"Crystal was sitting in a boy's lap while he messed with her hair," Ian added. "It was gross."

"Was she okay?" Amy asked, unable to hide her concern. "Did it look like she'd been crying?"

"Who?" Jeff asked.

"Crystal."

"Uh, I don't know."

"Was she still there when you left?"

"I think so. There was also a boy who was following Megan around like a puppy on a leash."

"Anybody we know?"

"No." Jeff shook his head. "But he's on the junior varsity squad because he was wearing a jersey. They let the boys do that on Friday nights. His number was fifty-four, which means he's probably a linebacker."

"Did Megan seem interested in him?"

"I don't know. You'll have to ask her."

"Was she mad when you and Ian showed up?"

"Why would Megan be mad that we went to Pizza Palace?" Ian asked. "I like pizza more than she does."

"It's way past your bedtime," Amy responded. "Take a quick shower, brush your teeth, and put on your pajamas. I'll be upstairs in ten minutes and expect you to be ready for lights-out."

Ian ran to the kitchen door, stopped, and looked back at Jeff.

"Thanks for taking me, Dad. It was a blast."

"You're welcome," Jeff replied. "Now, get upstairs."

"He'll never forget what happened tonight," Jeff said as soon as Ian left. "Catching that ball was a thrill. The kicker for Loudon County really had a strong leg. He also kicked a forty-two-yard field goal. That doesn't happen much at the high school level."

"And you're sure Crystal was fine when you left the pizza place?"

"Other than looking and acting like a fool. Did you see how much makeup she had on? I know you were upset with Megan, but there was no comparison between her and the other girls." Jeff paused. "Why are you so interested in Crystal?"

Amy bit her lip and didn't answer.

After Ian was tucked into bed, Amy and Jeff waited in the kitchen for Megan to come home. The clock ticked past 11:30 p.m. Jeff yawned for the third time in less than a minute.

"You can go upstairs if you're tired," Amy said. "I'm wide awake."

"Yeah, I'm beat," he replied. "Are you sure you don't want me to stay up with you?"

"No, I'll read a magazine."

Amy turned the pages of a home decorating magazine Natalie had lent her but couldn't focus on the words or the pictures.

Midnight passed without Megan returning, and Amy began to worry. She blamed herself for not asking Bethany's mother for a cell phone number. At 12:05 a.m., the door opened and Megan came dragging in. Her makeup was smudged and her hair slightly disheveled.

"Are you okay?" Amy asked.

"Exhausted," Megan mumbled. "I'm going to sleep."

"What about Crystal? Is she at home?"

Megan looked at Amy and rolled her eyes.

"Don't get me started on that. I have no idea where she is and I don't care. She ruined our evening."

"What happened? Where did she go?" Amy asked.

"Not now, Mom. You can interrogate me in the morning, but don't wake me up. I'm going to sleep till noon."

Megan stayed true to her promise to sleep away the morning. Jeff had a side job scheduled with Butch and left the house by 8:00 a.m. As soon as Ian woke up, he roared out of the house and into the neighborhood to play. When he returned at lunchtime, Megan still hadn't made an appearance.

"Mom!" he called out. "I'm starving!"

Amy was folding clothes on the bed in the master bedroom and came downstairs. Ian had pieces of dried brown grass stuck in his dark hair.

"What can I eat?" he asked.

"Start by washing your hands and drinking a big glass of water. You look like you've been rolling in a pile of hay."

Ian washed his hands at the kitchen sink.

"They let Bobby and me —" He stopped. "Is that right?"

"Yes."

"Bobby and me got to play in the game at the field behind the swimming pool."

Amy didn't try to correct the grammatical error caused by the sudden shift in his sentence.

"They have the goal line and out of bounds marked off with real lime. Because we helped put down the lime, they let us play. I got picked fifth. Bobby was last, but we ended up on the same team. I caught a pass, and after that, the boy playing quarterback threw three more to me. I couldn't run fast enough to score."

"Were you playing two-hand touch?"

"Uh, no. But you couldn't hit anyone in the head and had to arm tackle."

Amy wasn't sure about the modified rules for neighborhood football games played without pads and helmets, but Ian didn't show any signs of blood.

She opened the refrigerator door. "I went to the deli yesterday and bought turkey, ham, and roast beef. Which do you want?"

"All of them," Ian answered.

"Okay, get a plate and some bread."

Ian placed four pieces of bread on a plate. Amy prepared two sandwiches using all three meats, provolone cheese, a slice of tomato, and a brown mustard she knew he liked.

"Do we have any chips?" he asked as he chewed his first bite.

Amy placed a bag of chips on the table beside his chair. He ripped it open.

"This is good," he said after he'd eaten half of the first sandwich. "You make the best sandwiches in the world."

"I'm glad you like it."

Amy took a cup of yogurt from the refrigerator for herself and sat down beside him.

"Tell me more about the game last night," she said.

Ian provided a semi-intelligible account of

the game between the local high school and Loudon County. Amy knew the basic rules of football, but her ten-year-old son had already passed her in technical knowledge.

"The Cross Plains defensive backs had trouble tackling their running back once he got past the line of scrimmage. In the second half we started playing an eight-man front. That helped a lot because their quarterback couldn't pass it very good."

"Well. Pass it very well."

"When would I use the word 'good'?"

"You could say, 'The Loudon County player wasn't a good quarterback. He didn't pass it well.' "

"That's not right. He was a good quarterback running the option play. But he was a bad passer."

Ian finished the first sandwich and took a big bite from his second one. He showed no sign yet of being full.

"Do you know the name of the junior varsity player who was talking to Megan at the Pizza Palace?" Amy asked.

"Nate Drexel," a female voice responded from behind Amy.

Megan was standing in the kitchen door in her bare feet and wearing her pajamas. Her hair hadn't been combed and hung down in her face.

"We're just friends," she continued. "He's a tenth grader who's in my World History and

Algebra II classes. It was just somebody to talk to."

"Okay," Amy answered. "Are you hungry?"

"Just thirsty."

Megan poured a large glass of orange juice, then sat down at the table beside Ian and reached into the bag of chips.

"Can you tell me anything else about Crystal?" Amy asked, trying not to sound as anxious as she felt.

"She messed up the whole night for all of us," Megan said. "She left the restaurant without telling anyone where she was going and wasn't there when Bethany's mom showed up to take us home. We called everyone we knew but couldn't find her. Then her parents came and got in a big fight in front of everyone."

Megan looked at Ian's sandwich. "Can I have a bite?"

"I'll fix one for you," Amy said immediately. "Same as his?"

Megan lifted the corner of the bread.

"Leave it alone!" Ian said.

"I'm just looking."

"Just roast beef for me," Megan said to Amy.

Ian finished eating while Amy prepared a sandwich for Megan.

"I'm going over to Bobby's house," he said. "He's got a new video game."

"What kind of game?" Amy asked. "I don't

want you playing anything violent."

"It's all pretend, and his mom is the same as you."

"Then I'll call her."

Amy held the phone to her ear while she spread mustard on the bread and talked to Bobby's mother.

"Thanks, Nancy," Amy said as the call ended. "I'll do the same."

"Go ahead," she said to Ian. "Bobby's dad checked out the game and said it was okay."

"Jack Pickens likes to kill baby deer," Megan said.

"It's not hunting or war," Ian retorted. "It has something to do with trying to find a treasure."

"Those can be creepy if the role-play part is weird."

"How do you know about that?" Amy asked.

"Spend-the-night parties since I was his age."

Ian left the kitchen before his permission to play the new game could be revoked.

"Give up trying to control everything in Ian's life," Megan said to Amy. "He has to learn on his own."

"Did you learn anything last night?"

"Yes. The next time I want to do something, Crystal isn't going to be there. She left the pizza place with a sleazy guy none of us like. He's a junior and has his own car, but it's a piece of junk I wouldn't be caught dead in. I don't know what she was thinking. Alecia can usually talk sense into her, but not last night. Bethany sent me a text this morning that Crystal ended up at the guy's house all by herself. Her parents had to go pick her up."

"Was she hurt?"

Megan gave Amy an incredulous look. "He didn't beat her up, if that's what you mean. The guy is a jerk, but he's not some kind of psycho."

Amy didn't want the flow of information to stop. Megan took a big bite of sandwich.

"I was hungrier than I thought," Megan said when she swallowed. "And don't worry about me. I want to have fun, but I'm not going to do something stupid like Crystal. You didn't have to send Dad to spy on me."

"I didn't. Your father cares about you."

"It was Dad's idea?" Megan asked in surprise.

"Yes."

"Okay." Megan nodded.

Amy was mystified why it would be bad if she suggested parental surveillance but Megan could accept it if it was initiated by Jeff. She decided not to try to solve that conundrum.

"What will Crystal's parents do to her?"

"Probably ground her for a month, but it won't last."

"Why not?"

"Because she'll wiggle out of it."

Megan finished her sandwich.

"I'm going to take a hot bath and wash my hair," she said, "then read in my room. I have a book report due on Tuesday, and I haven't finished the book."

"What are you reading?"

"*The Lord of the Flies.* Have you read it?"

"Yes."

"I'm at the part where Simon gets killed because they think he's the beast."

"It doesn't get any happier."

Megan left the room. Amy thought about Golding's novel. Beneath the thin veneer of civilization, human nature could be murderously sinister.

Seven

On the Monday before the Thanksgiving holiday, Jeff lingered at home after the children walked out of the house to catch the school bus.

"Have you gotten an idea for a new book yet?" he asked as he poured a second cup of coffee.

Amy, still in her pajamas, was standing at the sink scrubbing the skillet Jeff had used to cook bacon and scrambled eggs. She turned off the water and faced him. She'd thought a lot about the fading flower verse from 1 Peter, but nothing had bubbled to the surface. She was starting to get frustrated, and Jeff bringing up the subject didn't help.

"No, and I'm expecting a call from Bernie Masters asking me the same thing. You know I can't force it; I have to wait on the Lord and trust him. Why?"

"Just wondering." Jeff shifted in place.

Amy waited. There was no subtlety in her husband. His ability to hide his thoughts and feelings was nonexistent. Usually Amy considered that a blessing. She'd much rather know what was going on inside his head than be left wondering.

"While you're on hold with the writing thing, would you consider talking with Ms. Burris? I'm doing the final inspection for the job at her house this morning, and I'd like to mention it to her."

"Working as Ms. Burris's maid isn't what I want to do," Amy said flatly. "You may not have noticed, but I've been slaving around here for the past two weeks getting the house cleaned up for the holidays. I don't want your mother to be embarrassed about the woman you married when she and your father come for Thanksgiving dinner."

"She likes you." Jeff paused. "It's your mother who sets her off."

"And we've solved that problem by telling my mother she can't come until Saturday."

Jeff took another sip of coffee. "Amy, I can't get the thought of you helping Ms. Burris out of my mind. How well did you know her when you worked for the law firm?"

"Not very well. We talked on the phone a few times when she needed to set up an appointment to see Mr. Phillips, and I saw her briefly when she came in for appointments."

Amy groped around in her mind for the right words to put an end to Jeff's persistent efforts to turn her into a part-time domestic.

"Would you consider helping her as a way to earn extra money to get us through Christmas?" he asked. "It would be like a trial work period for both of you. If it didn't work out, then you could quit. I could present it to her the same way. I'd hate to see a good opportunity wither away like flowers that have been cut."

Poised to deliver an emphatic retort that would forever squelch the subject of working for Ms. Burris, Amy abruptly shut her mouth instead.

"Will you at least talk to her?" Jeff finished.

Amy tried to open her mouth to reply, but her heart wouldn't let her.

"What did you say?" she asked, stalling for time.

"Which part?"

"The last."

"That it won't take a lot of your time and would be a trial work period. If Ms. Burris was a poor woman who couldn't pay you, I bet you'd consider helping her because you're a Christian. Just because she can pay doesn't mean it isn't worthwhile."

"No, about dead flowers."

"Uh, the chance for a job won't last long, just like grass or flowers that have been cut and have to be thrown out in a few days. It's just a figure of speech. What do you call it?"

"A simile."

Tension had Amy's insides tied up in knots.

She knew there was only one way to relieve the pressure.

"You win. Tell Ms. Burris I'll come over and talk to her."

"Great." Jeff brightened up. "When would be a good time?"

"Whatever suits her. Are you satisfied now?"

"I'm only asking you to consider it for a month or so. I wasn't sure I should even bring it up, but I couldn't get it out of my mind, and —"

"Go," Amy said with a wave of her hand. "I don't want you to be late for work."

As soon as Jeff was out of the house, Amy plopped down in one of the kitchen chairs. The easing of tension in her stomach was temporary. The prospect of having to ring the doorbell at Ms. Burris's house and talk to her about cleaning her house brought it back.

After taking a shower and getting dressed, she called Natalie and told her what happened.

"Did he quote the verses?"

"No, but he came close enough that it got my attention. Ever since we found out that the cost of Megan's dance lessons is going up, Jeff has wanted me to get a part-time job cleaning houses."

"Dance lessons can't be that expensive."

"They're not," Amy admitted, "but there are much bigger bills coming due that Jeff and I can't cover in our budget. We're going to be in a tight squeeze beginning in January, and my income from writing isn't going to cover the gap."

"I'm sorry. It cuts down the excitement of being a writer, doesn't it?"

"Yeah."

"I have an idea," Natalie said. "Why don't I hire you to clean my house? And I bet Sophie Melton and Kristen Land would use you, too."

Amy felt her face flush.

"Cleaning houses for you and your friends would be tougher on me than working for a stranger like Ms. Burris."

"It's just an idea. I wasn't trying to put you down."

"You're sweet to offer, but something inside tells me I have to see if Ms. Burris will let me work for her. If that doesn't pan out, I'm not sure what I'll do."

"Luke did a photo shoot for Ms. Burris's family at her house last year. He said it's a huge place for one woman to take care of."

"I may be the answer to that need."

Amy's cell phone beeped. It was Jeff.

"Gotta go," she said. "That's Jeff calling."

Mustering as much resolve as she could, Amy accepted the call.

"I just left the Burris house," Jeff said. "Ms. Burris is willing to meet you at two thirty this afternoon. That should give you time to talk to her and still be home when Ian gets off the bus."

"Okay. Did you go over any of the details with her?"

"No, but she seemed excited to meet you. She remembers you from the law office but hadn't made the connection between us. Before I left she mentioned hiring me to do some odd jobs around the place. There's always something that needs fixing in an old house."

"You can fix the toilet, and I'll clean it," Amy said.

Jeff was silent for a moment.

"Are you sure you're okay with this?" he asked. "You changed your mind so fast it kind of threw me off."

"It threw me off, too, but I'm not upset with you. I need to follow through with this and see where it leads."

The call ended, leaving Amy with a smidgen of guilt soiling her conscience. She knew she'd been hard on Jeff but couldn't think of a way to apologize over the phone. She resolved to make it right before they went to sleep that night.

It was an overcast day that matched Amy's mood. To get to Ms. Burris's house, she followed the same route she used to go to the law firm. It seemed longer than eighteen months since she'd logged off her computer and cleaned out her desk. She'd been a good secretary. Her work at Jones, Barrington, and Phillips was boring and mundane when typing a long document but challenging when rushing to prepare something for court.

The law firm was old-fashioned and stodgy enough that Mr. Phillips expected his personal secretary to wear dresses, skirts, or nice slacks. The senior lawyer always came to work in a coat and tie, even after some of the other attorneys adopted business casual attire on days they didn't go to court or meet with clients. As she turned onto McDonald Street, Amy knew dresses wouldn't be her working wardrobe at the Burris home.

Up ahead, she could see the two-story brick house with the large holly bushes and white gazebo. The front yard was billiard-table flat and carefully manicured. The outside trim of the house had a fresh coat of white paint. The new windows installed by Jeff's crew blended perfectly with the style of the house. Amy knew her husband made sure each window was mounted as carefully as a painting in a frame. She pulled into a semicircular driveway that looped in front of the house. Her car looked out of place, unless, of course, it was the maid's vehicle. She walked up a brick sidewalk to the front door. There was a huge lion's-head brass knocker, but she pressed the button for the doorbell and waited. No one came, and Amy checked her watch. It was 2:31 p.m. The door opened.

Ms. Mildred Burris was just as Amy remembered from the last time they'd crossed paths at the law office. Short, with carefully coiffed white hair and a wrinkled face, she was wearing a dark blue dress with a single strand of pearls around her neck. Her blue eyes almost matched the color of her dress. She squinted slightly at the afternoon sun that was shining in her face.

"Come in, come in," Ms. Burris said in a soft Southern voice. "I remember you from Harold Phillips's office. I knew you were special then, just not how much."

Puzzled, Amy followed the older woman into a small parlor to the left of the entrance hall. The furniture didn't look as old as Amy would have expected. Ms. Burris had done more remodeling at the house than just replacing the windows.

"Why don't you sit there," Ms. Burris said, pointing to a yellow chair with beautiful floral upholstery.

"That's almost too pretty to sit on," Amy said.

"One of my great-nieces helped me pick it out."

Ms. Burris sat to Amy's right on a love seat. The upholstery on the love seat was more subdued than the chair but picked up some of the same colors. Amy glanced around the room. There were three paintings on the walls, each one intriguing enough that Amy wanted to step closer for a better look. A wooden secretary desk in the corner looked like an antique. The low table in front of the love seat had an interesting swirl design in the wood around its edges. If Amy had to clean a house, this would be a nice one to keep tidy.

"I love this room," Amy said.

"You're sweet, but it's just a shadow, isn't it?"

Amy raised her eyebrows. "I'm not sure what you mean."

Ms. Burris smiled, which made her blue eyes almost close.

"Tell me about you," Ms. Burris said, scooting back in the love seat. "I want to hear everything you want to share."

"I worked at Jones, Barrington, and Phillips for twelve years after my husband and I moved here from Jacksonville, Florida. We have two children, a fourteen-year-old girl and a boy who's ten. The last six years at the law firm I was Mr. Phillips's secretary. I left my job there a year and a half ago to devote my time to writing. I've written two novels and hope to start a third one soon."

"I read the article in the paper about you. I think it mentioned that you'd worked for Harold. Your picture caught my eye, and your husband showed me a photo of you and the children on his phone."

When Amy's first novel was released, the

paper printed a local interest piece about her that included a shot of Amy sitting at her computer pretending to write.

"Yes, there was a kind quote from Mr. Phillips mentioning how proud he was of my accomplishments."

"Harold doesn't dish out praise very readily, does he?"

"No, ma'am, he doesn't. Anyway, I'm looking for a part-time job because writing inspirational romance novels isn't very profitable, at least at first. I'm very punctual and reliable. Mr. Phillips can verify that. And I'm a hard worker —"

"Especially when you put your head on the pillow at night," Ms. Burris said with a smile. "Not many people learn more about God's kingdom while they're asleep than awake."

Amy's mouth dropped open. She felt an immediate mixture of shock and a hint of anger at Jeff. He knew how much she valued her privacy.

"Did Jeff tell you about my dreams?"

"No," Ms. Burris replied with a wave of her hand. "But I like him. He's a good man."

"Then how did you know?"

"I saw you asleep with your head on a stone and Jacob's ladder reaching up to heaven. The interpretation seemed clear enough to me."

Stunned, Amy didn't know what to say. Ms. Burris sat on the love seat and blinked her eyes. The old woman didn't seem in a hurry to help her.

"When did you see me?" Amy asked.

"One afternoon while your husband was here. I wasn't sure what to do about the vision, but when he asked if you could come over to talk to me about a job, I knew it wasn't just so I could show you around the house. We needed to meet. Would you be kind enough to tell me a little bit about your dreams? When did they start?"

Ms. Burris's tone of voice was the same as if she were asking Amy to share tips about growing roses. Opening up to Natalie had been a huge step, but she was Amy's closest friend. Amy had been talking on a personal level with Ms. Burris for only five minutes.

"I'm not sure," Amy began. "I've had dreams since I was a little girl, but I'm not comfortable —" She stopped.

"I totally understand. We've just met." Ms. Burris held up her hand. "I've not been blessed in the same way as you, but the older I get, the smaller the gap seems between this world and the next. I'm beginning to understand why the apostle Paul said he longed to depart this life for what lies ahead. I want to go, too, but not because I'm sick. My health is good. But the glimpses I've had of what awaits us are so wonderful that it's almost more than my heart can bear. That's exciting, isn't it?"

Amy couldn't believe what she was hearing.

"Did you think you're the only person who walks with the Lord?" Ms. Burris continued.

"No, ma'am," Amy responded quickly, then added, "But I've lived as if I were. Part of it has been self-protection because of the way people reacted to my dreams when I was a child. I didn't want anyone to think I was crazy."

"You're not crazy, but you can't deny you're different."

It was a simple, sobering truth that Amy had never directly faced. The words went straight into her heart.

Ms. Burris smiled, and Amy realized she might have bigger problems with fear and pride than her reluctance to clean a stranger's bathrooms.

"The gifts of the Lord are like fruit trees," Ms. Burris said after a few moments passed. "Branches grow in new directions and fresh fruit is produced. We don't control the process. Our job is to remain connected to the trunk and share the fruit with those in need."

"I'm not sure what that means."

Ms. Burris leaned forward slightly. "Chapter 15 of the gospel of John isn't just a metaphor about a vine with branches. It's a true description of the spiritual life. Your gift is growing in a new dimension, isn't it?"

Amy immediately thought about Noah,

Natalie's flowers, and Crystal.

"Yes," she said. "I've started receiving glimpses of the future in my dreams, and I don't like it. I just want to enjoy the Lord's presence and let him love me."

"I understand. I'd feel the same way."

The look in the old woman's eyes convinced Amy that Ms. Burris really did understand.

"But there's a bright side to glimpsing what lies around the corner," Ms. Burris said cheerfully. "Because of the vision I saw, we're having a nice talk today. Would you like a cup of coffee or hot tea? It was rude of me not to offer something when you arrived, but I was so excited to meet you."

"I don't drink coffee in the afternoon, but tea would be nice."

Amy followed the older woman to the kitchen. It, too, had been modernized with new appliances and updated cabinets. A large island covered with decorative tiles was in the center of the room. There was a sunroom at the rear of the house. After the tea brewed, they went to the sunroom and sat in wicker chairs with comfortable, green-striped cushions. Colorful birds swooped in to eat at decorative feeders that were outside the sunroom windows.

They talked for more than an hour about Amy's life and family. When Natalie's name came up, Ms. Burris wanted to know all about her and suggested the three of them get together for lunch. The older woman deflected Amy's questions to her about herself. Then they prayed together. After Ms. Burris said, "Amen," Amy couldn't remember when she'd felt so refreshed and encouraged. Standing at the front door about to leave, she turned around.

"Ms. Burris, if you'll let me, I'd really love to come to work for you."

EIGHT

Amy wouldn't tell Jeff the details of her visit with Ms. Burris until after supper, when both children were upstairs in their rooms doing homework. She checked the stairwell to make sure they wouldn't be disturbed.

"Why all the mystery?" Jeff asked when they were seated on the couch in the family room. "You're either going to work for her or not."

"No," Amy replied. "It was so much more than that. Five minutes into our conversation I was on the verge of telling her my deepest, darkest secrets."

"Deep, dark secrets? What have you done that I don't know about?"

"Nothing," Amy replied. "But you know how hard it is for me to trust other people with private information."

While Amy talked, Jeff's normally impassive face revealed an unusually complex range of reactions.

"Did she say anything about me?" he asked.

"Nothing except you were a good man. But

I already knew that."

"I'm glad she didn't have a vision of me with horns or something."

"She's not like that. When the Lord gives her insight into a person or situation, her response is to pray in secret or use the information to help in a practical way. That's what she was doing with me. She wasn't freaked out by the fact that I have dreams. She wants to help me."

"Did she give you a tour of the house?"

"Just the downstairs. We ended up in the sunroom."

"That's a neat place. The kitchen is first-class, too."

Amy paused. "Why do you think an older woman like Ms. Burris has gone to all the trouble to remodel her entire house?"

"She never told me."

"I'm sure she has her reasons," Amy said and shrugged. "We spent at least an hour talking in the sunroom, and then we prayed together. It was a sweet time."

"Did you talk about the job?"

"Not much, but before I left I told her I'd love to work for her. She smiled, wrinkled her eyes, and told me she'd call me."

"Do you think she'll hire you?"

"Probably. But mainly because she wants us to spend time together. Scrubbing the floors would be a secondary reason. And after meeting her, I'm sure she'd let me set up my schedule so that I could do what I need to for the kids."

"Sounds good. I hope she calls soon."

The house phone in the kitchen rang. Both Jeff and Amy jumped.

"Do you think?" Jeff asked as Amy shot up from the couch and went into the kitchen.

The caller ID showed an unfamiliar local number.

"Hello," Amy said.

"Is this Mrs. Amy Clarke?" a male voice asked.

"Yes."

Jeff came to the opening between the kitchen and the family room.

"This is Neil Branch. I'm running for the school board in the special election to replace a member who moved away and had to resign. I see that you have two children currently in the system."

"Yes, I do."

"I'd appreciate your support on December 4. Turnout is expected to be low, so every vote will be important."

Jeff was making gestures in an effort to get Amy to let him know what was going on.

"It's nothing," she said to him.

"I'm sorry," Branch said. "What did you ask me?"

"I was talking to my husband. Thanks for your willingness to serve. I'll mention to my husband that you called."

Amy hung up the phone.

"That was a man named Neil Branch. He's running for the school board."

"I know Neil. He works for the insurance agency that wrote the policy for our house and cars. I'd vote for him."

The following morning Amy and Natalie met at the coffee shop. Amy couldn't wait to tell her about Ms. Burris.

"It sounds like the two of you were cut from the same piece of cloth," Natalie said after Amy told her about the visit.

"There are differences. She's not a dreamer, but there is a lot I can learn from her about the way she responds to what the Lord shows her. For the first time in my life, I met someone I can really open up with —" Amy stopped. "That didn't come out right."

"I know what you mean," Natalie reassured her. "There are things you and I can discuss because we both have young children. With Ms. Burris, you can share spiritual experiences."

"But I want to talk to you, too. It felt good to finally tell you about the living room the other day. It wasn't healthy for me to keep everything bottled up inside."

"Did you tell Ms. Burris about the verse from 1 Peter, the one about the flowers of the field?"

"No, it didn't come up."

"I've thought about it a lot. Do you still believe it might have something to do with your next novel?"

"Maybe."

"Well, I think *The Flowers of the Field* would be a neat title for a book. Maybe I could do a painting for the cover."

"That would be awesome!" Amy responded. "Of course, the publisher would have to approve it, but it would be fun for us to do something creative together. Oh, and I forgot to mention one of the most important parts of my meeting with Ms. Burris. I told her about you, and she wants the two of us to come to her house for lunch."

"I'm not sure it would be safe for me to be in the same room with you and Ms. Burris."

"Why not?"

"You'd talk about my secret sins as if they were printed in a newspaper."

Amy anxiously awaited Ms. Burris's call. One day, two days, a week passed by. Several times Amy picked up the phone but didn't have the confidence to enter the number. The next step was up to Ms. Burris, and for whatever reason, the older woman wasn't ready to take it.

One Saturday evening a week and a half before Christmas, Jeff, Amy, and Ian went to the local theater playhouse for Megan's Christmas dance recital.

"How long will this last?" Ian asked.

"A couple of hours," Amy replied.

"Why does Megan have to be one of the last people to dance?"

"Because the more advanced students perform at the end."

"That doesn't make any sense. They ought to have the best dancers at the beginning before everyone gets bored to death."

"Good point," Jeff said.

"The little girls go first," Amy said, cutting her eyes at Jeff.

"Are you going to make Megan come to my football games when I'm in middle school?" Ian asked.

It was a tough question. Jeff glanced at Amy and raised his eyebrows to let her know he wasn't going to answer it.

"If she doesn't have another school commitment, we'll encourage her to come," Amy said.

"I had another commitment tonight," Ian replied. "Bobby wanted me to spend the night and play video games."

"That's not school-related."

Ian gave up and stared out the window. It was a ten-minute drive to the playhouse theater, which was located in a building that formerly housed an Italian restaurant. The parking lot was filling up by the time they arrived. Inside, the beginning dancers scampered around in white and pink leotards. Ms.

Carlton used the older girls to help teach the younger students, and Amy knew some of the little girls were in a group led by Megan.

"There's Tiffany Cline," Amy said, pointing to a petite blonde who was holding her mother's hand. "She's one of Megan's girls."

They sat on folding chairs toward the back of the room. Ian sat between Amy and Jeff so his fidgeting wouldn't bother anyone else. After the younger girls danced the crowd would thin out, and they could move closer to the stage if they wanted to.

Ms. Carlton, a slender woman in her fifties, had run the studio so long that it had become a local institution. Mothers sent their daughters for dance lessons because it had been part of their own lives growing up. The instructor welcomed the crowd, and the show began. Amy and Jeff had been to enough Christmas programs that the routines were familiar. Some of the smaller girls came out and froze with stage fright.

"Why aren't they moving?" Ian asked.

"They're scared," Amy replied.

"Then they ought to sit on a bench or something."

Amy heard Jeff chuckle.

Halfway through the program there was a ten-minute intermission that gave the parents of younger children who'd already performed a graceful opportunity to leave. Amy gave Ian money for a snack. When he returned, they moved up to some open seats on the third row. To Amy's left was a blond-haired young man in his early thirties.

The older girls performed both group and solo routines. Megan was part of an ensemble that reenacted the angels announcing the birth of Jesus to the shepherds. It was a graceful piece performed to contemporary Christian music. Megan brought feeling to the performance and, to Amy's eye, danced flawlessly. After a quick change in the back, Megan came out for her three-minute solo. It was a free-flowing routine about a snowflake that falls from the sky, then melts in the winter sun.

"Did you approve that outfit?" Jeff whispered.

Amy stared straight ahead and shook her head. The costume was too low-cut for her taste, too. Amy was always nervous when Megan performed, but concern that Megan would turn the wrong way and accidentally reveal too much caused additional anxiety. Amy breathed a sigh of relief when Megan melted on the stage and the music ended. When the applause died down, Amy leaned over to Jeff.

"I'll bring up the outfit issue with Ms. Carlton," she said.

"If you don't, I will."

There were two more solo performances. Both of the girls wore costumes that Amy considered out of bounds for teenagers. It appeared an unfortunate trend was under way. When the show was over, Megan came bounding out, still wearing her snowflake outfit.

"You danced beautifully in both pieces," Amy said, giving her a hug.

"Ms. Carlton let me help design the costume," Megan said. "How do you like it?"

"Uh, it's very realistic," Amy answered as she gave Jeff a look to let him know it wasn't a good time to criticize. "And you really sold the story."

The blond-haired man who'd been sitting on their row stepped closer. Megan turned around.

"Mr. Ryan! I didn't think you'd really come."

Megan introduced the teacher to Amy and Jeff. Even in a North Carolina winter, he exuded an unmistakable West Coast vibe. He shook Jeff's hand.

"I never would have guessed that a studio in a town like Cross Plains would have such a high-level program, especially for contemporary dance," Ryan said.

"Ms. Carlton has been running the studio for years," Amy said. "Have you been interested in dance for a long time?"

"Since I was a teenager. A girl I dated in high school dragged me to a dance class because she needed a male partner, and I was hooked. My buddies on the soccer team made fun of me, but it's not bad being one of the few males in a world dominated by beautiful girls."

"You don't dance now, do you?"

"No. I blew out my right knee in a skiing accident, so all I can do now is watch and appreciate a good performance."

Megan was hanging on the teacher's every word.

"I've enjoyed having Megan in my World History class," he said. "She's a great student."

"She takes after her mother," Jeff replied.

Ryan turned to Amy.

"And Megan tells me you're a novelist. I like to write, but I've never had the discipline to finish anything longer than a short story, and nothing I've written has been published."

"I'm just getting started."

"Landing a book contract is a big deal. Congratulations."

Amy could see how this good-looking male teacher would be popular with the students.

"What brought you to Cross Plains?" she asked. "Megan said you came from California."

"She did?" Ryan looked at Megan.

"That's what Bethany and I guessed," Megan replied, blushing. "I think I told my mom you looked like you were from California, and I heard you talking to some of the boys about surfing."

"Actually, I'm from Colorado, but I've spent time in the San Diego area, too," Ryan replied. "When I was in college, I'd ski in the winter and go to California to surf in the summer. That life ended when I hurt my knee and had to start paying back student loans."

"Can we go home now?" Ian asked, pulling on Amy's arm.

"Don't interrupt," Amy said.

"I need to leave myself," Ryan said. "Nice meeting you."

Megan went to the dressing room to get the rest of her clothes. While they waited, Amy complimented Ms. Carlton on another good program but didn't bring up Megan's costume.

"I thought you were going to say something to her about Megan's outfit," Jeff said when the dance teacher moved on.

"It bothered me as much as you, but I'll do it later when she's not dealing with the stress of putting on a big program."

"I can't believe Mr. Ryan came to the recital," Megan said when they were in the car. "Bethany will be sick with jealousy."

"Why?" Jeff asked.

"All the girls have a secret crush on him. I mean, he's like something from a magazine."

"Remember what your dad and I mentioned the other day —"

"I know, I know," Megan interrupted, then

stared out the window.

They rode the rest of the way home in silence.

Three days before Christmas Amy was in the family room wrapping presents. Outside, the wind whistled through the leafless trees. Jeff was at work, and Megan and Ian were spending the afternoon with friends. The phone in the kitchen rang. Amy quickly finished tying a bow and ran to answer it.

"Hello," she said, slightly breathless.

"Amy?" a male voice asked.

"Yes."

"This is Harold Phillips. I hope I didn't interrupt anything."

Amy stood up straighter at the sound of the familiar voice.

"No, sir. I was wrapping Christmas presents."

"You always did a great job of that for me," the lawyer said.

When she worked at the law firm, Amy wrapped presents that Mr. Phillips gave to his family, clients, and friends. His favorite gift for other people was a sleeve of golf balls. He even gave them to his wife, complete with her initials embossed on them.

"I'd like to talk to you about something important," he said.

"Okay," Amy replied slowly as her mind

raced in several directions at once. "I'm listening."

"At the office."

Amy's hair was gathered into a loose ponytail, and she wasn't wearing any makeup.

"I'm in no shape to come downtown," she said.

"How about two this afternoon? That will give you time to get ready."

"What's this about?"

"Will two o'clock work for you?"

Amy knew it was impossible to pry information from the lawyer if he didn't want to give it out over the phone. She glanced at the calendar on the wall of the kitchen. She knew it was empty for the afternoon but checked anyway.

"Yes, sir."

"Good. I'll see you then."

Amy lowered the receiver, then grabbed her cell phone and sent Jeff a text message. He didn't reply. She returned to the family room and continued wrapping presents. Mr. Phillips didn't seem upset. He wouldn't have been able to hide his emotions if a mistake she'd made while working there had come to light and cost the firm a lot of money. And he didn't give any indication that he wanted to talk to her about employment. Amy returned to the kitchen and dialed the main number for the law firm.

"Jones, Barrington, and Phillips," an unfamiliar voice answered.

"Is Mr. Phillips's secretary available?"

"Just a minute, I'll connect you to Emily Ashburn."

Amy hung up as soon as the receptionist put her on hold. She'd have to wait until 2:00 p.m. to find out what was on Harold Phillips's mind.

While Amy was eating a salad for lunch, Jeff called, and she told him about the brief conversation with Mr. Phillips. One of his first questions was the same one she had.

"Yes, I called the law firm and made sure Emily was still there," Amy said. "And Mr. Phillips didn't sound upset, so I don't believe they've uncovered some huge mistake I made before I left."

"Let me know what it's about," Jeff said. "I'll keep my cell phone with me."

Amy had trouble trying to choose an outfit for the meeting. It didn't seem right to dress too casually, but it wasn't necessary to show up wearing her best clothes for a job interview. In the end, she put on an outfit she'd worn while working for the firm. As she got dressed, she realized one benefit of a writer's life was a cheaper wardrobe. Amy's clothes budget had plummeted since she could wear workout clothes all day at the house. She checked herself in the full-length mirror. Nothing had changed in her appearance over the past eighteen months, but she knew she'd changed inside, some of which she was still trying to sort out. She left a note on the refrigerator door so Megan and Ian would know approximately when she'd be home.

Driving to the law firm, Amy passed Ms. Burris's house. A large, decorative wreath hung on the front door. Amy touched her cell phone that was beside her on the passenger seat of the car. She wanted to call, but it just didn't feel right. She needed to trust Ms. Burris and didn't want to be pushy.

The law firm was only a couple of minutes from the Burris home. Most of the cars in the parking area at the rear of the office were familiar. Amy parked next to Mr. Phillips's silver Mercedes. Brick pavers formed a path around the side of the house to the front door. The law firm had maintained the landscaping of the old mansion, and Amy always enjoyed the sights and smells of each season. Early winter meant beds of brightly colored pansies smiling upward from beside the walkway. Today the pansies danced in the wind.

The name of the law firm was engraved on a square brass plaque beside the large wooden front door. Nelson Jones, one of the original founders of the firm, had been dead for twenty-five years. Bill Barrington, the second named partner, retired shortly before Amy was hired. Now in his eighties, Mr. Barrington and his wife spent most of the year at their beach house on the Outer Banks. That left Mr. Phillips as the only named partner practicing law with the firm. There were four younger partners, but the law firm name never changed. Amy suspected ambition by the other lawyers to have their names at the top of the letterhead and engraved on a new brass plate was quickly squelched by Mr. Phillips. He believed keeping the same name for decades communicated stability and prestige to clients and the community at large.

Amy was slightly nervous as she pushed open the front door but much less fearful than when she'd arrived years before for her initial interview. At that time, she was trying to convince Ms. Kirkpatrick, the firm administrator, that a year and a half of experience working for a CPA firm in Jacksonville qualified her for employment at a law office.

The firm reception area was the foyer of the house. There wasn't much space for seating; however, there were three conference rooms adjacent to the reception area, and clients were efficiently funneled into the conference rooms for meetings with the lawyers. An attractive young woman in her twenties sat behind a shiny wooden desk in the foyer. Amy looked at the familiar grandfather clock to the right of the front door. It was 1:58 p.m. Mr. Phillips valued punctuality and didn't like to be interrupted early or kept waiting. Amy introduced herself to the receptionist, who gave no indication she knew about Amy's former association with the firm.

"I have an appointment with Mr. Phillips at two o'clock," Amy said.

"I'll let him know you're here."

Amy sat in a leather side chair. There was a collection of regional and national magazines on a low table along with the current edition of the *Wall Street Journal.* Amy sat with her hands folded in her lap. She knew she wouldn't have to wait long. As the clock struck the hour, Mr. Phillips entered the reception area. Sixty-two years old with white hair and rugged good looks, the lawyer was comfortably perched atop the legal community in Cross Plains. The local judges gave Mr. Phillips an extra measure of respect when he appeared in their courtrooms. He greeted Amy with the smile he reserved for people he wanted to persuade or influence.

"Nice to see you," he said, extending his hand. "We'll talk in my office."

Amy saw the receptionist watching them as they left the foyer. Amy steeled herself for whatever important matter justified being summoned to the law firm. When in full-manipulation mode, Mr. Phillips almost always got his way.

The senior partner's office was in the former dining room. Entering the office, a visitor faced a bank of six tall windows with an expansive view of the side yard. The lawyer's desk was to the right with a small sitting area at the opposite end of the room. Amy's workstation had been behind Mr. Phillips's office in a converted butler pantry that led to the dining room on one side and a hallway on the other.

"How does it feel to be back in the office?" Mr. Phillips asked when they were seated.

"Fine," Amy replied, then stopped. She didn't want to say more than necessary.

Mr. Phillips sat back in his chair and crossed his legs. "I was reviewing some trust documents the other day and thought about you."

"Was there a problem?" Amy asked anxiously.

"No, no, but you typed them and your signature was at the end as one of the witnesses."

Amy waited. Mr. Phillips cleared his throat.

"How is the writing career progressing?"

"Fine. I enjoy it."

"I know you resigned your job to pursue a writing career, but I couldn't get the thought out of my mind that you might be interested in coming back to work here in some capacity. Emily is pregnant, and her doctor has ordered her to go on bed rest until the baby is born. After that she'll be on FML for at least a couple of months. I need a replacement until she returns. Also, we've brought in a new associate who is rapidly expanding his practice and would benefit from working with an experienced person like you. The firm could hire a temp, but you'd be infinitely more useful."

Amy's mind was racing. She knew what Jeff would want her to do, but her heart was unsettled.

"Taking care of your work is a full-time job," she said.

"Things have changed a bit since you left. Emily is primarily a word processor, and you've always been a fast, accurate typist. I bet you can finish a book in a month."

"Not exactly. It's different from transcription."

Mr. Phillips continued as if he'd not heard her. "And I think you'll like our new associate. His name is Chris Lance. He graduated from law school in Chapel Hill a year and a half ago. Some of these young lawyers believe they can type as fast as they can dictate, but I know you can show him how to be more efficient. There would be an increase in your salary and full benefits without a waiting period."

"I need to think about it and talk to Jeff."

"Certainly, and I'm not asking you for a ten-year commitment. I need help for the time Emily is going to be out, and we'll be evaluating the situation with Chris after six months or so. But if you do this and want to stay at the firm, I will make sure there's a place for you."

Amy was shocked at how accommodating Mr. Phillips wanted to be.

"This is very kind of you," she said. "I'll let you know as soon as possible."

"By tomorrow?"

Amy knew better than to try to negotiate for an extension of time.

"Yes, sir."

Mr. Phillips stood and escorted Amy back to the reception area as if she were an important client. Once she was in her car, Amy phoned Jeff and told him about the meeting.

"What do you think?" she asked, slightly out of breath.

"That he's realized how good he had it when you worked for him."

"Working for Mr. Phillips would be temporary. He's not getting rid of Emily. He wants me to break in the new associate named Chris."

"Do you really believe Mr. Phillips would give Emily her job back if he preferred you to her?"

"No," Amy admitted. "He'd either lay her off or shift her someplace else in the firm."

"Exactly. I think it's a great opportunity. Even if it only turns out to be for six months, your salary will help us out a lot, not to mention the benefits. What would dependent health coverage for the kids cost at the law firm? It might be cheaper than the amount I'm going to have to pay here."

"I don't know. I'll have to talk to Ms. Kirkpatrick, but I know I'd be covered as part of my compensation package." Amy paused. "But this feels like I'm going backward, not forward. And it will be so much tougher finding time to write my next book if I'm working forty hours a week."

"You did it before, and you can do it again. And you don't have a deadline on an option book."

"I will if the publisher likes the concept and exercises the option."

"When that happens, I'll do what I can in the evenings and weekends to give you time to write. And the kids are old enough to fend for themselves at night. Neither one of them wants you hovering over them."

"I'm not hovering —"

"Sorry, that didn't come out right. You're a mother who cares."

Amy could already tell from Jeff's tone of voice that he really wanted her to accept the job and was probably worried he'd say the wrong thing and push her into turning it down.

"Let's talk later," she said. "I don't have to let Mr. Phillips know until tomorrow."

Amy started the car and left the law firm parking lot. She turned onto McDonald Street and slowed as she approached Ms.

Burris's house. The elderly woman's car was parked in front of the garage. Amy turned into the driveway. It was time to be pushy.

Nine

Amy admired the wreath on the door for a moment before pressing the door chime. Showing up unannounced wasn't polite, but she hoped Ms. Burris wouldn't mind. She brushed her hair away from her face and adjusted her glasses. The door opened.

"Come in," Ms. Burris said. "I didn't know it would be you, but I'm glad it is."

Entering the foyer, Amy caught a glimpse of a tall Christmas tree in the living room. There was a large ceramic angel perched atop the tree.

"May I see your tree?" she asked.

Ms. Burris was already at the door of the parlor where they'd talked before but stopped and turned toward the living room.

"Yes, we can sit in there if you like."

The tree was placed in front of a double window that overlooked the front yard. It was covered with many unusual ornaments, some homemade, others expensive and ornate.

"It's a pretty tree," Amy said. "Who helped

you decorate it?"

"Katelyn, one of my great-nieces, came for a visit with her husband. She's got an artistic eye."

Ms. Burris sat at one end of a leather sofa. Amy sat across from her in a Queen Anne wing chair. She glanced around the room again and cleared her throat.

"I've been waiting for your call. Have you made up your mind about the job?"

"I'm sorry I haven't gotten in touch with you. I'm still praying and asking the Lord about it," Ms. Burris responded.

"Okay."

"Has something else come up?"

"Yes." Amy nodded. "And I need to let them know by tomorrow."

Ms. Burris sat quietly with her hands folded in her lap. Amy glanced down at the edge of the woolen rug that covered part of the floor. Mr. Phillips hadn't told her to keep the job offer from the law firm secret.

"I got a phone call from Mr. Phillips this morning asking me to come into the office and meet with him," she said. "I just left there. He wants me to return to work at the law firm, temporarily, while his secretary is on maternity leave, and possibly long term if I want to."

"And you don't want to go back to Egypt when you've started on your journey to the Promised Land."

"Yes," Amy said with relief. "That's a very accurate way of putting it. Jeff and I need the money and benefits, but that's not the only thing that's important, is it?"

Amy waited, but Ms. Burris didn't speak.

"Would the Lord tell you what I'm supposed to do?" Amy asked.

"He might, but my job is usually to confirm what he's already shown someone."

"I know what my husband wants," Amy sighed. "For him, the law firm represents financial stability."

"Which makes sense. It's a blessing to be married to a man who thinks about his family first."

It was a simple statement, but Amy had never applied it to Jeff. She had to admit that Ms. Burris was right.

"Yes."

"Would it make it easier for you if I told you I wasn't going to ask you to work for me?" Ms. Burris asked.

"That's not the way I want to decide."

"Good. All I can say is that my heart is telling me you have an important job to do. I don't know whether it's here with me or for Harold Phillips. But wherever you end up and whatever you do there, I believe it's time for your light to shine brighter than it ever has before."

For some unknown reason, Ms. Burris's softly spoken challenge took Amy's breath away. Not hiding her light was an idea familiar to her since childhood, but hearing the words at that moment, Amy knew there was a mature, much bolder expression for it.

"Yes, ma'am," she managed after a moment.

"The Lord really loves you," Ms. Burris said and smiled. She pointed at the presents under the tree. "He's given you gifts that many long for but didn't receive. Do you have a minute for a cup of tea?"

"Yes, that would be great."

The two women sat in the kitchen at a table nestled in the space created by a bay window.

"I've also thought a lot about Natalie," Ms. Burris said. "Do you think she would like to come over for a visit?"

"She'd love that, especially if she could have a tour of the house. She's a wonderful interior decorator."

Once again, they finished the visit by praying together. Amy felt a holy hush that reminded her of what she experienced in the living room.

"Thanks for letting me drop in unannounced," she said as she stood to leave.

"Let me know what you decide to do about the job offer from Harold Phillips."

"I will."

"And don't forget about our lunch with Natalie. Give me a few days' notice so I can plan something special."

■ ■ ■ ■

When Amy arrived home, Megan was sitting at the kitchen table eating a cup of yogurt.

"Where have you been all dressed up?" Megan asked in surprise.

When Amy told her, Megan's face grew serious.

"You'd go back to work at the law firm so I can keep taking dance lessons?"

Amy resisted the temptation to reply in a way designed to make Megan feel guilty.

"I'll go back to work if it's what I believe I'm supposed to do. Your dad and I want to find a way for you to continue dance whether I'm working outside the home or not."

"If you do go back to work at the law firm, I'll help out with Ian."

"You will?"

It was Amy's turn to be surprised.

"Yes, so long as it's not all the time. I know you don't want him coming home to an empty house, and it will cost money if you have to send him to an after-school program every day."

"I don't want to take advantage of you, but that would be great," Amy said. "Even two afternoons a week would help a lot."

"Monday and Wednesday would be the best. I won't have anything after school on those days, and dance class is going to be on

Tuesday and Thursday beginning in January."

Ian came into the kitchen. He didn't notice Amy's outfit. He opened the refrigerator door and poured a big glass of milk.

"What's for supper?" he asked. "I'm starving."

Amy looked at the clock. There wasn't time to put together a regular meal.

"Frozen pizza?" she asked.

Ian looked startled.

"Get used to it," Megan said. "Mom may go back to work."

When he got home, Jeff showed enough sense not to question why they were eating pizza from a box for supper. Amy scraped together the makings of a decent salad, which everybody but Ian ate. Because Amy's trip to the law firm was already out in the open, it was a topic of conversation during the meal.

"Are you going to keep writing books?" Ian asked as he blew on a piece of pizza to cool it.

"I hope so," Amy answered. "I haven't started a new one yet."

"Okay." Ian nodded. "Then it would be good to make money in a real job until you do."

Amy glanced at Jeff. "Like father, like son."

Jeff shook his head. "I didn't say anything to him."

After the children had cleared out, Amy and Jeff stayed in the kitchen. She brewed a pot of decaf coffee.

"After I left the law firm I went by to see Ms. Burris," Amy said as the water began to trickle down through the grounds.

"What did she have to say?"

"Not much and a lot," Amy replied.

"Huh?"

Amy leaned over and kissed Jeff on the cheek.

"She made me appreciate you more."

"I like that. Has she already hired someone to help her around the house?"

"Not yet. She's still praying about offering the job to me."

Amy saw Jeff's jaw clench, then release.

"Ms. Burris believes it's time for my light to shine in the darkness."

"That's easy to interpret," Jeff said. "What could be darker than a law office?"

"You really want me to work there, don't you?"

"Yes, because your light is so strong."

"And not because it will be a lot more money along with benefits?"

"Yes, but for every reason I can think of, it seems like the best decision. You want to work for Ms. Burris so you can spend time with her. You can do that whether you work for her or not. Her house is almost within walking distance of the law office."

Amy took her coffee up to the writing room to pray. However, instead of closing her eyes, she stared out the window at the darkening winter landscape. The sandhills region of North Carolina was dull and drab from December to March. It lacked the crisp starkness of New England or the softer hues of the Deep South. The brown landscape perfectly matched Amy's mood. She tried to encourage herself with the thought that Mr. Phillips held her in such high regard he extended a job offer designed to lure her back to work. But that was exactly how Amy felt — lured back to the daily grind of word processing by the need for money. Ms. Burris could quote a verse about light and darkness with a wrinkled smile on her face and a twinkle in her blue eyes, but Amy was the one who was going to have to leave her attic retreat and return to life in the ordinary world.

She turned on her computer and opened a new document. At the top of the page, she typed "Chapter One." Beneath the two words was a white ocean of blank space. Amy stared at the page. If she could fill the void with words that thousands and thousands of people would buy and read, she could reclaim her freedom.

But that wasn't going to happen tonight.

As she lay in bed listening to Jeff's regular

breathing, Amy knew what she was going to do. She turned onto her side and closed her eyes. No confirming dreams put heaven's stamp of approval on the next step of her life.

The following morning she told Jeff her decision.

"I'm accepting the job. I'll call Mr. Phillips around nine o'clock and let him know."

"Are you sure this is what you want to do?"

"I believe it's what I'm supposed to do."

Jeff hugged her. Feeling the gratitude in his embrace, Amy hugged him back.

After Jeff left for work, Amy called the law office. The same young female voice answered. This time Amy had a face to go with the greeting. Soon she'd know more about the young woman at the front desk.

"This is Amy Clarke. Is Mr. Phillips available?"

"Just a minute, please."

Mr. Phillips was appreciative and efficient. He brought Ms. Kirkpatrick in on a conference call and suggested that Amy return to work between Christmas and New Year's Day. When Mr. Phillips mentioned the amount of her salary, Amy's mouth dropped open in surprise. It was a ten percent increase in base pay.

"Prepare a compensation summary for Amy that also includes full benefits beginning immediately," Mr. Phillips said to the office administrator.

"She'll have to be treated as a new hire subject to the sixty-day waiting period for health insurance," Ms. Kirkpatrick said.

"I already talked to the other partners about that. We'll fund a supplemental policy to bridge the gap."

"Then I'll call about it today. Amy, I have all your information in your old personnel file. Any changes in your health?"

"No, just a year older."

"We all are. Mr. Phillips, since the office will only be open for three days next week, do you want to wait until after the New Year's holiday for her to start?"

"No," Mr. Phillips said. "We've agreed on the day after Christmas. And we'll pay her for the New Year's holiday."

"Yes, sir. Anything else?"

"No, that should cover it."

"Amy, I look forward to seeing you then," Ms. Kirkpatrick said. "And by the way, I loved your book. I had no idea all that creativity was hiding inside you. Most of the ladies at the office have read it. It was a sweet story."

"Thanks," Amy said. "I finished a second novel a few weeks ago. It will be released next year."

"I think we're done here," Mr. Phillips interjected.

"Yes, sir," both Amy and Ms. Kirkpatrick responded.

The call ended. Amy took a deep breath and phoned Natalie.

"Can you meet me for coffee?" she asked. "I have some news to share with you."

"Uh, the boys are here. I don't think you want me to bring them."

"Let me see if Megan will watch them for an hour or so."

"Okay. What's going on?"

"I'd rather talk in person."

Amy went upstairs and knocked on Megan's door. She received a sleepy acknowledgment.

"Do you want to earn some money babysitting this morning for Natalie?" Amy asked.

Megan rubbed her eyes. "Yeah, I still haven't bought Dad a Christmas present."

"How long will it take you to get ready?"

"Thirty minutes if no one is going to see me except Ben and Noah."

Amy called Natalie, then checked on Ian. He was in the midst of a complex construction project with tiny building blocks.

"I'll be back in an hour and a half," Amy said. "Will you —"

"I'll be okay," he said, not looking up from his work. "I promise not to put a plastic bag over my head or turn on the oven."

During the short drive to Natalie's house, Amy told Megan that she'd accepted the job at the law firm.

"I start December 26," Amy said.

"What is Mrs. Graham going to pay me?" Megan asked, turning toward Amy. "I hate having to wake up early during Christmas break."

"You know she'll be generous. She always is."

Ben tolerated Megan, but Noah loved her. The younger of the two boys grabbed Megan's hand as soon as they entered the house. His over-the-top excitement brought a grudging smile to Megan's face. He led her upstairs to his room.

"I'll give you the money to pay Megan," Amy said as soon as she and Natalie were out of the house. "She needs some cash to buy Jeff a Christmas present."

"What's going on?" Natalie asked as Amy backed her car out of the driveway. "Pre-Christmas depression can be worse than post-Christmas blues."

"This doesn't have anything to do with Christmas," Amy replied. "I'm going back to work at the law firm."

"What?" Natalie asked.

By the time they'd taken a couple of sips of coffee, Amy had shared most of the story.

"Mr. Phillips mentioned a salary increase yesterday," Amy said, "and this morning when I talked to the firm administrator, I found out it's going to be more than I would have guessed. Jeff is going to be thrilled."

Natalie stared at her for a moment. "But

you're not."

"I don't know. Part of me feels trapped. Another part is relieved that I can help out financially." Amy took a sip of coffee. "I stopped by to see Ms. Burris on my way home yesterday. I wanted to find out what she thought."

Natalie perked up. "What did she say?"

"That she wasn't ready to offer me a job cleaning her house, and wherever I went to work I was supposed to let my light shine. Jeff had no problem interpreting what that meant."

"It does make sense," Natalie said thoughtfully. "What could be darker than a law office?"

"A coal mine or a maximum-security prison are the only things I can think of," Amy replied glumly.

"I'm sorry."

"Thanks for coming to my pity party," Amy said. "Oh, on a brighter note, Ms. Burris mentioned again that she wants the three of us to have lunch together at her house, probably after the holidays. Maybe I can squeeze an extra half hour out of Mr. Phillips so I don't have to eat and run."

"I'd love to meet her."

"And I can't wait to share her with you. But brace yourself. There's no telling what she might say to you. She thinks outside the box."

"Hanging around you is good preparation."

"You give me too much credit for being spiritual."

"I'm entitled to my opinion." Natalie took a long sip of coffee. "And you also let your light shine through your books. The feedback you get from readers is the tip of the iceberg. You have no idea how many desperate women in a dark place have read *A Great and Precious Promise* and found the strength to go on. Most of them didn't take the time to send you an e-mail, but someday you'll know about every one of them."

Amy thought about Sanford Dominick's obituary. In the end, God determined what mattered in life.

"Not that you're proud or anything like that," Natalie continued. "Getting puffed up would be a real problem for a lot of people, but whether you realize it or not, you're more confident than you used to be. I mean, Mr. Phillips treated you as an equal."

"It wasn't at that level, but his attitude was different," Amy admitted.

"And I believe you're going to have more respect at the law firm than you did before."

"I doubt it. Most people will think I came back to work because I failed as a writer."

"No way." Natalie leaned forward in her chair. "You're going to walk into that office the first morning with your head held high."

Amy smiled and saluted. "Yes, ma'am."

■ ■ ■ ■

When she had returned home following her time with Natalie, Amy called Ms. Burris and told her about her decision.

"I'll be praying for you," the older woman replied.

"Thanks, I'll need it."

"Yes, you will."

The phone call ended with Amy wondering what, if anything, Ms. Burris wasn't telling her.

Christmas came with considerably less stress than would have been the case if Amy were unemployed. She'd not received a paycheck, of course, but the fact that a second income would soon flow into the house made the extra expenses of the holidays easier. Christmas Eve morning Amy received a call from Bernie Masters.

"Happy Hanukkah," Bernie said.

"I didn't know you were Jewish."

"I'm not, but for some reason a lot of people think I am, so I've gone ecumenical in my holiday greetings. I may say, 'Ho, ho, ho,' to the next person I call."

"I have a Christmas surprise for you," Amy said.

"News that you've started a new book would be the best present you could give me."

"Not yet. I'm still praying about it."

"Well, pray more."

"I will." Amy took a deep breath. "I'm going back to work at the law firm. My old boss contacted me and asked me to fill in for a few months while his new secretary is out on maternity leave."

"I think that's great," Bernie replied.

"You do? Why? I'll have less time to write."

"And less financial pressure forcing you to write. Your writing needs to flow from your heart, not from the threat of a deadline. Writers are like snowflakes and zebras. No snowflake has identical crystals, and every zebra has a different pattern of stripes. It's important to understand how you're wired to make sure the creative circuits don't short-circuit. Your waters can't be agitated by life circumstances."

"Why didn't you say that before?"

"Would you have listened? If you remember, I told you to reconsider quitting your day job when you first mentioned it."

"Yes, you did. I forgot about that."

"Most of us need to be self-taught. We refuse to learn from a teacher."

"What else do you want to teach me?"

"Nothing at the moment, but be careful when you ask a person like me, who has an opinion about everything, a question like that. Listen, I caught Dave Coley on the phone this morning. His assistant must be out for the holidays, and he answered. He thinks *The Everlasting Arms* is going to solidify your brand and mentioned an interest in exercising the option for a third book. I told him that was positive news, but we need to see a bigger marketing push for *A Great and Precious Promise* and expect a full-court press for *The Everlasting Arms.*"

"Did that upset him?"

"No, he wouldn't expect me to say anything else. But then he surprised me by tossing out a few things that are already in the works. They're going to run a nice promotion for the e-book version of *A Great and Precious Promise* that provides a teaser for *The Everlasting Arms.*"

"I like that."

"And they're going to purchase front-of-store placement in some of the larger Christian bookstores for the new novel when it releases. That's the sort of thing that will move units."

"Okay."

"You know I've been harping on you about starting another book, but it's not a bad strategy to let the buying cycle continue to run on the first two novels. If you make the publisher and your readers wait, it can fuel pent-up demand and cause a new release to pop up the charts — so long as it doesn't stretch too far out."

"How far out is too far?"

"I don't know, but I think the chances are good that Dave will bite on a new novel early in the process without seeing the finished product."

Amy's head was spinning. She still wasn't exactly sure what Bernie wanted her to do.

"I'll let you know as soon as I have a concept for the next book," she said.

"Don't do that," Bernie responded.

"Why not?"

"You don't buy the first pair of shoes you try on, do you? Make sure the idea fits the direction you want to go before you get my wheels turning on ways to promote it."

Bernie Masters was an enigmatic jumble of encouragement, instruction, confusing advice, and tough love.

"You should be a character in a book someday," Amy said.

"If that happens, I don't want it to be an inspirational romance novel. I want to be in a murder mystery. Everyone thinks I get killed, but I come back in the final pages to take my revenge."

Amy chuckled. "One of your other clients will need to write that one. I'd make you the man who finds true love after searching in vain in all the wrong places."

"That last part wouldn't be fiction. Talk to you soon."

TEN

The night before she returned to work, Amy lay in bed with her eyes open and stared unseeing at the ceiling. The law firm culture was familiar to her; she wasn't venturing into the unknown, but she couldn't shake a sense of apprehension at what lay ahead. She prayed a brief prayer, turned onto her side, and fell asleep.

And went to the living room.

The familiar walls enveloped her with peace, and Amy entered the place of rest where she wanted to stay forever. Eventually, she felt herself being pulled away. When she did, somber words echoed from the breathing walls and surrounded her:

> Have nothing to do with the fruitless deeds of darkness, but rather expose them. It is shameful even to mention what the disobedient do in secret.

Amy woke up. It was 3:05 a.m. She slipped out of bed and climbed the stairs to the writing room. She didn't know the exact location of the verse she'd heard but quickly found it with the help of a concordance. She turned to the passage in Paul's letter to the Ephesians and read it several times.

The intensity of the message was similar to the way she received the titles for *A Great and Precious Promise* and *The Everlasting Arms.* But there was an added sense of foreboding that troubled her. The verse fit precisely with Ms. Burris's challenge that she let her light shine in the darkness, which made Amy wonder if it had anything to do with her writing at all. She sat in her chair as the inner debate went back and forth. She reread the verses from 1 Peter chapter 1 about the flowers of the field. Which would it be? What direction was the Lord leading her?

Turning on her laptop, she typed in a large font on a fresh page:

DEEDS OF DARKNESS
A Novel
by
Amy Clarke

Seeing the title, Amy felt a strong desire to start writing well up within her. The feeling confirmed her decision. *Deeds of Darkness* would be her next novel.

Every book consists of random words placed in a new order, but when the concept is right, the creative process is a journey of discovery, not a laborious effort. Naming the book was the first step. Where it would go, she didn't know. How she would get there, she wasn't sure. But in her heart, Amy knew the words she'd heard in the living room would be the foundation for her next novel.

Jeff was out of bed and preparing a hot breakfast before Amy came down for a cup of coffee.

"Don't spoil me with a fancy breakfast," she said as she stirred in cream and sugar.

"I will today," Jeff replied. "You're a working woman."

Amy leaned over and kissed Jeff on the cheek.

As she waited for her coffee to cool, she debated whether to tell Jeff about her dream. She didn't want to hurt his feelings by excluding him, but it didn't seem right to launch into something that serious so early in the morning.

After giving instructions for the day to a sleepy Megan, who would be watching Ian, Amy went out to the garage and started her car so it could warm up. Back in the kitchen, she packed a salad for lunch and put it in an airtight container. Eating out every day was a quick way to knock a big dent in her salary, and she'd already committed to Jeff that she wouldn't do it more than a couple of days a week. That way she wouldn't feel guilty if she occasionally brought home Chinese or fast food for supper.

Amy poured a fresh cup of coffee in a travel mug and checked herself again in the downstairs bathroom mirror. At least she had a short commute. It would have been harder to drive a long distance to report for duty. Less than ten minutes later she reached the law firm. There weren't assigned spaces for the staff, but Amy often parked near a massive oak tree. Pulling into the familiar spot seemed the right thing to do.

Inside the office, the young receptionist was turning on her computer and looked up with a wide-eyed expression on her face.

"Oh, I brought my copy of your book to work," she said, reaching into her purse and taking out a copy of *A Great and Precious Promise.* "I had no idea who you were when you came to see Mr. Phillips. I mean, you told me your name, but I wasn't thinking about books. I knew you'd worked here in the past before you became a writer. Would you sign my copy of the novel? I thought it was fantastic. My mother liked it, too. And she's so picky."

Amy hadn't anticipated a gushy greeting from a fan at 8:25 a.m.

"I'd be glad to sign your book," she said, taking a pen from her purse. "What's your name?"

"Sorry, I'm Janelle Watson. I came to work right after you left."

Janelle handed Amy the book. The pages had enough wear to show they'd been read. Amy wrote Janelle's name and a brief word of encouragement before autographing the book on the title page.

"Thanks for reading it," Amy said as she handed the book back to the receptionist. "If you'd like to get a signed copy for your mother, I'd be glad to do that, too."

"That would be awesome," Janelle replied. "Her birthday is the middle of next month. It's always hard finding something special for her because it's so close to Christmas. Are you working on another book?"

"I just finished one that will be released next year and hope to start another one soon."

"Ms. Kirkpatrick said you wrote this one while you were working here."

"Not exactly. I wrote it at home."

"Sure, but you had to be thinking about it. When I start a good book I get totally caught up in what's going on and think about it whenever I have a free minute. That doesn't always happen, but it did with your book. You drew me in with the first chapter. If it's not a nuisance, I'd like to ask you some questions about it sometime. Maybe we could have lunch together."

"That would be fun," Amy said as the

grandfather clock struck the half hour. "Is Ms. Kirkpatrick here?"

"Yes, ma'am."

Amy, who had started to move on, stopped. "Hold it," she said. "My name is Amy. I'm not old, famous, or one of the bosses. Please don't call me 'ma'am.' Okay?"

"Sure."

"But thanks for letting me know how much you've enjoyed the book. It means a lot."

Amy adjusted her glasses as she walked down a long hallway to the firm administrator's office. Doris Kirkpatrick had been with the law firm for more than thirty years. Her job duties had grown from bookkeeping to general oversight of financial and personnel matters. Her primary mission was to make things run smoothly so the lawyers could concentrate on billable hours. Amy tapped the open door lightly with her knuckles. The gray-haired woman glanced up from her desk.

"Back again?" she said with a smile. "You've changed a little bit since the first time you stood in that doorway."

"I was twenty-one."

"And I was forty-one, which is still older than you are now."

Amy sat down.

"I met Janelle. She seems sweet."

"A bit scatterbrained at times, but she makes a pleasant first impression on the phone."

Ms. Kirkpatrick opened a thick manila folder. "We need to add a few items to your personnel file before you get started."

Amy signed the papers. She knew everything Ms. Kirkpatrick had prepared would be correct. In less than five minutes, Amy was officially an employee.

"Anything I need to know before I get started?" Amy asked.

"I don't think so. I'm here if you need to talk. I can help with most things, except changing Mr. Phillips's mind."

"Some things don't change," Amy said with a smile. "How about staff turnover in the past year and a half?"

Ms. Kirkpatrick went over departures and arrivals at the firm. There were four new employees. Chris Lance was the only new lawyer.

"I didn't know Susan resigned," Amy said, referring to a paralegal who worked for one of the partners.

"It was a sudden move. Her husband got a job offer in Raleigh."

Amy paused. "How did Emily feel about me coming back?"

Ms. Kirkpatrick raised her eyebrows. "That's a loaded question, but she had no choice but to take a leave. Her obstetrician ordered bed rest for the final three months of her pregnancy. She's been gone since December 19, so Mr. Phillips has a serious backload of work. I asked Emily to leave you a detailed memo of work in progress."

"Then I'd better get to it." Amy stood up.

Unless he had an early morning hearing in court, Mr. Phillips arrived at the office precisely at 9:00 a.m. During the years she worked for him, Amy would organize and lay out correspondence and pleadings pertinent to the day's responsibilities on his desk so he could quickly review them as soon as he came in. She'd also remove all junk mail and spam that made it past the firm's Internet filter so that his computer desktop was focused and uncluttered.

Amy went into her former office. Next to the computer screen Emily had positioned a big photo of herself and her husband, Rob, taken on the beach at Cancún following their wedding. A smaller photo of Emily with her pet schnauzer sat beside the phone. Amy put the pictures in the bottom drawer of the desk. She hadn't thought about bringing photos from home to personalize her workstation.

She turned on the computer but was locked out. The password had been changed. The promised memo from Emily was nowhere to be seen. It would be like Emily to "accidentally" forget to prepare the document. Before buzzing Ms. Kirkpatrick, Amy typed in a couple of password possibilities. When she entered "Lawrence," the name of Emily's dog, the computer allowed her to log in. There was an e-mail to Amy from Emily with a Word doc attachment and photo at the top of the in-box.

Hey Amy,

The attached memo will get you started. Call me if you need anything. I'll be flat on my back going crazy at home. Please pray for me and my baby. See ultrasound photo.

Emily

Amy read the e-mail three times. In a few sentences, Emily Ashburn went from being a conniving coworker who overtly tried to undermine Amy and steal her job to a scared first-time mother with a high-risk pregnancy. Emily was only a few years younger than Amy, and she and her husband had been trying to have a baby for almost a decade.

Amy printed out the grainy black-and-white photo of the unborn child, a boy, then bowed her head and prayed. She wrote a reminder on a Post-it note to "pray for Emily and her baby boy" and placed it in a spot between her keyboard and the desk where she would see it each day. She slipped the ultrasound photo into the top drawer of the desk as an additional reminder.

Emily had left a very thorough and helpful summary of the status of Mr. Phillips's practice. Amy wasn't the only one who had undergone change since leaving Jones, Barrington, and Phillips.

By the time Mr. Phillips arrived, Amy had opened and laid out his morning mail, performed housekeeping duties with his e-mail inbox, and pulled two files he would need for client meetings scheduled that morning. The strict formal organization required by the office was different from the free-flowing schedule of creative freedom Amy had enjoyed for the past eighteen months at home, but like an astronaut on the moon, she had to conform to the rules of the world in which she found herself. She was sitting at her desk when Mr. Phillips buzzed her and asked her to come into his office. She picked up a notepad and walked through the door that connected the two rooms.

Mr. Phillips was wearing a charcoal-gray suit, white shirt, and yellow tie. He had a cup of coffee in his hand. Amy knew which chair he preferred his assistant to use when she came into his office. She sat down with pen held to paper. The older lawyer looked at her.

"Good morning, Amy," Mr. Phillips said. "Welcome back."

"Good morning. Thanks."

Amy waited. Mr. Phillips cleared his throat.

"Did I tell you my sister in Wilmington read your book?"

"No, sir."

"She thought it was a very credible first effort."

Amy pressed her lips together in a tight smile.

"I'm glad she liked it."

Mr. Phillips shifted in his chair. "I have to admit you surprised me when you accepted my offer to come back to work. I thought the legal profession had lost your skills forever."

"The timing was right," Amy replied. "And I'm grateful you called. It meant a lot that you were willing to bring me back with a raise and benefits even if it proves temporary."

"Poor negotiation skills on my part," the lawyer grunted. "I know better than to open with my best offer, but I was afraid we wouldn't tempt you with anything less. At least it worked."

"And I'm ready to get to it. Emily left me a detailed memo of your work in progress. Is there anything I need to know before I get started? I saw that you have twenty-seven items in the dictation queue."

"Rule number one still applies."

"Don't miss any deadlines."

"Correct. And number two?"

"Make your life as a lawyer easier, not harder." Amy could still remember how wide-eyed she'd been when Mr. Phillips laid down his version of the Ten Commandments for secretaries. She pointed to the desk. "Do you still want me to sort the morning mail before —"

"Yes, yes," Mr. Phillips interrupted. "I like

to know if there are any fires that have to be put out first thing."

"What about priority between your work and what I do for Chris Lance? I didn't have anything from him in my queue, and Emily didn't mention his work in her memo."

"We'll create a new rule for that. My work always takes precedence unless you clear it with me first. You know more about some aspects of practicing law than he does and can tell what's critical and what can wait. I'll serve as gatekeeper for his work."

Amy wasn't sure how working for the two lawyers was going to play out.

"We'll sort out the kinks," Mr. Phillips continued.

"Sounds like fun," Amy spoke without thinking.

Mr. Phillips gave her a startled look.

"Sorry," Amy said.

"You don't have to tell me I'm a prima donna," the senior partner said with what passed for a smile on his gruff face. "Just promise you won't put me in one of your books and turn me into an ogre."

Amy held up her right hand. "I promise."

ELEVEN

One advantage of being busy was that time spent at the office passed quickly. Most of what Amy had to do involved matters started by Emily. She didn't find any of the smoldering fires Mr. Phillips hated in the initial projects listed in the memo.

Midmorning Amy began the process of whittling down the backlog of dictation. Mr. Phillips was meticulous in his recording. He provided the spelling of obscure legal terms and inserted precise punctuation that conformed to the rules of grammar the senior partner had learned in high school. Amy usually followed his instructions; however, in the case of a mistake or difference of opinion, she always highlighted her change. Mr. Phillips had an uncanny ability to remember what he'd said and recognize any deviations. She took a break a few minutes past noon and went to the large kitchen at the rear of the house to eat lunch.

Several women were sitting at a round table

eating. Each one of them, including Janelle, had a copy of *A Great and Precious Promise* open in front of them as if reading the book during lunch. The room was completely quiet. Amy stopped in the doorway.

"Okay," she said. "What's going on here?"

Betsy Gamble, a real-estate paralegal, looked up from the book with a startled expression on her face.

"Ladies!" she exclaimed. "It's Amy Clarke, the author!"

Every woman put down her copy of the book and turned to stare. Amy rolled her eyes, and everyone in the room burst into laughter.

"Welcome back," one woman called out.

"We're proud of you," Betsy added.

"Sit by me," said Val Jenkins, a legal assistant whom Amy had helped train. "I saved you a place. We were worried Mr. Phillips had so much for you to do that you weren't going to be able to stop for lunch."

The gracious reception by the women touched Amy. Natalie had been right. They didn't view her as a failure for coming back to work. She signed a few books and answered questions in between bites of salad. Amy noticed that two women weren't present.

"Where are Cynthia and Nora?" she asked Betsy in a low voice.

"Not everyone wanted to be part of the fan club." Betsy shrugged. "They made some excuse about needing to take an extra thirty minutes and eat out today. I think it's their loss. Don't let it bother you."

Amy's relationships with Cynthia and Nora had always been chilly. Surrounded by women who seemed genuinely glad to see her, it was easy for Amy to overlook their slight. The normal lunch break was only half an hour long, so they quickly finished. Amy thanked the group for their kindness.

"If you hadn't come back, Val and I might have had to do double duty," said Sally Compton, another legal assistant. "We're grateful to you."

"I'm still excited from meeting you this morning," Janelle added.

Amy rinsed the plastic container for her salad in the sink and headed back to her office. When she turned the corner into her work area, she almost collided with a tall, sandy-haired young man with clear blue eyes. He stuck out his hand and touched her right shoulder to avoid running into her.

"Excuse me," he said. "I'm Chris Lance."

Amy introduced herself.

"I recognize you," Chris replied.

"From the photo on the back of my book?"

"You've written a book?" the young lawyer asked with a puzzled look on his face.

"It's a romance novel. Most of the female staff know about it. I thought you might have heard about it or seen a copy."

"I'm not into books with a half-naked woman draped across a bare-chested man on the cover," the lawyer replied with a smile. "But I know they sell or they wouldn't be on the shelves. Congratulations."

"It's not that kind of romance novel," Amy replied, feeling her face flush. "It's inspirational. You know, with a Christian message."

Amy could tell the lawyer didn't completely grasp the precise nature of her writing genre. He held up a DVD in a plastic case.

"I saw you in the video taken when Sanford Dominick executed his last will and testament several years ago. You signed as the notary public. Do you remember doing it?"

"Oh, yes." Amy paused. "Mr. Dominick was a character."

"So I hear. Like someone you'd put in a book. Mr. Phillips has asked me to work on the administration of the estate and told me you could provide clerical support."

"Filling out the forms to file with the clerk's office?"

"I wish it was going to be that easy. At least one competing will has surfaced, and there are rumors flying around that there may be other heirs wanting a piece of the estate. One of Dominick's daughters is alleging her father wouldn't have left the majority of his estate to a much younger woman he met and married six months before the will was signed unless there was improper influence."

"It was an unconventional will signing," Amy admitted. "I can't remember the details. Was his new wife in the video?"

"Bleached-blond hair and all. I know Mr. Phillips brought in a videographer to record the proceedings in hopes it would bolster the legitimacy of what was taking place, but I'm not sure that's the way a jury will view it. It's going to be hard for some folks to get past how the people in the room look, except you, Mr. Phillips, and the witnesses, of course."

"The wife's son from a previous marriage was there, too."

"You can see him for a few seconds. He was the product of her second marriage. Was he some kind of bodybuilder?"

"I don't know, but he was a big man."

"I met Natasha, the wife, but I've only talked to her son on the phone."

"The obituary in the newspaper said they were still married at the time of his death."

"But it left out that they hadn't been within five hundred miles of each other for over two years. She's been staying in a condominium in south Florida, and Dominick was holed up with twenty-four-hour nursing care at the house he owns out in the country on the east side of town. There are at least two alleged illegitimate children who have their hands out wanting to be bought off. Bill McKay is the executor who's going to have to sort it out."

"The lawyer?"

"Yes. You may not remember, but Mr. Phillips asked him to serve as executor even though this firm prepared the will. I'm sure Mr. Phillips anticipated there might be a problem down the road and didn't want us to be disqualified by a conflict of interest. There's a lot more money to be made fighting for the will than serving as executor, and McKay will do whatever Mr. Phillips tells him. But this case is going to end up in front of a judge and jury."

Bill McKay, an older man, was a sole practitioner. He had a business clientele and never went to court. He referred all litigation to Jones, Barrington, and Phillips.

"What a mess."

"Which is why I need some help. I've worked with Mr. Phillips on two other estates that had problems, but nothing like this."

Chris Lance was young, but he didn't seem to lack confidence. He handed her the DVD.

"First thing for you to do is review the DVD and write a memo for the file about your independent recollections. That way your thoughts and impressions become work product for purposes of your deposition."

"I'll be deposed?"

"Yes, and I don't know how many times. We should be able to consolidate all the claims, but something new can always pop up outside our control. We're at the beginning stages."

"The priority for my work will be subject to Mr. Phillips's approval."

"I understand where I fit in the firm hierarchy," Chris replied with a grin. "But this is a big case, and if I'm right, it will only get bigger."

"Is there a paper file?"

"In a cabinet outside my office. It's on the second floor at the back next to the small conference room with the fireplace in it."

"That used to be Bud Carrier's office."

"So I've been told. Did you ever work with him?"

"For a year or so before he took an in-house job with a bank in Cary."

Chris pointed to the DVD that Amy had placed on her desk.

"Any idea when you will get a chance to watch the DVD and prepare a memo of your recollections?"

"I have a backlog of dictation from Mr. Phillips that will keep me busy for two or three days. And he will be passing along new work now that he has someone to type it. I'll check with Mr. Phillips. If he agrees, would the middle of next week be soon enough?"

"Yeah." Chris paused. "I was going to dictate something for you myself on a different matter with a lower priority. I'm fast on a keyboard, but Mr. Phillips wants me to get used to dictating more."

"Send it along."

Chris left, and Amy resumed her place in front of the computer screen. She'd worked with four different lawyers during her tenure with the firm and could adapt to different personalities and work styles. Fortunately, she'd never worked with one who yelled and threw files, and Chris Lance didn't seem to come from that mold.

By 3:00 p.m., she'd placed several pieces of correspondence, a draft of a commercial lease, a revision of a buy-sell agreement for a local group of doctors, and some answers to interrogatories in a breach-of-contract lawsuit on Mr. Phillips's desk. The file for each matter was positioned beneath that item. She was revising interrogatory answers when Mr. Phillips returned to the office from a meeting.

"Did you do the letter to Frank Norris?" he asked, sticking his head through the open door between their offices.

"Yes, sir. It's here."

Mr. Phillips picked it up from the corner of Amy's desk and read it.

"Did you change anything?"

"No, sir. If I do that I'll mark it as a draft and show you what I've done."

"Of course you will," he said as he turned to the second page of the letter. "Emily wasn't as careful about that as you are. This is ready to go."

"Do you want it sent in the mail and as an

e-mail attachment?"

"Yes, both." Mr. Phillips signed the letter and handed it to Amy. "Did you meet Chris?"

"Yes, and he told me the Dominick estate is going to be litigated."

"I knew that from day one," Mr. Phillips grunted. "Whenever there is that much money lying around, people are going to try to grab some. There's enough at stake to justify two lawyers working on it. Natasha may be flaky, but she pays the bills. The whole scenario is a recipe for a will contest."

Having multiple wives, mistresses, and illegitimate children didn't help, Amy thought.

"Chris wants me to watch the DVD of the signing and prepare a memo of my recollections. I told him I would have it done by the middle of next week."

"That's fine."

By 4:30 p.m., fatigue started to hit. Amy had arrived in the morning with a full tank of adrenaline but wasn't used to the grind of an eight-hour workday. The last thirty minutes dragged by, and she found herself making mistakes that wouldn't have happened earlier. Mr. Phillips was still at his desk when the clock finally reached 5:00 p.m.

"Good night," Amy said, standing in the hallway door of the senior partner's office.

Mr. Phillips glanced up at her and checked his watch.

"I won't ask you to work over on your first

day," he said.

Amy bit her lower lip.

"Thanks."

The following Monday was the first day back at school for Megan and Ian. When Amy turned onto their street after work the house wasn't on fire, and there weren't any ambulances in the driveway. She walked into the kitchen and kicked off the shoes that had imprisoned her feet all day, then went to the bottom of the stairs.

"Megan! Ian!" she called out. "I'm home!"

Ian came running out of his room and rocketed down the stairs.

"Hey, Mom," he said and launched into a rapid-fire account of a new video game that a lot of his friends had received for Christmas and was now spreading faster than the flu through the school.

"Where's Megan?" Amy asked when Ian paused for breath.

"I think she's in her room," Ian said, "and I want to use my Christmas money to buy it."

"We'll have to check it out first," Amy said.

She headed up the stairs and knocked on Megan's closed door.

"Who is it?" her daughter responded.

Amy tried the doorknob, which was locked. A quick image of Megan bent over with her hands on her stomach flashed through her mind.

"Your mother. Please open the door. Are you sick?"

There was no immediate answer. Amy knocked again and waited. Finally, the knob turned, and the door swung open. The blinds were closed, the room dark. Megan was wearing an old pair of pajamas. Her long hair was in a floppy ponytail.

"What's going on?" Amy asked. "Did you throw up?"

"This has been the worst day of my life."

"Why?"

"Nate Drexel embarrassed me in front of the whole school. Is there any way you and Dad could send me to Broad Street Christian? I know there aren't many kids in the high school, but at least I wouldn't feel like everyone is looking at me when I go down the hall."

"What did he do?"

Amy could see that her daughter's eyes were red from crying.

"I sent him a text message asking him a question. He pretended to respond to me but copied a couple of his buddies as a joke instead. What he wrote about me was horrible. By the end of the day it was all over the school. There were juniors and seniors who didn't know I was alive before Christmas looking at me and laughing."

"What did the text say?"

"Don't make me tell." Megan hung her

head. "How much is the tuition at Broad Street Christian? Could you afford it now that you're working?"

"We'll talk to your dad after supper. I'm sorry this happened."

"Just get me out of the high school. I'm never going back."

Amy stepped forward and wrapped her arms around Megan, whose arms hung limply at her sides.

"Do you want to come to the kitchen while I fix supper?" Amy asked.

"No, I'm going to stay in here. I'm not hungry."

Amy went downstairs with a heavy heart. She'd prepared a meat loaf the previous evening and put it in the refrigerator. While she waited for the oven to warm up, she racked her brain for a way she could help Megan. The cruelty of teenagers seemed to have no boundaries. While the meat loaf cooked, she peeled and cut up carrots. She was also perplexed why she would remember a picture from the living room while standing at the door to Megan's bedroom. It would have helped to know something in advance of the problem Megan would face so Amy could have warned her.

Jeff came into the kitchen when the main dish was about twenty minutes away from coming out of the oven.

"How was work?" he asked after giving

Amy a longer than usual hug and kissing her firmly on the lips. "I thought about you. And prayed, too."

"You should have prayed for Megan."

Amy told Jeff about the text-message disaster. His face grew dark.

"I'm going to call the boy's father," he said.

"Don't you think we should ask Megan first? We really don't even know what happened."

"You believe her, don't you?"

"Yes. I mean, I have no reason not to."

Jeff paced back and forth across the kitchen.

"Why don't you go upstairs and talk to her?" Amy suggested. "Maybe you can get more out of her before we decide what to do."

After Jeff left the kitchen, Amy walked to the bottom of the stairs and listened until she heard Megan's door open and close. She put four yeast rolls on the cooking rack beside the meat loaf and set the timer. The phone rang.

"Mrs. Clarke, this is Greg Ryan, one of Megan's teachers. I met you and your husband at the dance recital."

"Of course, I remember."

"Is this a bad time to call?"

"Actually, we're in the middle of a crisis."

"Did Megan tell you about an incident at school involving a text message?"

"Yes, but we don't know the details," Amy

replied. "She's devastated and wants to transfer to a private school."

"She has a right to be upset. I reported the matter to the administration, and action is being taken against the boy who did this. When I left the school a few minutes ago, he and his parents were meeting with the principal, one of the counselors, and the junior varsity football coach."

"Thanks," Amy replied gratefully. "My husband and I weren't sure what to do."

"It know it will be rough on Megan, but in a day or two students will be talking about the punishment given to the boy, not what he did to her. Everyone who knows Megan realizes it was a cruel lie."

Amy paused, struggling with whether she really wanted to know more.

"What do you think will happen to the Drexel boy?" she asked.

"I'm not sure, but there will probably be at least a short-term suspension. Some of the worst punishment for student athletes comes from the coaches. The counselor involved in the disciplinary process should be in touch with you soon, but I didn't want you to have to wait in the dark."

"Okay."

"And encourage Megan to come back to school tomorrow with her head held high. I'd like to call a couple of her friends and suggest they rally around her as soon as she walks through the door."

"That would be wonderful. She's close to Bethany —"

"And Sadie and Alecia. Ninth-grade girls travel in such tight packs that sometimes there isn't any air space between them."

"You're right." Amy allowed herself to relax a little bit. "My husband and I really appreciate what you're doing."

"It's one of the reasons I became a teacher. Tell Megan I expect to see her on the front row during third-period World History."

Twelve

Amy went upstairs. Megan and Jeff were sitting beside each other on the bed.

"Mr. Ryan is awesome," Megan said after Amy told them about the phone call.

"I still think I should call Nate's father," Jeff said.

"Please don't, Dad. It will only make it worse."

"How?" Jeff asked.

"Maybe it would have been necessary if the school hadn't stepped in," Amy offered. "But I think it's okay if we wait to see how the disciplinary process plays out before deciding if there's anything we should do on our own."

"Mom's right," Megan said.

"Don't gang up on me." Jeff held up his hands. "I'm not going to fight both of you."

"This isn't an argument," Amy replied. "All I'm suggesting is to wait. Mr. Ryan is right that the focus on Megan will quickly go away. Nate's punishment will replace it along with all the other drama that's poised to jump out of the dark and stir up trouble on a high school campus."

Jeff turned to Megan. "Five minutes ago you wanted me to find out what it would take for you to transfer to Broad Street Christian. Is that still what you want me to do?"

"No." Megan shook her head. "I don't want to leave my friends."

Jeff shrugged his shoulders.

"And you'll be able to go to school tomorrow?" Amy asked.

"Yeah, Bethany and Alecia texted me right before Dad came up. They're going to be my posse."

"Okay," Amy said. "Are you hungry? The meat loaf is sitting in the oven, and the rolls are going to get hard if we don't eat soon."

"Starving," Megan said. "I'll be right down."

Supper passed uneventfully. After the emotional roller-coaster ride of the past hour and a half, Amy was content to eat in silence. Following the meal, the children left the kitchen. Jeff stayed behind to help Amy clean up.

"Can we go to bed at eight o'clock?" Amy asked as she put a plate in the dishwasher. "I'm exhausted."

"Whatever you need to do. When Megan was born I didn't realize we might have an evening like this."

"And she's only fourteen."

Once the kitchen was tidy, Amy fixed a cup of hot tea and took it into the family room. Jeff turned on the computer. Amy propped her feet up on the coffee table, took a sip of tea, and closed her eyes. The only sound in the room was the quiet tapping of Jeff's fingers on the keyboard.

"I wish I'd drafted Calvin Johnson of the Lions," he muttered after several minutes passed. "My wide receivers are so inconsistent going into the play-offs."

Amy chuckled.

"What's funny?" Jeff asked, glancing over his shoulder. "I'm in big trouble with my team this week."

"I'm just glad you're upset about fantasy football instead of talking to Nate Drexel's father on the phone. Every so often I have to turn down the heat on the characters in my books and give them a chance to act normally. We need the same thing in our lives right now."

Amy went upstairs and took a bubble bath. Afterward, when she went into Megan's room to tell her good night, Megan was sitting cross-legged on the bed with her Earth Science book open in front of her.

"Big test tomorrow about weather," she said. "Did you know most hurricanes form off the coast of Africa?"

"No. Don't stay up too late."

"I won't."

The bubble bath had made Amy feel like a normal person and revived her spirits. Jeff was downstairs watching a TV show. After she kissed Ian good night, Amy went upstairs to the writing room and turned on her laptop. She'd written much of *A Great and Precious Promise* between 9:00 p.m. and 11:30 p.m.

Amy read the Bible verse from Ephesians and stared at the title page. Megan's crisis proved there was no shortage of evil that needed to be exposed to the light. But a novel had to be based on a broad theme that could be fleshed out in connected scenes. And where was the romance in darkness?

Then an idea popped into her head.

The worst aspects of fallen humanity often appeared in the vulnerability of people in love. To portray that in the lives of her main characters would be a perilous journey, much more daunting than the circumstantial obstacles overcome in her first two novels. But it might be the path to greater literary success. Amy began typing:

> Alone, Roxanne listened to the dull roar of the cheap white-noise machine she'd bought with a roll of quarters she'd been saving for the next trip to the Laundromat. Flickering lights from the liquor store across the street pulsed through a crack in the ragged curtains. Each flash reinforced the harassing voices that hov-

ered like hyenas at the edge of her mind. She stared wide-eyed at the ceiling. It would take more than imaginary waves crashing onto an electronic beach to give her a full night's rest.

The liquor store lights illuminated a bottle of prescription sleeping pills on the nightstand. A single pill would knock her out, but there was no guarantee she would wake up in time to make it to work by six thirty in the morning. One more failure to clock in and she'd be fired. And if Roxanne didn't have a job, the two children asleep in the adjoining room might be taken from her. Unless they ran again.

She rolled onto her side and let her right arm flop across the bed. The emptiness triggered a tear mixed by sadness and frustration to run down her cheek onto the pillow. Another followed, cruel drops in an hourglass of sorrow. She heard the baby whimper and wiped her cheek with the back of her hand. She crawled out of bed. It probably wasn't anything serious, but it didn't take much for her to bring him into bed. His sighs and coos when they cuddled were one of the few comforting sounds in her world.

Amy stopped typing and stared at the words that had poured out of her. She'd never considered writing a third person novel.

She'd written her other two from the first person perspective, telling her tale from a vantage point inside the main character's head. From that perspective it was easy to communicate feelings and emotions. Third person writing was more challenging. The story would unfold through the lens of a camera recording the words and actions of the characters. Feelings would be revealed by conduct and word choice and emotions gleaned gradually, not imposed by blunt force. But even in the third person perspective the intense mental torment of Roxanne, the abandoned woman in the night, was like a sledgehammer breaking down a door.

Amy stared out the window into the night. No neon lights intruded into the writing room. Amy and Roxanne had little in common, but that didn't mean the door to the character's soul was shut. Imagination is the key to many doors. And Amy sensed she was ready to follow Roxanne into the darkness and lead her toward the light.

Amy opened a new document and brainstormed as many ideas and possibilities for the story as came to mind. Some produced immediate affirmation; others she left on the page but doubted they'd make the final cut. It was midnight when the third yawn in less than a minute interrupted her concentration. She'd planned on going to bed early and ended up staying up later than normal. She saved her work and closed the computer.

Jeff was lying on his side asleep. He'd left the bathroom light on for her. Amy felt guilty that their last conversation of the day had been about fantasy football. She brushed her teeth, put on her pajamas, and crawled quietly into bed.

"Were you writing?" Jeff asked.

"Yes. I started a new novel. I thought you were asleep."

Jeff rolled over so they faced each other in the darkness.

"I may have dozed for a few minutes, but I didn't want to go to sleep until I told you that I love you."

Amy reached across and gently touched his face. When she did, the tragedy of Roxanne's loneliness and the void in her marriage bed hit Amy with renewed force.

"I love you, too," Amy said, her voice cracking slightly. "Thank you for always being there for me, for us."

Jeff took her hand in his and kissed it.

"And I always will be," he said. "Good night."

"Good night."

Jeff's regular breathing resumed in a matter of seconds. Amy lay awake. The world she was about to enter with this new novel was not a place she wanted to visit in real life. It was much better to lie in bed with an honest, uncomplicated man who installed replacement windows for a living.

The following morning Jeff had to leave early because his crew was going out of town for a big commercial job.

"Will you be late for supper?" Amy asked as she poured a cup of coffee.

"It depends on how much we get done. This is either a three- or four-day project. Mr. Crouch wants us to be finished in three days, but I don't know if that's possible."

"Then I'll plan on picking up Megan from dance practice and Ian from after-school care."

"Thanks." Jeff gave Amy a quick kiss and turned toward the door. He stopped with his hand on the knob. "When did you dream about a new book?"

"The night before I went back to work."

"Do you think that's a sign?"

"Of what?"

"That you were supposed to return to the law firm. Once you made the decision, you got an idea for a story."

"Maybe, but don't worry. I'm not going to quit my job."

"Me, either."

Megan came downstairs a few minutes later. She was dressed more nicely than usual. Amy guessed it was an outfit designed to boost self-confidence.

"Do you want a banana on your cereal?"

Amy asked.

"Yeah. Where's Dad?"

"He had to leave early for work."

Amy fixed a bowl of cereal for Megan, cut up a banana on top, and added milk. Megan was sitting at the kitchen table with a far-off look in her eyes.

"Are you ready to face what's waiting for you at school?" Amy asked.

Megan looked up at her. "Mom, that's not very helpful. I know I have to go, but I'm not looking forward to it."

"Sorry, I thought your friends were going to meet you —"

"Yes, but it's still going to be tough."

"Do you want me to drive you to school?"

"No. That won't make any difference."

Amy gave up. She left the kitchen and called upstairs for Ian, who came down jumping two steps at a time.

"Thanks, Mom," he said when Amy fixed his cereal for him.

"I'll be picking both of you up today," Amy said. "Don't forget you're going to after-school care with Tommy and his brother."

"Yeah, he says it's a lot of fun. They have good snacks and a bunch of stuff to do."

After Megan and Ian left the house for the bus stop, Amy had several minutes before she needed to leave for the office. She checked her makeup. It was as good as it could be at age thirty-six and a half. After pouring a cup of coffee in a travel mug, she called Natalie's cell phone. Her friend had been out of town during the holidays visiting family in Ohio.

"Are you driving car pool this morning?" Amy asked.

"Yes, I'm on my way to pick up Braxton. He had a cold yesterday and stayed home, but Kim claims he's better and is sending him to school. All I need is for Braxton to dump a cupful of germs on Ben and Noah so they end up sick."

"It's that time of year."

"How's work? I thought about you a bunch."

"I felt like a hippie who had to reenlist in the Marine Corps."

"Ouch. Is it terrible?"

"Not really."

Amy told her about the women bringing their copies of *A Great and Precious Promise* to the kitchen during lunch on the first day.

"That's cool. They realize you're a celebrity."

"I wouldn't go that far, but it made me feel special. There's a lot of work to do. In addition to my responsibilities for Mr. Phillips, I've been assigned to help a fresh associate."

"What's the new lawyer like?"

"Okay for now."

"Any interesting cases?" Natalie asked, then quickly added, "I guess you can't tell me."

"No, but there's at least one litigation matter I'm sure will be all over the papers when it gets going. Of course, the reporters won't get it right. At least I admit my writing is fiction."

Amy started to mention Megan's crisis but decided not to over the phone.

"When can we get together?" Natalie asked. "I know you're crazy busy."

"I'm not sure, but I want to set something up with Ms. Burris. I'll try to figure that out and let you know."

"You're a sweetie. I'm here at Kim's house now." The phone was silent for a moment. "And here comes Braxton. Kim is stuffing tissues into the pocket of his coat. It looks like Dallas has a red nose, too. I can't hold my breath all the way to school, and I'm more worried about the kids than myself. Pray for me!"

"I will. Talk to you later."

Amy hung up the phone and smiled. If only the worst challenge in life were the threat of a runny nose. She sipped coffee as she drove to the office. After the late night spent in the writing room, she needed a jolt of caffeine to get going.

"Good morning, Janelle," Amy said when she entered the reception area.

"Good morning," the receptionist replied in a slightly breathy voice. "I called my mother last night and told her about you. I didn't mention your offer to sign a book for her. I want it to be a surprise. She'll be thrilled."

"Let me know. I always keep a few copies in the trunk of my car."

"Oh, and Chris came in earlier and asked about you. Should I buzz him or do you want to check in with him?"

"I'll go upstairs and see what he wants."

Amy checked her watch as she climbed the stairs to the second floor of the office. It would take at least fifteen to twenty minutes to organize the mail and computer in-box for Mr. Phillips before he arrived.

The staircase went up ten steps to a landing and then another six steps to a wide hallway. During the mansion's previous existence, the hallway led to six bedrooms, an upstairs study, and a second-story atrium. Several partners had their offices on the second floor. The room that served as Chris Lance's office had most likely been a child's bedroom. The door was closed, and Amy knocked.

"Come in!" the younger lawyer responded.

Even though the office was small, it still had a nice view of the yard and a pair of enormous live oak trees. Chris's desk was positioned to the right of the door so he could look out the window.

"Janelle said you wanted to see me. I only have a few minutes because I have to get everything ready for Mr. Phillips when he arrives."

"Sure."

Chris swiveled around in his chair and picked up a file that was on a credenza behind him. On the corner of the lawyer's desk Amy saw a photograph of a young woman in her twenties with dark hair, a young man in his twenties also with dark hair, and a chestnut-colored horse. She stared at the picture. It looked vaguely familiar.

Then she remembered.

She'd seen the same image during the visit to the living room when she saw the vase of flowers that turned up in Natalie's house. Chris turned around and opened the file.

"I know you probably haven't had a chance to look at the DVD of the will signing, but there's also a CD that contains a conversation Mr. Phillips had with Dominick and Natasha around the same time as the preparation of the will. There's a note from Mr. Phillips in the file that the purpose of the conversation was to negate claims of undue influence. I listened to it last night and think it might help our case. I'd like you to transcribe it."

He handed the CD to Amy.

"How long is it?" she asked, forcing her gaze away from the photo.

"About five minutes."

"Is this the only copy?"

"Yes."

"And the DVD you gave me? Is there a copy of it?"

"No, and we need to have backups. You can do it at your desk, or we can send it out for a professional to do it."

"Let's keep it in-house. I don't think it's a good idea for either of these to leave the office."

While they talked, Amy glanced again at the picture on the desk.

"I'm not trying to be nosy, but who is in the picture?" she asked, pointing to it.

Chris reached across and picked it up.

"My wife, Laura, and her older brother, David. They grew up around horses on a farm in Virginia." Chris stared at the photo for a moment. "David died about two years ago in a car wreck. This was the last time they were together."

"Don't worry about David," Amy said. "He's in heaven."

Startled, Chris stared at her.

"What?"

Amy felt her face flush. She covered her mouth with her hand, but it was too late to take back her words.

"I mean, I'm sure he's in heaven," she said.

Chris narrowed his eyes.

"I don't see how you can claim to know what's happened to someone who died," he said. "My wife is more religious than I am, and even she's not sure where her brother is today. I'm not convinced he's anywhere at all."

"I apologize," she said. "I shouldn't have offered an opinion."

"Why did you?"

Amy could tell Chris Lance was about to turn lawyer on her, and she wanted to withdraw from the awkward situation before his cross-examination intensified.

"It was a sense. That's all."

"Based on what? And don't claim women's intuition. That wouldn't cover something like this."

"No, it's not intuition. I've been a Christian since I was a little girl."

"That doesn't explain anything, either."

"It's hard to explain."

"Try. Are you a psychic?"

"No, I don't believe in that."

"But it looks to me like that's what you are. Talking to the dead, stuff like that, is what psychics claim to do."

"I don't talk to the dead." Amy looked at her watch. "I really need to go downstairs and organize Mr. Phillips's mail. Forget what I said."

Chris stared at her for a moment. "That's not possible. And even though it doesn't have anything to do with your job, I would appreciate an honest answer from you."

"May I go now?"

"Whatever," Chris said with a wave of his hand.

Amy fled down the stairs. She could see that Chris had one of the traits common to successful trial lawyers — a dogged determination to ask questions until every rock was turned over and the ground beneath it carefully inspected.

"Why did I do that?" she muttered to herself when her right foot touched the main floor of the mansion.

Letting her light shine sounded nice when talking to Ms. Burris and Natalie, but turning it on a photograph in a skeptical lawyer's office wasn't fun. Amy had felt strangely drawn to the man in the picture, but it wasn't until Chris mentioned his deceased brother-in-law's name that the final piece of a jigsaw puzzle dropped into place. She knew in her heart that David was with the Lord.

Amy reached her desk and tried to compose herself. Instead, an unexpected wave of emotion swept over her. The wonderful truth that the young man was in heaven was so sweet and tender and powerful and comforting that it suddenly overwhelmed her. And for a moment, the goodness of God in preparing a place for his children was greater than the embarrassment she felt over the conversation with Chris. Amy dabbed her eyes with a tissue. This was not the way she'd imagined her morning would begin.

After saying a quick prayer for Emily and her baby, she started opening Mr. Phillips's mail.

THIRTEEN

Amy made it through the rest of the day without seeing Chris Lance. She ate lunch at her desk and continued to whittle down the backlog of Mr. Phillips's work. By 5:00 p.m., she estimated she would be caught up by midday on Wednesday. Of course, new batches of dictation continued to be channeled by the senior partner into her queue. Immediately after she logged off her computer to go home, Mr. Phillips buzzed her phone and asked her to come into the office.

"Amy," he said without looking up from some papers he was examining on his desk, "I have a meeting this evening with the board of directors for Plaxo Industries. I need you to come and take notes."

Amy swallowed. "Jeff is working out of town, and I have to pick up Megan from dance class and Ian from his after-school program."

Mr. Phillips looked up. "Can someone else do it? There's a chance this meeting will get contentious, and I want an accurate record of what's said and who says it. I can't referee and write at the same time."

In the past, Amy had almost never turned Mr. Phillips down when he asked her to perform extra duties, and she hated to refuse so soon after coming back to work. She struggled for a tactful way to respond. There was a knock on the door.

"Come in!" Mr. Phillips barked.

It was Chris Lance. He saw Amy and started to back away.

"No, stay," Mr. Phillips said. "Chris, you claim to be a fast typist, don't you?"

"I get by pretty well," Chris responded slowly.

"We're about to find out. You're coming with me to a corporate board meeting this evening and taking notes on your laptop."

Chris glanced at Amy, and she knew he suspected what had happened shortly before he came into the room.

"Yes, sir. I'll be glad to do it."

"Good," Mr. Phillips said. "We'll leave in fifteen minutes."

"Thanks," Amy said to Chris, who ignored her.

Driving away from the office, Amy knew she had to develop a backup plan for child care in case Mr. Phillips asked her to work late again. She'd simply not thought about it yet.

She picked up Ian first.

"How was after-school care?" she asked as soon as he was seated in the car.

"Okay, I guess. Ms. Bolton made me do my homework first. That took over an hour before I got to do anything with my friends."

"But it also means you don't have any schoolwork to do after supper. How were the snacks?"

"Good, but they ran out of brownies, and I only got one." Ian put his backpack on the floorboard of the car. "Tommy didn't tell Ms. Bolton the truth about his homework. We're in the same math class and both of us had fifty problems to solve. He told her he didn't have any homework. Should I have tattled on him?"

Amy thought about the exposing the deeds of darkness verse from Ephesians but wasn't sure if it applied to Tommy's math homework.

"That's a hard one," she said. "What do you think is the right thing to do?"

"I wanted to tell on him because I was mad that he got out of the work when I didn't. But then I thought that he'll get in trouble at school if he doesn't do it before tomorrow. Ms. Bolton talked about something she calls the 'honor system.' That means it's up to us to tell her the truth about stuff like homework."

"Were you glad you told her the truth?"

"Yeah. I would have felt bad if I'd lied

about it."

"I'm proud of you."

Ian was silent for a moment. "Do you and Dad always tell the truth?"

"We try to."

"It's hard to think about you telling a lie."

Living up to a child's expectations of adult conduct was tough. Amy wondered again about the wisdom of saying something to Chris Lance about his deceased brother-in-law. She was trying to tell the truth, but there was no way for Chris to verify it.

They reached the dance studio. Amy left Ian in the car while she went inside. Megan had already changed out of her leotards and was wearing her school clothes. Ms. Carlton handed Amy an envelope.

"Here's the bill for January. Sorry about the increase, but I had to sign a new lease on the studio, and the rent went way up. Also, the practice mats were worn out and needed to be replaced."

"I understand," Amy said. "We appreciate what you do for the girls."

The instructor patted Megan on the shoulder. "Working with dancers like Megan makes it all worthwhile. I know it's early to think about the future, but she could do something serious with dance if that's what she wants. A lot of girls learn the steps; Megan dances from deep inside." Ms. Carlton looked at Amy. "I guess she gets that level of artistry from you. It just takes a different form."

"We're proud of her."

Amy and Megan moved toward the door.

"How was school?" Amy asked when they were out of earshot of Ms. Carlton. "Did things calm down?"

"I don't want to talk about it in front of Ian."

The short ride home took place in silence. Once they reached the house, Ian went into the family room and turned on the TV.

"Where do you want to talk?" Amy asked Megan as they stood in the kitchen. "We could go up to your room."

"Not now." Megan brushed past her toward the stairs.

Amy stared after her for a few seconds, then began preparing a chicken casserole. While she worked, she went through several possible scenarios for Megan's day at school. None had a happy ending.

After putting the casserole in the oven, Amy changed into more comfortable clothes. The door to Megan's room was closed, and Amy paused for a moment to listen. She could hear Megan talking in a low voice on the phone but couldn't understand what she was saying or whom she might be talking to. Megan's decision not to communicate was one of the toughest challenges Amy had faced as a parent.

The casserole was starting to bubble when the phone rang. It was the high school. Amy picked up the phone and peeked into the family room to make sure Ian was still watching TV.

"Hello," she said.

"Mrs. Clarke?" a female voice asked.

"Yes."

"This is Madeline Robbins, one of the counselors at the school. I think we met during ninth-grade orientation at the beginning of the year."

Amy remembered Ms. Robbins, an attractive black woman in her thirties.

"Yes."

"I met with Megan today during her second-period study hall, and she told me you're aware of the texting incident that occurred yesterday involving Nate Drexel."

"We know there was a text but not what it said."

"I have it here."

The counselor read the text. Amy's eyes opened wide, and her face grew pale.

"That's bad," she managed.

"The administration agrees. Nate will be given in-school suspension for ten days and won't be able to participate in spring sports activities. My question for you and your husband is whether you want him to apologize to Megan. Any apology would be supervised by me and take place in the school office, but we didn't want to make this part of the disciplinary process unless you wanted us to."

Amy was impressed with the suggestion. "I'll need to talk to my husband when he gets home. What does Megan know about the punishment or the possibility of an apology?"

"I told her about the suspension when I met with her but not about sitting down with Nate."

"How did she seem to you? I picked her up at dance class, and she didn't want to talk to me about anything. She's been in her room ever since."

"I won't minimize the emotional trauma. Megan seems like a confident young woman, but this has been very hard on her. It helps that she has a group of good friends. They seem supportive; however, too many students think making fun of a ninth-grade girl is cheap entertainment. That's not the culture we promote at the school, but it's a sad reality."

"Yesterday Megan wanted to transfer to Broad Street Christian where she went to elementary school."

"That's definitely an option. I'd like to stay in close contact with her for the next couple of weeks. She has an appointment to see me again tomorrow. Time will tell."

Amy was surprised that the counselor didn't discount the possibility of pulling

Megan out of the public high school.

"Thanks for what you're doing. I'll talk to my husband and let you know about the apology."

The counselor gave Amy her direct number at the school.

"I'd encourage you to include Megan in the discussion about the apology. She'll likely oppose the idea at first, but I think it would be a good thing to do."

Amy hung up the phone. The timer went off, signaling the casserole was done. Jeff came into the kitchen from the garage.

"How's Megan?" he asked. "I thought about her the whole time driving back to Cross Plains."

Amy told him what she knew, leaving out the specific wording of the text. Jeff's anger was buried deep, but when aroused, it was hard to keep caged.

"Let's try to talk to her after supper," Amy suggested. "Will you go upstairs and see if you can get her to come down and eat?"

Amy and Ian set the table while they waited for Jeff and Megan.

"What's going on with Megan?" Ian asked. "She spends all her time in her room, and I heard her crying when I went to the bathroom to brush my teeth last night."

"Someone hurt her feelings at school," Amy said.

"Was it Nate Drexel?"

"How did you know?"

"His little brother is in Ms. Duncan's class, and he told me on the playground that Megan was going to get Nate kicked out of school. I told him he was crazy."

"Megan can't make anything happen. It's up to the principal to decide how Nate is punished."

"What did he do?"

"I can't tell you."

Ian rolled his eyes. "I know about more stuff than you think."

"What kind of stuff?"

"I can't tell you."

Before Amy could correct Ian's attitude, Jeff returned to the kitchen with a solemn-faced Megan in tow. It was another meal eaten in silence, but Amy was thankful that Megan was present and had an appetite. She liked chicken casserole and ate two helpings. Without any conversation at the table, supper was over quickly. Jeff told Ian he would pay him five dollars to clean up the garage.

"But, Dad, you always put away your tools," Ian said.

"Then it will be an easy five bucks. Stay there until seven o'clock."

"Is that so you and Mom can talk to Megan about Nate Drexel?"

"What do you know about that?" Megan asked, a horrified look on her face.

"Just what his little brother said on the

playground," Amy responded. "And most of that wasn't correct."

Ian opened his mouth, but before any words came out, Jeff spoke.

"Out to the garage!" he said. "Now!"

Ian retreated from the kitchen, and in a few seconds they heard the door to the garage close.

"Ms. Robbins called me late this afternoon," Amy said to Megan and then told them about the conversation.

"I like her," Megan said. "I didn't know what they were going to do to Nate. I wish they would start the in-school suspension tomorrow. That way I wouldn't have to see him in English class."

"He's in your English class?" Amy asked. "I thought he was in the tenth grade."

"And World History. He failed English Composition last year and had to take it again."

Amy looked at Jeff. "It might be a good idea to ask the school to take him out of Amy's classes."

"All the trouble started in English," Megan said, "and I can't stand the thought of him staring at the back of my head. I don't care so much about World History. Mr. Ryan can look out for me in there."

"I'll talk to the principal about it," Jeff said.

"What do you think about the personal apology?" Amy asked Megan.

"I don't want to do it. If he apologized, he wouldn't mean it. He's just sorry he got caught and is in a bunch of trouble."

"Ms. Robbins thought it was a good idea," Amy said.

Megan didn't respond.

"What if the counselor brought the junior varsity football coach to the meeting?" Jeff asked. "Nate probably cares more about football than anything else, and it would be hard to admit what he did in front of Coach Nichols."

"Yeah." Megan nodded. "And Mr. Ryan could come."

"Dad and I would be there —" Amy began.

"Getting parents involved doesn't help," Megan interrupted.

"We'll decide that later," Jeff said, then turned to Megan. "Look at me."

Megan, her eyes wide, gave him her full attention.

"Did you know that I think you're a wonderful daughter who is beautiful on the inside and the outside? And if there was any way I could take this pain and embarrassment away from you and put it on myself I'd do it in a second? I thought about you all day and wished I could solve this as easily as I did with a Band-Aid on a cut when you were a little girl."

Amy watched Megan tear up. She sniffled and nodded. Jeff stood, pulled her to her feet, and wrapped his strong arms around her. She didn't try to resist. As Amy watched in admiration, Megan closed her eyes and leaned her head against her father's chest.

"No matter what happens, remember how much your mother and I love you," he said.

Megan nodded. She and Jeff separated.

"Do you have any homework?" Jeff asked.

"Not much." Megan wiped her eyes. "I have to research a report for World History. Mr. Ryan is going to give me suggestions for sources, but I want to show him I've done some of it on my own."

"Use the computer in the family room," Jeff said. "I'll do my work after you finish."

Megan left the kitchen.

"I'll call Ms. Robbins," Amy said. "It's easier for me to take care of it at work than it is for you to take a phone call when you're at the top of a ladder."

"Tell her I'll be there," Jeff said. "I'll sort that out with Megan later. Tonight wasn't the time to do it."

"You don't think I should be at the meeting, too?"

"I'll leave that up to you."

Amy hesitated. "I'll stay away. I might start crying and become a distraction."

"Okay."

Amy edged closer to Jeff.

"But can I have one of those hugs?" she asked.

Jeff opened his arms wide.

"I saved one especially for you."

After Megan finished her research and Jeff logged on to the family computer, Amy slipped up to the writing room.

Writing the first chapter of a novel was like attending a party where Amy didn't know anyone. The best way to break the ice was to start asking questions. At Amy's imaginary get-together she didn't begin with typical questions about work or family. The most important piece of personal information she wanted to know about someone who was going to walk through the pages of her book was what the character feared most.

Amy read again what she'd already written. Roxanne certainly felt the ache of loneliness because the other side of the bed was vacant, but being left alone wasn't her primary fear. Her economic status was dire, but poverty alone wouldn't cause the woman to toss and turn at night. Her health wouldn't be an issue; Amy didn't want to write a doctor/hospital story.

Then Amy had a writer's epiphany. Even though she and the main character lived in radically different worlds, they shared the same greatest fear — that something horrible would happen to their children. A wrenching ache that only a mother can feel welled up in Amy's heart. That was it. She let the mixture of compassion and anxiety and dread and love she felt become more real in her mind. Amy quickly typed a few key phrases to capture the moment. When a powerful emotion swept over her, she knew there was an opportunity to create scenes that could produce a similar response in her readers.

Deeds of Darkness would have many tentacles, but for Roxanne they would be rooted in a life-and-death threat to her children.

Amy scrolled down to a fresh page and continued typing character notes. Roxanne would also be a mixture of weakness and strength — strong enough to try to make it on her own but frustrated because her stubborn determination couldn't guarantee security for her family. Somewhat shy around others, she would have an active thought life and, like Amy, would view solitude as both an enemy and a friend. Amy smiled wryly. Writing this novel might involve visiting more unexplored facets of her own subconscious than she realized.

As she considered possible endings for the story, Amy considered an unexpected twist. What if the gut-wrenching challenges faced by Roxanne eventually destroyed her? Amy shuddered. She'd never considered writing a novel with a tragic ending, and it was a disconcerting scenario. But there was no denying that some of the greatest works of fiction didn't end with "and they lived happily ever after."

Amy turned off her computer. She was standing at the edge of a dark literary forest and didn't want to take another step into the forbidding woods.

Not yet.

Fourteen

The following morning Amy phoned the high school and talked to Ms. Robbins.

"That sounds like a good plan," Ms. Robbins replied to Amy's suggestion. "I'll speak with Coach Nichols and Mr. Ryan, then contact Nate's parents and set up a time for the meeting."

"Even though I won't be there, I'll be praying."

The call ended with Amy grateful she had an ally inside the walls of the schoolhouse. The counselor had figured out a way to let her light shine in the darkness.

Amy organized Mr. Phillips's mail and then settled in at her desk. She'd finished a short piece of dictation when she looked up and saw Chris Lance standing in her doorway. She slipped the listening buds out of her ears.

"Thanks for agreeing to go to the corporate meeting with Mr. Phillips last night," she said. "I was in a jam because I needed to pick up my children. I hope it didn't run too late."

"About ten thirty," Chris replied flatly. He handed her a flash drive. "I took seven pages of notes. Would you clean these up so they can go into the file?"

"Certainly."

Chris reached into the pocket of his shirt, took out a small envelope, and handed it to her. Amy's name was written in a woman's cursive on the front.

"This is from Laura. I told her what you said when you saw the picture in my office, and she started to cry."

"I'm sorry." Amy felt her face flush. "I was way out of line and shouldn't have said anything. I know it was a tragic loss. Please —"

"I don't know what she wrote in the note," Chris interrupted her. "But she isn't mad at you. She made me promise to give this to you first thing this morning."

Chris left, and Amy fingered the sealed envelope. She looked around to make sure she was alone and opened it. The note was written in a graceful script on an embossed card:

> Dear Amy,
>
> I can't tell you how deeply your words about my brother touched me. I shared my faith with David several times over the past few years. He listened politely but never gave any sign that he believed. I

always thought there would be other chances to talk and then he was killed.

Yesterday I was thinking about him, missing him, and wondering where he was. I knelt in front of the chair where I have my devotions every morning and asked God to somehow let me know the truth.

When Chris came home last night and told me what you said, I burst into tears. I've never had something so supernatural happen in my life! Praying will never be the same for me. I know God hears and answers!

I can't wait to meet you in person and give you a hug. Thank you, thank you.

Fondly,
Laura Lance

P.S. I'm so excited you're going to be working with Chris. Please pray for him!

Amy reread the note. It seemed like it was written to someone else, not her. She slipped it into her purse. Putting the flash drive into the USB port of her computer, she brought up the notes Chris took the previous night. Cleaning up the notes didn't demand her total concentration, and a private part of her brain continued to think about Chris, Laura, and David.

Shortly before noon she received a call on

her cell phone. It was Bernie Masters.

"I need to speak with the next great American novelist," Bernie said.

"Then you called the wrong number. If you want to talk to Amy Clarke, it will have to wait. I'm typing answers to interrogatories for my boss. Can I call you back on my lunch break at noon?"

"You got it."

Amy took the salad she'd fixed for lunch to her car and drove a couple of blocks to a city park. It was too cold to eat outside, so she stayed in her vehicle and called Bernie. He answered immediately.

"Tell me you're not just typing answers to interrogatories for a living," Bernie said.

"And memorandums of law, correspondence, pleadings, buy-sell agreements, employment contracts with noncompete provisions, and briefs that are long, not short."

"Are you trying to make me feel guilty?" Bernie asked. "Several priests have tried and failed. Seriously, how are you holding up in the working world?"

"In some ways it's easy, like riding a bike, but I'm not the same person I was when I left a couple of years ago." Amy thought about the note she'd received from Laura Lance. "But for now I'm sure it's the right thing to do."

"And what about your own writing? Has

being around other people on a regular basis primed your pump?"

"That's not how it works with me, but I've started a new novel."

"Yes!" Bernie shouted into the phone. "You don't have to give me credit so long as you mention me in the acknowledgment section of the book and let me negotiate your next contract. What's the hook?"

"I'm at the preliminary stages. I've only written part of the first chapter, but I've jotted down a bunch of character notes and plot possibilities." Amy paused and took a deep breath. This was going to be the first time her concept had left the privacy of her mind and the attic writing room. "It's going to be third-person point of view with a female protagonist. She's a young woman —"

"I saw that coming," Bernie cut in before Amy could continue.

"What? Both of my main characters have been young women."

"Going third person. Your writing style in the other books gave it away. It was like the main character was a superhero struggling to get out of her ordinary clothes and express herself in a broader way. That usually happens best in third-person perspective. It will also allow you to develop the arcs of other characters who've been shuffled to the side."

"I thought you liked my books."

"Of course I do, but what kind of agent

would I be if I didn't want you to grow?"

"Why didn't you say anything?"

"Amy, you're not the kind of woman who likes tough love. I have to treat you with kid gloves, not boxing gloves."

Amy wanted to disagree, but she knew he was right.

"Do you have a working title? I know that's a big deal for you."

"Yes," Amy spoke slowly. "It's going to be called *Deeds of Darkness.*"

"Whoa," Bernie responded. "That's bold, but I'm willing to track with you. Imagine you just entered an elevator on the ground floor of a building, and the publisher comes in behind you, presses ten, and says, 'Hey, Amy, tell me what you're working on.' "

Bernie had trained Amy enough that she'd already given this question some thought. She took a deep breath.

"A young mother with two small children is left alone after her husband is wrongly sent to prison. She moves to a small border town in southern Texas where no one knows her past. She gets a low-level clerical job working at the local sheriff's department and learns about corruption in the town connected to illegal smuggling of drugs and people across the border. When she starts asking questions, the bad guys get nervous and file charges against her in family court alleging that she's an unfit mother. She tries to flee the town but is caught and brought back. Her children are taken from her and placed in foster care at a secret location. She realizes the only way to reclaim her children is to bring down those behind the charges against her and the corruption in the town. In the final third of the book, her husband gets out of prison and comes to help. But he makes things worse."

Amy stopped.

"Go ahead," Bernie said. "How does the arrival of the husband on the scene make things worse?"

"I can't tell you. The elevator reached the tenth floor."

"You've got me hooked." Bernie chuckled. "Do you know yourself what happens?"

"I was thinking the husband might go postal in his anger and resentment over all that's been wrongly done to him and his family. I'm not sure he makes it to the end of the novel."

"That's understandable. What about the mother and the kids?"

Amy hesitated. "It may not turn out happy for anyone. I can't decide if the mother dies trying to save her children or one of the children doesn't make it."

"That's pretty harsh. If both the mother and father die, the children would end up in foster care anyway. And it's always risky to kill a kid. Men readers don't care so much, but women get attached to the little critters even when they're not real."

"I thought about that, but something inside tells me I have to consider all options."

Bernie was silent.

"What are you thinking?" Amy asked after a few moments passed.

"I'm not sure this is a book that will fit in Dave Coley's stable. He's a traditional publisher who likes to play it safe. He'd rather hit a bloop single than swing for the fences. He'll be expecting another inspirational romance piece."

"There will be romance. The main character will visit her husband at the jail. I thought working through the challenges in their relationship with bars between them would be a powerful metaphor."

"Careful, you're going literary on me. What about the Christian stuff?"

Amy knew that Bernie Masters kept matters of faith in a dented file cabinet in one corner of his brain. He wasn't antagonistic, just uninterested.

"I thought the main character could become a Christian in the midst of her struggles. Communicating that to her husband would be part of their personal challenge."

"I get it. She tells him, 'Your body and your soul are behind bars, and only Jesus can set you free.' That could work nicely and avoid objections from general market readers. I mean, any guy who's unjustly locked up has a built-in excuse to call out to a higher power. Then, if he kicks the bucket, the Christian reader will be okay with it because the guy will be sitting on a cloud in a white robe and playing a harp."

"That's not exactly the way I'd set it up, but it's the general idea. The deeds of darkness would begin before the story opens with the imprisonment of the husband and continue to the very end of the novel. But bad things don't stop happening in people's lives just because I reach my maximum word count for the book. The denouement will have a degree of triumph but not be totally tidy."

Bernie was silent again.

"Does that make sense?" Amy asked. "You know what I mean by denouement, don't you?"

"It's French for wrapping up the third act with a big boom so you can bring down the curtain. And you'd better be glad I'm thicker-skinned than you are. I didn't say anything because I'm still trying to get my head around this new idea. Are you sure some bad guys in Texas haven't kidnapped my sweet, innocent Amy Clarke and shipped her south of the border?"

"No, and I wasn't trying to insult you." Amy felt embarrassed. "I got carried away."

"In more ways than one, but I have to

admit this is an intriguing, original concept. I'm sure there's something similar out there, but nothing comes to mind off the top of my head. Have you tried to see if there is another book whose author could accuse you of stealing?"

"No, but I'm sure there will be enough that's unique about the story to make it my own."

"I'll do some checking. How soon can you put together a three-page synopsis?"

"For you to show Dave Coley?"

"Maybe, but there are a couple of people in New York who might consider a story like this."

Amy sat up straighter on the seat of her car.

"Are you serious?"

"I joke with you about a lot, but not that. With the release of *The Everlasting Arms,* we'll be able to establish your track record in the Christian market and have two published novels as writing samples for a big-time editor to review. Writers try to cross over all the time. When a book does cross over, the difference in advance money is significant. You could quit being a legal secretary once and for all."

Amy's head was spinning. "But I'm not going to include any profanity or write something that goes against my own morals."

"We don't have to tell them that going in. I

wouldn't pitch it as pulp fiction written according to a sleazy formula. I'd describe it as a sophisticated, insightful character piece in which the plot is strong enough to actually make the reader want to turn the page. This could be big."

Amy knew Bernie's job as an agent was to hype his clients to publishers, but she felt her own level of excitement rising.

"I'll get to work on the synopsis," she said. "Cecilia was okay if I didn't stick strictly to it because the story will take new twists and turns as I get to know the characters. Will it be the same way with another company?"

"It varies, but most editors are so overworked and underpaid they don't have time to micromanage. However, if you venture outside the Christian bubble, you'll have to toughen up. Editorial feedback, when it comes, can be brutal."

"I work in a law firm."

"Lawyers are nice compared to some of these people."

"But I'll be able to write what I want?"

"So long as you can convince the decision makers it will drive sales. Remember, regardless of what they say about their love of books, publishers are driven by sales figures. Otherwise, they lose their jobs."

The call ended and Amy ate a few bites of salad. Her mind was racing so fast that her stomach didn't mind being ignored.

■ ■ ■ ■

Mr. Phillips was out of the office all afternoon. Amy was up-to-date in transcribing his dictation and decided to review the video of the Sanford Dominick will signing. She loaded the DVD into her computer. In the opening image she saw herself in the downstairs conference room. Her hair was shorter, and she was wearing a maroon outfit she later donated to the local clothes closet. She looked directly into the camera lens and spoke.

"This is a video of the signing of the last will and testament of Sanford B. Dominick, taking place at the law offices of Jones, Barrington, and Phillips in Cross Plains, North Carolina."

She then walked out of the room, which remained empty for a couple of minutes until Mr. Phillips ushered in Mr. Dominick along with his wife, Natasha, and her son, a man whose name Amy couldn't remember. Amy and two other women who worked at the firm brought up the rear. Mr. Phillips positioned everyone at the table so their faces were visible to the camera. He asked everyone in the room to introduce themselves and give their name, age, and address. The son's name was Manfred, but everyone called him Freddie.

Tall and slender with a full head of white

hair, Sanford Dominick looked the part of an aging World War II hero, but as the tape continued to roll, there was no question that his mental capabilities had started to fade. When asked to name his children, he missed one. Amy winced. She'd remembered the meeting was awkward but not the details. When Mr. Phillips corrected him, Mr. Dominick looked puzzled for a moment before nodding his head.

"Yes, and this is my wife, Natasha, and my newest grandson." He pointed to Freddie, a muscular young man in his early twenties.

"Your stepson," Mr. Phillips corrected him. "What is his name?"

"Frankie," Mr. Dominick replied.

Mr. Phillips looked at the camera for a split second.

"Isn't it Freddie?" he asked.

Dominick nodded.

"Please answer out loud," Mr. Phillips said.

"Freddie, that's right. And Michael Lancaster is one of my grandsons," Mr. Dominick continued. "And he has two children, Emma and Jacob. Jacob is a baby."

"That's correct." Mr. Phillips beamed as if congratulating an astute student. "And how many times have you been married?"

Mr. Dominick knit his eyebrows as if this were a very complex question.

"Uh, three, no four. That's right, four."

"And the names of your wives starting with

the first one."

"Lillian," Dominick replied quickly, then paused and looked at Mr. Phillips. "What was the name of the one I only stayed married to for a year? You helped me get a divorce from her."

Mr. Phillips waited until it became obvious Mr. Dominick could not recall the woman's name.

"Kitty," the lawyer replied.

"That's it." Mr. Dominick slapped his hands together with a smile on his face. "I was glad to get out of that one. She about drove me nuts with all her —"

"We don't need to go into the reasons for the divorce," Mr. Phillips replied. "Who did you marry after Kitty?"

"Selena," Mr. Dominick replied with a faraway look in his eyes. "Sometimes I really miss her."

"Sonny!" Natasha cried out. "How can you say something like that in front of me?"

Mr. Dominick turned and saw his wife beside him. A surprised look crossed his face, and Amy suspected the old man had forgotten for a moment where he was and who was in the room with him.

"And did you and Selena get a divorce?" Mr. Phillips asked.

"Yes. How much did that cost me?"

"I can tell you later, but it's not important for this meeting."

Mr. Phillips looked down at a legal pad, an indication that he was ready to move on. In his present state of mind, Sanford Dominick was the kind of witness a lawyer didn't want to keep on the stand too long. Amy could see Mr. Phillips flipping pages as he abandoned questions. He slid a copy of the will across the table.

"Have you read your last will and testament?" Mr. Phillips asked.

"Yes. You gave it to me the other day, and I took it home."

"Who will receive most of your estate under the terms of this will?"

Mr. Dominick frowned.

"You changed it after we talked to Natasha, didn't you?" he asked. "It's different from the other one. How many times have you changed my will?"

"A few, but only when you wanted me to. Mr. Dominick, I need you to tell me in your own words who you want to receive most of your estate."

"My wife," Mr. Dominick replied and motioned toward Natasha. "Her."

"Do you mean Natasha?"

"Yes, yes." The old man yawned and rubbed his nose.

"What about your children and grandchildren?" Mr. Phillips asked. "What do you want them to receive?"

"It's all in there," Mr. Dominick replied,

touching the will. “They get some money, but I want my wife to have everything else.”

“Is anyone making you set up the will this way?”

Mr. Dominick looked puzzled again. “No.”

“Have you been subject to undue influence?”

“I’m not under the influence. I haven’t had anything to drink since a glass of wine last night with dinner.”

“Mr. Dominick, in your previous will, you left most of your estate to Selena. Now that you’re divorced from her, do you want to change that?”

“Yes.”

Mr. Phillips looked relieved that any remaining affection Mr. Dominick felt toward Selena wasn’t going to taint the current estate plan.

“And how do you want to change it?”

“So most everything goes to Natasha.”

“Did Natasha pressure you to do this?”

“She asked me about it quite a few times, but I haven’t been feeling too good and didn’t come down to see you until the other day. When was that?”

“Last Wednesday. What day is it today?”

Mr. Dominick shook his head. “You got me there.”

Mr. Phillips glanced toward the camera. “Mr. Dominick, are you signing this will because it’s what you want to do or what Natasha wants you to do?"

"Yes."

Mr. Phillips waited, but Mr. Dominick seemed satisfied with his answer and showed no indication of explaining. Mr. Phillips cleared his throat and glanced at the camera before focusing on Mr. Dominick.

"Do you have any questions?" he asked the elderly gentleman.

"No."

"Are you ready to sign this will in front of these witnesses and Mrs. Clarke, who is a notary public?"

"Yeah, let's get this over with. I'm hungry. It's time for lunch."

Amy watched Dominick initial each page, then sign the last page of the will, which was then witnessed and notarized.

"Do you want me to keep the will for you in our office?" Mr. Phillips asked.

"No, I'll take it with me."

Amy knew this was not according to the script. Mr. Phillips liked to keep wills in the firm vault to ensure they weren't lost, destroyed, or tampered with.

"Wouldn't you like to keep it safe here at the law firm?" Mr. Phillips asked again.

"No." Mr. Dominick took the will and handed it to Natasha. "Let's go. I'm starving. And talking about wine has made me thirsty, too."

Mr. Dominick got up and left the room.

Natasha and Freddie trailed along behind him. Natasha was talking to Mr. Dominick as the door closed, but the microphone didn't pick up the conversation. Mr. Phillips looked at the camera and motioned to Amy.

"Turn that thing off."

Amy walked over to the camera, and the picture went blank.

FIFTEEN

The CD of the conversation between Mr. Phillips, Mr. Dominick, and Natasha lay on the top of Amy's desk. Chris wanted her to transcribe it, but she'd spent enough time with the Dominick family for one day. She slipped it into a drawer and opened a new item of dictation to transcribe.

Late in the afternoon her phone buzzed. It was Chris.

"Can you come to my office for a minute?" the young lawyer asked.

"As soon as I finish a letter that Mr. Phillips wants to send out in the afternoon mail."

Amy printed the letter and took it into the senior partner's office.

"Here is the settlement letter for the plaintiff's lawyer in the Worthington case," she said.

Mr. Phillips read it while she stood before him.

"It galls me to no end to offer money on this case," he groused, "but the client doesn't want to fight. Did you read the answers to our discovery requests?"

"Just enough to make sure I had the names right for the letter. It looks like a nuisance suit."

"That's exactly what it is, and I hate to reward a gold digger."

Amy's mind immediately went to Natasha Dominick, but she kept her mouth shut. Like many lawyers, Mr. Phillips had no qualms about applying a different standard of morality to his clients than he did to the people on the other side of a lawsuit. He scribbled his signature at the bottom of the letter and handed it to Amy.

"Maybe they'll get greedy and reject the offer," he said. "That will force Bob Worthington to spend the money to fight. It may cost him the same in the end, but at least a victory will protect his reputation. I don't want word to get out that he's an easy mark."

Amy folded the letter on the corner of Mr. Phillips's desk and slipped it into an envelope.

"I'm going upstairs," she said. "Chris wants to see me in his office."

"What do you think about our new associate?"

Amy knew this question would be coming, but she hadn't expected it so soon. Mr. Phillips wouldn't be satisfied with an evasive answer.

"He's smart and not easily intimidated by a

challenge. And I don't think he'll give you any pushback —"

"Not if he wants to work here."

Amy stopped.

"Go ahead," Mr. Phillips said.

"He's an accurate typist. His notes of the meeting you went to last night at Plaxo Industries were detailed and clean."

"That's surprising considering how messy the meeting was. Print the notes and give me a copy before you go upstairs."

Amy pointed to a stack of papers on the corner of Mr. Phillips's desk.

"They're in there. Do you want me to pull them out?"

"No." Mr. Phillips waved his hand. "But check back with me before you leave to go home."

"Yes, sir."

Amy took a steno pad with her. She didn't know formal shorthand but had developed her own style of abbreviations that worked well if she didn't wait too long to transcribe them. The door to Chris's office was open. He motioned for her to come in and sit down. His face didn't reveal any emotion.

"Did you get a chance to watch the DVD and transcribe the CD in the Dominick will case?"

"I watched the DVD this afternoon and made a few notes but haven't listened to the CD. I'll try to get to it tomorrow."

"It's more of the same. What did you think of the video?"

"Since I don't remember anything that happened before the camera started recording, I can't help out there. Mr. Dominick came to the office off and on for years, so I was around him quite a few times. He was a smart but impulsive man. It was obvious in the video that he was declining."

"Mentally?"

"Yes." Amy nodded. "His mind was jumping all over the place."

"Yeah, that's what I thought, too."

"But he knew Natasha was his wife and wanted to leave most of his estate to her."

"That's the only part Mr. Phillips focused on. He thinks the video will prove the case. I'm not so sure."

Amy decided to take a chance and offer a perspective on the senior partner.

"Mr. Phillips knows there are issues in the case. Saying that to you is his way of putting pressure on you to deliver what he wants."

"I already feel it." Chris touched a brown mailer on his desk. "And this didn't help. I received a packet of information today from a Georgia lawyer who represents a man claiming to be Dominick's illegitimate son."

"Mr. Dominick had a reputation as a womanizer."

"This is the third notice that has floated in from illegitimate children — two putative sons and one putative daughter," Chris said.

"Has there been any DNA testing?"

"Dominick was embalmed using formaldehyde, which contaminates any sample. One of the claimants wants to have him exhumed anyway. Another is seeking hair and fingernail samples. Natasha isn't very happy with either request."

Mr. Dominick had a full head of snow-white hair in the DVD. If there was a hair-brush of his remaining in the house, it would be a treasure trove of chromosomal data.

"Can they search the house?" she asked.

"I'm not sure, but the illegitimate offspring don't pose the only challenge to the will. There are also caveats from two of his legitimate children." Chris paused. "And a competing will supposedly executed after the one prepared by Mr. Phillips."

"What a mess."

"That's what happens when twenty million dollars is at stake."

"Twenty million dollars?" Amy raised her eyebrows. "I had no idea there was that much money involved. Where did it come from? I knew Mr. Dominick owned a couple of houses, but I never knew how he made his money. He spent most of his time being a war hero."

"The majority of his assets are from an import/export business he started after he got back from the war. His main job was to schmooze with clients. Apparently, he was very good at it."

It was slightly past five o'clock when Amy left Chris's office and walked downstairs. She went in to see Mr. Phillips.

"You wanted to see me before I left for the day?" she asked.

"Yes." The older lawyer motioned for her to sit down. "I saw Mildred Burris when I was eating lunch at the country club today. She mentioned that you've been spending time with her."

"Yes, I've visited her a couple of times in the past month or so."

Mr. Phillips cleared his throat. "Now that you're working here again, I'm not sure that's a good idea."

Amy's mouth dropped open. "Why? She's been extremely kind to me."

"I don't want to jeopardize client confidentiality or have an appearance of impropriety."

"I would never say something to Ms. Burris or anyone else that violates the rules. We talk about our faith, not what happens here." Amy paused. "And she's a client of the firm."

"Was a client," Mr. Phillips responded with a slight grimace. "I'm going to send her a letter ending our professional relationship. It's not something I want to do, but I don't see a way around it. Given your recent personal contact with her, I didn't want you to be surprised when it shows up in your queue."

"Why?"

Mr. Phillips cleared his throat. "She's going to be an adverse witness in the Dominick estate litigation."

"What does she know about it?"

"It seems she and Sonny were romantically involved many years ago, and when his health declined, she started visiting him and recommended the home health nurse who stayed with Sonny when he couldn't care for himself. My information is the two of them convinced him to execute a new will shortly before his death. The lawyer who prepared the will came to the house where it was executed."

"Who gets Mr. Dominick's estate under that will?"

"Most of it goes to his children and grandchildren. Natasha still receives a life estate in the condo in Florida where she lives, but not much cash. Upon her death, the condo reverts to the estate. There is also a sizable bequest to a nonprofit organization that Mildred supports. I think she's on the board of directors. The home health nurse, a woman named Beverly Jackson, also gets a tidy sum. The will was prepared by a sole practitioner about fifty miles east of here. I have no doubt Sonny wasn't competent by then. The last time we met, he had trouble remembering my name. And we'd known each other for almost thirty years."

Amy was stunned. By everything. She

especially had trouble imagining Ms. Burris involved in a romantic relationship with Sanford Dominick.

"I don't want to risk anything that would create an ethical issue or a conflict-of-interest problem for the firm," Mr. Phillips continued. "When church people get together to talk and pray, it can be an information download."

"I'll keep my mouth shut."

Mr. Phillips stared at Amy. Her anxiety shot up as she anticipated his next statement.

"Just make sure your name doesn't come up in this case except to bolster Sonny's competency to sign the will I prepared and you typed. Understood?"

"Yes, sir."

It took every second of the drive home for Amy to unwind. And she had no one in her life she could talk to about what had just happened. Not Natalie. Not Jeff. And of course not Ms. Burris, who was the one person who could provide her with a helpful perspective.

At home Megan and Ian were sitting at the kitchen table doing homework. It reminded her of the days when they shared crayons.

"Why are you working in here?" she asked.

"So I don't have to go into Megan's room to ask her a question about social studies," Ian replied.

Megan was reading a book and had a yellow highlighter in one hand. It made her look like a college coed. For Amy, the jump from crayons to college prep was far too quick.

"How was school?" Amy asked her.

"Okay," Megan replied curtly.

Ian closed his book. "I'm done. I'll shoot baskets in the driveway while you talk about secret stuff."

"Did you finish the section about urban planning?" Megan asked.

"Yeah."

Megan grabbed Ian's book and asked him a few questions that he answered while tapping his feet against the floor. Amy watched in amazement.

"That's enough," Ian said. "You're harder than Ms. Burkholder."

"We'll have a review after supper," Megan said.

Ian put on his jacket and ran out of the kitchen.

"He's studying urban planning in the fourth grade?" Amy asked. "The last time I checked he was learning about the Lost Colony."

"It's part of the unit on economic development and growth over the past hundred years. They skip around in the text. It's not chronological."

"Thanks for helping him."

"I told you I'd do it."

Megan sounded grown up. Amy hoped her maturity would continue into their next conversation.

"Did you talk with Ms. Robbins?" she asked.

"Yeah. She's going to set up a meeting for Nate and me. Mr. Ryan and Coach Nichols are going to be there, too. It may not do any good, but I want to show Nate I can sit in the same room with him and look him in the face without crying or having a nervous breakdown."

Megan's expression as she sat at the table seemed resolute enough.

"I think Dad can come," Megan said slowly. "But I don't want him to say anything unless he clears it with Ms. Robbins first. Both of Nate's parents are going to be there."

Amy bit her lower lip at being excluded.

"Your father doesn't know what the text message said. And I don't think he should find out in a roomful of people."

"Ms. Robbins told me that won't be the point of the meeting. It has to do with Nate making a serious apology. She's not going to let him get off with an 'If I hurt your feelings, I'm sorry' kind of thing."

Amy was impressed with the counselor. Learning how to deliver a bona fide apology was something few adults knew how to do. And Ms. Robbins wasn't just teaching Nate. At some point in her life, Megan would also need to know what to do when she wronged someone.

"Okay," Amy said. "I'm going to cook spaghetti with meat sauce for supper. Does that sound good to you?"

"I had it for lunch at school, but it was so bad it made me want to barf. Yours will get the bad memory out of my brain. Will you put mushrooms in it?"

"I bought some fresh ones the other day."

"Yummy."

Megan left the kitchen. Amy took the ground beef out of the refrigerator and put a large pot of water on the stove to boil the pasta. At times, Megan was like a plate of wet spaghetti noodles — impossible to unravel.

After supper, Amy, Jeff, and Megan discussed the upcoming meeting with Nate at the school. Megan immediately tried to set limits on what Jeff could do.

"You will not tell me what I can and can't do as your father," Jeff said in a tone of voice that left no room for debate. "I'm glad you believe I should be at the meeting, but I was going to come anyway."

"Okay," Megan replied in a mousy voice. "I'm going up to my room."

After Megan left, Amy turned to Jeff.

"Way to go," she said.

"It all goes back to our responsibility to let Megan know we care about her. She felt secure when we set boundaries for her as a little girl, and she needs to know that there are limits to her wishes, even in a situation like this."

Amy leaned over and kissed Jeff on the cheek. "How did you get to be so smart?"

"You're smart; I'm practical."

Later, while sitting together in the family room, Amy told Jeff about *Deeds of Darkness* and her conversation with Bernie Masters. Jeff's eyes widened as Amy gave him the "elevator pitch."

"I'd read that book," he replied. "Are you going to have any action in it?"

Amy knew what Jeff meant. She'd never written a fight scene, and the idea made her chuckle.

"What's funny?" Jeff asked.

Amy punched her fist into the air. "I guess I could describe someone throwing a punch, but if you want a bunch of scientific details about what happens to the bone structure of the nasal cavities when a person's face is crushed, this won't be the book for you."

"No, but if the bad guys are as evil as you say they are, they will try to dish it out and deserve to reap what they sow."

"That's biblical." Amy nodded.

"I've been reading my Bible some during breaks at work." Jeff smiled.

Upstairs in the writing room, Amy expanded the elevator pitch into a synopsis. She thought about Bernie's warning against killing both

Roxanne and her husband and knew the agent was right. The mother and father couldn't both die. She toyed with the idea of killing Roxanne and keeping the father alive, but his tangential connection with the main thrust of the story made that an unappealing option. However, she couldn't get away from the possibility that one of the children might not make it through the final chapter alive. Amy had never allowed a child to play a main role in either of her other novels, much less be a tragic figure. In her books children were rarely seen or almost never heard.

Amy stopped typing.

What if one of the children in her new novel wasn't a toddler but rather a teenage niece whom Roxanne took in and adopted after the young girl was abandoned by her parents? The adoption would bolster reader sympathy for Roxanne and her husband and would be a poignant subplot. The niece would be an interesting mix of tough-knocks maturity forged by difficult life circumstances and a loving, sacrificial attitude toward her baby cousin. Thinking about the niece and her possible willingness to put her own life in serious jeopardy for her cousin, Amy felt a rush of emotion. It could be a powerful plot twist. She quickly wrote down a few notes to capture her thoughts and feelings.

That night, after Jeff fell asleep, Amy lay in bed and thought some more about the world of her new novel. A mixture of excitement and apprehension bubbled to the surface. If she'd heard the verse from Ephesians about exposing the deeds of darkness prior to writing *A Great and Precious Promise,* she never would have turned on the computer and typed "Chapter One." The first and second novels sprang from gentler seeds. Now she was ready for a deeper, more serious challenge.

After all, it was all make-believe.

SIXTEEN

The night before Megan's meeting with Nate Drexel, Amy spent an hour praying in the writing room. Her heart was still unsettled when she lay down and fell asleep.

And went to the living room.

Peace recognizes no foes in the courts of the Lord. The truth that God prepares a table for his children in the presence of their enemies finds its ultimate fulfillment in the place where he reigns supreme. When awake, Amy was an unwilling mystic, but during her nighttime visions, she knew that to doubt would be foolish.

As the dream came to an end, a new series of pictures and images flooded her mind in rapid succession. Each one was indelibly printed on her memory, but only for a split second. Once the impressions stopped, she couldn't specifically recall any of them.

After she woke up, Amy lay on her back wishing she could hold on to the wisps of the nighttime encounter that slipped through the fingers of her mind as soon as she left the living room. But there remained a gulf between the two realms.

"I'll be at the school at three thirty," Jeff said to Megan as they ate a bowl of oatmeal the following morning.

"Okay," Megan replied. "I wish I could stay out of school until then. It's going to be hard to think about anything else."

Amy was eating a grapefruit she'd sectioned with a sharp knife.

"Look to Ms. Robbins for guidance," Amy said. "That's her job."

"Or Mr. Ryan," Megan replied. "I stayed after class yesterday, and he told me about a similar situation that happened when he was in high school. Later, the boy did something worse and ended up in jail."

Amy wasn't exactly sure how that related to Megan. She turned to Jeff.

"Call me at work as soon as the meeting is over. Do you want me to pick up Ian?"

"No, I'll be off the clock, and there's no use going back for an hour or so. I'll get him."

Megan went upstairs. Jeff finished his oatmeal, too, but continued to stare at the empty bowl.

"What are you thinking?" Amy asked.

Jeff looked up at her. "That I don't want to lose my temper. I've tried to imagine everything that could be said so I won't be caught off guard, but that's no guarantee it won't happen."

Amy went to the door to make sure Megan couldn't hear them.

"Then you need to know exactly what Nate sent in his text," she said. "Megan didn't want me to tell you, but it's not something you should find out for the first time in a roomful of people."

Amy repeated the message to Jeff. She saw red streaks come up the sides of his neck. He picked up his spoon and began tapping it against the bowl.

"If you knew, why didn't you tell me before now?" he asked in a tense tone of voice.

"Maybe I should have. I didn't want to upset you more than you already were, but when you mentioned your concern about surprises, I knew I couldn't keep quiet."

"If I'd done something like that, my father —"

"I know," Amy interrupted.

Jeff glanced up at her. "It's going to take a lot to convince me this boy is sorry enough for what he's done."

"Do you think you should go to the school early so you can talk to Ms. Robbins? I've been so impressed with her during our phone calls."

"No. Just pray that I say and do the right thing."

"Maybe you shouldn't go."

"No, I'm committed to it."

Amy bit her lower lip. "Then don't dwell on the text all day. It's not something I want rolling around in your mind. And no matter what's said in the meeting, promise me you won't lose your temper and do anything rash."

"Like you said, there will be a roomful of people," Jeff said. "That will help keep me in check."

Ian came into the kitchen.

"I'm going to pick you up from after-school care," Jeff said.

"Cool. Can we go by the new indoor batting range? Bobby's dad took him. They have machines that pitch the ball at different speeds."

"Sure, I'll put your bat in my truck."

"And leave it there when you go to the high school," Amy said quickly.

Jeff gave her a strange look.

"I don't think I'll need it in the meeting."

Jeff left the house. Megan returned to the kitchen while Amy was helping Ian look for a missing schoolbook.

"Here it is," Ian said while lying on his stomach in front of the washing machine. "It was down here."

"What is it doing there?" Amy asked.

"I put it on top of the machine when I was putting my dirty socks in for you to wash and must have knocked it off."

Once the children were bundled up, Megan stopped and gave Amy a hug.

"Bye, Mom, I love you," Megan said.

"I love you, too."

"What did you do wrong?" Ian asked Megan.

"Nothing," Amy replied immediately. "Either one of you can tell me you love me anytime you want to and for no reason at all."

After the children were gone, Amy went upstairs and turned on the old clock radio Jeff had brought into their marriage. She stood in front of the bathroom mirror listening to the local news while putting the finishing touches on her makeup:

"A Cross Plains man was reported missing by his wife after he failed to return home from a trip to a convenience store last night. Carl Fincannon, age sixty-one, a retired policeman, was last seen at approximately 8:30 p.m. His abandoned car was found near the intersection of Selmer and Castile Streets on the west side of town. He left the house wearing a brown coat, khaki pants, and a red N.C. State cap. Anyone who has information about his whereabouts is asked to call the police or sheriff's department."

Amy was about to apply a final dash of eye shadow to her right eyelid when the announcer mentioned that the missing man was wearing a red cap. An image from her previous night's trip to the living room flashed across her mind. The announcer moved on to the weather report. Amy turned around and stared at the radio.

She'd seen that cap.

In addition to the N.C. State letters, it also had a snarling wolf, the team mascot, embroidered on the front. In her dream, the cap was lying on the ground not far from a place where a residential street crossed a narrow stream. Amy knew the place because the road was a shortcut from the downtown area to a row of buildings rented by various doctors behind the hospital. Jeff and Amy's internist had his office in one of those buildings.

Amy's cell phone was on the sink in front of her. She picked it up and started to dial the number for the police information line the announcer had given but stopped. What would she say to the person who answered the call? How would she respond to a request for the source of her information? She returned the phone to the sink and stared at herself in the mirror. The police department probably received lots of bogus calls when a plea went out asking for help locating a missing person. Amy's hat information would fit neatly into that category.

But what if her call was taken seriously? She didn't feel right about causing a patrolman to waste his time driving over to the street near the hospital to see if a red hat was lying on the ground. What if the patrolman was needed elsewhere on legitimate police business? Amy hurriedly finished getting ready and went downstairs.

As soon as she was in the car, she knew she wasn't driving directly to work. She backed out of the driveway, left their neighborhood, and turned in the direction of the hospital. It was a cold morning, and the thought of a man spending the night outside made Amy shiver even though her car heater was blowing full force. The tragic plight of Mr. Fincannon's wife, who undoubtedly didn't sleep all night, was also sad.

About the time Amy usually arrived at the office, she turned onto the street she'd seen in the dream. Her heart beat a little faster. Up ahead was the bridge. It was little more than two low concrete sections that kept cars from drifting off the roadway. A garbage truck passed going the opposite direction. Amy slowed and pulled onto the grassy shoulder of the street. There was no sign of a red hat. She sighed with relief.

And felt a huge wave of guilt.

How could she be relieved that the dream wasn't real? Wouldn't it be better to deal with the awkwardness of providing helpful information about the missing man than hiding in anonymity? Leaving her car running, Amy got out and looked up and down the grassy shoulder. The roadway was slightly built up, and beyond the edge of her car it sloped sharply down to the waterway, which was lined with bushy trees and other vegetation. Even in winter it was hard to see through the thicket to the water. There was plenty of trash that needed to be picked up but nothing out of the ordinary.

She crossed the narrow street to the other side. No red hat. A large tree obstructed her view, and Amy took a few steps toward the bridge to get a better look into the shallow ravine. When she did, she saw something brown that looked like a fallen limb. She stared more intently. It wasn't a tree limb.

It was a man's leg.

An hour later a slightly disheveled Amy walked through the front door of the law office.

"How are you?" Janelle asked with concern.

"Okay. Just late," Amy replied.

"I know that. How is the man you rescued? All it said on the Internet was that he was taken to the hospital."

Amy's mouth dropped open.

"It's on the Internet?"

"Yeah. My friend who works in the ER called me and told me a woman who works at our office helped the police locate a missing man who had a stroke or something. She probably wasn't supposed to say that because of HIPAA, but we're real close."

"I didn't rescue anybody," Amy said, still

somewhat in shock.

"Then what happened?"

"I saw a leg in the bushes and called the police."

"That would have scared me to death, and I would have screamed my head off," Janelle said, rubbing her arms with her hands. "I mean, it sounds like something out of a book. Maybe you should include it in your next novel."

"I'd better get to work." Amy moved forward in the direction of her office. "Is Mr. Phillips here?"

"No, he's meeting with a client in Raleigh this morning."

"That's right. I forgot."

"Which is understandable. What should I say if a TV reporter or someone from the newspaper calls and wants to talk to you?"

"Uh, connect them to my voice mail."

Amy made it to her office and closed both doors. She was barely seated when someone knocked on the hallway door.

"Who is it?" she asked.

"Chris."

"Come in."

The young lawyer slowly opened the door.

"Is what I'm hearing about you and the man who was missing true?"

"I don't know what you heard, but I placed a 911 call this morning on my way to work that led to the police finding Mr. Fincannon.

He was barely conscious after spending all night out in the open. Fortunately, he was wearing a heavy coat."

"How did you find him?"

Amy told as brief a version as possible.

"It's remarkable that you stopped your car," Chris replied thoughtfully. "Where do you live?"

Amy told him.

"Is that the way you normally come to work?" Chris asked with a puzzled expression on his face. "I'm still new to town, but that doesn't make sense."

"My internist has his office in a nearby building behind the hospital."

It was the answer Amy had given to the police. She'd not lied and claimed she was going to see the doctor. She'd merely mentioned the fact and left it alone.

"And you had a doctor's appointment this morning?"

"Don't start in on me," Amy bristled. "I'm not in the mood to be cross-examined. And if you don't like it, you can complain to Mr. Phillips."

"Okay, okay." Chris held up his hands. "There's no need to start a war. It's a great thing you did. But it made me wonder if your psychic powers were involved."

"I do not have psychic powers!" Amy snapped.

Chris opened his mouth, then closed it. He

stepped out of the tiny office and quietly closed the door behind him. Amy put her head in her hands and leaned her elbows on her desk.

The rest of the morning she came out of her office only to go to the bathroom and return. Two phone calls from one of the main reporters for the local paper went into her voice mail. There was no way she was going to talk to the press. During her lunch break, she left the office through a back door and drove to the park. As soon as she turned off the car's engine, Jeff called her cell phone.

"What is going on?" he asked. "I was on a job, and the woman we're working for asked me if I was your husband."

Amy sighed and told Jeff everything. She'd never been so transparent with him about the living room, but today she didn't have the emotional reserve to be evasive. He listened until she finished.

"That is weird," he said.

Tears stung the corners of Amy's eyes. It was exactly the kind of reaction she'd feared. Jeff didn't say it in a malicious way, but the words stood on their own. Amy was tempted to hang up on him.

"But it worked out for good. You probably saved that man's life."

Amy sniffled.

"Are you okay?" Jeff asked.

"No."

"Do you need to go home?"

The thought of sitting at home with nothing to do wasn't the answer.

"No, I may as well stay at the office. Mr. Phillips was out this morning, but he'll be back this afternoon." Amy paused. "Nobody knows what I told you. The police were more interested in helping Mr. Fincannon than questioning me. But Chris Lance, the young lawyer at work, got very nosy, and I was rude to him."

"I'm sure he deserved it."

"I don't know. What do you think I should do about the reporter from the newspaper?"

"Given how you feel, I don't think you should call him. This has been traumatic for you, too."

Jeff's understanding tone started to calm Amy down.

"And you're not going to say anything to anybody?"

"Only that I'm proud of my wife."

"Okay, thanks. I'll see you later this afternoon."

"Yes, and don't forget to pray for Megan's meeting with Nate Drexel at the school."

"Of course. I need something else to think about."

Amy was at her desk when Mr. Phillips returned to the office. She'd left the door cracked open so she could see the senior partner when he entered. He put his leather briefcase in the corner where he always kept it and came toward her. Amy focused her attention on the computer screen in front of her.

"Have you finished the first draft of the buy-sell agreement for Kit Austin?" Mr. Phillips asked.

"Yes, sir, but I haven't printed it out."

"Get it to me so I can correct it. Kit and I are going to discuss it at three o'clock."

"Yes, sir."

Mr. Phillips left the doorway. Amy relaxed and brought up the document so it could be sent to the printer. Her phone buzzed.

"Mrs. Fincannon is on the phone," Janelle said. "She really wants to talk to you. I tried to put her off, but —"

"It's okay," Amy interrupted. "Tell her I'll be with her in a minute and park her on my line."

She retrieved the document Mr. Phillips wanted from the printer and took it to him.

"Thanks," he said, staring down at something else he was reading on his desk. "What's this I hear about you calling 911 this morning? Janelle mentioned it when I came by her desk."

"I saw something beside the road and notified the police. It turned out to be a man who had a stroke, got confused, and left his car. He'd spent the night outside. They took him to the hospital."

"Lucky for him you came along. It was cold outside last night."

"Yes, it was."

"How's he doing?"

"I'm not sure. His wife is holding on my line."

Mr. Phillips looked up.

"Then don't stand there talking to me. Take the call."

"Yes, sir."

Amy returned to her office and picked up the phone. Mrs. Fincannon was a soft-spoken woman with a country accent.

"I'm so glad you found Carl," she said. "The specialist who's doctoring him thinks he's going to pull through, but it will take awhile to find out what he's lost the use of. I was having chest pains, and the doctor made me come home and lie down for a little bit. Our daughter is up there now. She called me a few minutes ago and said he knew her face and spoke a few words. He even asked about our new grandbaby who is only six weeks old."

As she listened, Amy's emotions were a swirling tornado.

"That's encouraging," she said, deciding it was best to keep her comments short.

"I'm going back up there later, but I had to call you first. I'm worn out with worry and haven't slept a wink since he took off for the store last night. Thank goodness I made him take off his lightweight jacket and put on his heavy coat. Normally, I wouldn't have said a thing, but for some reason it popped out of my mouth. I think the Lord was looking out for him then and sent you down the street this morning to find him."

"I agree."

"Good, 'cause that's what I told the fellow from the newspaper. I don't think it would be right to say it just happened. My mother always told us God has his hand in a lot more than folks are aware of, and I sure don't want to miss a chance to give him the credit he's due."

Tears formed in Amy's eyes.

"Yes, ma'am. You're right," she managed.

"Well, I won't keep you," Mrs. Fincannon said. "But I'd like you to come see Carl when he gets to feeling better. I'm sure he'd like to thank you himself. He's a good man. We've been married forty-one years. Our anniversary was two weeks ago. We have three daughters and eight grandchildren."

Amy held a tissue to her eyes.

"That would be great," she said with a sniffle. "Please let me know a good day and time, and I'll be there."

The call ended. Amy slowly lowered the phone to its cradle.

Seventeen

Amy was interrupted at 4:15 p.m. when Janelle buzzed her.

"Your husband is here," the receptionist said.

"At the office?" Amy asked in surprise.

"Yes, he stepped back to the restroom."

"I'll be right out."

Jeff never came to the office. Amy's sense of foreboding about what had happened during the meeting at the school increased as she walked to the reception area.

"Mrs. Fincannon seemed like a nice lady," Janelle said cheerfully when Amy came into the foyer.

"Yes." Amy glanced down the hallway toward the bathroom that had been designated for male use.

"My friend at the hospital said it looks like Mr. Fincannon is going to make it."

"That's what his wife told me. I'm going to see him when he feels better."

Janelle lowered her voice. "I told her you

were an author, and she's going to buy your book."

"I appreciate that."

Jeff opened the door of the bathroom and came toward her. He had a sober look on his face.

"Is anyone in conference room 3?" Amy asked Janelle.

"No, it's available until a deposition that starts at five o'clock."

Amy motioned to Jeff. They went into a conference room that had been used as a sitting room when the mansion was a private residence. It contained a shiny wooden table surrounded by six chairs. A vase of fresh flowers rested in the center of the table. A large bookcase lined one wall. The other walls were decorated with paintings, including a portrait of Mr. Jones, one of the founders of the firm.

"How did the meeting go?" Amy asked Jeff as soon as the door was closed.

"It's hard to know," he replied.

"What do you mean? Did you get upset?"

"Yes. Can we sit down?"

They sat across from each other.

"But you didn't do anything to Nate, did you?" Amy asked.

Jeff gave her a puzzled look. "I didn't punch him, if that's what you mean. Although if we'd been the same age, I probably would have thought about it. I'd think you'd be more interested in Megan than him."

"Of course I am. I want to know everything. I'll shut up and listen."

Jeff rested his large hands on the table. "I know how you like everything in chronological order. Ms. Robbins gave a short speech, but after that Mr. Ryan took over the meeting. I guess they'd planned it that way in advance. Coach Nichols was there with a scowl on his face. He didn't say anything, but I know Nate is dreading what's in store for him on the practice field. The football team is in an off-season training program, and Nate will probably be running wind sprints until he throws up for the next few weeks. His parents were there. Nate's mother looked like she was about to cry but kept quiet. Nate read an apology that sounded like he'd written it himself. After he did it once, Mr. Ryan asked him to read it again. It was a good move. The second time around it seemed like he was thinking more about what he was saying."

"How did Megan react?"

"She didn't cry, and at the end when Nate asked her if she would forgive him, she told him yes. That's when Ms. Robbins talked for a minute about what forgiveness looks like. She mentioned not bringing up the incident again and made Nate promise nothing like that will happen in the future."

"Did his father say anything?"

"He pulled me aside at the end and told

me he was sorry Nate had hurt Megan. He believes he's learned his lesson. I have no idea if that's true, but I don't think he'll be trying to hang around Megan again. Oh, and I spoke with Ms. Robbins about the English class. She's going to check Nate's schedule and discuss the situation with the teacher. If a change can be made, they'll do it. Otherwise, the teacher will be on the lookout for any problems."

"Where's Megan now?"

"I took her out for an ice cream and then dropped her off at the house."

Amy smiled. Father-daughter ice-cream trips had been a tradition to celebrate triumphs and ease hurts since Megan was little.

"And I'm on my way to get Ian at afterschool care when I leave here. Remember, I promised to take him to the batting cages."

"Right."

"I guess that's it. I'm sure I'll remember more by the time you get home." Jeff paused. "Did you hear anything else about the man you found this morning? Is he going to make it?"

Amy told him about the phone call with Mrs. Fincannon.

"That's good," Jeff said. "I'm still trying to get my head around what you did."

"Me, too, but I think Mrs. Fincannon had the right attitude."

"Are you going to call the newspaper reporter?"

"No, she said it better than I could."

"Don't worry about fixing supper," Jeff said. "I'm going to cook hamburgers on the grill."

Relieved at the news about Megan, Amy returned to her office. The last item in her dictation queue was from Chris Lance. It was the first project he'd sent her and was more than twenty minutes long.

It was the first draft of a brief — a written legal argument addressed to a local trial judge in a lawsuit about the breakup of Westside Lighting, a wholesale company. Chris talked very fast and, unlike Mr. Phillips, gave no punctuation, paragraph separation, or help with spelling. It was similar to a stream-of-consciousness novel in which the author ignores the rules of grammar and composition for the sake of artistic freedom. If she'd received something like this from one of the partners, Amy would have wondered if it was a test of her competency. With Chris, she suspected it might be his way to get back at her for cutting him off earlier in the day.

The dictation software allowed her to slow down Chris's voice so she could keep up. The process made him sound like the bass singer in a gospel quartet. Close to 5:00 p.m. she reached the midway point of the brief.

"And as a third ground for finding that the alleged verbal agreement between the parties is unenforceable, the Court's attention is directed to page twenty-one of the deposition of Michael Baldwin, the former manager for both the Fayetteville and Cross Plains stores."

Amy stopped the dictation. She'd been inside the Cross Plains store. Even though it was a wholesale company, Jeff had used his connections in the local building industry so they could purchase track lighting for the high ceiling in their family room at a big discount. The man who'd helped them with their purchase was Michael Baldwin. Amy remembered him because of his distinctive handlebar mustache and thought at the time he'd make an interesting character in a book. Now she remembered him, not as a salesman, but because she'd seen him in a dream.

And he hadn't left a good impression.

There was a knock on her hallway door.

"Come in," she said.

It was Chris. Amy pulled the buds from her ears.

"Are you making progress with the brief in the Westside Lighting case?" the young lawyer asked.

"Yes."

"I know I put my thoughts out there pretty fast."

"It reminds me of a James Joyce novel."

"Who?"

"James Joyce, the Irish novelist and poet."

"What did he write?"

"*Ulysses* is his most famous novel."

"I thought that was written by Homer, the Greek guy."

"That was the *Odyssey.* Ulysses is the Latin name for the hero."

"I was an economics major in college." Chris shrugged. "Since you're a published author, I didn't want to insult your intelligence by providing punctuation and spelling."

Amy couldn't tell if Chris was being sincere or sarcastic. She tried to keep her response professional.

"I've worked for several lawyers over the years," she said. "Periods and commas aren't essential, but it would help to know when to start a new paragraph or the spelling of unusual names or terms."

"No problem. Just get me the first draft, and I'll mark it up." Chris paused. "Did you say anything about my dictation to Mr. Phillips?"

"No."

"Thanks."

Chris cleared his throat.

"And, uh, I'm sorry for the way our conversation went this morning. You know, the one about the man you found."

"I remember."

"I was talking about it to Laura at lunch, and she really let me have it. Let's put it behind us. Chalk it up to my ignorance. I know as much about religion as I do James Joyce and ancient Greek literature."

It seemed to be a day for apologies.

"Thanks," Amy said.

"And if there's anything else you want to tell me" — Chris paused — "either personal or about a case, let me know."

Amy raised her eyebrows.

"Did Laura make you promise to ask me that?"

Chris shifted his weight on his feet.

"Was it that obvious?"

"Yes," Amy said, smiling slightly, "but as a wife, I commend the humility and the effort. Please pass that along to Laura."

Amy thought again about Michael Baldwin. She hesitated. But it didn't seem right to bring it up to Chris. Not yet.

Smoke and flames shot up from coals piled in a pyramid in the center of the charcoal grill. Amy went into the kitchen and found Jeff molding hamburger patties in his hands. Jeff's hamburger patties were always perfectly symmetrical. Amy thanked him and kissed him on the cheek.

"You're welcome," Jeff replied. "But I enjoy cooking on the grill."

"That doesn't make it less sweet."

Amy went upstairs to change. Megan stuck her head out of her bedroom door.

"Mom!" she called out in a loud whisper.

"Where's Dad?"
"Downstairs in the kitchen."
"Can I talk to you?"
Amy went over to Megan's room. Megan pulled her inside and shut the door.
"What did Dad tell you about the meeting at school?" she asked.
"He thought it went well."
"I was scared to death. If Mr. Ryan hadn't stepped in, I'm not sure what Dad would have done."
"What are you talking about?"
"You know how he looked at me the other night when he told me I wasn't going to tell him he couldn't come to the meeting? Today, before anyone said anything, he pointed his finger in Nate's face and told him how upset he was about what he'd done to me and my reputation. Nate turned as white as a sheet, and his mother started crying."
"Did he raise his voice?"
"He was loud. I thought he was going to grab Nate and shake him or punch him. That's when Mr. Ryan interrupted and took over the meeting. He turned everything toward the real reason why we got together. When Nate read the apology, he looked at Dad more than he did me. His hands were shaking. I had to say I forgave him or Dad might have gone off on him."
Amy was bewildered.
"Please don't say anything," Megan contin-

ued. "I don't want him to get mad at me. Has he ever lost his temper so badly that it scared you?"

"No," Amy answered. "And he's cooking hamburgers on the grill for supper to make things easier for me."

Megan pushed her hair behind her ears. "He was better by the time we got in the car to leave the school. He even took me out for ice cream, but the whole thing freaked me out."

"I think it will be okay."

"I hope so."

Supper was subdued. Ian loved hamburgers and french fries. He focused all his attention on his food and finished two hamburgers before Amy could eat one. His appetite was the sign of an impending growth spurt.

"Can I take a plate of fries up to my room?" he asked. "I'd like a snack while I do my homework."

"May I," Amy corrected him.

"May I?"

"Yes."

"Do you want to tell your mother about the meeting at school?" Jeff asked Megan.

"Uh, we already talked. I'm just glad it's over."

Megan left the kitchen. Amy waited a few seconds until her footsteps couldn't be heard.

"Can you give me a more detailed version

than what you told me at the office?" she asked.

"I may." Jeff smiled.

"This isn't funny," Amy replied flatly.

"It wasn't much of a joke, but there's no reason to get upset."

"You did."

Jeff was about to eat a french fry but returned it to his plate.

"Is that what Megan told you?"

Amy chose her words carefully. "She said you were overly stern with Nate."

"He needed to hear it, and I think it made a strong impression on him. At least I hope so."

"I know you were doing what you thought needed to be done, but it shook Megan up. She's not seen that aggressive side of you."

"I was doing it for her," Jeff said with a puzzled look on his face. "She's our daughter, and her reputation was dragged through the mud."

"I understand, but in a few days you might want to revisit how it made her feel."

Jeff threw his hands up in the air. "Women are impossible to figure out at any age."

"That's true, but we appreciate a man who tries and doesn't give up."

While Jeff was on the computer, Amy sneaked up to Megan's room. She was on the phone and quickly ended the call when Amy entered.

"Dad doesn't realize how you felt during the meeting and would feel terrible if he knew how much it upset you," Amy said.

"What did you tell him?" Megan asked sharply. "I told you to keep it secret."

"Nothing except that at times you were uncomfortable with his approach."

"Is he going to corner me?"

"No, but he may bring it up. When he does, listen to what he says and then explain your feelings."

Megan shook her head. "I was talking to Mr. Ryan when you came in a minute ago. He called to check on me and said I should be careful not to make Dad mad."

"This isn't about worrying that your father will get mad. You need to talk it through with him so there's nothing between you." Amy paused. "And Mr. Ryan shouldn't be calling you on your cell phone. How did he get your number?"

"He has everyone's cell number in case he needs to get in touch with us. He was worried about me."

Amy wanted to press the issue but didn't. Megan had gone through more than enough stress for one day. At least she didn't try to hide the fact that the teacher contacted her.

"Okay. Do you have any homework?"

"Yes, but it's going to be hard to force myself to do it. I hate algebra."

"I did, too."

"You did?"
"Yes. I barely made a B–."
Megan smiled.
"Thanks, Mom."

Amy looked over the railing into the family room. Jeff was staring intently at the computer screen. She needed to work on the synopsis Bernie wanted.

Deeds of Darkness continued to evolve in Amy's mind and on her computer screen. The age difference between Roxanne and her niece was now only twelve years, which opened the door to interesting opportunities for tension between them as they competed for dominance in a household with no man present and for the love of Roxanne's baby.

Amy felt confident that the basic plotline of smuggling people and property across the Mexican border was solid. Public concern over border security was a constant news item, and it was plausible that events like those presented in the story could actually take place. A sophisticated smuggling operation would also be fertile ground for internal plot possibilities between the villains and everyone else.

The more she thought about the relationship between Roxanne and her husband, the more Amy liked the drama created by a man wrongly removed from his family and thrown into jail. Devastated by her husband's false imprisonment, Roxanne would then be challenged to confront a more immediate evil when she learned that children as young as her son were being illegally transported across the border. As a mother, she could not allow that sort of wickedness to go unopposed, even if she stood little chance of defeating a cruel, powerful enemy. In the fight, the niece would play a key role as an ally, but one whose interaction with Roxanne would be laced with underlying antagonism.

The great unknown remained the degree of personal sacrifice the family would have to make to overcome the deeds of darkness. Amy completed the four-page synopsis without including a tidy conclusion, but she made it clear that victory for Roxanne would come only at a high cost.

Eighteen

As usual, Jeff was out of bed before Amy the following morning. When she shuffled downstairs to get her first cup of coffee, Jeff had the morning paper open on the kitchen table. Instantly, Amy was fully awake.

"What does it say?" she asked.

"That you're a hero who avoids the spotlight," Jeff replied.

Amy rubbed her eyes and put on a spare pair of glasses she kept in the kitchen. The brief article was on the second page toward the bottom. The headline and text read:

LOCAL MAN SUFFERS STROKE — SURVIVES COLD NIGHT IN DITCH

Cross Plains resident and retired police officer Carl Fincannon, age 61, was reported missing Wednesday evening after he failed to return from a trip to a convenience store. His abandoned car was found a few hours later near the intersection of Selmer and castile Streets. The search for Fincannon continued through the night until his body was spotted in a ditch early Thursday morning by local resident Amy Clark.

An emergency crew responded to Clark's 911 call, and Fincannon was taken to nearby Memorial hospital where he is being treated for a stroke and exposure. Fincannon had walked almost a mile from the place where he left his vehicle. Paul Moran, shift supervisor for cross Plains EMS, stated, "Mr. Fincannon was in the early stages of severe hypothermia when our crew arrived." Temperatures in the area fell into the upper twenties last night.

Clark was unavailable for comment, but Fincannon's wife, Betty Jean, expressed the family's appreciation to Clark, the EMT responders, the local police, and the medical staff at the hospital. Fincannon is currently in ICU at Memorial hospital. His condition is listed as serious.

"They spelled our name wrong," Jeff said when Amy looked up from the page.

"I noticed that."

Jeff came over and gave Amy a hug.

"Even without an 'e' on the end of your name, you did great."

"Mrs. Fincannon's deepest appreciation was to the Lord, but I guess that didn't make it past the editor."

Jeff pointed up. "He knows."

When Amy checked her voice-mail messages at work, the next to last one was from Mildred Burris asking her to call.

With a heavy heart Amy had typed and sent the letter Mr. Phillips dictated to Ms. Burris informing the elderly lady that the firm could no longer represent her. The voice mail didn't mention the letter. Amy glanced at the clock. She barely had time for a short conversation before opening and organizing the morning mail for Mr. Phillips. Wondering if Ms. Burris had seen the morning paper and suspected the truth about Carl Fincannon, Amy closed both doors to her office and dialed the number.

"It's Amy Clarke. You left me a voice mail yesterday afternoon."

"Yes. I have a couple of dates for our luncheon with your friend Natalie. Would either this Friday or next Tuesday at noon work for you?"

Amy made a spur-of-the-moment decision to disobey Mr. Phillips.

"Either day is fine with me, but let me check with Natalie and get back to you later today."

"All right."

Amy hesitated. She needed to get busy, but a question she'd been mulling over on the way to the office wanted to leap off the end of her tongue.

"If God shows me something, does that mean it's going to happen, or can it be changed?" she asked.

"I have a principle," Ms. Burris replied. "Information is for intercession first. God can certainly reveal events that are going to take place no matter what, but I don't assume that to be the case. Prayer is always in order. However, don't use prayer as an excuse not to act."

"Okay."

"And don't forget to call Natalie."

"Yes, ma'am."

The call ended. Amy glanced at the clock. There wasn't time to phone Natalie and prepare for Mr. Phillips's arrival to the office.

It was late morning before she had a chance to get in touch with her friend. By that time, four people from the office had stopped by to give Amy a copy of the article in the newspaper. When they asked for more details, Amy described Mr. Fincannon's leg. That seemed to satisfy their curiosity. None questioned why she was near the hospital so early in the morning.

By 11:00 a.m., Natalie would have finished her workout at the gym and returned home.

"Kim Green ran out to the car this morning and told me about you finding the man who spent the night in the ditch," Natalie said as soon as she answered the phone.

"Yes," Amy sighed. "The Lord prompted me to drive down that road."

"I knew it," Natalie responded. "But of course I didn't say anything to Kim. She's such a blabbermouth."

"And I appreciate it. I'm still sorting the whole thing out. But that's not why I called. I talked to Ms. Burris about the three of us getting together."

When given a choice of days, Natalie immediately selected Friday.

"Why Friday?" Amy asked.

"It's sooner."

"Okay."

"What should I wear?" Natalie asked. "You'll be dressed up for work."

"Ms. Burris is fairly formal, and she's going to make this an occasion. Wear something with flair. Don't be boring like me."

Friday morning Amy was working at her desk when her phone buzzed. It was Chris Lance.

"Can you come to my office for a minute?" he asked.

"Yes."

Amy removed her earbuds. She'd given the young lawyer the first draft of the brief in the Westside Lighting case two days earlier and had not heard anything else from him. As her feet hit the treads on the stairs, they alternately called out "Michael" and "Baldwin." Ever since her discussion in the call with Ms.

Burris, Amy had been praying about what she'd seen in the living room concerning the mustached man. Was this a situation for prayer only or was she called to act?

She'd even pulled Baldwin's deposition from the file and read it. According to his sworn testimony, he left the lighting company on good terms for a better job with a large floor-covering outlet in Fayetteville and harbored no bias against either party. Shortly before his employment ended, he overheard a conversation between the three owners about the need to finalize the terms of their buy-sell agreement in writing. It all seemed straightforward enough, but Amy had her doubts. And one of the worst things that could happen to a lawyer was to inform a judge that testimony presented as truthful was, in fact, a lie.

Chris swiveled in his chair when Amy appeared in the doorway.

"Come in," he said.

Amy sat down across the desk from the lawyer. He handed her a stack of papers.

"I marked up the Westside Lighting brief. I hope you can decipher my comments."

Amy glanced at the top sheet of paper, which was covered in red ink. There were lines drawn to the side and words scribbled down the margins. Something about it all struck her as humorous, and she started to chuckle.

"What is it?" Chris asked.

Amy turned one of the pages to the side and studied the words that crawled along the edge. She spoke slowly.

"Does this say, 'The Court in *Delray, supra,* ruled that the contract was unenforceable on grounds that are clearly distinguishable from our case'?"

"Yes."

"Then we're good here."

"Are you sure?"

"I've been translating lawyer scribbles for a long time. I'll let you know if something doesn't make sense."

Amy turned to the third argument, the one based on the testimony of Michael Baldwin. Chris had left it largely intact.

"Are you sure you want to rely so heavily on Michael Baldwin's deposition?" she asked, trying to sound nonchalant about it.

"That's my strongest argument. I even thought about moving it to the front of the brief."

"I agree, but if he's not telling the truth, it could put you in a bad spot."

"He doesn't have an ax to grind with anyone, and his testimony is consistent with what our client claims."

"Yes, I saw that."

Chris and Amy stared at each other for a moment.

"When do you think you can make the corrections?" Chris asked.

"Unless Mr. Phillips gives me a project I'm not expecting, I should be able to have something to you by the end of the day."

"That would be great. I'm coming in tomorrow morning to work on this case."

Amy left Chris's office, taking her secret information with her.

Shortly before noon Amy sent Mr. Phillips an e-mail reminding him that she'd be gone for at least an hour. Thankfully, he didn't pry into the reason why she requested the change in her normal schedule.

When she arrived at Ms. Burris's house, Amy found Natalie sitting in her car in the driveway.

"How long have you been here?" Amy asked.

"A few minutes."

"Why didn't you go inside?"

"I wasn't sure I should until you got here."

Amy glanced sideways at her friend as they approached the front door.

"Were you scared to ring the doorbell?"

"Yes."

"Then I think I did a terrible job of describing Ms. Burris to you. She's like a friendly grandmother. It would have been fun for you to meet her without me around."

"Oh, does Ms. Burris know about the man you found?"

"I don't know, but if she doesn't bring it up, please don't mention it. I want this time to be about other things."

"Okay."

Amy pressed the doorbell. It took a minute or so for Ms. Burris to open the door. The elderly woman had dressed up for the occasion and was wearing a yellow brocade dress with an emerald necklace around her neck. It was the first time Amy had seen her since the allegation surfaced at the law firm about her decades-old romantic relationship with Sanford Dominick and her recent influence on his estate plan. The possibility that two people so different in their later years could have been attracted to each other when younger seemed as strange to Amy as anything she'd written in either of her books.

"Come in, Amy," Ms. Burris said with a smile. "And you must be Natalie."

Natalie extended her hand, but Ms. Burris reached out and gave her a gentle hug.

"Handshakes are for men who meet each other at a business lunch," Ms. Burris said. "Let's go directly into the sunroom."

As they followed Ms. Burris through the house, Natalie looked from side to side and craned her neck as she tried to see into all the rooms they passed.

"You have a lovely home," she said to Ms. Burris's back.

"I'll give you a tour later. There's no need

to try to see everything now."

"I'd love that."

"Natalie is a fantastic decorator," Amy said.

They reached the sunroom. Light snacks of cheese, fruit, and sparkling water were laid out on a glass table. The birds that lived in the backyard were out in force and surrounded the sunroom, almost making it feel like an aviary. Ms. Burris served each of them a small plate of fruit and cheese. Amy nibbled one of the cheeses and licked her lips.

"What is this?"

Ms. Burris glanced at Amy's plate.

"That's a Hittisau. The other two are Appenzeller and Flosserkase."

Amy sampled the other two cheeses. She'd never imagined something as common as cheese could be so exotic. Natalie put some Hittisau on her plate.

"I'm glad I don't have to spell it to eat it," Natalie said. "I could make a meal of this."

"The Appenzeller is stronger," Amy said.

"Yes, it's often used in fondue," Ms. Burris said.

"How did you learn about cheeses?" Natalie asked.

"I did some traveling in Europe when I was younger."

Amy wondered if that was when Ms. Burris spent time with Mr. Dominick. Amy put a tart, crisp grape in her mouth. The fruit was deliciously fresh.

"This is wonderful," she said.

Ms. Burris smiled and pointed at the glass table.

"Everything God creates is good. That's the fruit. But he gives us the ability to create wonderful things as well. That's the cheese."

Amy nodded.

"Tell me about you," Ms. Burris said to Natalie.

Natalie took a sip of water and gave a one-paragraph summary of her personal background before launching into information about her family.

"Not so fast," Ms. Burris interrupted. "There's more to you than what you've said. Amy has dreams in the night. What are your dreams during the day?"

Amy saw her friend's eyes widen. She had no idea what was going through Natalie's mind.

"Nothing but silly thoughts," Natalie said after a few moments passed.

"Like Amy, you're a creative person, too."

"I like to decorate."

"But that's not all, is it?"

Natalie glanced nervously at Amy before she answered.

"I've never shared this with anyone except Luke, but I have an idea for a series of children's books. I've written part of the first story and painted a few watercolor illustrations."

Amy's mouth dropped open. "I think that's fantastic. Why didn't you tell me about this?"

"I didn't want you to think I was trying to be a copycat or compete with you. I've wanted to write and illustrate children's stories for years, but I kept pushing it away. Then, when you got a contract for your first novel, it gave me the courage to try. I thought if —" Natalie stopped.

"Amy Clarke could get a book published, there is a chance for me." Amy finished the sentence with a smile.

"Sort of like that," Natalie admitted sheepishly. "But I'm super-proud of you and know it's a long shot for me to get my foot in the door with a publisher."

"When can I see what you've done so far?" Amy asked.

"Not until the first book is finished. I've written most of the text, but I have three more illustrations to complete. You won't give me a sneak peek of your novels."

"And now I'm sorry," Amy said before turning to Ms. Burris. "You should see what Natalie does with watercolors. If Jeff and I ever bought a house at the beach, I'd have her paintings in every room."

"The stories are set at the beach," Natalie said. "They're about a family with three children who discover things in nature while on vacation."

"That sounds great," Amy said. "Authors

who weave educational information into children's books have a big niche."

The women continued to talk and nibble the fruit and cheese. Every time she looked at Natalie, Amy couldn't keep from smiling. Ms. Burris took them into the kitchen where they fixed a salad from an expansive array of ingredients that included several kinds of fresh seafood. Amy loaded her salad with crab, not the imitation stuff squirted through a nozzle and shaped by a machine, but succulent, moist meat that tasted as clean as the arctic waters it came from.

After they'd fixed their salad plates, the women returned to the sunroom. There were four yellow finches thrusting their sharp, pointed bills into the tiny openings in a birdseed sock. Ms. Burris said a blessing for the food, and they began to eat. The short prayer made Amy want to make sure they left enough time at the end of the luncheon to pray again. No one spoke for a few moments while they savored the food.

"Amy, are you working on a book?" Ms. Burris asked.

Amy swallowed a bite. "Yes. I just started."

Natalie raised her eyebrows. Amy made a split-second decision.

"And I'd like to run the concept by both of you."

Beginning with the dream and the verse, Amy laid out the inspiration for the story and ended with her elevator synopsis. The other two women listened without interrupting her.

"My agent is more excited about this book than either of the other two," Amy said. "And Jeff even seemed interested, which is a first. What do you think?"

Natalie looked at Ms. Burris and didn't say anything.

"What is it, Natalie?" Amy asked.

"I'm just not sure," Natalie said slowly. "It sounds, uh, so different from anything else you've written. But I'm sure I'll love it when I read it."

"There will be a different kind of depth to the characters," Amy explained. "Brainstorming the plot has shown me the potential that's in the story when I open myself up to more possibilities."

"Possibilities to show the deeds of darkness?" Ms. Burris asked.

"Yes, and how the light dispels the darkness."

"I missed that in the summary."

"It will be there," Amy replied, shifting in her chair.

The women continued to eat; however, for Amy the salad had lost some of its appeal. The disapproval from the other two women about the direction of the new novel hung heavy in the air.

"Tell me what you really think," she blurted out. "Now is the time before I invest a year of my life writing this book. I've never shared my ideas so early in the process. After today, I'm going to be second-guessing myself every time I turn on the computer."

"I didn't mean to upset you," Natalie replied immediately. "And I trust you enough to know that you'll use the gift God has given you in the best way possible. Don't let me discourage you; I'd never do that."

Amy bit her lower lip. "But it's so easy for me to feel insecure, especially when I consider doing something different from what I've done before."

"I agree with Natalie that you're sincere and talented," Ms. Burris said calmly. "However, my question is whether the verse from Ephesians is the basis for a new novel or preparation for what you're going to face in your own life."

Amy felt like she'd been hit in the stomach with a baseball bat. She didn't breathe for a few seconds.

"Are you sure about that?" she managed.

"No," Ms. Burris said. "But you asked us what we really thought, and I felt that I should mention it. Would either of you like something else to drink?"

"Water, please," Amy mumbled.

Ms. Burris left for the kitchen. Amy immediately turned to Natalie.

"Is she right? My agent and Jeff didn't have a problem with the concept. And I know I wouldn't write something that dishonored the Lord."

"Please, Amy. You can't expect me to be the Holy Spirit for you."

Even though Natalie was right, Amy felt put off. Ms. Burris returned with Amy's water and then asked Natalie a question that took the conversation in another direction. Amy didn't participate. She silently followed the other women as Ms. Burris gave Natalie a tour of the house. When it was time to leave, Amy didn't ask Ms. Burris to pray.

"Are you okay?" Natalie asked as they walked toward their cars.

"How could I be?"

Nineteen

A much less confident Amy returned to the office and tried to focus on her work. Late in the afternoon her cell phone vibrated. Usually she didn't answer during the day unless it was Jeff or one of the kids, but Bernie's picture appeared. Hoping for an emotional lift, Amy quickly closed the door between her work area and Mr. Phillips's office.

"You answered," Bernie said with surprise. "Is your boss playing golf this afternoon?"

"No, but he should be back shortly. He had lunch with a client, then went directly into a full-fledged meeting."

"So the client buys lunch and gets billed for the time."

"Yes."

"Pretty soon you may be able to afford filet mignon for both of us," Bernie replied.

"What do you mean?"

"The synopsis you sent me for the new novel was dynamic. I shot it out of the cannon to acquisitions editors at four of the big six and hit bull's-eyes with two of them."

The publishing industry was dominated by six companies with global distribution capabilities.

"If we play this right, we may be looking at an auction for your services."

"An auction?"

"We set up a conference call and parade you around the paddock like a prize broodmare. The bidders weigh in with competing offers. When the bidding stops, we decide which stable will have the benefit of your services."

Amy didn't like the analogy.

"What about Dave Coley? Did you talk to him?"

"Not yet, but he wouldn't be able to pay the entrance fee for this kind of sweepstakes."

"I still want to let Dave and Cecilia read the synopsis for the book. I trust her instincts, and they took a chance on me when no one else would."

"And you've rewarded them with two novels that are better than most of the titles they bring to market. This is the way it works, and they know it."

Amy didn't doubt Bernie's knowledge about the publishing industry, but that didn't make it feel right.

"Don't fret. I'm going to send it over to Dave eventually," Bernie continued. "But I wanted to see if I could get a nibble from

New York before defaulting to plan B. And I got a lot more than a nibble. One of the editors bought a copy of *A Great and Precious Promise* and read it before calling me back."

"You're kidding. What did she think about it?"

"That it was an excellent first effort but only showcased a hint of your potential."

"And she understands I'm a Christian."

"As plain as if you stuck a Bible verse beneath your face on a billboard. Look, these editors know the kind of writers who get contracts from Christian publishing companies. It's self-evident. The issue is whether a person has enough storytelling chops and writing ability to produce a book that can stand on its own outside the Christian ghetto. Most can't and won't ever get the chance to try. You're about to become part of a small minority. This could be a big deal in every way. Think about reaching an audience beyond white-haired ladies who think coffee with caffeine is a strong drink."

"It's tempting," Amy said, then quickly added, "That's not the word I wanted to use. I mean, it's an opportunity I need to pray about."

"Pray quick, because we have to strike while there's an open door. If sales of *The Everlasting Arms* go into the toilet, this door will close and there won't be a keyhole on our side.

Right now, the acquisitions editors in New York can spin up sales projections to present to a publication committee without having to back them up with facts. Once the second book is released, there will be hard numbers that can't be manipulated as easily."

"How quick are you talking about?"

"A week or two. That will give me time to run the new novel past Dave Coley even though I know what his reaction will be. Also, do you think you can churn out a few chapters to show that you've got the ability to write with the big boys and girls?"

The reaction from Ms. Burris and Natalie at lunch was like a ball and chain wrapped around Amy's creativity. If she was going to produce anything, it would take a mammoth effort.

"Maybe I could send you two chapters in two weeks," she said tentatively. "It goes slower at the beginning because I'm just getting to know the characters."

"Take the characters out to dinner and make it three chapters so it's a nice round number. The prospects of a fatter contract, a bigger advance, and a broader stage should motivate you."

"How large could the advance be?"

"It depends on whether we can generate healthy competition. Two or more publishers bidding for your services could push it to around one hundred thousand dollars per book on a three-book deal."

"Are you serious?" Amy's mouth dropped open.

"Yes. Advances aren't what they used to be, but fresh voices with concepts that have curb appeal are always hot. The editor I talked with is already thinking about how to market you."

"What did she say?"

"We didn't get into specifics, but it's healthy that she's looking ahead."

The call ended, leaving Amy to process what Bernie told her. There had been something different in the agent's voice. He'd never treated her in such a professional manner.

The interest by the acquisitions editors in New York didn't erase the reservations about the new novel expressed by Natalie and Ms. Burris at lunch, but it sure helped. Amy decided she would consider what they'd said, but until she received a clear signal from the Lord that she was on the wrong track, she would continue in the same direction.

Ian was at Bobby's house and Megan was with Alecia. Amy stood in front of the open refrigerator door wishing that Jeff would call and tell her they were going out for supper. Friday night was the time she most wanted to avoid the kitchen. Dining at a restaurant, even if it was only a step above fast food, felt like a reward for making it through another week. She stepped back and let the refrigerator door slowly swing shut, then took out her cell phone and stared at it. The phone vibrated. It was Jeff.

"That is weird," she said. "I had my phone in my hand hoping you'd call."

"I can sense your desires within a twenty-five-mile radius of the house. Also, I know how much you like to eat out on Friday night because you've told me at least two hundred times during our marriage."

"Don't say too much. You'll lose your brownie points. How far away are you?"

"About ten minutes. I told the kids to leave you notes so you'd know where they were."

"They did."

"Where would you like to go? We can swing by and pick up Megan and Ian on the way. How about Mexican? I thought we could go to Los Reyes."

Amy would agree to any suggestion, so long as someone else cooked the food and brought it to the table.

The Mexican restaurant was a casual place. Amy changed from her work clothes into blue jeans and a sweater she knew Jeff liked. As she buttoned her jeans it seemed she'd lost a couple of pounds since returning to the law office. Even though she'd always been a healthy eater, working kept her from snacking during the day. She sent Megan a text about the plans for supper and called Bobby's mother to relay the message to Ian. Jeff arrived covered with Sheetrock dust and took a quick shower. As soon as they were in the car, Amy took advantage of the few moments they would have alone.

"I need to tell you about my lunch with Natalie and Ms. Burris."

When she mentioned Natalie's desire to publish children's books, Jeff interrupted.

"Do you think she has a chance?"

"She's a good artist, and illustrations are the key with children's books. A decent story with great illustrations has a better shot than a good story with lousy pictures. And if I can get a publishing contract, then she could, too. But that's not the main thing. I told Natalie and Ms. Burris about my new novel, and they didn't like it."

"Why?"

Amy explained as best she could the women's concerns.

"It really shook my confidence," she said.

"Yeah, but you're the writer, and you should do what you think is best."

"I also got a call from Bernie. He sent the synopsis for *Deeds of Darkness* to some acquisitions editors with publishers in New York and received encouraging feedback, especially from one woman."

As Amy repeated the rest of the conversation, she saw Jeff's fingers tighten on the steering wheel. She hesitated before mentioning the possibility of a six-figure advance but felt that it wouldn't be right to hold back important information. Jeff didn't try to hide his shock.

"Amy," he said, then shut his mouth.

"I know what you're thinking," she said, "but I can't let money dictate what I do."

"Bernie isn't talking about money dictating what you do." Jeff shook his head. "If that's how much a publisher would pay, I'd rather you make a hundred thousand dollars than another writer. I can't imagine that much money landing in our bank account. What would we do with it?"

Amy hadn't thought that far ahead, either. They turned into the driveway at the Pickenses' house. Ian and Bobby were throwing a football in the front yard. Ian ran over to the car and opened the door.

"Let Bobby's mother know that you're leaving," Amy said.

Ian yelled at Bobby, "Tell your mom that my parents picked me up, and I wasn't kidnapped by Mexican drug dealers."

"What are you talking about?" Amy asked when Ian was inside the car.

"You told Mrs. Pickens that we were going to eat Mexican food for supper," Ian answered.

"And why did that make you think about being kidnapped by Mexican drug dealers?"

"I don't know."

"Don't even joke about that," Amy said.

Ian didn't respond. He was making a face at Bobby through the car window. Amy thought about her new novel. When Ian became the object of a fictitious plot to kidnap him and drag him across the border, Amy disliked the idea more than Natalie and Ms. Burris.

Amy woke up Saturday morning at the usual time, but then, realizing she didn't have to go to work, she rolled over and slept blissfully for another thirty minutes. When she awoke again, Jeff's spot in the bed was empty. She went downstairs and found him in the kitchen drinking coffee and reading his Bible. Amy poured a cup.

"Mind if I sit down?" she asked. "I don't want to intrude."

"It's okay." Jeff slid the Bible away.

"What are you reading?" Amy asked after she sat next to him.

"Doing my own study," Jeff replied cryptically. He took a sip of coffee. "I've had second thoughts about the way I handled the meeting the other day at the school."

"Did Megan say anything to you?" Amy asked.

"No. What got me started was the verse you're using in your new book, the one about exposing the deeds of darkness. It made me ask myself about any darkness in me. The first thing that came up was how I felt toward Nate Drexel and what he did to Megan."

After fifteen years of marriage, Jeff could still surprise Amy. Ninety-five percent of the time he was completely predictable, but when he varied from his usual pattern, the results could be startling.

"What he did was terrible," Jeff continued. "But I went into the meeting thinking it was my job to make sure he knew how bad it was. That's God's job, not mine. Trying to impose my will even if I'm sincere and it's for a good cause isn't the way real repentance works."

"Where did you find that?"

"In Romans it says that God's kindness leads to repentance. There was nothing kind in my heart or mind when I walked into the door of the school. I'm not even sure what God's kindness would have looked like."

Amy took a bigger sip of coffee. "I admire a man who can repent before eight o'clock in the morning."

"It shows that the stuff you hear in your dreams isn't just for you to use in your novels."

"That's what Ms. Burris said," Amy replied, sitting up straighter. "She told me the deeds of darkness might have a practical impact on my life. It wouldn't be limited to inspiration for a work of fiction that teaches a lesson."

"And it may not apply to you. I doubt you

have any big, bad, dark spots," Jeff said.

"I do," Amy replied.

"Name one," Jeff shot back.

"Charging too much on the credit card," Amy said. She thought of a few others but didn't continue.

"That's not in the dark. I see what you spend every month, and I only brought it up when things were so financially tight before Christmas."

"Every woman has areas of insecurity where darkness likes to hide."

"Don't get superspiritual on me," Jeff said. "And don't make anything up. I can tell in half a second if you're not on the level."

Amy smiled. "It's good to have a personal lie detector test in the house."

Jeff shook his head. "You're the most honest person I know."

Amy leaned over and kissed him on the cheek.

"You're wrong, but you might want to share some of this with Megan. It would help her, too." Amy glanced at the clock on the wall of the kitchen. "I'm going to take her to dance practice at nine. I'll report back to you later about my sins."

While getting dressed, Amy thought about her fears that lived in the dark. Those things might not be actions, but that didn't mean they weren't deeds of darkness. Jeff's attempt to paint her as pristinely pure was sweet, but darkness hid in every human heart.

Even hers.

TWENTY

After she dropped Megan off at dance practice, Amy returned home. Jeff and Ian were in the garage cleaning out the back of Jeff's truck. She pulled in behind them.

"Mom, you're going to have to move your car," Ian said. "Dad and I are going to leave as soon as we're finished."

"Where?" Amy asked Jeff.

"Over to Calvin Harris's place in the country."

"To ride four-wheelers!" Ian added excitedly.

Calvin was a man who worked on Jeff's crew. Depending on the season of the year, his idea of fun often involved the death of a wild animal.

"There won't be any guns," Jeff said, anticipating Amy's next question. "Several fathers are bringing their sons to ride on a closed course. There will be helmets for everyone, and Ian will be with an adult. I'm not going to let him get in with a teenage driver."

"Tell her about the mudholes," Ian said.

Hands on hips, Amy stood with her head tilted to the side. She raised her eyebrows.

"It's part of the fun," Jeff said. "They fill up some low spots with water to make it muddy so the four-wheelers will slip and slide a little bit."

"What if you get stuck?"

"There's a winch they hook onto a tree to pull us out. But most of the trail is through the woods. There's even a place at the top of a hill to get out and enjoy the view."

"What happens to the mud that gets thrown up by the tires? Where does it go?"

"Ian is wearing old clothes, and I have a different outfit for him on the floorboard of the truck. There's an old hunting cabin nearby where he can clean up and change when we finish."

"Does this cabin have hot water?"

"Not unless we fire up the propane water heater. I'll ask Calvin to do that if he hasn't already thought about it."

Amy wasn't buying Jeff's idyllic interpretation of the planned activities. Nothing from her hidden memory bank of nighttime visions flashed into view with warning signs around it, but there was still a mother's normal concern about dangerous activities.

"Don't be running all over the place alone," Amy said to Ian, whose eyes were electric with excitement. "And wear your seat belt."

"The driver and passengers are strapped in with a four-point harness," Jeff said. "It will be safety first and fun second."

"Dad's bringing the video camera so we can show you what happens," Ian said.

"How long will you be gone?" Amy asked.

"Until late this afternoon," Jeff replied. "We're going to cook over an open fire for lunch. With a quiet house all to yourself, I thought you could get a lot of writing done."

"Why didn't you tell me about this earlier?"

"It was a last-minute discussion at work yesterday, and Calvin only confirmed everything with me after you left with Megan. I didn't want to mention it to Ian and get his hopes up if we weren't going to go."

Ian came over and gave Amy a hug.

"Don't worry, Mom. Bobby has a video game with four-wheelers in it. I've been practicing, but it's going to be way more fun to do the real thing."

Jeff and Ian got in the truck and backed down the driveway. Amy knew they were about to create a memory that Ian would never forget. She went inside the quiet house and poured herself a second cup of coffee. If she didn't have to write, she would enjoy putting her feet up in the family room and staring absentmindedly out into space. Instead, she carefully carried the cup of coffee up the steep stairs and turned on her computer.

After bowing her head for a brief prayer, Amy started working in earnest on the first chapter of the new novel. Typically, the chapters in her books were between three thousand and four thousand words. Writing nine thousand to twelve thousand words in two weeks while continuing to work at the law office, fulfill her duties as a wife and mother, and overcome the seeds of doubt sown by Natalie and Ms. Burris was daunting. Adding to the pressure was the fact that it always took longer to complete the early chapters of a manuscript. The setup of the story, like the foundation for a house, needed to be solid so it could support the remainder of the novel. It was also important to layer in foreshadowing of events that would be revealed at a later time.

Amy had done a lot of brainstorming in preparing the synopsis and written a rough draft of the opening scene. Much of that scene could be used; however, it didn't include the teenage niece. The first thing she did was rewrite the scene to include the niece sleeping on a mattress on the floor of the second bedroom beside Roxanne's baby boy. The presence of the older girl immediately created another basis of sympathy for Roxanne. Not only was she a young mother cruelly deprived of a husband's love and help, she was willing to share the slender crust of bread she had left with a vulnerable girl in even greater need. A good story is built on a protagonist the reader wants to root for — a person whose budding goodness can be fully forged in the furnace of affliction provided by the plot. Based on that formula, Roxanne was an ingot with unlimited potential.

The identification Amy felt with the main character as she wrote was encouraging. She was able to transfer her own feelings directly to the page, particularly when describing the sense of abandonment Roxanne experienced because her wrongly imprisoned husband was absent from the family. To communicate emotion at a deep level so early in a story was a new phenomenon for Amy.

After writing almost fifteen hundred words, she saved the file and closed her laptop. She glanced at a digital clock on a small desk against the wall. She'd been working almost three hours; however, the intensity of her concentration made the time pass quickly.

Driving to the studio, Amy decided to take Megan out to lunch. It wouldn't be as dramatic an outing as Ian's four-wheeling adventure, but it would send a message to Megan that Amy wanted to be with her and do what she wanted to do. When Amy arrived at the studio, she came face-to-face with Greg Ryan.

"Mr. Ryan," Amy said in surprise.

"Mrs. Clarke, how are you?" Ryan smiled broadly. "I stopped by for a few minutes to watch Megan and one of the other girls dance. Megan told me about the routine they were working on, and it sounded cool."

Amy nodded her head. Ryan glanced over his shoulder.

"I'm sure Megan told you about the meeting with Nate Drexel."

"Yes."

"How did she feel about it? I haven't had a chance to follow up with her."

Amy was determined not to say anything negative about Jeff.

"There were some positives. We'll see what happens from here. Megan appreciated you being there for her."

"She's a great kid, and it's easy to want to help that kind of student." Ryan lowered his voice and leaned in a bit closer. "I know your husband was upset, and I don't blame him. I tried to imagine how I'd feel in his shoes."

Megan came running up. She'd changed from her leotards into street clothes.

"Thanks for coming, Mr. Ryan," she said. "I'll let you know when Ms. Carlton schedules the real performance."

"I hope I can make it. I know you'll be fantastic." Ryan nodded to Amy. "Nice talking to you."

The teacher left. Megan ran over and picked up her gym bag.

"Isn't he the best ever?" Megan said when she returned.

"Who else did he come to watch?" Amy asked.

"Molly Prichard," Amy replied. "She's in his senior seminar class. I hope he's still at the school when I'm a senior. It would be awesome to have him one-on-one."

"Where would you like to eat lunch?" Amy asked once they were in the car. "Dad and Ian went four-wheeling."

Megan was texting on her phone. She looked up.

"What did you say?" she asked.

"I'd like to take you out for lunch. What sounds good to you?"

Before Megan answered, Amy's phone beeped. It was Jeff.

"Hello," she said.

"We're on our way to the hospital," Jeff said. "It looks like Ian may have broken his left arm."

"What?"

"He hit his arm on a tree."

"Are you in an ambulance?" Amy asked frantically.

"No, I'm taking him. I should be at the ER in less than five minutes if you can meet us there."

"I'm on my way."

"What happened?" Megan asked.

"Ian may have a broken arm. We've got to go to the hospital."

"Can you take me home first?" Megan

asked. "It's not that far out of the way, and you could be stuck at the hospital for hours."

Amy stared at Megan as if her daughter were an alien transported into the car from another planet.

"Are you serious?" she asked in a shrill voice.

"What can I do to help? And you know there will be a huge wait. When Crystal broke her arm last year, it took the doctor four hours to set it."

"Ian is your brother!"

Megan turned away and looked out the window. Amy sped out of the parking lot. Neither spoke.

"All right," Amy said abruptly when they reached the entrance to their neighborhood. "I'll drop you off at the house. But I can't believe you don't care more about your brother."

"I care, but there's nothing I can do. When he comes home and needs something, I'll be there for him."

Amy let Megan out of the car at the end of their driveway. Glancing in the rearview mirror, she saw Megan with her cell phone to her ear walking nonchalantly toward the house.

It was an eight- or nine-minute drive to the hospital. When Amy pulled into the parking lot for the emergency room, Jeff's truck was already there. She rushed through the sliding glass doors that opened in front of her and into the waiting room. There was no sign of Jeff or Ian.

"I'm Amy Clarke," she said to a young man seated behind the intake desk. "My husband just brought in my son, Ian. They think he may have a broken arm. Where are they?"

The man yawned and looked at a computer screen while he moved a handheld mouse. Amy fidgeted.

"In triage room 3. One of the nurses will need to take you back there."

"Then get one up here right now!"

The man didn't respond but picked up the phone.

"It'll be a minute," he said.

Amy fumed as she stood beside the desk. From where she stood, she could see that the young man was playing a game of solitaire on the computer. She made a mental note of his name. She would either report him to the hospital administration or use his name for the most evil character in her next novel. In a few moments a blond-haired nurse in scrubs appeared behind the young man.

"Mrs. Clarke?" she asked.

"Yes."

"Come with me."

The nurse led Amy past a row of glass-faced cabinets filled with medical supplies.

"How is he?" Amy asked as soon as she was beside the nurse.

"They've taken him to radiology."

"So his arm is broken?"

"The doctor and radiologist will review the X-rays and let you know."

"Did you see his arm?"

The woman glanced sideways at Amy.

"Yes."

"Was the bone sticking through the skin?"

"No, if it's broken, it's a closed fracture."

Amy had been totally focused on getting to the hospital. The reality of what had happened to her little boy suddenly hit her. Tears flooded her eyes. She grabbed a tissue from her purse as they walked.

"He's a brave fellow," the nurse said when she saw Amy's tears. "He sat very still on the examining table when Dr. Hostettler checked him."

"Which arm is it?" Amy sniffled.

"The left. It looked like the injury is to one of the lower bones."

"Could he move it?"

"Not really."

They reached the radiology department and turned a corner. Amy almost bumped into Jeff, who was standing beside the door to the room where the X-ray machine was located. His shirt and pants were covered in mud. Through a clouded glass she could see Ian. He was wearing a T-shirt and standing in front of an X-ray machine. A female technician was beside him and gently touched Ian's arm to move it into position. Amy saw Ian wince in pain.

"What happened?" Amy demanded.

"He was riding in the back of a four-seater when it popped over a big rock and slid into a tree. Ian's arm was resting against the outside of the roll bar and got hit."

"Who was driving?"

"I was."

The technician turned Ian around for another scan.

"I wasn't going fast, probably less than five miles an hour. It was a freak accident. I'm sorry."

Everything about Jeff's body language and tone of voice communicated sincerity, but Amy wasn't ready to give up her right to be angry with him.

"Then what?"

"We were close to the beginning of the course, so I was able to get him out quickly. We kept an ice pack on the arm during the drive to the hospital. He was a real trouper with the doctor. You would have been proud of him."

The technician brought Ian out of the X-ray room. His jeans were muddy. Amy realized they must have cut off his shirt.

"Hi, Mom," Ian said in a slightly shaky voice. "I think I broke my arm."

Amy wanted to hug him but was afraid to touch him. The nurse who'd brought Amy to the radiology department came up to them.

"I'll take you back to the examination room to wait," the nurse said. "Dr. Hostettler talked with Dr. Fletchall, the orthopedist on call. He should be here shortly to discuss treatment."

They reached the examination room.

"You can lie on the bed or sit in a chair," the nurse said to Ian.

"I want to lie down," he replied. "I feel really tired."

"The adrenaline is wearing off," the nurse said to Amy and Jeff. "And the pain medication is taking effect. We've also given him a mild sedative."

The nurse helped Ian onto the bed. He stretched out and the nurse gently positioned his arm.

"I'll get a fresh cold pack," she said. "Let me know if you need anything else."

Ian lay on the bed with his eyes closed. Amy couldn't tell if he was breathing. She stepped closer to the bed and saw the slow rise and fall of his chest.

"He may be asleep," Amy said softly to Jeff.

Ian opened one eye and shook his head but didn't speak. He closed his eye. The nurse returned with a cold pack and placed it on Ian's lower arm.

"Leave it on for five minutes and then remove it for a couple," she said to Amy.

Amy's phone, which was in her purse at

her feet, beeped, and she took it out. It was Natalie. She motioned to Jeff and stepped out into the hallway.

"I'm at the hospital with Ian," Amy said softly. "They think he broke his arm."

"I know," Natalie replied. "Megan called to let me know and asked me to pray for you."

"She did?" Amy asked in surprise.

"Yes. And she wanted the phone number of the woman who is in charge of the prayer chain at the church so she could let her know, too. How is Ian?"

"He just got out of X-ray, and we're waiting for the orthopedist to get here. It looks like his left arm is broken. He and Jeff were riding on a four-wheeler, and Ian's arm hit a tree."

Amy looked through the open door. If she didn't know something was wrong, she'd think her son was taking a Saturday afternoon nap.

"How are you holding up?"

"Starting to calm down now that I'm here and can watch him. I know kids break their arms, but I wasn't prepared for this."

"No premonition in a dream like you had for Noah's field trip?"

Amy hadn't even thought about that possibility. Natalie's question was a good one.

"And that doesn't make any sense," Amy said. "Why would I be able to tip you off and not get anything in advance for my own son that he was going to be in danger? I mean, I'm glad I could warn you, but it doesn't seem fair."

Natalie was silent for a moment. "Maybe it's because there was no way to suspect the field trip might be hazardous. Everyone knows getting on a four-wheeler can be risky."

"But Ian was so excited I didn't have the heart to try to stop them when Jeff told me about it this morning. I really didn't have much time to think it over and react."

"Don't blame yourself," Natalie said quickly. "Or Jeff, either. I'm sure he feels terrible."

Amy could see Jeff sitting in the chair with his head bowed.

"Yeah, I need to say something to him. I didn't yell or anything when I got here, but I'm sure he's wondering when I'm going to blow up."

"I've never seen you blow up."

"My blowups are like icebergs. Most of them are hidden beneath the surface."

"Which may not be good for your health. Listen, call me if I can do anything. Can I bring over supper tonight? I have beef stew cooking in the Crock-Pot, and there's no way we can eat it all."

Natalie was a true friend. Amy could receive help from her without hesitation because her kindness was motivated by pure love.

"That would be great," Amy said. "I'm not

sure how long we'll be here, and Jeff loves beef stew."

"Consider it done. Let me know when you get home, and I'll hop right over."

Amy returned to the triage room. She touched Jeff on the shoulder. He looked up in her face.

"I know this was an accident," she said. "And I don't blame you."

He put his hand over hers.

"Thanks."

Fifteen minutes later a gray-haired doctor came into the room and introduced himself as Dr. Fletchall. He turned on a light box mounted on one wall of the room and slipped an X-ray beneath a clip at the top. Seeing how small Ian's arm looked caused Amy's emotions to swell once again.

"You can see it best on this one." He pointed to a hazy line in one of the lower two bones in the arm. "He has a fracture of the ulna. It's what we call a greenstick fracture because it resembles what happens when you try to break a green stick. It's cracked up the bone on one side but doesn't go all the way through. That's good news. The better news is there isn't any indication of damage in the area of his growth plate. He should heal as good as new with proper splinting."

"Thank God," Amy said.

"Yes," Jeff said.

"How did this happen?" the doctor asked

Jeff. "It would take a fairly hard blow to do this."

Jeff described the incident in the four-wheeler. Ian opened his eyes.

"Was he wearing a seat restraint and helmet?" the doctor asked.

"Yes, sir," Ian replied in a soft voice.

"Good," the doctor said, then faced Jeff and Amy. "Young bones don't do very well when they come in contact with tree trunks, but they bend a lot more than ours. I've asked the orthopedic nurse to prepare material for a fiberglass cast."

"Are you going to have to set it?" Amy asked.

"Nothing drastic. Only enough to make sure it's aligned properly." The doctor turned to the bed and pointed to the lower part of Ian's arm without touching it. "His arm is rotated outward more than it should be. I'll need to correct that."

"What will you do to it?" Ian asked.

"Make sure it heals straight." The doctor glanced sideways at Amy. "I think I'll give him something stronger to put him in a twilight state. That way he won't remember anything."

"How long will he be in the cast?" Jeff asked.

"Probably four weeks or so. I'll have you bring him in after a couple of weeks for a recheck."

The doctor left, and a nurse returned to give Ian a shot. He whimpered slightly, but by the time Dr. Fletchall and the orthopedic nurse came back to set and cast the arm, he showed no sign of discomfort. The care the doctor used when handling Ian's arm comforted Amy.

"Will the place where the break occurred be stronger?" Amy asked.

"No, the research doesn't support that theory. Is your son interested in any sports?"

"All of them," Jeff replied. "But he loves football the best."

The doctor glanced up.

"Then I'll see you at some point in the future after the cast removal."

When they left the hospital, Ian sat in the backseat of Amy's car and leaned against the door with his eyes closed. He was sound asleep when she pulled into the driveway. Jeff carried him upstairs. They met Megan on the landing at the top of the stairs.

"How is he?" Megan asked.

"He'll be fine in a month or so," Amy replied. "Thanks for calling Natalie and the prayer coordinator at the church. I really appreciate it."

"I did what I thought you would do."

"And I apologize for saying you were selfish. You wouldn't have been able to do anything at the hospital."

"It's okay."

Amy covered Ian with a sheet and tucked him in.

"He'll need a pain pill in two hours even if we have to wake him up," she said to Jeff.

Amy went downstairs while Jeff showered and changed into clean clothes. He was still upstairs when Natalie arrived with the beef stew.

"That smells yummy," Amy said, lifting the lid on a large container. "But you gave us too much. Is there enough for your family?"

"And the neighbors on both sides."

"Can you stay for a minute?" Amy asked.

The two women sat at the kitchen table while Amy told Natalie about Ian's injury and treatment.

"I'm sorry I brought that up about your dreams," Natalie said when Amy finished. "I was thinking out loud. I didn't want to upset you."

"It's okay. I thought about it while I waited for the doctor to finish with Ian. I can't expect the Lord to reveal everything bad that's going to happen to my family. No one goes through life with that kind of information. But I do want to see what God wants to show me and hear what he wants to tell me."

"You've changed," Natalie said.

"How?"

"When you warned me about Noah's field trip and saw the vase of flowers in my house, you didn't want to know anything at all about the future."

"Yeah, and I'm still not sure I can handle it, but I don't really have a choice, do I? Ignoring my dreams isn't an option."

After Natalie left, Amy cooked a batch of corn muffins. Megan liked Natalie's beef stew, and Jeff finished three bowls before licking his spoon and pushing the empty bowl a few inches away from him.

Amy checked on Ian several times during the night and gave him pain medicine. She fell into a sound sleep at 4:00 a.m. and woke up to gentle pressure on her left shoulder. She cracked her eyes open and jumped. It was Ian.

"What are you doing out of bed?" she asked.

"I'm hungry. Did I eat supper last night? I don't remember coming home from the hospital."

Amy went downstairs and fixed a snack that she brought up to his room. The following morning he felt so much better after breakfast that Jeff said it was okay for Amy and Megan to go to church while he stayed home with Ian. Amy hesitated until Megan spoke up and said she wanted to go.

"We'll only be gone an hour and a half," Amy said. "I'll keep my phone on vibrate so you can text me if I need to come home."

"Don't worry," Jeff said. "While you're gone, I'll help Ian take a bath."

Before the church service started, Amy fielded questions from several people about Carl Fincannon.

"I didn't hear anything about that," Megan said as the last person left and they headed to their seats.

"You've had plenty to deal with in your life this week."

"You were dodging those people's questions. I can tell when you're not telling the whole truth."

"And I can tell when you're not telling the whole truth," Amy replied. "That makes us even."

Shortly after they sat down, Amy glanced around the sanctuary. Most of the faces were familiar. A young couple in their late twenties who were seated a few rows ahead of Amy raised their hands when the pastor recognized first-time visitors. The woman turned to the side as a packet of information was passed to her by one of the ushers. When she saw the woman's profile, Amy gasped.

Twenty-One

During the sermon, a debate raged inside Amy. Every so often, she shifted in her seat so she could see the woman, and her heart raced ahead a few beats. Megan seemed to be paying attention to Reverend Harbough's sermon based on the story of the woman who touched the hem of Jesus' garment and was healed. As much as she wanted to follow along, Amy didn't have the ability to concentrate on anything except the image that flashed through her mind each time she saw the young woman's silhouette.

At the end of the service, Reverend Harbough invited anyone who wanted to receive prayer to come forward. The woman slipped from her row and made her way down front. Distance diminished the uncomfortable compulsion Amy had to speak to her. The music from the final song ended, and everyone started toward the aisles. Megan was in front of Amy. When she reached the aisle, she turned around.

"Is it too late to go to the front and ask someone to pray with me?" she asked Amy.

"No. What's on your heart?"

"The yucky stuff that has happened to me at school has made me feel sick on the inside. I know it's not the same as the woman in the story, but I want Jesus to take the bad feeling away."

Even though she wanted to get out of the sanctuary as quickly as possible, there was no way Amy could deny Megan's request. They wove their way through the crowd. A trained group of prayer counselors had positioned themselves near the pulpit platform. The young woman Amy saw at the beginning of the service was on the right receiving prayer. A middle-aged woman who was one of the volunteer leaders with the youth group came over to Amy and Megan.

"Hi, Megan," she said with a kind smile. "How can I pray for you?"

While Megan talked, Amy's attention was distracted. The volunteer leader and Megan bowed their heads to pray. Amy closed her eyes for a few seconds and then opened them to make sure the young woman to her right hadn't left. An older couple who had been members of the church for a long time were praying for her. They didn't seem to be in a hurry. Amy closed her eyes and focused on Megan, who was sniffling. Amy pressed a tissue into her hand. The youth leader finished praying and gave Megan a hug.

"Thanks for coming forward," the woman said. "It took a lot of courage. Is there anything else you want me to pray about with you?"

Megan hesitated. Amy glanced over at the young woman who was standing with the older couple. Her eyes were now open.

"No, I guess not," Megan said.

"I'm here for you," the woman said, then motioned to Amy. "And I know your mother is, too."

"What?" Amy asked.

"You're here for Megan."

"Yes, of course."

Amy and Megan turned away at the same time as the young woman. She had been crying and held a wad of tissues in her hand. Their paths crossed at the beginning of the aisle.

"Good morning," Amy said, her mouth dry.

The woman looked at her with red eyes.

"Hello," she said.

They took a couple of steps together.

"I'm Amy Clarke, and this is my daughter, Megan."

Megan gave Amy a questioning look.

"Uh, I'm Stacy Kennedy," the woman said. "We're in town visiting a friend from college who goes to this church."

Amy was unable to let the conversation die a natural death.

"Who's your friend?"

"Kat Brown. She was Kat McCollum when we were in school together."

Amy knew the dark-haired, petite woman. She was married to a man who worked for an engineering firm. They had two small children and a baby on the way.

"Kat's pregnant, isn't she?"

"Yes."

"You're going to have a baby boy," Amy blurted out. "And he's going to have red hair."

The woman stopped in the middle of the aisle and stared at Amy. Megan continued for a second and then returned to her mother's side.

"How can you say that to me?" the woman asked, her lower lip trembling. "Do you know what I've been through?"

"No." Amy swallowed. "But you're pregnant right now."

The woman turned and walked rapidly down the aisle without looking back.

"What are you doing?" Megan asked Amy. "That was crazy!"

Amy stayed where she was, as immovable as if her feet were stuck in cement. She watched Stacy reach her husband, who was waiting with Kat Brown and her spouse. The two women had their heads close together. Kat looked over her shoulder at Amy with a deeply troubled expression on her face before heading toward the exit.

"Why did you say that?" Megan asked.

Amy sighed. "I saw that young woman in a dream the other night. She had a smile on her face and was holding a baby with red hair. The baby was wrapped in a blue blanket."

"Why do you think it was her?"

"I saw her face from the side during the service and just knew." Amy pointed to her heart. "I had to say something to her."

"She didn't have red hair," Megan said.

"Neither did her husband."

"And what you said really upset her."

"I know."

"This is too weird." Megan started walking down the aisle.

Amy followed at a slower pace. Several people greeted her before she reached the door, and she mumbled in reply. In the parking lot, Megan was talking to a group of her friends. Amy got in the car. She leaned her head against the rest and closed her eyes.

What happened in the church was exactly the reason Amy didn't want her nighttime trips to the living room to change from times of personal encouragement and experiencing God's love to a download of bizarre information. She hated talking to strangers. She didn't want to upset people. She didn't want to be weird. She didn't want to embarrass her family. She didn't want to open her mouth and say something wrong. She didn't want to ruin someone's life.

But Stacy Kennedy had looked so happy as a mother. There was nothing in the picture that flashed before Amy's eyes that communicated anything negative. And few earthly joys can compare with a woman welcoming a wanted child into the world. The pressure of the message in Amy's chest when she stood at the front of the church made her think she would explode if she kept silent. She tried to imagine how she would feel if she'd not said anything, but it didn't compute. Megan opened the door on the passenger side of the car and got in. Amy braced herself for another onslaught.

"Promise that you won't ever say anything crazy like that to one of my friends," Megan said.

"I wasn't trying to be crazy," Amy said, her mind going back to how she'd felt as a little girl who innocently talked about her wonderful dreams. "I wanted to encourage her."

"You don't do that by freaking someone out."

"I'm glad you went forward for prayer," Amy said, trying to change the subject.

"Yeah." Megan looked out the window of the car.

"How was church?" Jeff asked Amy and Megan when they came inside the house.

"Part good, part superweird," Megan replied as she continued through the family room and up the stairs.

Jeff stared after her.

"Where is Ian?" Amy asked.

"Asleep in his bed. The second dose of pain medicine made him drowsy."

"Do you think he'll be able to go to school tomorrow?" Amy asked, talking unusually fast.

"Not if he has to take the pain medicine. He's not complaining, but I don't want him to be uncomfortable." Jeff motioned to the stairwell. "What's Megan talking about?"

Amy plopped down on the sofa in the family room and told him about Megan going forward for prayer and what happened with Stacy Kennedy. Jeff's eyes grew bigger.

"Talking to strangers is taking things to a new level," he said.

Amy hadn't told Jeff about her conversations with Chris Lance at work, but approaching someone whose name she didn't know was even more outside the box.

"I know," she said. "And it didn't go over well at all."

Amy put her head in her hands. "Megan said I was acting crazy, and part of me agrees with her."

Amy waited for Jeff to speak, but he didn't. The phone rang in the kitchen. Amy didn't look up.

"I don't want to talk to anyone," she said.

Jeff answered the call.

"Just a minute," he said, then came to the opening between the kitchen and the family room. "It's Kat Brown. She says it's important."

Amy shook her head. "Tell her I'm unavailable."

Jeff relayed the message and was silent as he listened to a response.

"She didn't," Amy heard him say before growing silent again.

"Okay, I'll let her know. Bye."

Jeff returned to the family room.

"Is she going to report me to Reverend Harbough?" Amy asked.

She could see herself being summoned to a Tuesday night meeting and dragged in front of all the leaders of the church where she would be subject to a Salem-style witch-hunt inquisition that resulted in her banishment from the church and complete humiliation from one end of town to the other.

"She didn't mention it but wanted to let you know they bought a pregnancy test at a pharmacy on the way home from church, and Stacy Kennedy is pregnant. She and her husband have wanted to have a baby for years but weren't sure they could because of three miscarriages. A couple of weeks ago her doctor told her the chances of her conceiving again were remote. That's why Stacy went forward for prayer this morning. She wanted the Lord to touch her and either heal her or take away her desire for children."

"She was already pregnant?" Amy asked flatly.

"Yeah, that's a safe bet," Jeff replied. "But she didn't know it."

"Why did she get mad at me?"

"Kat said she thought you were eavesdropping on the prayer time and barged in with a well-meaning but badly timed attempt to give Stacy hope."

"I didn't hear anything."

"I made that clear to Kat." Jeff paused. "Oh, and she said to let you know there are several redheads in Stacy's husband's family. He would love to have a redheaded son."

Amy glanced up at the ceiling. The phone in the kitchen rang again. Amy shook her head. She felt partially vindicated but not confident enough to speak to anyone. Jeff answered the call.

"It's Natalie," he said. "She saw you at church with Megan but says you left in a hurry, and she didn't get a chance to talk to you."

"Tell her I'll call her later," Amy said.

After he hung up the phone, Jeff returned to the family room. Amy followed him with her eyes. He sat on one end of the couch, and Amy, her feet tucked beneath her, sat on the other end. Neither of them spoke.

"Everything turned out okay," Jeff said in a hopeful tone.

"For now," Amy replied. "But what if Stacy Kennedy has another miscarriage? For all I know, I could have been seeing her holding her baby after he's died and gone to heaven."

"Is that what you really believe?"

Amy was silent for a moment. "No, but I don't want my life to be a series of extremely awkward encounters with strangers whom I tell something I believe is from God that I saw in a dream but may not make sense to them. They'll look at me like I'm crazy or get mad. On top of everything, I may be wrong in my interpretation of what I think I saw. How would you like to live under that kind of a cloud?"

"I wouldn't, but don't let your imagination run away with you. This wouldn't be happening to you if God wasn't going to show you how to handle it."

"That's a very practical and easy thing for you to say."

Jeff opened and closed his mouth. Amy continued to fume.

"You were excited when you started receiving inspiration in the night that helped you become a writer," Jeff said.

"Yes, but it was still a private thing. No one knows about that but you, the kids, and Natalie." Amy paused. "And now Ms. Burris. This is totally different."

"It's different, but not totally," Jeff replied. "It's still connected to your relationship with the Lord and the way he made you. Do you realize how blessed I am to be married to a person like you? I work with my hands for a living, and I'm proud of what I do because I do it well. But I'm married to a woman who goes to heaven in her dreams, writes books that encourage people from one end of the country to the other, helped save a man's life earlier in the week, and today shared a word with a young woman who'd lost all hope of ever having a child. That's pretty amazing."

While Jeff talked, Amy's eyes filled with tears. She wiped them away with the back of her hand.

"Is that what you really believe?" she asked. "You're not just saying that to try to make me feel better?"

"I'm not going to lie to you."

"I know," Amy sighed. "And as long as I have you backing me up, I guess I'm going to be okay."

"I don't plan on going anywhere, no matter what you do or say."

Amy scooted over on the couch until she was beside Jeff. He put his arm around her, and she rested her head on his shoulder.

Later, carried on the wings of Jeff's unconditional love, Amy went upstairs to the writing room. But instead of turning on her computer and trying to work, she propped her legs up on the ottoman, closed her eyes, and took a nap. No dreams interrupted her afternoon rest.

The following morning Ian felt well enough to go to school.

"Don't let anyone touch your arm," Amy warned as she buttoned up his shirt.

"Why didn't I get one of those white casts so my friends can write on it?" Ian asked. "That's what Ricky Little had when he broke his arm. By the time they cut it off, the cast was covered with so much writing and drawings that you couldn't see any white. He took it home and put it in his room. It stunk terrible."

"It smelled terrible," Amy replied. "And the doctor said you didn't need a plaster cast. But that doesn't mean you don't have to take care of your arm so it will heal properly."

"So long as it's okay by the time baseball season starts."

After hearing Dr. Fletchall's comment about the dangers of football, Amy thought it might be better to encourage Ian to play a less inherently violent sport like baseball.

"I bet it will be. That's still a couple of months off, isn't it?"

"I'm not sure. You'd have to ask Dad."

During her drive to the office, Amy phoned Natalie.

"Did you hear what happened in church

yesterday?" Amy asked when her friend answered the call.

"Yes, I saw Megan go down front. I was thrilled. It's so special when a teenager is willing to step out and be noticed in front of the other kids."

"That was great, but I meant about Kat Brown's friend."

"I haven't heard anything about it."

Amy described her encounter with Stacy Kennedy and Kat's subsequent phone call to the house.

"And you're worried Kat is going to talk about what you did?" Natalie asked when Amy finished.

"Don't you think I should be? Even if Kat means well, I'm going to end up looking like a fortune-teller. That's what Megan thought."

"She said that?"

"No, she just said I was acting weird and crazy."

Natalie was silent for a moment. "I'm sitting at the computer and checked Kat's Facebook page. She didn't say anything about it on there. Do you want me to call her for you? I know her pretty well from the mission trip we took together to Mexico."

Amy had forgotten the connection between Natalie and Kat.

"Would you? I know it's a long shot to expect her to keep quiet, but it would make me feel better if you tried."

"Sure, I'll call her this morning. She's so busy with her kids that she doesn't have time to spread a story."

"That would be great. If you reach her, let me know what she says."

Amy arrived at work. For the first time since she'd returned to the law firm, she felt like her tiny office was a sanctuary. She was sorting through Mr. Phillips's morning mail when her phone vibrated. It was Natalie.

"I talked to Kat," Natalie said. "She hasn't told anyone about your conversation with her friend Stacy."

"Are you sure?"

"Yes, because Stacy asked her not to. She wants to believe what you told her is going to come true, but she's been so disappointed in the past when she got her hopes up and ended up having a miscarriage that she wants to keep everything confidential. Kat wondered if you would keep quiet, too."

"Did you tell her I would?"

"Yes. She understands how vulnerable you feel and respects you a ton for stepping out to share with someone you don't know."

"She does?" Amy was stunned.

"Amy, everybody isn't looking for a stone to throw at a person who is trying to obey the Lord."

"I guess I am being a little paranoid," she said.

"I'm not judging you, and don't let what

Megan said get under your skin, either. What did Jeff say?"

Amy told her about the conversation on the couch in the family room.

"Now you're making me jealous," Natalie replied. "I'm not sure Luke would say something like that to me — even if he had three days to prepare."

"I need to thank Jeff again," Amy said. "We were so busy getting Ian ready for school this morning that I forgot to mention it. And I appreciate you calling Kat. It takes a huge load off my mind."

"And I'll be praying that Stacy doesn't lose this baby."

Amy remembered Ms. Burris's words that divine information was often given for purposes of prayer and intercession.

"Me, too. Oh, and the beef stew was awesome. Jeff ate three bowls."

Amy sent Jeff a sweet text message before putting her phone in her purse. For the first time since she'd received word that Ian had hurt his arm, she was able to relax. Ian was going to be okay, and it didn't look like her Sunday morning encounter with Stacy Kennedy was going to blow up in her face.

That left Michael Baldwin.

Twenty-Two

Tuesday morning Amy was sitting at her desk when she received a call from Carl Fincannon's wife.

"They've moved Carl to a regular room," Mrs. Fincannon said, "and he asked me to call and see if you could stop by to see him."

Amy didn't mention that she'd spent Saturday afternoon in the ER with Ian.

"What if I swing by during my lunch break?" Amy replied. "I only get thirty minutes, so I couldn't stay long."

"I don't want you to skip your lunch."

"That's fine. A missed meal gives me an excuse to eat a piece of chocolate later tonight."

"Okay. He's in room 3259."

Amy jotted the room number down on a slip of paper.

"I'll see you around noon," she said.

On the way to the hospital, Amy passed the spot where she'd found Mr. Fincannon. She slowed down to take a look. When she did, she saw a flash of red caught in a bush not far from the water. She pulled onto the shoulder of the road, got out of the car, and carefully descended the bank. It was the red cap she'd seen in the dream. She held on to a limb and pulled the cap free from the bush. It was well-worn and dirty.

Amy parked in the main lot and took the elevator to the third floor. Room 3259 was at the end of the hall on the left. The door was cracked open. She knocked. Mrs. Fincannon answered.

"Come in."

Amy pushed open the door. Mrs. Fincannon was sitting in a recliner chair beside the bed. Her husband, an overweight man with slightly red cheeks and a head full of white hair, was sitting up in bed with his meal tray in front of him. His plate of food was empty, and he was sipping tea through a straw in a plastic cup.

"You must be Amy." Mrs. Fincannon smiled, getting up from her chair.

"Yes. It's good to see you."

Mrs. Fincannon gave Amy a long hug.

"Thanks so much for coming by."

Carl Fincannon placed his tea on the tray. Amy held up the cap.

"Don't tell me —" He stopped.

"Does this look familiar to you?" she asked.

"It's my cap!"

Betty Fincannon stared at the hat for a moment and then burst into tears. Amy handed the cap to Carl, who put it on his head and pulled it snug.

"Betty, I didn't know you loved this hat so much," he said. "You've been after me for years to get a new one even though this one was broken in just the way I like it."

"Don't be silly." Betty sniffled. "It's not the hat. But it reminds me how blessed we are Amy came along and found you in that ditch."

Carl looked at Amy. "And I want to thank you from the bottom of my heart. The last thing I remember was feeling dizzy when I checked out at the convenience store. I don't know why I left my car or how I walked almost a mile before passing out. The doc said if you hadn't found me, I wouldn't have made it."

"I'm thankful I did," Amy said. "How are you feeling?"

"Almost back to normal, except my right arm doesn't want to follow orders. I may have to learn how to cast my fishing line with my left arm." He pointed to the empty tray. "And what they serve for food in here is barely enough to keep me alive. I can't wait to get home and fry up a mess of fish."

"The doctor wants him to lose weight," Betty said. "I've already thrown out a trash bag full of junk food at the house. And we're going to be broiling our fish for a while."

"But you don't know where I keep everything," Carl responded with a wink.

"I used the step stool to get to the top shelf of the closet near the garage," Betty retorted. "That stash alone almost filled up one bag."

"Oh." Carl's face fell.

"And we're both going to change our eating habits. I won't make you do anything I'm not willing to join in with."

Listening to the couple playfully argue made Amy smile.

"I have a couple of recipes for broiled fish that my husband likes," Amy offered. "Just because it's broiled doesn't mean there's no flavor."

"Pay attention to her," Betty said to Carl. "Or I'll tell her to take that cap and keep it as a souvenir."

Carl fingered the bill of the cap.

"No, it fits your head perfectly," Amy said.

The twenty minutes Amy had to spend with the couple flew by. When it was time to leave, she received another long hug from Betty Fincannon and a final word of thanks from Carl.

"Stay in touch and let me know how you're doing," she said.

"And don't forget to send me those fish recipes," Betty said.

"I have your address in here." Amy patted her purse.

The image of Mr. and Mrs. Fincannon

together in the hospital room stayed with Amy on her return to the office. She spoke a brief prayer of thanks as she pulled into the law firm parking area.

Later that afternoon Chris came downstairs to Amy's office. He had the brief in the Westside Lighting case in his hand and laid it on the corner of her desk.

"I finished the brief on Saturday. The cover letter for the judge is on top. I've signed everything, including the certificate of service. Will you make the copies and send it out?"

When she looked at the cover letter, Amy got a queasy feeling in her stomach.

"It's not due until Wednesday, is it?" she asked.

"No, but there's nothing else to change, and I'm tired of looking at it. I'm sure you reach that point with your books."

"There is a time to stop editing," Amy admitted.

"That's where I am."

Chris left, and Amy read the brief a final time. When she reached the argument that relied on Michael Baldwin's deposition testimony, she jotted down her concerns on a legal pad. But there was no way she could substantiate or dispel her uneasiness without performing her own investigation of the case. That wasn't possible without Chris's cooperation or bringing in Mr. Phillips. The prospect of talking to the senior partner stopped Amy.

She took the documents to the copy room, made the service copies for the other attorneys, and put them in the mail. She left the original brief and letter to the judge in the basket for the firm's runner to take to the courthouse. With one last glance over her shoulder, she returned to her office.

Amy's life moved forward smoothly for the next week and a half. Ian's arm healed quickly, and he received a good report from the doctor at his follow-up appointment. She stayed busy at work but faced nothing out of the ordinary and didn't have any awkward conversations with Chris. She and Mr. Phillips settled into the type of familiar routine the senior partner liked, which meant Amy did everything she could to anticipate his wishes and meet them without expecting him to notice or thank her.

Even though she had to constantly push aside a nagging inner voice of doubt, Amy finished the first three chapters of *Deeds of Darkness* and sent them off to Bernie. Along with the chapters, she included a revised synopsis that reflected the current direction she wanted to take with the novel. Three days later Bernie called during her lunch break.

"Is this a good time to talk?" he asked.

Amy was in the kitchen at the law office. She had another twenty minutes before she needed to return to work and log on to her computer.

"Yes, let me take my salad back to my office."

"I'll talk while you walk," Bernie said. "First, I sent over the sample chapters and synopsis for the book to Dave Coley. He called the next day and told me that your new direction is not something they'd be interested in publishing."

Amy knew this was possible, but the sudden harshness of it stunned her. It reminded her of all the rejection letters she received when she sent her first novel to more than twenty publishers. She quickly closed the door of her office.

"Is there any chance of talking it over with them? Did Cecilia take a look at what I've written?"

"I don't know about Cecilia, but Dave is the one holding the key to the printing press. What he says goes."

Amy wasn't going to accept a partial explanation.

"What did he specifically say?"

"The usual blather about the concept not meeting their needs at this time. It was a brief conversation, and he was on autopilot while we were talking. I think he was probably reading his e-mails."

Amy was having trouble absorbing the news. She'd been so thrilled to land an initial contract that to move on so casually didn't seem right. It was like two people getting a divorce without making any effort to save the marriage. In particular, she'd spent so much time working with Cecilia that it was hard to think of the relationship with her ending so abruptly. They'd become long-distance friends, a common occurrence between authors and editors.

"Can I call Cecilia and talk to her?"

"If you do, keep it personal. Let me handle the business side of things. That's why you hired me."

"If I sign with another publisher, are they still going to promote my first two books?"

"Sure. They want to make money on what you've delivered, and if *Deeds of Darkness* is a best seller, they'll probably try to catch the wave of popularity it generates. It's all about units shipped and not returned. If a new publisher dumps a bunch of money into marketing and promotion, Dave Coley won't complain. He'll turn on his adding machine and crunch some numbers."

"Okay," Amy replied with resignation.

"Can I move on to some good news?"

"Yes."

"I also sent the sample chapters to the editor in New York who was interested in the concept when I pitched it to her. She's taken her response up the ladder. That doesn't guarantee she's ready to offer you a contract and cut a check for a fat advance, but you're definitely on her radar."

"What does that mean for now?"

"That you need to turn on your computer and type like a million people can't wait for the release of your next novel. The sooner the manuscript is done, the quicker we can get down to brass tacks."

"Did you send the synopsis to any other editors?"

"Yes, but I haven't heard back yet. If you were further along with the writing, I'd light a fire underneath them and let them know if they don't act they'll lose the chance to land you. But since you're still a few months away from finishing the first draft, that won't work now."

"A few months? Now that I'm working full-time, it will take eight or nine months for me to complete the first draft."

"You did three bang-up chapters in two weeks. What was the word count on the stuff you submitted?"

"About ten thousand words."

"Multiply that by ten or eleven, and you've got a bona fide novel. That doesn't compute to eight or nine months."

"But my writing process isn't linear. The book will continue to evolve as I get to know the characters better and new wrinkles pop up for the plot. Then I have to go back and revise what I've written."

"Draw a straighter line. Look, I'm d
I can for you, and I need you to do you
Amy didn't like the new, harsh task
side of Bernie, but she knew he was pro
her for her own professional good.

"I'll put my nose to the grindstone,
said.

"Good girl. When you do, you're goin
produce diamonds."

The call ended with Amy shaking her h
at Bernie's final comment. She laid her
phone on her desk and pulled up the dic
tion queue on her computer.

While she'd been at lunch, Chris had se
her information related to the Dominic
estate litigation. Amy started typing. The firs
part was a summary of all the parties currently involved in the case. Chris wanted her to organize the information into a flowchart he could use as a visual aid during depositions and when presenting the case to the judge. The first step for Amy was to type out the data in narrative form. She'd worked on it for about fifteen minutes when she heard Chris say, "A year after he returned from World War II, Dominick was engaged to a woman named Mildred Burris. Dominick's father worked in a mill owned by Ms. Burris's father. For unknown reasons, Dominick abruptly broke off the engagement. Ms. Burris is a former client of the firm and serves on the board of directors for the

econd Chance Foundation, a local charity
hat is a beneficiary under the disputed will
xecuted shortly before Dominick's death."

Amy rewound the dictation and listened again. It was one thing for Ms. Burris to date Sanford Dominick. That was hard enough for Amy to imagine. But for them to be engaged was the stuff of fiction. She left her desk and went into Mr. Phillips's office. The lawyer was sitting at his desk and looked up.

"I was transcribing a memo for Chris," she said. "Did you know Mildred Burris and Sanford Dominick were engaged to be married?"

"Not until the other day. It's hard to believe, isn't it? Mildred is an odd duck, but she's about as straitlaced as they get."

"Odd duck?"

"I know Mildred means well, but she's a religious fanatic. Now that I know more about her history, it makes sense as a way to atone for her earlier sins with Sonny." Mr. Phillips paused. "You've cut off contact with her, haven't you?"

Amy had been so caught off guard by the revelation from Chris she hadn't considered what might happen if she started a conversation about Ms. Burris with Mr. Phillips.

"No, sir," she admitted. "A friend and I had lunch with her a few weeks ago. The luncheon was something Ms. Burris and I discussed before you talked to me. She wanted to meet my friend Natalie. The three of us were only

together for an hour or so."

Mr. Phillips's face darkened. "I can't control what you do with your free time, but I certainly have the right to decide if you're going to work here another minute."

"Yes, sir. I understand."

"And I want to keep you as an employee. You're an outstanding secretary."

"Thank you." Amy licked her lips.

"Is ongoing contact with Mildred Burris more important to you than keeping your job?"

Like a witness withering under cross-examination, Amy was being backed into a corner from which she knew there was no escape.

"No, sir."

"Then will you promise to stay away from her until this estate matter is concluded?"

"That could take years."

"And it probably will."

Mr. Phillips might say he couldn't control Amy's free time, but every word from his mouth spoke otherwise. Her shoulders slumped in surrender.

"Yes, sir, I won't have any contact with Ms. Burris. All I ask is that I be able to give her a reason. It would be terribly rude to simply ignore her."

"What would you say?" he asked.

"That I can't communicate with her because I'm working here, and the need to avoid the appearance of impropriety related to the litigation of Sanford Dominick's estate requires it. She's already received your letter discharging her as a client, so it won't be a total shock."

"Did she mention the letter when you had lunch with her?"

"No, Sanford Dominick didn't come up."

"Or the letter?"

Amy felt a rush of anger rise up inside her.

"No! And I've agreed to what you want! Why do you have to keep on attacking me?"

"I'm not attacking," Mr. Phillips said with the steady calm that had kept him in control of countless courtrooms, especially after he'd gotten his way. "I'm clarifying. And I'm satisfied. I appreciate your cooperation. Anything else?"

"No," Amy muttered.

"Good."

Mr. Phillips returned his attention to the documents on his desk. Amy went to her office and put her head in her hands.

Twenty-Three

Amy's emotions swirled as she drove home. She'd never secretly wished the firm would lose a case, but it would be more just for Sanford Dominick's children and grandchildren to inherit his estate than the bleached-blond Natasha. At home Jeff's questioning expression when he saw her gave away his suspicions that something bad had happened at work, but all Amy could tell him was that she'd had a difficult conversation with Mr. Phillips.

"Would it help if you went upstairs to the writing room after supper?" Jeff asked. "You can get your mind on something besides the office. I'll help Ian with his homework."

"I'll try," Amy replied. "But I'm not sure if I'll be able to focus."

Upstairs, Amy turned on her computer and tried to channel the frustration she felt into her main character. Toward the beginning of many books, the protagonist has a crossing-the-threshold moment in which she has to choose whether to go forward into the unknown or maintain the status quo. Even if the character initially refuses the call to adventure, an author can create circumstances that overwhelm the character's will. But Roxanne didn't need to be manipulated. Her seething rage at the injustice visited on her family fueled her decision to confront the evil in the local sheriff's office. As Amy rapidly typed, Roxanne crept into a restricted area of the sheriff's department and found a folder that hinted at the illegal activity she suspected.

When she finished the writing session, Amy stood and stretched. Between the stress of the law office and the concentration required to write, her brain was a frazzled mush. But she was satisfied with what she'd accomplished. The inciting incident for *Deeds of Darkness* rang true.

She went to Ian's bedroom and peeked inside. He was already asleep. The cast on his arm prevented him from lying on his preferred side, so he'd had to adjust. With his mouth slightly open, he was a picture of the total relaxation only children possess. Watching Ian, Amy made a note to use what she saw when describing the carefree sleep of the baby boy in her book. His lack of concern would be a nice juxtaposition to Roxanne's fear and anxiety. Amy kissed Ian on the forehead. Once he was sound asleep, there was little chance a gentle kiss would awaken him.

Megan's light was still on. Amy knocked and entered. With her legs propped up on the bed, Megan was lying on her back on the floor and holding a textbook in front of her face.

"Why are you reading like that?" Amy asked.

"I have a chapter test tomorrow in history, and if I get in a different position, I can remember what I read. World War I was a huge mess. What were the European politicians thinking?"

Amy didn't attempt an answer.

"Is the test essay, multiple choice, or fill in the blanks?" she asked.

"All of the above, but GR tells us the essay questions in advance."

"GR?"

"Mr. Ryan. Bethany and I have been calling him GR for Greg Ryan."

"But not to his face."

Megan lowered the book to her chest and gave Amy an exasperated look.

"No, but now that you've brought it up, we might give it a try."

"There's no need to get sassy with me."

Megan rolled her eyes and went back to studying the book.

"Good night, Mom," she said.

"Good night."

Amy backed out of the room in retreat. Jeff was in the family room watching TV. When Amy approached she saw that he'd fallen asleep.

"Do you want to go to bed?" she said in a normal tone of voice, hoping she wouldn't startle him.

"Uh, yeah," Jeff mumbled, opening his eyes and rubbing them. "This show is almost over. Did you get a lot of writing done?"

"Yes, but I don't feel right abandoning the family for the entire evening. I can't do this every night of the week. It's not fair to you or the kids."

Jeff stood up and stretched. "There will be plenty of nights when you won't be able to grab this much time, but when you can, I want you to do it. Finishing this book is your number one priority."

"You sound like you've been talking to Bernie."

"He has his reasons for pushing you along," Jeff said, looking Amy in the eyes, "and I have mine. If you get a big contract, you can quit working at the law office and never go back."

"Yeah." Amy thought about her conversation with Mr. Phillips. "I need to remember that."

In the middle of the night, she had a divine dream.

Even as a grown woman, Amy experienced

a childlike wonder each time she came into the living room. Stress peeled off her soul like dead skin. If God's mercies are new every morning on earth, they are even more magnificent when revealed in glory. Faint voices of praise fluttered at the edge of her hearing.

Bathed in thankfulness, Amy's heart felt renewed. Just as she reached the point of overflowing gratitude, she felt herself being pulled away, and a rapid succession of images flashed across her mind. Once again, she couldn't slow them down. The next thing that happened was auditory, not visual. She heard an unfamiliar name accompanied by a sick, sinking feeling in the pit of her stomach: *Larry Kelly.*

Amy woke up lying on her back in the darkness. Usually she felt refreshed after a trip to the living room. Tonight it took a few moments for the nauseous sensation to go away. She couldn't think of anyone she knew named Larry Kelly. Jeff was asleep on his side with his back turned toward her. She turned on the lamp on her nightstand and wrote the name Larry Kelly on a piece of paper.

When she came downstairs the following morning, Jeff was alone in the kitchen preparing scrambled eggs and cooking bacon for breakfast.

"Smells good," she said, glancing at the bacon sizzling in the skillet.

"It's been awhile since I gave the kids

something hot for breakfast. Ian can eat bacon with one hand."

Amy poured a cup of coffee and took a sip. "Do you know a man named Larry Kelly?" she asked, trying to sound casual.

Jeff poured milk into the bowl where he'd put the raw eggs.

"There's a guy named Richard Kelly who works as an inspector for the building authority, but I think he goes by Ricky. Why?"

"I heard the name in a dream last night. I thought maybe he was someone who'd been arrested recently, and I saw his name in the paper."

"Not that I remember," Jeff said as he added salt to the egg mixture.

"Maybe I can use the name in my new novel. I haven't identified the bad guy who is the sheriff of the fictitious county on the Texas border."

"Sheriff Kelly works for me." Jeff turned his attention to the bacon and used a long fork to expertly turn over the strips. "Do you think this is too done?"

Amy peered into the skillet. "Ian likes it crisp; Megan limp. I'd take a couple of pieces out for her."

"What about you?"

"None for me, but I'll eat a bite or two of eggs if the kids leave any."

Amy went upstairs to get dressed for work. When she returned to the kitchen, Ian was scraping more scrambled eggs onto his plate with a large plastic spoon. Megan wasn't in sight.

"These eggs are great," Ian said to Jeff.

"Your dad makes the best breakfast on earth," Amy said with a smile. "Where's Megan?"

"Already come and gone back upstairs. She didn't want any breakfast but asked for a cup of coffee."

"And you let her have one?" Amy asked.

"Yeah, she caught me off guard. She added creamer and sugar like she knew what she was doing. If I didn't know better, I could have sworn it was you."

Megan returned to the kitchen and put an empty coffee cup in the dishwasher.

"When did you start drinking coffee?" Amy asked.

"At school. Mr. Ryan has a pot in his room every morning and shares it with a few of us. It's an acquired taste."

"Yes, it is," Amy said. "And I don't want you relying on caffeine to jump-start your day."

"You and Dad do."

Amy glanced at Jeff, who shrugged.

"If you drink a cup here, don't have another one at school," Amy said. "One cup is enough."

"How many do you have?" Megan asked.

"I'd like some coffee," Ian popped up

before Amy could answer. "Bobby's grandmother lets him drink it with breakfast when he spends the night with her."

"No, you're too young," Amy said to him, then turned to Megan. "And one cup is enough at your age."

"Then I'll wait until I get to school where drinking a cup of coffee doesn't start World War III," Megan replied.

Amy spoke to Ian. "And remember, you shouldn't increase your caffeine intake while your broken arm is healing."

"What?" Ian asked.

"Caffeine isn't good for your bones," Jeff said. "The doctor told you to stay away from soft drinks for a few weeks? It's the same with coffee."

"How are your bones?" Ian challenged.

"Strong enough," Jeff said.

Jeff held out his arm. Ian wrapped his good arm around his father's bicep, and Jeff lifted him a few inches off the floor.

"Stop," Amy said. "We don't need two broken arms."

Jeff lowered Ian and moved his arm back and forth.

"My arm feels fine," Jeff said.

"It's not you I'm worried about."

Jeff was still at the house when the children left to catch the school bus. He rinsed the breakfast dishes at the sink and washed the skillet by hand. Amy dried the skillet with a dish towel.

"Megan throws me a curveball when I least expect it," Amy said as she hung the skillet on a hook above the stove.

"Coffee now, beer later," Jeff said.

"How can you be so nonchalant about it?" Amy asked. "That sort of thing is serious."

"You don't have to tell me."

Jeff was right. His father had battled a drinking problem, but he'd been sober for twenty years.

"And at the right time, I'll tell Megan about my dad," Jeff continued. "She knows him as a kind, gentle man. A totally different side came out when he'd knocked back too many drinks. He was a real Jekyll and Hyde. It might be better to ask him to talk to her."

"He'd do it. Did you ever apologize to Megan for the way you acted at the meeting with Nate Drexel?"

"I tried, but she cut me off and told me everything was okay. I think she realized I was upset because I cared about her."

During the drive to the office, Amy thought about Larry Kelly. It was a decent name for the evil sheriff in *Deeds of Darkness.* But in her heart, she suspected that wasn't the only reason she'd heard the name in the night.

She logged on to her computer. The firm paid a lot of money so the employees could access a massive national database and find personal information on just about anyone. When Amy was first trained to use it, she was stunned by the breadth of data revealed in the reports. The scope of personal privacy was a lot smaller than most people thought.

It was routine practice for Amy and the other staff at the firm to run a search on opposing parties, witnesses, and potential jurors. Amy typed in the name Larry Kelly and waited. The program came back with hundreds of matches. She would need more specific information to conduct a meaningful search. Adjusting her glasses, she closed the program and began organizing Mr. Phillips's mail.

In her dictation queue was a memo regarding a new matter for the Thompson Trust. Raymond Thompson and his company had been Mr. Phillips's biggest client for years. After Mr. Thompson died, control of his assets was transferred to a family trust. Mr. Phillips served as trustee, and his duties for the beneficiaries consumed a considerable amount of his time.

In the memo, Mr. Phillips revealed that he'd received a letter from a solicitor in London who represented a man named Vernon Carville. Mr. Carville claimed his deceased father served in the military with Mr. Thompson, who, like Sanford Dominick, was a World War II veteran. While Sonny Dominick was hacking his way through the jungle trying to avoid Japanese patrols, Raymond Thompson was hanging out in pubs making friends with British officers. Carville claimed his deceased father, a retired British officer, had a business relationship with Mr. Thompson involving mineral interests in Nigeria. In the memo, Mr. Phillips indicated there was nothing in the firm files about this type of investment, and it would have to be reviewed carefully.

It all sounded suspicious to Amy.

"No," she said out loud.

"What are you talking about?" a male voice asked.

Chris Lance was standing in the doorway.

"Nothing," Amy said.

Chris shook his head. "That avoidance strategy isn't going to work with me. Out with what you're thinking about unless it's personal. What are you working on?"

"A memo from Mr. Phillips about the Thompson Trust."

"Yeah, he talked to me about that. It has to do with Nigerian oil and mineral rights. What's the problem?"

"Nothing specific, just a creepy feeling. I've read about how much corruption there is in Nigeria and all the Internet scams that originate there. If Mr. Thompson had business interests there, they could be shady."

"The British lawyer says Thompson and Carville paid pennies for oil and mineral rights that have been dormant for years. The government changed so many times that approval to move forward never happened until a few months ago. Now there are wells in the southern part of the country that are producing oil, and Carville says the Thompson Trust will be receiving money for its share."

"That would be good."

"Yes," Chris said. "So why would you think it might be bad?"

"Like I said, it's just a feeling."

"You may be right."

"I don't understand," Amy replied. "You just agreed that it would be good."

"The trust will have to spend money to make money. That's where the big issue comes in. And as trustee, Mr. Phillips is feeling some heat about it."

Amy knew the beneficiaries of the trust weren't an easygoing group.

"If that feeling gets specific," Chris continued, "I want to know why, okay?"

"All right." Amy nodded. "Oh, I'm glad you came by. One of the lawyers on the other side of the Westside Lighting case filed a supplemental response to your motion. It was served on Mr. Phillips because he's the lead counsel of record. I put it on his desk."

"What did it say?"

"I didn't read it."

"Make me a copy, and I'll review it later."

After Chris left, Amy began checking the

Thompson Trust memo for typographical errors. The door between her office and Mr. Phillips's office was cracked open, and she heard the senior partner come in. A few minutes later she heard him explode.

"What? This is outrageous!"

Amy sat up straighter and wondered what she'd done wrong. The next thing she heard was Mr. Phillips's voice on the phone.

"Chris! Get down to my office. Now!"

Mr. Phillips was often intense and intimidating, most recently toward her. But losing his temper was not something she'd witnessed more than a handful of times during the years she'd worked at the firm. She could hear him muttering as he waited for Chris to arrive. Amy got up to close the door between their offices but hesitated. As she stood beside the door, she heard Chris come in.

"Yes, sir," Chris said in a voice that didn't try to hide the young lawyer's apprehension. "You wanted to see me."

"Sit down and read this!" Mr. Phillips roared.

Amy found herself not wanting to breathe. She shifted her weight from one foot to the other. Each passing second felt like a minute.

"I had no idea —" Chris began in a voice that was even more unsteady than when he'd entered the office.

"If I thought you did, you wouldn't be sitting in that chair!" Mr. Phillips interrupted with a loud voice. "I would have sent Ms. Kirkpatrick upstairs to lock you out of your computer and escort you off the premises immediately!"

"Yes, sir."

Mr. Phillips was silent for a moment.

"You realize the judge is going to grant their request for sanctions, including attorney's fees."

If Chris responded, Amy couldn't hear it. Mr. Phillips continued.

"You've dragged the reputation of this firm, which I've spent almost forty years building and protecting, through the mud. The other judges will know about it before the end of the day. There is no way to estimate how much damage this will do to our credibility in every case we argue for who knows how long."

"Yes, sir," Chris replied in a weak voice. "Do you want me to file a response with the court informing the judge that no one else in the firm knew about Baldwin's testimony? Under the circumstances, I should take sole blame for the submission of perjured testimony."

At the mention of Michael Baldwin's name and perjured testimony, Amy felt herself grow light-headed.

"I signed the brief, too!" Mr. Phillips raised his voice again.

"Yes, sir, but —"

"Get out!" Mr. Phillips barked. "I'm going to call a meeting of the partners and discuss what we should do. Notifying our malpractice insurance carrier will be one of the first steps. If we don't reach an agreement with the client, we will most certainly be sued, which will be all over the local newspaper."

"Do you want me to resign from the firm?" Chris asked from a different spot in the room that Amy guessed was close to the door.

"We'll make that decision, not you."

Amy heard the door open and close. The phone on her desk buzzed. She almost fell down reaching for it.

"Yes, sir," she said breathlessly.

"Notify the partners to drop what they're doing and meet me in the main conference room in five minutes. If anyone tries to give you an excuse, let me know immediately."

"Yes, sir."

Amy's heart was pounding in her chest as she made the calls. Three of the partners were in the office and available to meet. The fourth was out of town at a hearing in a neighboring county.

Twenty-Four

After Mr. Phillips left for the meeting with the other partners, Amy slipped into his office and checked his desk for the supplemental response. It wasn't there. He'd probably taken it with him to the meeting. She didn't know specifically what had happened in the Westside Lighting case, but it was obviously much worse than she'd imagined. She returned to her desk and plopped down in her chair. She felt a mixture of guilt and sympathy. Guilt toward herself because she'd not spoken up and strongly warned Chris to be careful about relying on Baldwin's testimony, and sympathy for the young lawyer, who was now probably sitting in his office staring out the window with a stunned look on his face.

Not able to do any work, she sat in front of a blank computer screen and prayed for the men in the conference room. An hour later she heard Mr. Phillips return to his office. The light for the senior partner's phone came on, but Amy couldn't hear who he was talking to or what was said. That call ended, and he buzzed her. She jumped up and went into his office. Amy felt like her eyes were bugging out of her head.

"What are you working on for Chris Lance?" Mr. Phillips asked before Amy could sit down.

"I just finished a long memo he dictated about the Dominick estate litigation."

"Give it to me. I'm going to take over responsibility for some of his work. If you see anything in his files that doesn't look right, let me know immediately."

"Yes, sir." Amy swallowed.

Mr. Phillips looked down at his desk. Amy remained where she was. Mr. Phillips glanced up.

"Anything else?" he asked.

"No, sir."

Amy returned to her desk feeling sick to her stomach. Several times she'd come to the brink of warning Chris about Michael Baldwin, but fear held her back. Now it looked like he was going to lose his job, and it was her fault. She paced back and forth across her tiny office a few times, then picked up her phone and buzzed Mr. Phillips.

"What is it?" he asked in a gruff voice.

"May I come in for a moment?"

"Why?"

"I need to tell you something."

"All right, if you can make it quick."

Not entirely sure what she was going to say, Amy returned to the senior lawyer's office. He wrinkled his forehead and stared at her.

"I know there was a problem with the testimony from Michael Baldwin in the Westside Lighting case," Amy began. "I overheard part of your conversation with Chris about it."

"Which should not be discussed with any of the staff."

"Yes, sir." Amy paused. "I'm not exactly sure what happened in the case, but I believe I made a mistake as well."

"How?"

"When I was typing the motion and brief, I had a serious question in my mind about Michael Baldwin's testimony but didn't mention it to Chris or to you. I should have spoken up about it."

"What did you suspect?"

"That Baldwin had been paid by someone to say what he did in his deposition, and the truth was going to come out eventually."

Mr. Phillips raised his eyebrows. "Did you read the supplemental response we received this morning?"

"No, sir."

"Were you aware Chris didn't review the financial documents in our possession, which should have let him know something was seriously wrong?"

"No, sir."

"Then how did you reach that conclusion?"

Amy rested her hand on a chair to steady herself.

"I had a dream about it. And sometimes my dreams are about actual people and events."

Mr. Phillips's mouth dropped open, and he raised his eyebrows.

"I've had vivid dreams since I was a little girl," Amy continued, "but it's only been in the past few months that there have been connections to real situations. I don't expect other people to base what they do on my dreams, but if I'd warned Chris, he might have done some digging and not been deceived by Baldwin."

"Tell me exactly what you saw in your dream."

Amy took a big breath. "Jeff and I met Baldwin when we bought some lights for our family room a few years ago. I remember him because he has a big handlebar mustache and puts a lot of wax on it. In the dream I saw Baldwin and a man I didn't recognize. Both of them were dressed in black. The man handed Baldwin a check that was the size of those huge checks they print when someone wins the lottery. Baldwin turned around and suddenly realized a crowd of people was watching him. He got a shocked look on his face. That was it."

"I'm not sure what to think about that,"

Mr. Phillips said with a puzzled look on his face.

"Did someone pay Baldwin to lie?"

"Yes, and there was a poorly executed effort to hide what happened. We obtained financial records in discovery that should have led to questions, which in turn would have led to the truth. Chris was so excited about Baldwin's testimony that he didn't do his homework."

"I should have warned him." Amy's lower lip trembled. "And if the firm fires Chris, it will be my fault."

"If Chris is fired, it won't be because of anything you did or didn't do. Our decision whether or not to terminate Chris won't be because of your dream."

"He's not been fired?"

"Not yet, although it's still under discussion. The immediate plan is to scale back his responsibilities and closely supervise anything he does." Mr. Phillips stopped and stared at Amy. "All of which is none of your business."

"Yes, sir, but I appreciate you letting me know. It takes some of the load off my mind."

"At least you feel better," Mr. Phillips grunted. "Now, get back to work."

"Yes, sir."

When Amy reached the door to her office, Mr. Phillips called after her.

"Amy!"

She turned around.

"Have I been in one of your dreams?"
"No, sir."
"Good. Keep it that way."

Amy finished the day without seeing Chris, but the compassion she felt in her heart for the young lawyer never left. Several times she found herself offering up a quick prayer for him and his wife, Laura. She continued to pray during her drive home.

It was an afternoon when Megan was going to watch Ian, and they were at the kitchen table doing their homework when Amy walked through the door. Ian had taken his arm out of the sling and was resting it on the table.

"What's for supper?" Ian asked as soon as Amy came through the door. "Megan is starving me."

"Only because I wouldn't let you climb on top of the counter to get into Dad's stash of candy and offered you fruit instead," Megan replied.

Megan sounded almost exactly like Amy.

"Megan is right," Amy said. "If you don't want to snack on something healthy, you can wait for supper. I'm fixing spaghetti and salad."

"I'm done." Ian closed his book. "Call me when it's time to eat."

Ian ran out of the kitchen. Amy knew he would bound up the stairs two steps at a time.

"Thanks for watching him," Amy said to Megan.

"He's a good kid, most of the time."

Amy gave Megan a puzzled look. Megan closed her book and snapped the cap on top of her highlighter.

"Are we doing anything as a family Friday night?" she asked.

"I don't think so."

"I'd like to get together with friends."

"Where?"

"At Mr. Ryan's house. We're going to make homemade pizza with all kinds of cool toppings. Then he's going to show old videos from when he was a teenager and went surfing and snowboarding."

"How big a group will be there?"

"It depends on who ends up coming. You know how people are. They'll say yes then bail if something they think is going to be more fun comes along. But I think this will be cool."

"How many people did he invite?"

"I don't know, but it was probably a bunch. He's superpopular."

"Any other adults?"

"Please, Mom, I'm not hiding anything from you. Is it okay if I go? Alecia's mother is going to pick me up and bring me home, so there's nothing you have to do but say yes."

"Let's check with your dad."

Megan crossed her arms in front of her chest.

"Which means I have to be cross-examined all over again."

"He may have questions I didn't think of."

Megan stormed out of the kitchen, leaving her schoolbooks behind. Amy took the ground beef out of the refrigerator and turned on the skillet. Staring at meat as it cooked in a pan seemed like a nice thing to do. The meat might spatter a bit, but she could always adjust the heat and avoid getting burned. Interacting with Megan was not so easily controlled.

After supper, Amy, Jeff, and Megan sat around the kitchen table, and Megan repeated her request in a humble tone of voice.

"Sounds fine with me," Jeff said.

"Thanks, Dad." Megan cut her eyes at Amy. "I knew you'd understand."

"So long as you're home by eleven o'clock," Jeff added. "There's no reason for you to be out any later than that."

"Eleven o'clock?" Megan responded. "The party won't start breaking up until at least midnight."

"Party?" Jeff asked.

"You know what I mean."

"No, I don't, and whatever you want to call it, your time at Mr. Ryan's house ends at eleven o'clock. If Alecia's mother lets her stay later than that, I'll pick you up. Agreed?"

"Okay, I guess that's better than having to miss it."

Megan left, and Jeff turned to Amy.

"We can't keep her in a bubble," he said, "and a teacher-sponsored event is better than a lot of the alternatives. Mr. Ryan seems like a nice guy who is genuinely interested in his students."

"I hope you're right," Amy agreed reluctantly.

Jeff logged on to the computer, and Amy went upstairs to the writing room. She stared at a blank screen for a few moments before setting her laptop aside. Taking paper from the top drawer of her desk, she wrote Ms. Burris a note briefly explaining why she had to cut off contact between the two of them. Amy hoped Ms. Burris would receive the news with grace. With a sigh, she folded the note and put it in an envelope to mail the following day.

Returning to her computer, she read the last few pages she'd written in *Deeds of Darkness.* When composing the first draft of a novel, Amy worked carefully and deliberately. Reading her words, Amy felt herself being drawn into the story. She reached the final line and immediately knew what she wanted to write about next. An hour and a half later she saved her work and turned off the computer. It had been a much more productive evening than she would have guessed possible when she climbed the stairs.

"You know one of the things I miss most about going back to work?" Amy asked Jeff as they were getting ready for bed.

"Helping me with the yard?"

"No, but I'll plant flowers as soon as it's warm enough."

"Will you water them?"

Amy took care of indoor plants but had a well-earned reputation of allowing outside flora to wither in the summer heat.

"Probably not, but you'll show me how much you love me by doing it for me."

"If that's your love language, I'll buy the biggest watering can on the market and fill it up to the top."

"You're sweet." Amy smiled. "But I was thinking about Natalie. I really enjoyed sitting at the coffee shop and talking to her after the kids went to school. We could relax and people-watch without having to worry about the clock."

"I can't help you there." Jeff paused. "But why don't you meet her for lunch once a week or so? You'd have to make it short, but it would be better than nothing. I'm sure Natalie misses you, too."

Amy glanced at the clock on the nightstand. "She and Luke go to bed later than we do. I'm going to call her."

Natalie was surprised at Amy's late-night phone call but quickly agreed to meet with her the following day.

"I'll pick you up," Natalie said. "Since you only have thirty minutes, there's not enough time to go to a restaurant, so I'll bring you something to eat."

"No," Amy protested. "I'm not trying to turn you into my private caterer."

"Hush. Where can we go that's quiet?"

"How about the park across from the Presbyterian church? I go there a lot by myself and eat in the car."

"Drive-in, take-out dining it is. I'll see you tomorrow. And thanks for calling. I've missed you, too."

When the lights were turned off, Amy lay on her back in the darkness. She wanted to see Natalie and was glad it worked out for them to get together. But in the back of her mind, she knew she was also trying to compensate for the loss of Ms. Burris. The older woman had been in her life only a short time, but it was amazing how many times she'd thought about a phrase Ms. Burris shared with her. One thing Amy intended to do was encourage Natalie to continue her own relationship with the elderly woman. Natalie could then tell Amy about it.

A secondhand drink of godly wisdom was better than no drink at all.

The following morning Amy finished organizing Mr. Phillips's mail and was transcribing letters when she looked up and saw Chris standing in her doorway with a stack of files in his arms. Nothing about his face revealed the trauma of the past twenty-four hours. Amy pulled out her earbuds.

"Mr. Phillips wants to go through these files," Chris said, putting them down on the corner of Amy's desk.

"He mentioned that to me yesterday."

Chris glanced past Amy's shoulder toward Mr. Phillips's office.

"He's not in yet," Amy answered the unspoken question.

"Then you know what happened in the Westside Lighting case?"

"My door was cracked open, and I overheard your conversation with Mr. Phillips."

Chris hung his head for a moment, then cut his eyes to the side.

"I had no idea," he said.

"But I did, and I told Mr. Phillips I should have mentioned it to you."

Chris looked up in surprise.

"How?" he asked.

Amy knew an apology would be small consolation to the young lawyer, but it was all she had to offer. She told him about her dream. He listened without showing any emotion.

"I should have said something to you," she said, "and I'm sorry."

"What did Mr. Phillips say?"

"Not much about the dream. He believes you should have reviewed the financial records more closely."

"Yeah. When I was hired, I emphasized my background in economics and financial matters. That came back to bite me big-time in this situation." Chris lowered his voice. "I guess you can't tell me whether I'm going to lose my job?"

"No, but the fact that you're still here this morning is a good sign. The firm hasn't fired a lawyer during the years I've worked here, but when a staff member is let go, it always happens fast."

Chris pointed to the files on the corner of the desk.

"There's work that needs to be done in these cases, but I'm locked down until I'm told specifically what to do."

"Mr. Phillips's calendar for the morning is blocked out for 'Review of CL Files.' He'll probably want to go over some things with you in person later in the day."

"I'll be here," Chris said, "unless I'm escorted off the premises."

Chris turned to leave.

"Oh," Amy said. "I finished your chart of the parties and witnesses in the Dominick estate litigation. There's a copy on Mr. Phillips's desk, but I made another one for you."

Chris unfolded the chart. Amy had printed

it out and taped the chart together so it could be hung on the wall.

"I like this," he said. "We may do a version of this as an exhibit for the jury. It's hard to follow all the players without a roster."

"Sounds like a good idea."

Chris paused. "What do you think about that case?"

"I was shocked that Mildred Burris and Sanford Dominick were engaged. She was a client of the firm for years, and I've met her several times. I never would have imagined them as a couple."

"Did you ever talk to her about Dominick?"

"No, there was no reason to."

"Does she trust you?"

"Uh, I guess so."

"Would you be willing to talk to her about the case?"

Startled, Amy said, "I can't. Mr. Phillips ordered me to cut off personal contact with her until the case is over, and I put a note telling her that in the mail room this morning. He was concerned about a conflict of interest or ethical problem."

"There's no conflict of interest because she's no longer a client of the firm. And she's not a party to the litigation."

"But she may be a witness to the will prepared by the lawyer from the eastern part of the state."

"Which still doesn't mean we can't conduct

informal discovery." Chris paused. "How did you feel when Mr. Phillips ordered you not to have any contact with Ms. Burris outside the office?"

"He's the boss."

"Sounds like a slave boss. Anyway, I wouldn't expect you to disregard what he told you unless he changes his mind."

"I wouldn't feel right trying to trick Ms. Burris into giving me information."

"That's not the goal. But it would be helpful to have an idea what took place between Ms. Burris and Dominick both in the past and more importantly prior to his death. I don't want another repeat of the Michael Baldwin fiasco."

Amy hesitated.

"At least don't send the note until I can talk to Mr. Phillips about it," Chris said. "If he changes his mind, he'll be upset that you already closed the door on communication."

Amy felt trapped. Mr. Phillips was capricious enough to react exactly the way Chris suggested.

"All right. I'll retrieve the note and hold it for now."

"And let me know if you have any insight into that case or any other. I've learned my lesson and promise not to give you a hard time about it."

After Chris left, Amy went to the law firm mail room. The note was still in the bin for delivery to the post office. She took it out and stuck it in her purse.

Exactly at noon, Natalie sent Amy a text that she was in front of the office to pick her up. Amy logged off her computer. She passed Janelle's desk on the way out the front door.

"If Mr. Phillips asks about me, I'm out to lunch with a friend," Amy said to the receptionist.

"He's been in a meeting with the other partners most of the morning," Janelle responded in a low whisper. "Something big is going on. Do you know what it is?"

"Yes, but I can't say anything about it."

"They're not going to lay off staff, are they? I've been here the least time of anyone."

"That's not it. Besides, you do a great job. I wish I could talk to people on the phone as easily as you do. Several clients have mentioned to me how pleasant you are, and you route the calls very efficiently."

"Really?" Janelle brightened up. "No one's ever said anything like that to me. I mean, Ms. Kirkpatrick gave me a little bit of positive feedback at my review but nothing specific."

Amy left the office, glad she could at least brighten Janelle's day. Natalie was parked behind a Mercedes owned by one of the partners.

"I have a special surprise for you," she said

when Amy opened the passenger door. "Get in."

"Something smells good." Amy glanced over her shoulder into the backseat. "I thought you'd whip together a salad, but you've been baking."

Natalie pulled away from the office and drove to a red light. The park was to the right, but when the light turned green Natalie took a left.

"This isn't the way," Amy said.

"It is for where we're going."

"Tell me."

"Be patient."

Natalie took two more turns. Amy suddenly realized what she had in mind.

"We're not going to Ms. Burris's house, are we?" she asked in alarm.

"And we're almost there."

Natalie turned onto Ms. Burris's street. Her house was the second one on the right. Amy held out her hand.

"Stop!" she said. "I can't see her. At least not until some things at work are cleared up."

"What in the world are you talking about?"

"It's confidential, but Mr. Phillips made me promise not to have any contact with Ms. Burris."

Natalie pulled the car to the curb.

"He can do that?" she asked incredulously.

"Maybe not legally, but I have to agree to what he says if I want to keep my job."

"That's crazy."

"Does Ms. Burris know we're coming?" Amy asked.

"Of course she does. I wouldn't barge in unannounced. She thought it was a wonderful idea. I could tell when you called me last night that you were stressed out, and I thought this would be a good way for you to be encouraged."

"You could hear the stress in my voice?"

"Of course. You hide what's going to happen in one of your books a lot better than you do your own feelings."

Amy took the note she'd written Ms. Burris from her purse and showed the envelope to Natalie.

"I wrote this last night telling Ms. Burris I couldn't see her. I was going to mail it today. One of the things I wanted to ask you to do was to keep meeting with her. Some of the bits of wisdom she comes up with really stick with me, and I thought you could share what she said with me."

Natalie shook her head. "You're serious about this, aren't you?"

"Totally. I promised Mr. Phillips." Amy hesitated. "But the reason I didn't send the note in the noon mail was because one of the other lawyers talked to me this morning and wants a chance to try and change Mr. Phillips's mind."

Natalie, who had picked up her cell phone

to call Ms. Burris, dropped it in her lap.

"What?" she asked.

"I can't tell you why the other lawyer wants to talk to Mr. Phillips, but he does."

"I'm not following this. I thought lawyers were supposed to be logical."

"And they aren't afraid to disagree. The goal is to argue until the best idea wins out."

"Where does that leave us?" Natalie asked. "I have a meat pie with a puff-pastry topping in the backseat that isn't going to be fit to eat if it isn't hot."

Without saying another word, Amy grabbed her own phone from her purse and punched in a number she knew by heart but rarely called. She silently prayed the person would answer. As soon as the call went through, she started talking rapidly.

"Mr. Phillips, this is Amy. Do I have your permission to eat a quick lunch with Ms. Burris at her house? A friend set it up without knowing there might be a problem. We'll only be there a few minutes, and I promise to be completely discreet. It would be socially embarrassing to cancel without an explanation or to give one with my friend present."

Amy had never delivered such a fast speech to the senior partner. Usually she chose her words carefully and spoke slowly. Mr. Phillips didn't immediately respond.

"We're parked outside Ms. Burris's house, and I would appreciate an answer now," Amy concluded in a rush.

"Go ahead. But avoid any topics related to firm business."

"Yes, sir. Thanks so much. I really appreciate it. I'll see you back at the office. Bye."

Amy ended the call before Mr. Phillips could change his mind or say anything else.

"I'm turning off my phone," she said to Natalie. "Let's go inside. The aroma from that pie is making me so hungry my stomach is about to start eating itself."

Twenty-Five

In addition to the meat pie, Natalie had also prepared a fruit compote that Amy carried to the front door. Ms. Burris let them in.

"I was watching through the parlor window," she said. "I know we don't have much time, so everything is set up in the kitchen."

Instead of the sunroom, the women went to the large kitchen where Ms. Burris had laid out bright floral china on a small round table covered with a woven tablecloth. Natalie and Amy placed the food in the center of the table, and the three women sat down.

"I'll pray," Ms. Burris said.

Expecting a quick blessing, Amy bowed her head and closed her eyes. A few moments of silence passed. Amy wondered if she'd heard incorrectly and Ms. Burris had asked her to pray. She opened her eyes. The other two women looked like they were waiting. Amy cleared her throat.

"Heavenly Father," Ms. Burris said right before Amy was going to speak, "thank you for bringing us together today so we can eat this food and bless your daughter Amy, whom you love with an everlasting love that can never be shaken. Encourage her with your abiding presence and give her the faith that comes by hearing your voice and believing your Word. May every force of evil arrayed against her and her family be cast down in defeat. Release the full measure of the creative gifts you've placed within her and grant her favor and success in all she does. Show Natalie and me how we can best help her as friends. In Jesus' name, amen."

"Thank you," Amy said when the older woman finished. "I needed that."

"That's what friends are for — to pray in ways that aren't influenced by direct involvement in difficult circumstances."

It was one of Ms. Burris's statements that Amy knew she'd think about after the luncheon was over.

Amy served the fruit, and Natalie dished out the meat pie. Amy savored a bite of pie that included a few slivers of flaky crust.

"This is delicious," she said to Natalie. "I knew it would be good, but this is over the top. How many times have you made it?"

"This is number two. I made it for Luke and the boys a few weeks ago. When the boys didn't turn up their noses at it, I knew I was onto something good."

"Better than good," Amy replied as she

swallowed her second bite. "This crust is amazing."

The women ate in silence for a few moments. Amy glanced at a clock on the wall of the kitchen beside an antique china cabinet. She had to be back at work in fifteen minutes.

"Thank you for doing this," she said. "Even though we're rushed, it's worth it."

"You're worth it," Ms. Burris replied.

Ms. Burris's words were delivered with such a deep sense of motherly affirmation that tears suddenly rushed to Amy's eyes. She sniffled.

"What's wrong?" Natalie asked.

Amy wiped her eyes and pointed to Ms. Burris.

"She did it. What I never got from my mother." Amy picked up her purse to get a tissue.

"She didn't understand," Ms. Burris said as she reached over and touched Amy's arm, "but that didn't keep it from hurting."

Natalie looked puzzled.

"I'll explain it to you later," Amy said, blowing her nose.

Ms. Burris turned to Natalie and asked her a question. The conversation went in a new direction. A short time later Amy and Natalie had to leave.

"That was great," Amy said during the drive back to the law office.

"I'm glad you enjoyed the pie," Natalie replied.

"It was delicious, but —"

"I know you didn't mean the food," Natalie interrupted with a small laugh. "It had to do with your mother not understanding your unique relationship with the Lord. When parents don't put their stamp of approval on something, it makes it tough for children to believe it's valid. If my mother hadn't encouraged me to draw and sent me to art class, I never would have graduated from crayons."

Thinking about Megan's love of dance, Amy resolved to be a better encourager.

"And I'm glad for you, not jealous." Amy smiled. "But even though Ms. Burris prayed for me, the lunchtime wasn't all about me. It's neat that you've completed two more illustrations for your book. One more and you're done."

"Yeah, but right now I'm putting off the last one because then I'll have no excuse to keep it hidden away. If I hadn't opened my big mouth the first time we met with Ms. Burris, I could finish and put it in a closet and not worry whether it's any good."

"I'm sure it's adorable."

Natalie reached a stop sign and turned left toward the law office.

"I want to ask you a question before I drop you off, but I'm afraid to do it," Natalie said.

Amy turned sideways in the seat. "Don't be

silly. What is it?"

Natalie took a deep breath. "I'm pretty sure the illustrations for my book are decent, but if the story needs a lot of work, would you be willing to help? I'd be glad to give you credit as the writer —"

"Joint credit with you," Amy interrupted. "And I'd love to do it. Not having to crank out a hundred thousand words to finish a book sounds like a vacation to me."

"Great." Natalie smiled. "Then I'll start on the final illustration this afternoon. I know exactly what I want to do. It's a sunset scene at the end of the day, and the children are walking up the beach toward their house."

They reached the office, and Amy got out of the car.

"Have a good afternoon," Natalie said. "Maybe we can get together this weekend, and I'll show you the book and illustrations."

"I'd love that. Call me."

When Amy left the office, she'd tried to encourage Janelle. Returning, Amy felt encouraged herself. She was a few minutes late clocking in at her computer, but that could easily be taken care of by staying over at the end of the day. She peeked into Mr. Phillips's office. The senior partner wasn't there.

Amy's big project for the day was preparing Chris's files for Mr. Phillips to review with the young associate. To her eye, Chris seemed like a conscientious attorney. He documented his work with memos, kept detailed billing records, and prepared comprehensive report letters to clients. If she hadn't known he was a recent law school graduate, Amy would have guessed he'd been practicing at least four or five years. Nothing jumped out as a mistake or evidence of sloppiness. Amy suspected Mr. Phillips already knew Chris was doing a good job, which was the most likely explanation why the young lawyer hadn't been fired for failing to catch Michael Baldwin's false testimony. She finished her review and carried the files into Mr. Phillips's office. The senior partner had returned and was on the phone. He motioned for her to put them on his credenza. She laid them out in alphabetical order and turned toward her office. She heard the phone receiver click.

"Amy," Mr. Phillips said, "what do you think about Chris's work?"

She faced him and gave her opinion.

"Yeah, that's what I found when I spot-checked the files he's worked on over the past few months," Mr. Phillips said. "The recent disaster was a very unfortunate aberration that is going to cost the firm a lot of money and prestige, but we'll get through it."

"Yes, sir."

"Any other thoughts about Mr. Lance?"

"I think he's a good writer."

"Better than I am?" Mr. Phillips asked with a glint in his eye that let Amy know he wasn't completely serious.

"Different," she replied. "You're the most precise writer I've ever known. With you, every word has a purpose."

"And you think a well-placed compliment will buy you a pass for ambushing me about your luncheon with Mildred Burris?"

Amy swallowed. This time no glint in Mr. Phillips's eye indicated any playfulness.

"Thank you very much," she began. "Nothing business-related came up. If it had, I was ready —"

"Forget it," Mr. Phillips said with a wave of his hand. "I've had second thoughts about trying to fence you in. All I ask is that you be extra careful. I trust you'll know where to draw the line."

"Yes, sir." Amy hesitated. "There's one other thing."

"What? You already got what you wanted."

"I wouldn't feel right trying to get information informally from Ms. Burris about the Dominick litigation, either."

"Who suggested that?" Mr. Phillips sat up straighter in his chair.

"Chris mentioned it. He didn't think there would be a conflict of interest, because Ms. Burris is no longer a client of the firm; or improper contact with an opposing party, because she's not named in the litigation."

"Hmm, he has a point," Mr. Phillips said.

Amy held her breath and waited.

"But I don't like it. If we want to ask Mildred anything about Sonny Dominick, it needs to be in a deposition where she can have counsel present to represent her if she chooses to do so."

"Thanks. I know Chris may bring it up this afternoon, and I didn't want it to look like I went behind his back."

"Even though you did?"

"I wasn't trying to —"

"I don't expect you to be a lawyer," Mr. Phillips interrupted, "but you'll be a better assistant if you speak your mind and let me decide what I think about it."

Amy's door was closed when Chris arrived for his meeting with Mr. Phillips. A few minutes before 5:00 p.m., Mr. Phillips returned some of Chris's files to her office and placed them on her desk.

"The thirty-four-minute dictation piece I just sent you covers the cases I went over with Chris. I'd like that on my desk first thing in the morning."

Amy glanced at the clock on her computer. It would take at least an hour and a half to transcribe that much dictation.

"Is it okay if I come in early in the morning?" she asked. "I won't be able to finish today."

"Whatever it takes. Oh, and I talked to Chris briefly about Mildred Burris. As I told you earlier, you can see her if you like, but steer clear of all topics directly or tangentially related to the Dominick matter."

Amy wasn't exactly sure what topics would be tangentially related to the Dominick estate but didn't want to say something that might prompt Mr. Phillips to revoke his permission.

"Yes, sir. Thank you."

Amy stayed a half hour past her normal quitting time to make up for her extra-long lunch break and to get as much of the dictation complete as possible. Mr. Phillips's ability to quickly grasp the status of a case and order next steps was impressive. It looked like Chris would be working more, not less.

On her way home, Amy called Jeff and asked him to bring Chinese takeout for supper.

"What does Megan want?" Jeff asked.

"The sesame chicken."

"I thought she liked Mongolian beef."

"That was three months ago. Everyone else gets the usual."

"How do you know I haven't expanded my culinary horizons?" Jeff asked.

"Go ahead, but before supper is over, I bet you'll wish you'd stuck with the sweet-and-sour pork."

Amy beat Jeff to the house. Neither Megan nor Ian was in sight when she came in through the kitchen.

"Megan! Ian!" she called up the stairwell.

"I'm in my room!" Ian responded through

the open door.

Amy waited, but there was no answer from Megan. She climbed the stairs. The door to Megan's room was closed. Amy tapped the door with her knuckles.

"Megan? Are you in there?"

Amy tried the doorknob. It was locked. She knocked more loudly.

"Megan! Are you asleep?"

Still no answer. Amy stepped down the hall to Ian's room. He was sitting in the middle of the floor building a spaceship. He balanced the spaceship against his cast while he placed another piece in position.

"Where's Megan?" Amy asked. "She didn't tell me she wasn't going to be home or leave a note."

"I don't know," Ian said. "As soon as she got here, she went to her room. I think she was feeling kind of sick."

Amy returned to Megan's room and banged on the door with her fist. No answer. Beginning to panic, Amy shook the doorknob. The door could be opened by inserting a nail into a small hole. Amy ran downstairs to the garage. Jeff kept different sizes of nails and screws in tiny bins above his workbench. She grabbed a couple of nails and raced back up the stairs. She tried to keep her mind from imagining something horrible. Her fingers trembled slightly as she inserted a nail into the hole and pushed until it clicked. She threw open the door.

Megan was lying on her back on top of the covers. Her head was tilted slightly to the side, and her mouth was open. Amy rushed up to her and shook her shoulders. Megan moaned.

"What's wrong?" Amy asked.

Megan's eyelids fluttered, then slowly opened. She moved her arms and yawned.

"Huh?" she said.

"Are you sick? Didn't you hear me knock on the door?"

Megan blinked her eyes a few more times.

"No. I passed out as soon as I got home. I was exhausted."

"But you never sleep that soundly, not even in the middle of the night."

Megan rubbed her eyes and tried to sit up but collapsed on the pillow. Amy felt Megan's forehead, but there was no sign of fever. Megan made another effort to sit up. Amy helped her, and she swung her legs over the edge of the bed.

"Why are you so tired?" Amy asked.

"I don't know, but I'm awake now. And I'm thirsty."

"Do you want me to bring you some water?"

"Yeah."

Amy left the room and raced to the kitchen. She was filling a glass with ice water when Jeff came in.

"Something's wrong with Megan!" Amy said. "She went to sleep when she got home from school, and I had trouble waking her up."

"Does she hurt anywhere or have a fever?"

"I'm not sure about pain, but she didn't feel hot."

Jeff placed the bag from the Chinese restaurant on the counter and accompanied Amy upstairs.

"Hey, Dad," Ian said when they passed his room.

"Hi, son."

Megan was lying down with her head on her pillow. She looked much the same as she did when Amy first opened the door.

"I had to unlock the door from the outside," Amy said. "She didn't hear when I knocked."

"Hey, sweetheart," Jeff said, walking over to the bed and sitting down. "Wake up."

Megan opened her eyes, saw Jeff, and smiled. He put his arm behind her back and helped her sit up.

"I brought you a glass of water," Amy said.

Megan reached for the glass. Amy steadied it so Megan could take a sip. Megan opened her eyes wider and took another sip. She took the glass from Amy and had a third drink.

"I don't know why I woke up so thirsty," she said. "What would cause that?"

"Diabetes," Amy blurted out.

"Diabetes?" Jeff asked in surprise.

"I don't know," Amy said. "But I remember my aunt Lacy was thirsty all the time before they diagnosed type 2 diabetes. They found her one afternoon passed out at the house. She was almost in a diabetic coma."

"I wasn't in a coma," Megan replied in a stronger voice. "I was asleep."

"Maybe, but it wasn't a normal afternoon nap," Amy said. "I'm going to schedule an appointment for you with Dr. Simmons."

"I'm not sick."

"You're going to the doctor," Jeff said. "No debate."

Megan stumbled downstairs. She began to revive as she ate supper. Amy watched her closely. By the time they finished eating, she seemed normal.

"I'm going to do my homework and go to bed early," she said with a yawn. "But I really don't think I need to go to the doctor."

"Are you sick?" Ian asked.

"No."

"Then why do you have to go to the doctor?"

"Dad and Mom are making me."

"That's right," Jeff said. "Which means you don't have to worry about the decision."

"I'll try to make the appointment as soon as school gets out," Amy said. "That way you won't have to miss any classes."

"I wouldn't mind missing sixth-period Earth Science. It's like something Ian would take. I always have trouble staying awake in that class."

Amy checked on Megan twice after supper. Both times she was sitting at the desk in her room doing schoolwork. On school nights, Megan usually went to bed around 10:00 p.m. When the clock passed 9:30 p.m. and she was still awake, Amy knocked on the door frame.

"I thought you were going to sleep early."

"No, I'm not that tired. I guess the nap I took this afternoon kicked in."

Amy went downstairs to the family room where Jeff was in front of the computer and told him what Megan said.

"Maybe she doesn't need to go to the doctor," Amy said. "She seems okay now."

"She wasn't when we got home. And if you're right about the possibility of diabetes, then something she ate may have equalized her system and caused her to perk up. I've been reading about the common symptoms of diabetes online. One is excessive thirst. She definitely had that. Did she have to go to the bathroom a lot today?"

"I didn't ask her, but I did hear her door open and close a few times after supper."

"And you saw how much she ate tonight. An increased appetite is another indication of a problem."

"Yeah, we know she loves Chinese food, but it won't hurt to get her checked out. I have to go into the office early in the morning to finish a memo Mr. Phillips dictated so I won't have to use more than an hour or two of sick time to take her to the doctor."

Jeff turned back to the computer. Amy wanted to tell him about the luncheon with Natalie and Ms. Burris, but it was clear his mind was elsewhere. Amy left him and climbed the stairs to the writing room. However, instead of working on *Deeds of Darkness,* she opened her journal and wrote an entry about the simple yet profound affirmation given to her by Ms. Burris. A wounded place in her heart had received a measure of healing.

The following morning Megan didn't exhibit anything except typical teenage grogginess and irritability.

The parking lot for the law firm was deserted when Amy arrived shortly after 7:00 a.m. She punched in the code to disarm the security system. The firm had long ago replaced the old key lock with an electronic system.

The mansion seemed especially large, old, and creaky when no one else was there. Glad it was daylight, Amy pushed away her fears and went into her office. Without distractions she hoped she could finish the dictation and leave plenty of time to organize Mr. Phillips's mail before he arrived. She was typing at a rapid pace when an unexpected sound at her doorway startled her. It was Chris.

"You almost gave me a heart attack!" Amy said. "Why did you sneak up on me like that?"

"I wasn't trying to sneak up on you. I saw your car in the lot and wanted to see what brought you in so early."

"Mr. Phillips wants me to finish a memo he dictated yesterday after he met with you. Basically, he's outlining what he wants you to do in several cases and who you're to report to about them."

"That's a relief. During our meeting it seemed like he was asking me questions so he could pass the cases off to someone else when I was fired."

"That's not what this is about."

"Okay. I'll look forward to getting it."

Amy waited for Chris to move on, but the young lawyer stayed put.

"Is there anything else?" Amy asked.

"Not for me. But when I told Laura you had a dream about Michael Baldwin, she made me promise that I would ask you to tell me anything you see or hear about me or my cases."

"How much did you tell her about the Westside Lighting case?" Amy asked. "That information is confidential."

Chris glanced at the door to Mr. Phillips's office.

"When I thought I might lose my job, I had

to give her a reason. I couldn't expect her to settle for vague generalities."

Amy remembered her promise to Mr. Phillips that she would let him know if Chris did anything improper. Breaching client confidentiality, even with spouses, was a big deal.

"You know we have to keep firm business within these walls."

Chris eyed her suspiciously.

"Are you going to blow me up in front of Mr. Phillips over something that minor? I came to you as humbly as I know how, and you're kicking me when I'm down. That doesn't seem like the Christian thing to do."

Twenty-Six

Chris returned to his office without a promise from Amy to keep her mouth shut. Obeying the rules was a part of working at a law office. No exceptions. Chris's final comment that he didn't tell Laura anything about the Westside Lighting case except what was already part of the public record at the courthouse kept Amy from immediately firing off an e-mail to Mr. Phillips. But she had doubts that Chris was telling the truth. His explanation sounded like an effort at backpedaling.

Amy sat at her computer. She really didn't want to cause more trouble for Chris. Brand-new lawyers knew how to do legal research and write briefs, but the nuts and bolts of the practice of law came from mentoring and experience. She wondered how much attention Mr. Phillips and the other partners had given to training Chris.

Amy finished the memo and put it on Mr. Phillips's desk. She also sent a copy as an e-mail attachment to Chris. He acknowledged with a simple "Thanks" that did nothing to ease the tension between them. Amy then called Dr. Simmons's office and scheduled an appointment for Megan at 3:45 p.m.

A few minutes later she heard Mr. Phillips arrive and begin moving around his office. He left a few minutes later without letting her know where he was going or what he was going to do. Amy double-checked his calendar and didn't see an appointment outside the office. A few minutes later Janelle routed a call for Mr. Phillips to Amy's desk. It was Ken Bell, a longtime client and one of Mr. Phillips's golfing buddies. Mr. Bell was a Southern gentleman who always treated Amy with respect.

"When do you expect him back?" Mr. Bell asked.

"I'm not sure. He was only here a few minutes then left without letting me know. I can try to reach him or you might want to call his cell phone."

"I'll do that. Oh, and he's thrilled to have you back at the office. He brought it up when we were playing the Old Sycamore course last week. Now that you're a big-time author, how did Harold convince you to come in and put up with him every day?"

"I needed to work. All he promised was a temporary position until Emily returns from maternity leave."

"I wouldn't try to lure you away from Harold, but if he ever fails to appreciate your skills, my son could use an administrative assistant at our business. Keep it in mind."

Mr. Bell developed commercial property. Amy had never met his son.

"Thanks."

As soon as the call ended, Amy buzzed Janelle.

"Did Mr. Phillips tell you where he was going or when he'd be back?"

"I overheard him tell Mr. Jessup that he had to go to an unexpected meeting about the Thomas Trust and would be out the rest of the day."

"That would be the Thompson Trust. Send his calls through to me if the person doesn't want to go to voice mail. I have to leave around three o'clock to pick up my daughter at the high school and take her to the doctor."

"Okay. And thanks again for what you said to me yesterday. It made me want to do an even better job."

Janelle's comment made Amy wonder if she should use a more positive approach with Chris.

Midafternoon Amy left the office and drove to the high school to pick up Megan. Cross Plains High was an uninspiring collection of squat brown buildings. The most imposing structure on the campus was the new gymnasium. The football team played at a municipal stadium five blocks from the school. If the team won the game, the players would walk back to the school in a celebratory parade. When they lost, they boarded buses and rode to the locker room without looking out the windows.

Amy parked in a visitor spot and went inside to the office. As she waited for Megan, Ms. Robbins, the guidance counselor, came in.

"I heard the page for Megan on the intercom and wanted to say hello," Ms. Robbins said with a smile. "Has she said anything about Nate Drexel recently?"

"No. Is there another problem?"

"Not that I know about. Nate was moved out of her English class, which will cut down on the number of times they are in the same room."

"That's good."

"What brings you to the school today?"

"Megan has a doctor's appointment."

Amy described the scene in Megan's bedroom when she got home from work the previous day.

"There is a history of diabetes in our family, and even though there's probably nothing to it, my husband and I thought Megan should have a checkup."

"Sure," Ms. Robbins replied thoughtfully.

"Is she taking any medication on a regular basis?"

"No."

Ms. Robbins lowered her voice. "You may want the doctor to run a random drug screen as part of any testing."

Amy couldn't hide her shock. Before she could say anything else, Megan came into the office.

"Let's go," Megan said.

Amy stared at Ms. Robbins, but there was no way to ask the counselor a follow-up question without tipping off Megan. The counselor simply nodded her head.

"Did you sign me out?" Megan asked.

"Yes," Amy said.

"Then come on. The last time I had a doctor's appointment I was late, and we had to wait an extra hour."

As they walked toward the front doors of the school, Amy tried to come up with a plausible reason why she needed to go back and talk to Ms. Robbins.

"We have plenty of time to make it to the doctor's office," Amy said. "I think I should check with Ms. Robbins about the Nate Drexel situation."

"There's nothing to talk about. He was booted out of my English class, and he's hanging out with Jessica Kraal. They're in the same homeroom, and she's wanted to date him all year. I don't know her, but Bethany says she likes to go after the 'bad' boys."

When they reached the front doors, Amy held back, but Megan pushed a door open and stepped outside.

"Mom!" she said, glancing over her shoulder at her mother. "Let's go!"

Amy reluctantly followed. They rode in silence to the doctor's office. On the way, they passed the spot near the little bridge where Amy saw Carl Fincannon's leg. She sent up a silent prayer for wisdom in handling her own dilemma.

Dr. Simmons had been Megan's pediatrician since birth. The white-haired doctor fit every stereotype of a kindly family physician. He always looked a child in the eye when he talked, and his calm voice had a soothing effect on fractious youngsters. Today Amy was the one who felt fractious.

After Megan was weighed and her height measured, they went to an examination room where a nurse took Megan's temperature and checked her blood pressure.

"Both within normal limits," the nurse said when she finished. "Dr. Simmons will be in to see you shortly."

"What are you going to tell Dr. Simmons?" Megan asked after they were alone.

"You need to speak for yourself," Amy responded. "And tell him the truth."

"Okay," Megan said slowly. "I'll shock him with the news that I took a nap when I got home after a long day at school, and you and Dad didn't think I woke up quick enough. Oh, and I was thirsty. After supper, I felt fine, and I feel great today."

"What happened at school yesterday?"

"Uh, the usual stuff. Alecia was out sick, but she came back today."

"What were her symptoms?"

"A sore throat, but she doesn't have strep so she wasn't contagious."

There was a knock on the door, and Dr. Simmons came in. He greeted both Amy and Megan before asking Megan to sit on the examination table.

"What brings you in today?"

"I'm not sure. My mom should tell you."

Amy cleared her throat and told him what happened.

"I'm not trying to play doctor," she said, "but my first thought was she might have diabetes. There is a history of diabetes in our family." Amy looked at Megan. "But if you think there might be another explanation, we want to hear it, of course."

"Diabetes type 1 can pop up at this age."

The doctor listened to Megan's chest, checked her ears, and looked down her throat.

"You've grown another inch. You're probably going to be about the same height as your mother. And you've also gained weight, which is a good thing. Have you noticed the need to go to the bathroom a lot more often?"

"No."

"Have you been hungrier than usual?"

"No."

"She ate a lot for supper last night," Amy interjected.

"Only because I love Chinese," Megan replied.

"Other than a craving for Chinese food, how has your appetite been?" Dr. Simmons asked with a smile.

"About the same," Megan said.

"Is that correct?" the doctor asked Amy.

"Yes."

"What about blurred vision?"

"No."

"Other than the nap you took yesterday, have you been sleeping a lot more?"

"No." Megan hesitated. "Sometimes I turn my light back on and read after Mom tells me good night."

"How long have you been doing that?" Amy asked.

"A few weeks, but you told me to tell the truth."

"Which is necessary for me to properly evaluate you," Dr. Simmons said. "It doesn't sound like you've developed type 1 diabetes, the most common variety for young people, but it's easy enough to check with a blood test. I'll send you down the hall to the lab so the technician can draw some blood. It's just a little prick in the arm. She might ask you to let a smaller child watch to see how easy it is. Would that be okay?"

"Sure," Megan answered.

"Thanks." The doctor turned to Amy. "We'll call if anything is amiss, or you can contact the office tomorrow afternoon after three o'clock for the results. In the unlikely event a problem shows up, we'll need to take another blood sample following an overnight fast."

"Will the test check for anything other than diabetes?" Amy asked, trying not to sound overly anxious.

"Yes, it will be a broad spectrum test, although I don't think there's going to be a problem with Megan's cholesterol level." Dr. Simmons patted Megan on the shoulder. "I saw your name in the program for the Christmas recital at Ms. Carlton's dance studio. One of my granddaughters has started going there. Her name is Candace Jordan. I was on call that weekend and couldn't come to see her."

"Candace was in my group." Megan perked up. "She's a sweetie."

"I think so, too." The doctor smiled.

And with that, he was gone. Megan hopped down from the examination table.

"Candace has great balance," she said. "And she's really learned how to point her toes. I had no idea she was related to Dr.

Simmons."

"I think her mother is Dr. Simmons's youngest daughter," Amy said distractedly.

They walked down the hall to the waiting area for the lab. No sooner had they sat down than an older black woman came to get Megan. Wanting to ask more questions about the scope of the blood test, Amy stood up to follow.

"You can wait here," the woman said. "The lab is cramped."

"Yeah, I'm fine, Mom," Megan said, then turned to the technician. "Dr. Simmons said you might want to use me to show a little kid it's not too scary to have blood drawn."

"Thanks, but right now you're my only customer."

Amy plopped down in her chair. There was a TV in the upper corner of the waiting area. It was tuned to a show featuring an abrasive female host who was more interested in listening to herself talk than interviewing guests. Amy fidgeted while the woman berated a mother whose fourteen-year-old daughter had taken the family car out for joyrides and caused three wrecks. Amy didn't want to be a negligent mother, but at the moment, that's exactly how she felt.

After leaving Dr. Simmons's office, they picked up Ian. As soon as he got in the car, he made a comment about the bandage on Megan's arm.

"What have you been shooting up?" he asked her.

"What did you say?" Amy asked sharply before Megan could respond.

"I'm kidding," Ian said.

"They took my blood at the doctor's office," Megan said. "You would have cried like a baby."

"No, I wouldn't. Mom, tell Megan how good I did when the doctor had to fix my arm."

"You did great."

"Because you were so doped up that you didn't know what was going on," Megan said.

Amy didn't want to hear another reference, joking or otherwise, to drugs.

"Stop it!" she said. "No one talks in this car until we get home!"

They were only a few minutes away from the house. Ian hopped out as soon as the car rolled to a stop. Amy and Megan went into the house together.

"What are you going to do now?" Amy asked her when they reached the kitchen.

"I'm not going to take a nap, if that's what you mean. None of my friends at school could believe you were making me go to the doctor just because I went to sleep. Sometimes I wonder what in the world you're thinking. You know the blood test is going to come back normal."

"How can you be so sure?"

Megan rolled her eyes and left the room.

Jeff was running late from work and came in as Amy was putting the final touches on supper.

"I need to take a quick shower," he said. "We got into some nasty places today in a cluster of rental units not far from the county recreation center. I couldn't believe people were living in there up until a few months ago. There were needles on the floors and all kinds of drug paraphernalia lying around —"

"Take your shower," Amy interrupted. "We need to eat before supper is ruined."

As soon as they were seated at the supper table, Jeff asked about Megan's trip to the doctor.

"He doesn't think I have diabetes, but they're doing a blood test anyway," Megan replied. "And do you remember the cute little blonde named Candace who was in the Christmas recital? I think she's either six or seven."

"Uh, there were a lot of little blond-haired girls hopping across the stage," Jeff replied. "It's hard for me to tell one from the other."

"Anyway, she's Dr. Simmons's granddaughter. There's going to be a special practice Saturday morning for the spring show, and I hope she'll be there."

"Saturday morning?" Amy asked. "I didn't know anything about that."

"Don't worry, I already have a ride."

"Who's taking you?" Amy asked.

"Mr. Ryan is going to pick me up. I told him I had to be home at eleven o'clock from the pizza party because I have dance class the following morning, and he said he'd like to watch. He's also going to pick up Molly Prichard."

"No," Amy said flatly. "We'll take you to dance practice. And you don't have to come home early from the pizza party because of dance practice."

"I only said that because I was too embarrassed to admit I have such a lame curfew for an adult-supervised event."

Jeff spoke. "Amy, don't forget we volunteered to be at the Connors' house at nine o'clock on Saturday to help them pack up for their move to Oklahoma."

"You volunteered," Amy corrected.

"Okay, but I'm sure Tammy could use the help."

Amy also remembered her commitment to spend time with Natalie going over her children's book.

"All right, but I also have to get together with Natalie."

After the meal was over, Amy and Jeff stood side by side in front of the sink doing the dishes. In a soft voice she told him about Ms. Robbins's suggestion that Megan be drug-tested.

"I could tell you were upset during supper," Jeff said.

"But what do you think? I didn't get a chance to talk to Dr. Simmons in private. And all he did was screen Megan for diabetes and check her electrolytes."

Jeff was scrubbing the pan Amy used to cook the main dish.

"I don't know. To falsely accuse Megan of something like that could cause a huge rift that might be very tough to heal."

"But what if it isn't false? Catching something early can be crucial to keeping it from becoming a bigger problem."

Jeff put the pan in the dishwasher.

"Let's keep our eyes open. If there's really a problem, she won't be able to hide it."

Amy wasn't so sure.

TWENTY-SEVEN

Megan's blood work at Dr. Simmons's office came back completely normal. When she called for the results, Amy asked in as casual a voice as she could manage if the test included a check for illegal or street drugs.

"No," the physician's assistant replied. "I don't see that on the doctor's order."

"Could that sort of test be run?"

"We'd need a new blood sample. Once the analysis is complete, the lab doesn't store the unused material. Would you like to schedule another appointment and bring Megan in?"

Amy hesitated. "Not at this time. I should have asked Dr. Simmons about it the other day."

"If you have reason to be concerned, it's better to know a problem exists than wonder."

"I know, but my husband wants to wait."

As soon as she spoke, Amy felt bad for criticizing Jeff to a stranger.

"There's no harm in talking to your daughter about drug usage," the woman continued. "A common mistake parents make is assuming a child won't experiment. Peer pressure can be a powerful force."

"Megan has a good group of friends," Amy replied with more confidence than she felt. "But I'll try to find a time to bring it up in a way that doesn't seem like I'm attacking her or don't trust her."

"What is your e-mail address? I'll send you the link to a website that will help you with the conversation," the woman said.

Amy gave her the information.

"This comes up a lot more than you'd think," the woman said. "And in good families. Don't be afraid. Take action."

"Okay, thanks."

Amy hung up. A minute later she received an e-mail with the link. Before she could go online, Mr. Phillips buzzed her.

"Come into my office," he said.

"Should I bring anything?"

"Something to take notes."

Amy picked up a steno pad. The senior partner had a thick file spread out in front of him. Amy sat down across from his desk.

"I've been working on the Thompson Trust for the past twenty-four hours," he said. "Are you aware a man named Carville from the UK claims his deceased father and Raymond Thompson had joint business interests in Africa?"

"Yes, sir. I typed a memo you dictated about it."

"Of course you did." Mr. Phillips rubbed his forehead with his fingers. "Mr. Carville and his solicitor flew to Raleigh yesterday, and I met with them at a hotel near the airport. They told me there are oil wells in production on the coast of Nigeria close to the area controlled by Thompson and Carville. However, to exploit them is going to require additional expense from Carville and the trust. The decision whether to spend the money is in my hands."

"Yes, sir."

"Carville is willing to put up his share of the additional development costs, and he's put the money in his solicitor's escrow account."

"How much?"

"Around a million dollars in US currency."

Amy pursed her lips.

"If Carville wasn't willing to put up his share, it would be an easy decision. I'd advise the beneficiaries of the trust to walk away from it." Mr. Phillips pointed to the documents on his desk. "I've looked over the paperwork, and Thompson owned seventy-five percent of this company. That means the trust would have to pony up three million dollars to see this thing through. Normally, I wouldn't recommend that level of risk, but the return would be ten times the investment."

The amounts of money Mr. Phillips was talking about were so large that they were only numbers in Amy's head.

"What do you want me to do?" she asked.

"I've located at least two firms that can examine the project and give us expert opinions about the risk. I want you to find out everything you can about the consultants and get back to me. There's no way this kind of decision should be made by us in-house."

Amy hesitated. "Mr. Phillips, I'm not trying to avoid work, but that sounds like something one of the lawyers should do."

"I'm putting Chris and Morgan Jessup on it as well. There can't be too much redundancy on something this important. Don't consult with either one of them. Report back to me."

"Yes, sir." Amy wrote down the names of the two consulting firms. "Would you need to talk to the beneficiaries of the trust about it?"

"That should only be done when I'm satisfied with the legal opinion I'm going to give. Based on past history, they won't agree, and I'll have to step in and make the call. It creates a very touchy situation. The firm is subject to liability whatever we recommend. The responsibility made it tough for me to fall asleep last night, and at this point in my career that's not the kind of pressure I want."

Mr. Phillips rarely showed weakness.

"Tell me what you want, and I'll do my part," Amy said.

"That's it for now. Get back to me with your recommendation by Friday morning."

Over the next few days, Amy was surprised at how much she enjoyed her new assignment. In between her normal dictation duties, she conducted research on the Internet, but more important, she contacted individuals and firms that had used the services of the different consultants. Coming up with a recommendation wasn't easy. She discovered there were clients who didn't like a consultant because they didn't get the answers they wanted; clients who were pleased with the consultant's opinion at the time it was given but dissatisfied when it didn't prove accurate in the long run; clients who were initially unhappy with a consultant but ultimately came to appreciate the advice; clients who didn't like anything about the consultant; and clients who thought the consultant was the repository of the highest level of business wisdom. Amy developed a spreadsheet to chart her results.

At home Megan had no further instances of unexplained afternoon sleepiness. Ms. Robbins's comment about possible drug usage didn't drop off Amy's radar, but it faded further in the rearview mirror. Ian received a good report on his arm from the orthopedist, and it looked like he might get his cast off early.

Thursday night after supper Amy went up to the writing room. Each stage in writing a book held its own unique challenges and pleasures. In the beginning, the freshness of meeting the new characters and discovering who they were intrigued her. During the middle section of a book, there was the ebb and flow of success and failure that lay along the characters' developmental arcs. And toward the end of a book, Amy often found herself typing as fast as she could to find out what happened next. Even though she generally knew the end of a story, the exact path the characters followed to get there held surprises for her as well as her readers.

In the opening chapters of *Deeds of Darkness,* the courage of Amy's main character in facing serious challenges made her someone a reader would want to root for. This was a key element for a successful novel. If readers didn't care about the characters, why would they want to spend time finding out what happened to them? And the teenage niece would have no problem attracting her own cheering section. Her mixture of toughness, tenderness, and neediness was sure to touch maternal hearts.

Friday morning Amy delivered her recommendation about the financial consultant for the Nigerian oil project to Mr. Phillips. He looked over the spreadsheet she'd printed out.

"This is an interesting approach," he said. "How many people did you interview?"

"Thirty-eight," she replied. "It's split fairly equally among the two companies."

"And you're recommending the firm in Miami even though you have the least information about them."

"Yes, sir. They've worked on two projects for clients in Africa, including one in Nigeria."

"I don't see where you talked to that client."

"I didn't. I couldn't get anyone to return my phone calls. I thought maybe one of the executives would talk to you. When I told the person on the phone I was an administrative assistant, it didn't get me past the gatekeepers."

"Maybe you should have said you were an author working on a book."

"There's nothing in my new novel about Nigerian oil companies. The setting is south Texas."

"It's still oil and gas territory." Mr. Phillips raised his eyebrows.

"Yes, but —"

"Don't let me interfere with that part of your life," Mr. Phillips interrupted. "Your information will go into the mix I'm getting from Chris and Morgan."

"I know you wanted us to work separately, but is there going to be a meeting to discuss what each of us found out?"

"Not with you, but thanks for what you did."

Disappointed, Amy returned to her office. She had no right to expect to be a direct part of the decision-making process, but she'd invested a lot of time and energy. Mid-afternoon, Chris Lance came by her office. He leaned against the door frame.

"I've not been avoiding you on purpose," the younger lawyer said in a casual voice. "But Mr. Phillips has kept me very busy. It looks like I've weathered the storm and will be staying at the firm."

"That's good news."

"I'm glad you think so. Oh, and I talked to him about my conversation with Laura about the Westside Lighting case. Did you say anything to him about it?"

"No."

"I didn't think so. He understood." Chris glanced down the hall. "I just came out of a two-hour meeting with Mr. Phillips and Mr. Jessup about the possible consultants for the Nigerian oil issue and the Thompson Trust. I saw your work. It was impressive."

"Thanks. What did Mr. Phillips decide to do?"

"Mr. Jessup and I both recommended the firm in Houston, so they're going to get the nod."

"Why? They had a lot of negative reviews from clients."

"But that was primarily the result of a man who's no longer with the firm. They have a specialist in foreign business analysis who is very impressive, and his clients rave about him. I didn't see that you talked to him."

"Who is it?"

"Dr. Claude Ramsey. He's a geologist who went back to school to get a degree in international finance. He knows a lot about oil and gas."

As soon as Chris left, Amy went to the website for the Houston firm and clicked the "Our Staff" tab. Midway down the page she saw Dr. Ramsey's name and clicked on his bio. The face of a middle-aged man in his late forties appeared on her screen. Something about his face seemed vaguely familiar.

Then Amy remembered.

She'd seen the same face the night she saw Michael Baldwin in the living room. She knew the two men couldn't be directly connected, but there had to be a reason why the geologist appeared with Baldwin in the dream. Amy read his curriculum vitae. Dr. Ramsey received his bachelor of science degree in geology from the University of Texas at Austin and his MBA and PhD in finance from Wharton School of Business in Philadelphia. She couldn't quibble with his academic credentials. He was obviously a very smart guy. But the number of letters after a man's name didn't guarantee moral integrity. That part worried Amy.

As she read the information on the website, the sick feeling Amy had when she saw Michael Baldwin in the living room returned. She wasn't sure why she felt nauseous, but it couldn't mean anything good. She knew she couldn't sit by idly and let another Michael Baldwin disaster fall on the firm. But with Baldwin, she'd seen a vivid picture that could be interpreted fairly easily. How would Mr. Phillips react if she went to the senior partner and urged him not to hire Dr. Ramsey because his name made Amy feel bad? She closed her eyes, bowed her head, and prayed. No answer came.

Troubled, Amy was on her way home from work when she received a phone call from Megan.

"Mom, where are you?" Megan demanded as soon as Amy answered.

"About five minutes away from the house. What's wrong?"

"We need to leave right now to go to Mr. Ryan's pizza party! It starts at five o'clock. I'm already late!"

"And when were you going to tell me that?"

"I did! You were probably thinking about

your new book or something."

Amy bit her lip.

"Be ready. I'll honk the horn, and you can come out to the car. Do you have his address? I don't know where he lives."

"Yes, just hurry! I'm supposed to help set up before everyone else gets there. I've already missed that part."

Amy tried to remember when Megan told her she needed to be at the teacher's house at 5:00 p.m. but couldn't. If she had, Amy would have made arrangements to leave work a few minutes early. She pulled into the driveway. Before she could honk the horn, Megan was out the door jogging toward the car. She was wearing her shortest skirt and a short-sleeved shirt. At least she'd not gone overboard with her makeup.

"Where's your jacket?" Amy asked as soon as Megan opened the car door. "You're going to freeze. It's supposed to get down into the forties tonight."

"This isn't a ball game. I'm not going to be outside, and I'm sure Mr. Ryan has heat in his townhome."

"And you're going to be home at eleven."

"No, you're going to pick me up at eleven. And don't come a minute early. If you do, you'll have to wait because I'm not coming out to the car. Let's go. And don't drive under the speed limit just to make me mad."

Megan's attitude was as bad as some of the

tantrums she pitched when she was three years old. However, sending her to time-out wasn't an option. Amy backed up the car.

"You could be more polite," she said.

"You get mad when Dad makes you late."

It was a true statement. Amy put the address in her GPS. It was a ten-minute drive. She and Megan rode in silence. The route took them within a block of the law office and then to the east side of town. The teacher lived in one of the nicer townhome communities in the area. Amy slowed as they drove past the pool and clubhouse. The pool was covered for the winter. Lounge chairs were stacked against the wall of the clubhouse.

"Bethany and I hope Mr. Ryan will have a pool party this summer," Megan said.

Amy didn't reply. Teenage pool parties were not something she was looking forward to.

"That's it," Megan said when they reached the back of the development. "I recognize his car."

Another female student was walking up to the front door of the townhome.

"That's Rita Fox," Megan said. "She's a junior. It's amazing that ninth graders like Alecia and me are getting to come to something like this. Before Mr. Ryan came along, Rita wouldn't know I was alive. He says it's important for students from every grade to get to know one another."

The words sounded fine in theory. Amy

could only hope the teacher knew what he was doing. She pulled into an empty parking spot beside a small, older-model car. A tall young man with dark hair got out.

"Mom!" Megan squealed. "It's David Springsteed. I had no idea he was going to be here. How does my hair look?"

"Great. Who is he?"

"He's a junior, too. You and Dad would love him. He's superpolite and goes to church and everything."

"Have you been talking to him?"

"No, but all of us think he's gorgeous."

"Megan, the difference between a ninth grader and an eleventh grader is too much. There's no harm in a little daydreaming, but —"

"Girls mature faster than boys," Megan said, cutting her off. "If I hop out now, I can go inside right after him. Bye."

Before Amy could say anything else, Megan was out of the car and up the sidewalk. The front door of the townhome opened, and Amy saw Greg Ryan. The teacher shook David's hand and looked past the student toward Amy's car. He motioned to her with his right hand, inviting her inside. Amy knew Megan would be furious if she crashed the party for even a minute, but her mother's curiosity was not going to be denied. She turned off the car's engine and got out.

TWENTY-EIGHT

Greg Ryan was wearing blue jeans and a casual shirt. He waited on the landing for Amy.

"Thanks for dropping off Megan," he said. "I know you're busy with work and writing."

"It was a quick turnaround. I'm sorry she's late. I didn't know she was supposed to be here to help set up."

"Don't worry about it. 'Late' is a relative word for kids. A party doesn't start until the right people get there. Come inside, and I'll show you around."

Amy followed Mr. Ryan into the townhome. It had an open floor plan. To the left was a combination living room/dining room/kitchen. There were several teenagers milling around. Megan looked up and saw Amy.

"Mom, what are you doing here?"

"I'll be leaving in a minute."

"I invited her in," Mr. Ryan added. "Megan, will you make sure there's plenty of ice in the bucket in the kitchen sink? If not, there are a couple of bags in the fridge."

Amy glanced around. For a single male, Ryan had decent taste in furniture and wall decorations.

"I like your place," she said.

"Thanks."

Ryan led Amy down a short hallway.

"The master suite is downstairs, and there are two bedrooms upstairs. I use one of those for a home office. Upstairs is off-limits for the kids. I'll keep them corralled down here."

He opened the door to a spacious bedroom decorated in dark blues and greens suitable for a man.

"Would you mind if I used the bathroom?" Amy asked. "I didn't get a chance to stop at the house when I picked up Megan."

"Use mine," he replied. "The kids are using the half bath down the hall."

"That's not necessary. I —"

"Mr. Ryan, can you come here?" a female voice interrupted them.

The teacher turned away and left Amy standing inside his bedroom. She stepped over to the bathroom. It featured a double sink and a Jacuzzi tub. While she was washing her hands, Amy looked at herself in the long mirror. She touched her right cheek just below her eye. A new wrinkle was definitely forming on her face. She sighed. Her mother had more crow's-feet around her eyes than a dusty corn patch. It didn't take a nighttime trip to the living room for Amy to know her future face.

As she dried her hands, Amy glanced down at the items spread out on the long sink. The teacher used the same brand of cologne as Jeff. Amy couldn't remember the last time Jeff actually applied it to his neck. She sniffed the cologne. Setting it down, she saw a set of shiny cuff links. They were gold with letters engraved on them. Amy picked one up and read "AKL." At the end of the sink in a small ceramic frame was a photo of the teacher with an older couple who were probably his parents. Mr. Ryan's father was bald. The passage of time is an unforgiving arbiter. When she left the bedroom, Mr. Ryan was waiting for her in the hallway.

"Thanks," Amy said. "I couldn't help noticing the cuff links on the sink."

"Oh, those belonged to my grandfather," Mr. Ryan replied. "I've only used them a couple of times, but I have to go to a formal dinner for the alumni chapter of my college fraternity next weekend and pulled them out."

"Where will that be?"

"Uh, Denver. I went to the University of Colorado."

"I thought the campus was in Boulder."

"That's the main campus. There's a branch in Denver."

The noise in the townhome had gone up a

few decibels as more young people arrived. A girl Amy didn't recognize looked up.

"Are you Mr. Ryan's girlfriend?" the girl asked, her eyes wide open.

Amy felt herself blush. "No, I'm Megan Clarke's mother."

"Megan Clarke?" the girl asked.

"She's a ninth grader," another girl said, then faced Amy. "I can tell you're her mom. You look just alike."

"And don't worry about my social life, Lindsey," Mr. Ryan said to the first student. "You have enough to keep up with yourself."

"Promise you'll tell us when you get a girlfriend?" Lindsey persisted. "We want to know who your type is."

Mr. Ryan shook his head and turned to Amy.

"Kids have an overly romanticized view of the life of a single teacher."

"I know. Thanks for showing me around."

"You're welcome," the teacher said. "I hope to see you in the morning when I pick up Megan for dance class."

"She's excited that you're coming to watch."

The teacher moved away and began talking to another cluster of students. Amy left. While driving home, she decided to ask Jeff if they could enlist Mr. Ryan's help in trying to determine if Megan was being influenced by the wrong kind of crowd at school. The group of young people assembled at the teacher's townhome seemed nice enough, but Amy wasn't naive. Deeds of darkness could come in packages that gave no hint of what lay inside.

Jeff was waiting for her in the kitchen.

"I apologize," he said as soon as he saw her. "I meant to come home early so I could take Megan to Mr. Ryan's house."

"She was extremely rude to me about it. I didn't remember her telling me."

"I don't think you were in the kitchen when she brought it up earlier in the week."

"That's okay, I'm glad I went. Mr. Ryan invited me in to see his townhome, and we talked for a few minutes. One of the girls there thought I was his girlfriend."

"Girlfriend?"

"Yes, which made me feel better because I found a new wrinkle under my right eye a few minutes earlier. Anyway, I think we should ask Mr. Ryan if he suspects Megan might be mixed up with students who are using drugs. He seems connected to what's going on with the kids."

"If he suspected something like that, don't you think he'd tell us?"

"I'd hope so," Amy said. "But maybe he's not tuned in to the issue. You wouldn't believe how the kids are pulling on him. He's like a rock star."

"Do you think he's handsome?"

Amy stared at Jeff for a moment. Her first reaction was to burst out laughing. She managed to stop herself.

"No, and it was silly for a student to suggest he and I might be a couple. Mr. Ryan is not my type; you are. That story has been written, and nobody is going to change it."

"I like it when you talk to me like that."

"Then I should do it more often." Amy paused. "What about me?"

"I think you're more beautiful than the day we got married."

"And the wrinkles don't bother you?"

Jeff leaned in close to her face and squinted. "I love you so much I have trouble seeing any imperfections."

Amy laughed. "Now we're both getting away from fact and into fiction."

Amy fixed one of Ian's favorite suppers — hot dogs topped with chili, cheese, chopped onions, and mustard. She warmed the buns by wrapping them in a damp cloth and steaming them for a few seconds in the microwave. Jeff liked an old-fashioned hot dog, too, and father and son could eat a platterful.

"You're the best cook," Ian said to Amy as he finished his second hot dog and reached for a third with his nonbroken arm. "Bobby's mom doesn't know how to do it like you do."

"I agree," Jeff added with a twinkle in his

eye. "These hot dogs are gourmet."

After Ian was in bed, Amy didn't go up to the writing room. Instead, she and Jeff sat beside each other on the sofa and watched a movie.

"I'll pick up Megan," Jeff said when the movie was over.

"But I already know where Mr. Ryan lives."

"My face is the only male face I want you to see this evening," Jeff replied. "Besides, if we're going to ask Ryan to spy on Megan for us, I should be the one to do it."

"It's not spying," Amy replied. "It's —"

"Spying," Jeff cut in. "But that doesn't mean it's bad or we shouldn't ask. Nine months out of the year Megan spends more time at school than she does anywhere else. My question is whether I'll be able to grab a moment with him while his place is filled with kids."

"I asked to use the bathroom."

"That might work for a woman, but I'll have to figure something else out."

Amy glanced at the clock. "Don't leave for another ten minutes. Megan threatened to stay in the house and not come out if we got there early."

"Then I'm leaving now. That will give me an excuse to crash the party and talk to the teacher."

Amy began to get anxious as the time passed

when she expected Jeff and Megan to return. The door to the garage didn't open until 11:30 p.m., and they came through the kitchen into the family room.

"Did you have a good time?" Amy asked Megan.

"Yeah, it was a blast. All the kids want to do it again soon." Megan looked at Jeff. "Mr. Ryan thinks you and Dad are cool, but that doesn't mean he needs extra chaperones. If he has a bigger party, he's going to ask Ms. Garrison, the P.E. teacher, to come."

"I helped carry out the trash," Jeff said. "Taking a black plastic bag filled with half-eaten pizza to the Dumpster is a skill most teenage boys haven't learned yet."

"You spent most of your time there talking to Mr. Ryan," Megan said. "What were you talking about?"

"There could only be one topic of conversation," Jeff replied. "I was asking Mr. Ryan to spy on you for us."

"Quit it." Megan rolled her eyes. "Anyway, thanks for letting me go. The party was breaking up at eleven, so I didn't really miss much. Oh, and Dad said it was okay, so Mr. Ryan is going to be here at nine in the morning to take me to dance class. He has to pick up Molly first."

Megan went upstairs. Amy and Jeff watched her go and remained quiet until they heard her door click shut.

"That was a risky move," Amy whispered. "She thought you were joking about asking Mr. Ryan to spy on her."

"Did you expect me to lie?"

"You know what I mean. What did he say?"

"He was surprised and concerned. Offhand, he didn't know anyone in her circle who's going downhill except Crystal."

"Megan saw that last fall during football season."

"And Ryan says they don't hang around each other much anymore. He mentioned that even though he's had casual contact with a lot of students, he doesn't know many of them very well. This party was a chance to be around them with their hair down a little bit."

"What was Megan doing when you got there?"

"Huddled in a corner with the other ninth-grade girls watching the older kids. It's tough for the various age groups to mingle. There's so much difference between them."

"That's what I told Megan. She came back at me with a line about girls maturing faster than boys."

"That's true enough. I'm still trying to catch up to you."

"Consider me caught." Amy yawned. "We'd better get some sleep. We have a busy day tomorrow."

"Are you still going to try to see Natalie?"

"Yes, for a late lunch. But I don't want to

shirk my duty at the Connors' house."

"We'll both drive. That way you can leave when you want, and I'll stay to make sure everything gets done."

"That would be nice," Amy said gratefully. "Since I went back to work, it's hard to see Natalie, and I don't want to cut into our family time on the weekends."

"There's not going to be much family time this weekend."

"What's Ian going to do tomorrow while we're not here?" Amy asked suddenly. "I feel like a terrible mother for not planning ahead."

"He's going to Bobby's house. I called Jack this afternoon. He's going to take the boys out in the woods and show them a tree stand he's set up for deer season later this year."

"This isn't going to involve a four-wheeler, is it?"

"No. They'll ride in Jack's truck, and I told him Ian can't climb the stand with one arm. There's also a little stream nearby where the boys can mess around for a while. It's just a chance to be in the woods before it gets warm and the bugs come out."

As she lay in bed, Amy spent a few anxious moments thinking about Dr. Claude Ramsey. She wasn't sure what could go wrong, but that didn't relieve the stress she felt. She offered up a quick prayer for either additional information or guidance in how to bring up the subject with Mr. Phillips. Nothing percolated up from her spirit. She fell asleep and slept through the night.

The following morning was more like a school day than a leisurely Saturday. Knowing he was going to be doing some strenuous physical activity, Jeff cooked a full breakfast, and the entire family gathered around the table.

"Remember, you're not going to be climbing any trees today," Amy said to Ian.

"She means you're not going to climb the tree stand," Jeff corrected. "Obey Bobby's dad."

"But he's going to let Bobby —"

"That's exactly the attitude I'm talking about," Jeff interrupted. "If you can't go along with the program, you can come with your mom and me to pack up the Connors' stuff. I'm sure there are some things a one-armed boy can put in boxes."

"Yes, sir," Ian said.

"Good. Mr. Pickens knows a ton of stuff about the woods. You'll learn a lot and have fun doing it. He's going to bring you home in time for supper."

"Bobby invited me to spend the night."

"All day is enough," Jeff said.

While Jeff talked with Ian, Amy nibbled a piece of wheat toast. It was nice when Jeff took over the parenting duties. Of course, managing Ian was a lot easier than managing the young woman who was eating her fourth piece of bacon.

"What am I supposed to do for lunch?" Megan asked.

"There are all kinds of sandwich fixings in the fridge," Amy replied.

"What if Mr. Ryan wants to buy my lunch?"

"That would be fine with me," Amy said, glancing at Jeff. "It would give you time to talk."

Amy could see Megan's mouth drop open.

"Sure," Jeff said. "But come straight home after you eat. I checked your room after you came downstairs, and you've got plenty of work to do cleaning and straightening up. I expect it to look decent by the time I get home this afternoon."

"Don't suggest that he buy your lunch," Amy added. "Let him bring it up."

Jeff reached into his back pocket and pulled out his wallet.

"Actually, it wouldn't be right for him to pay for your meal. He's trying to live on a teacher's salary. Here's twenty dollars. That should pay for both of you if you eat at a fast-food place."

Megan stared at the twenty-dollar bill.

"Let me have twenty dollars so Bobby and I can buy something," Ian said. "I know he'd like to go to the ice-cream place after we've been in the woods."

"Nice try, but no," Jeff responded.

Megan finished breakfast in silence. Amy

couldn't help smiling to herself at Megan's bewilderment with the puzzling turn of events.

"Do you want me to save you a cup of coffee in a travel mug?" Amy asked her. "You didn't have any with your breakfast."

"Uh, no, thanks. All I wanted was orange juice."

Shortly after Bobby and his father picked up Ian, Mr. Ryan came to get Megan. Amy opened the front door. She could see Molly Prichard sitting in the passenger seat of the car.

"Good morning," the teacher said. "Is Megan ready?"

"She should be down in a second. Would you like to come in?"

The front-door entrance opened directly into the family room. They stepped inside, and Amy looked up the stairs.

"Megan! Mr. Ryan is here!"

"Just a second!" Megan replied.

"Busy Saturday?" Mr. Ryan asked.

"Yes, Jeff and I are helping a family in our Sunday school class pack up for a move to Oklahoma, and then I'm going to spend some time with a close friend who's writing a children's book."

"There is lot of creative talent in this town. Are you working on a new book yourself?"

"Yes, it's in the beginning stages."

"That must be a challenge. Holding down

a full-time job and writing."

"And trying to be a good mom." Amy lowered her voice. "Jeff and I appreciate you helping us keep an eye on Megan. She's smart and strong-willed, but it's not paired up with wisdom yet. We want to make sure she doesn't make bad choices."

"Sure. But getting kids to let down their guard and talk isn't always easy. There's a lot of listening required first."

"I know, and I don't want to steal your time. You're already giving so much of yourself to your students. But if you'd like to take Megan to get a burger after dance practice, Jeff gave her money for lunch. Of course, if Molly is going along, that might not work."

"I'll play it by ear."

Megan came rapidly down the stairs. Her dance clothes were in a canvas tote with the studio logo on its side.

"Hey, Mr. Ryan. Bye, Mom," she said, then darted past her out of the house.

Mr. Ryan lingered for a moment. "If dance doesn't work out, Megan could probably be a track star."

Amy watched as Megan got in the backseat of the car.

When Amy and Jeff arrived at the Connor house, it looked like a cross between a haphazard garage sale and an episode from a TV show about a hoarder. Fortunately, a lot of people had shown up, and Tammy's best friend efficiently assigned people to specific tasks. While Jeff worked in the garage, Amy went to a child's bedroom.

Darla Connor was six years old and similar to her mother. A small child's opinion about what's valuable isn't logical, so Amy didn't try to separate junk from treasures. She treated everything except obvious trash as a keepsake, divided the items by type, placed them in boxes, taped them shut, and wrote a detailed description on top. Amy especially enjoyed folding the little-girl clothes. The years when she'd been able to treat Megan as a doll had been a lot of fun. Amy was getting close to finishing the room when Tammy and Darla came in.

"Darla can't find her bunny," Tammy said. "I know she had him this morning because she always sleeps with him. Normally, she leaves him alone during the day except at nap time, but all this activity is making her feel insecure."

Darla had a sad expression on her face. Amy, who was on her knees sorting through shoes, stood up.

"I know exactly where he is."

She went over to a stack of boxes in the corner of the room and found the third box down. On the top, she'd written *Darla's stuffed animals.* Tearing off the tape, she opened the box and took out a well-worn grayish rabbit with long, floppy ears. As soon as she saw the rabbit, Darla's eyes lit up. Amy handed the bunny to her.

"Hold him for a few minutes, and then we're going to put him in the car so he doesn't get lost during the long drive," Tammy said to the little girl.

Darla ran out of the room.

"Thanks, Amy, you're a lifesaver. We lost Bunny last week. It was a rough couple of days until we found him hiding behind the potato chips in the pantry."

"Darla is cute," Amy replied. "I look forward to keeping up with her through your photos online."

"Hey, I saw the pictures from the party Megan went to last night. That was the biggest pizza I've ever seen. They must have cooked it in sections."

"I'd like to see them. Who posted the photos?"

"Patty Springsteed. Her son David went to the party. Are you friends with her online?"

"No. What was Megan doing in the picture?"

"Being silly. David had his arm around her and another girl. If my computer wasn't already packed away, I'd show you."

"Oh, that's okay. You have plenty to do."

Twenty-Nine

The Connor family ordered multiple pizzas to feed the volunteers. When the food arrived, Amy excused herself and drove to Natalie's house. The contrast between the chaos at the Connor house and the serene organization of Natalie's home couldn't have been more dramatic. Natalie had fixed mini club sandwiches with different kinds of meat.

"Where are Luke and the boys?" Amy asked after she'd washed up and settled into Natalie's kitchen with a cup of hot tea in front of her.

"Out for a couple of hours getting something to eat and then going to the new park on Westover Drive."

"This is so much better than pizza with grease running off the top," Amy said after she ate a tiny sandwich in three bites. "I'm hungry."

"How are things going with Megan?" Natalie asked.

Amy decided it was time to tell her friend

about her concerns. That took the rest of the meal.

"Maybe we should pray for her time with Mr. Ryan right now," Natalie said when Amy mentioned enlisting the teacher as an ally.

Amy glanced at her watch. "Okay. They should be finished by now."

"Unless they're really having a good talk."

Natalie offered up a heartfelt prayer that perfectly mirrored what Amy hoped would happen.

When she finished, all Amy added was "Amen."

"If you write as well as you pray, your book isn't going to need much editing," Amy said.

"Are you ready to see it?" Natalie asked, her eyes lighting up.

"Yes."

"Do you want to see the illustrations first or read the text?"

It was a question Amy hadn't thought about. She hesitated.

"Let me see the pictures. If they tell the story well enough, the words aren't going to be as important. Where should we sit?"

"Right here is fine." Natalie hurriedly left the table.

Almost every time she sat in Natalie's kitchen, Amy saw something that gave her an idea for her own home. A new napkin holder that turned a routine object with a mundane purpose into an artistic piece caught her eye.

Natalie returned with a large leather portfolio. Beige-colored papers peeked out from its sides.

"This is exciting and scary at the same time," she said. "And you're my friend. I can't imagine what it's like to show something you've created to a total stranger."

"Much worse."

Natalie laid the portfolio on the table. She lifted one corner of the folder and slid out a single sheet of paper.

"This is my concept for the cover."

It was a beach scene with a house in the background and three children running along the top of a sand dune toward the ocean. It was a windy day, and the sea grass bowed before the breeze. The two older children were boys. The youngest was a girl whose long blond hair trailed along behind her. In the children's hands were buckets and nets. The boys were in shorts and shirts, and the girl was wearing a blue and yellow dress.

"I love it," Amy said simply. "And not just because I'd like to hang it on the wall."

"Why?"

"I love that you don't show the children's faces. Often it's best to ease into the characters and setting and give the reader's imagination a chance to kick in. That way they own the story, too. And your images are so generic that children who read the book can see themselves in the picture."

"That's good?"
"Yes."
"Yea!" Natalie responded.
Amy smiled. "I assume that's what you intended. How much physical detail do you give later?"
"Some, but the children remain images, not portraits. Watercolors allow soft edges. I tried not to cross the line of artistic ambiguity."
"Okay. And I like that they're wearing regular clothes. Children who spend a few days at the beach aren't in bathing suits every chance they get. Those who stay for weeks or months dress more like they do at home."
"Is it okay for the little girl to wear a dress?"
"Yes, especially for the cover. Also, it tells me she likes to think for herself."
"Yea again."
"Let me see another one."
One by one, Natalie brought out the paintings. Not only were they beautiful to look at, they told a visual story.
"I get it," Amy said after she saw the final image, a sunset similar to the cover, only from the perspective of the beach looking inland. "I especially love the pictures where the children are building the imaginary pirate boat from driftwood, and Sarah's encounter with the jellyfish."
"That makes me feel great." Natalie paused. "Now, the part I'm nervous and not excited about — the text."

"Don't be."

Natalie pulled a thin stack of papers from the portfolio. "I'm going to leave the room and clean the toilet in the boys' bathroom while you read it. I know you can't tell me everything that needs to be fixed on a first reading, but I'd at least like your impressions. There are pencil sketches of the illustrations on the pages where I think the words should appear."

"Are you really going to clean the boys' toilet?"

"Or find something to do. If you hear me pacing back and forth upstairs, try to ignore it."

Natalie left the kitchen. Amy picked up the pages. She knew her friend's anxiety was misplaced.

Until she read the first page.

The lighthearted serendipity of the paintings never made the leap to the printed words. Some sentences were stiff. Others were way too long for a children's book. Worst of all, the words didn't open a window to the innocent imaginations of the children that were the heart of the story. Amy started reading faster, hoping the writing would improve. But it didn't. She found only a handful of phrases that vibrated with vitality. She took a pen from her purse and put a star beside each one.

Amy could hear Natalie's footsteps as she

walked up and down the hallway on the second floor. Not sure what to do, she read the story again. It didn't improve the second time, but Amy's lowered expectations helped her appreciate the effort Natalie put into it. She put down the final page and looked again at the wonderful paintings. When she looked up, Natalie was standing in the doorway.

"I didn't hear you come downstairs," she said.

Natalie held up her shoes in her right hand. "I crept down quieter than Noah stealing an after-bedtime cookie."

It was the kind of sentence Amy had hoped to see a lot more of in the story but didn't.

"How bad is it?" Natalie continued.

"It has its moments," Amy responded, and immediately regretted her choice of words.

"But there aren't many of them." Natalie finished the thought before Amy could continue.

"I marked some of the sentences that really sing," Amy said, trying to keep a positive expression on her face. "But overall, I think it needs work."

Natalie stepped forward and slumped down at the table.

"Can you fix it?" she asked with a forlorn look on her face.

"It's a different genre. But I'm sure I can toss out a few ideas that might help."

"Anything you can do would be awesome.

Did anything come to you as you were reading?"

"Yes." Amy nodded. "Every time I looked at one of the paintings, it sparked an idea. The visual message is there. All that's lacking is to sync up what you've created using watercolors with the words on the page. In an illustrated book, less can be more. It's common for the narrative to be very sparse for several pages, then the writer tosses in two or three paragraphs that fill in the blanks and add texture to what the reader's mind has already visualized with the images."

"I read a bunch of children's books but never noticed that," Natalie replied.

"And it's necessary to resist the urge to explain everything. Make the reader, even a child, work a bit to follow the story. Overstating things slowed me down more than anything else. For example, building the pirate ship needs very little explanation once the children get started. You show it happening. The words come in when the kids are in their places, and Peter hoists the flag made out of their father's old Hawaiian-print shirt. That's the point where you show the children's imaginations in action. One of the best lines is at the end of that scene when you encourage readers to tell their own pirate story. It will segue into a nice discussion between parent and child."

"I tossed that in as an afterthought."

"It was a good one."

Natalie rested her elbows on the table.

"I'm overwhelmed," she said.

"Don't be. Here's what we'll do," Amy said. "Make copies of the paintings on a color copier. I wouldn't be able to sleep at night if the originals were at my house. And I'll take the text and begin to play around with it."

"What about your own book?"

"I can do this during my lunch break at work. And this will be a fun diversion at home that will perk me up when I need a break from my novel. Your book isn't the sort of thing that warrants several hours of writing at a sitting. Short spells may actually be better."

"And you'll take credit for the story."

"Maybe. It depends on how many of my changes make it into the final version."

"I know they will."

Amy smiled. "That means we'll split the million dollars received in royalties fifty-fifty. We could use the money to go in together and buy a fabulous house at the beach. Your family can use it for two weeks, then we'll come down for a joint week, followed by two weeks on our own."

"I like that idea." Natalie perked up. "And it's only right that it would be the beach since a beach story made it possible in the first place."

■ ■ ■ ■

Driving home, Amy hoped Natalie's light-hearted comments at the end of their conversation didn't give way to tears as soon as her friend was alone. Insecurity crouched on every writer's shoulder. Amy knew its condemning voice well.

When she pulled up to the house, Jeff hadn't returned yet. Amy went inside. There was no sign of Megan, either. She went upstairs. The door to Megan's room was closed. Amy turned the knob and pushed it open. Megan was lying on the bed, fast asleep.

"Megan!" Amy said. "Wake up!"

Megan rolled over and barely opened one of her eyes for a second, then closed it again. Amy shook her.

"Wake up! What did you take that made you fall asleep?"

"Take?" Megan mumbled. "Take what?"

"That's what I'm asking you!" Amy repeated in a loud voice.

Megan rubbed her eyes and opened them. It looked like she was having trouble focusing.

"Tell me what you've done, or I'm going to take you to the hospital."

Megan unsteadily forced herself to sit up.

"I was sleepy," she said.

"No, you were unconscious, passed out.

What did you do, and where did you go after dance class?"

"Uh." Megan hesitated for several moments. "Mr. Ryan dropped off Molly at her house, then we went to get a burger and shake for lunch." Megan yawned. "There were a bunch of people there who'd been at the school working on decorations for the prom."

"Who?"

"I'm not sure."

"Did you know any of them?"

Megan brushed her hair out of her face and yawned again.

"They were mostly juniors and seniors."

"Was David Springsteed there?"

"No, why are you asking about him?"

"Who did you talk to?"

Megan opened her eyes wider. "I mostly watched and listened. They were more interested in Mr. Ryan than me."

Amy took a deep breath. "Did anyone give you anything?"

"Give me something? Like what?"

"A pill."

"You think I took some kind of drug that made me sleepy?" Megan asked incredulously.

"Why else would you pass out on a Saturday afternoon? This wasn't a normal nap. There's a reason why it was so hard for me to wake you up."

"You think I would take a pill that someone from school gave me?" Megan repeated, shaking her head in disbelief.

"What am I supposed to think? You've never answered my question."

Megan stared hard at Amy. There was now no doubt she was fully awake.

"I didn't take any pills and never would. I can't believe you think I'm that stupid."

"I didn't say you were stupid, but I know how peer pressure works, especially with older and younger high school students."

"Mom, you're crazy. Or what's the word? Paranoid."

Amy felt steam about to boil out of her ears. If Megan were Darla Connor's age, Amy would apply a paddle to her bottom. But you couldn't spank a teenager who just used the word *paranoid.*

"I was sleepy," Megan said, perhaps sensing she'd pushed her mother too hard.

"So what's your explanation? Was dance practice hard?"

"Not really. Maybe it's my hormones."

It was such an unexpected answer that Amy's jaw dropped. She was speechless.

"If I'm paranoid, I guess you have the right to blame your hormones," she managed. "That's always a woman's prerogative. But if this keeps up, I'm going to take you back to Dr. Simmons for more tests."

"Fine. I've not done anything wrong, and I

don't have anything to hide."

"I'm just trying to figure out why you're so sleepy."

"Then I wish you'd stick to things that don't involve accusing me of being a terrible person. Now that I'm awake, would you please leave me alone?"

The last thing Amy saw as she left the room was Megan picking up her cell phone to send a text. She started to ask her not to send any text messages about their conversation to her friends, but that was an unrealistic request. Teenage girls were going to talk. It was as much a part of their DNA as emerging hormones.

Amy went to her bedroom and closed the door. Taking out her own cell phone, she punched in the number for Greg Ryan.

"It's Amy Clarke," she said as soon as the teacher answered.

"Hey, Mrs. Clarke —"

"Call me Amy. We'll save the formalities for the school campus. I came home a few minutes ago and found Megan passed out in her room. It was almost identical to the other day. After I got her awake and talking, I asked her if she'd taken any kind of drug. She got offended and denied it. She mentioned you ran into a group of older students while you were eating lunch. What did you see? Who did she talk to? Was she ever out of your sight? What sort of condition was she in when you dropped her off at the house?"

"Let's back up a bit," the teacher said. "Yes, we went to Jackson's Shake Shop after I took Molly Prichard home. During the drive and when we first got to the restaurant, I asked Megan to give me a rundown on her friends. I already knew most of them, of course, but I wanted to find out if there was someone on the list who would be a red flag. Megan considers a lot of people friends."

"Yes, she's much more social than I ever was."

"I don't know all the kids at the school, and a couple of names came up that I wasn't sure about. Both of them were boys. One was Keith Nelson, and the other was Bruce Peabody."

"She's known both of them since they went to Broad Street Christian School together. I'm surprised Megan considers them friends. Bruce is so shy that he usually keeps to himself. That may be why he's unfamiliar to you. And Keith's mother tells me that he's more interested in video games than girls."

"That's true of a lot of boys at the high school."

"Was Keith at the burger place today?"

"No. That was a group of juniors and seniors who'd been at the school getting the gym ready for the prom tonight."

"Yeah, that's what Megan told me."

"And to answer your questions, Megan

didn't leave the booth where we were sitting except to go to the bathroom with a mob of other girls. I don't know what happened during that time. Other than that she was sitting across the table from me while students came by to chat. During the drive to your house, she mentioned she was going to take a nap because nobody was at home and the house would be quiet. I let her out and waited in the driveway until she went inside, then left."

"She didn't have any problem walking into the house?"

"None that I could tell. She looked normal to me."

"What time was that?"

"Oh, about one fifteen. We spent a little over an hour at lunch. I'm sorry there's not more to tell. I know you're concerned, but it may simply be that her body is craving sleep right now."

"Yeah. Megan mentioned hormones."

"I don't know much about that. I grew up in a family of boys."

THIRTY

By the time Jeff came home, Megan was sitting in her room listening to music, texting on her phone, and reading a book — all at the same time. Jeff listened to Amy's story.

"It sounds like she took your question about using drugs better than I expected," he said.

"How can you say that? We haven't talked since."

"She could have left the house without telling you where she was going."

When she was a little girl, Megan ran away from home twice. But like Hansel and Gretel, she left a series of breadcrumb clues that made the incidents more cute than scary.

"I didn't even think about that."

"If she was connected to a bad network of kids, that could have been one of her first responses. She would flee to her 'friends' for support. Sending Bethany a text message telling her how terrible you are is probably a good thing."

"I'm not sure that's what she did. And why would that be good?"

"Because if Megan is telling her best friend that she isn't using drugs, it's the most reliable evidence we have, short of a drug test, that she isn't doing anything wrong."

"Yeah, I can see that," Amy admitted. "But how am I going to repair the damage between us?"

"I don't know. Women are complicated when it comes to getting upset with each other and sorting it out. Guys are more direct."

"Are you trying to blame it on hormones?"

"No way," Jeff said. "I've been married long enough not to fall into that trap. But I'll make sure Megan knows that if I'd been here, I would have asked her the same questions. She needs to realize that you and I are in this together."

"That would make me feel better." Amy looked at the kitchen clock. "Any word from Ian?"

"Unless he has to make another trip to the hospital, he should be here in an hour and a half."

"Why would he need to go to the hospital?"

"Sorry. That was a lame attempt at male humor."

Ian arrived home an hour later with his cast intact and a headful of stories about his day in the woods. There were bits of leaves in his hair, and the knees of his jeans were dirty.

"When Bobby and me are twelve, Mr. Pickens is going to let us go deer hunting with him."

"Hunting?" Amy responded, so surprised by the news she didn't bother to correct his grammar.

"We won't have guns or anything, but we can sit in the tree stand with him and wait for the deer to come close enough for him to get a clean shot."

"What about all the other hunters?" Amy asked. "They might see you and think you're a deer."

Ian held his hands up to his head. "Mom, I don't have any antlers. And we'll wear orange camouflage coats and hats. That's what I want for Christmas next year. Did you know deer can't tell the difference between green camouflage and orange camouflage? Mr. Pickens told me deer see a lot better at night than people do, but they don't see colors the same as us. But he says the most important thing for a hunter is to 'be still and not smell.' "

"What about deodorant?" Jeff asked with a straight face.

"I don't think Mr. Pickens uses it when he goes hunting," Ian replied. "But he probably takes a shower as soon as he gets home."

"I'm sure Bobby's mom appreciates that," Amy said.

Megan's appearance at the top of the stairs interrupted Ian's explanation about deer hunting.

"Go upstairs and take a shower," Amy said to Ian. "You brought home part of the woods in your hair, and I want you to smell good to people, not animals."

Megan and Ian passed each other on the stairs. Megan came into the family room.

"Did Mom tell you what she said to me?" she asked Jeff.

"Yes, and I would have asked you the same questions if I'd been here."

"None of my friends can believe you are treating me like this." Megan's voice got louder. "What have I done to deserve this? And who else have you talked to about it? How am I going to face Grandma and Grandpa Clarke and Granny Edwards?"

"We've not said anything to them and don't intend to," Amy said. "Your dad and I are going to believe you told me the truth this afternoon."

"And the only reason this came up was because we can't figure out why you've been so sleepy in the middle of the afternoon," Jeff added. "You don't always show us the proper respect, but there's nothing about your overall behavior that's out of line. You're a serious student, participate in youth activities at church, and are dedicated to dance. All of those positives make the possibility of a big negative in your life seem out of place."

Megan looked at Amy, who nodded. "I don't know what you've told your friends, but after listening to you, I've accepted what you said."

"Really?" Megan asked.

"Yes," Jeff and Amy responded together.

"Okay," Megan replied with a sigh. "I mean, I'm glad you care about me. I don't want that to stop. But I also want to know that you trust me."

"We do," Amy replied.

"And even though we trust you, we'll continue to ask you questions if we think we should," Jeff said. "Also, if you have questions, I want you to know you can talk to either one of us. Okay?"

"What kind of questions?"

"Anything." Jeff paused. "Although if it has to do with hormones, you should probably talk to your mom."

Supper was as close to normal as possible given the afternoon and evening discussions with Megan. Ian was so caught up with his day in the woods that he didn't notice any remaining tension between his parents and sister.

"Bethany invited me to come over to her house and hang out for a few hours tonight," Megan said as she took her plate to the sink. "Is that okay? Her mom is going to pick me up and bring me home."

Jeff glanced at Amy.

"Sure," Amy replied. "But there's no need for her mother to make two trips. I'll take you, and she can bring you home. How late will you be?"

"Maybe eleven or so. It will just be the two of us. Alecia can't make it."

Amy suspected the visit was set up by Bethany as an escape for Megan following her dramatic portrayal of the persecution she received at home. Amy and Megan left the house at 7:30 p.m. for the short drive to Bethany's house.

"I never got a chance to ask you how dance practice went this morning," Amy said as she backed the car down the driveway.

"It was good." Megan paused. "Except Molly was trying to show off for Mr. Ryan. When I was onstage she was sitting with him talking his ear off. Everyone knows she has a secret crush on him."

"Does he know it?"

"Probably, but he's cool about it." Megan turned sideways in her seat. "Dad said I can ask you any questions I want to. Is that really true?"

"Yes," Amy said, offering up a quick prayer for divine wisdom.

"Would you let Ian shoot a deer? He thinks it would be like something in a video game, but it wouldn't. It's a living creature with real blood in its veins. Crystal told me that after a deer is killed, the hunters have to cut out its guts and drag it from the woods. I can't imagine Ian doing something like that."

Amy kept a tight grip on the steering wheel.

"Ian didn't say anything about him killing a deer. Bobby's father invited him to come along on a hunt."

"And watch Bobby's dad kill a deer?"

"Yes."

Megan shook her head. "If Ian thinks it's okay to shoot a deer now, you're going to have a hard time telling him no later. You have to manage his expectations."

"I'll keep that in mind. Your dad will probably handle that one."

Megan faced forward. Amy relaxed.

"Has Dad ever killed a deer?" Megan asked.

"Uh, he had a great-uncle who took him and your grandpa Clarke deer hunting several times in South Carolina. That was a long time ago."

"Did Dad kill one?"

"I think he did. You can ask him about it if you want to know the details."

"Why would I want to know more about something gross like that?"

Amy didn't answer. They arrived at Bethany's house.

"Thanks for driving me," Megan said as she hopped out of the car. "I needed a night out."

"Sure," Amy said as she watched the confusing, complex bundle of humanity she knew as her daughter run up to the front door.

At home Amy went up to the writing room. The tension with Megan was hard, but it was perfect preparation for writing about conflict between Roxanne and her niece. Amy hadn't planned on a scene involving the niece as next in line, but when she introduced the idea, the characters took off with it. As she typed, Amy came face-to-face with the niece's feelings in a way she'd tried to avoid with Megan.

Amy tried not to be an overly self-protective parent, but it was tough not to hunker down in a defensive shell. In the novel, Roxanne and her niece ended up in a yelling match followed by a grudging ceasefire. Amy was careful not to let their reconciliation go too far. There had to be the seeds for future problems. Just as in real life.

Megan was home before 11:00 p.m. Amy heard her moving around in her bedroom and went down to see her.

"How was your time with Bethany?" Amy asked.

Megan let out a big yawn.

"Good, but I was ready to come home and go to bed. I'm really sleepy —" Megan's eyes suddenly opened wider, and she started speaking faster. "But there's no reason for it except I'd like to go to bed. The only thing I had at Bethany's house was a bowl of ice cream while we watched a movie. You can call her mom."

"It's okay. Good night."

Amy wasn't ready to go to sleep when Jeff turned off the light and rolled over. She lay on her back with her eyes open. Her concern about Megan, the issue at the office with Dr. Ramsey, how to fix Natalie's book, and lingering uncertainty about *Deeds of Darkness* ricocheted around in her head even though no answers could be found there. After forcing herself to breathe slowly and commanding the muscles in her arms and legs to relax, she drifted off to sleep.

In the middle of the night she went to the living room. None of the matters troubling her mind were addressed in her dream. Instead, something completely unexpected shot through her unconsciousness.

And it had to do with Mildred Burris.

The following morning at church, Amy kept turning over in her mind what she'd seen in the night. If she wasn't one hundred percent convinced of Ms. Burris's godliness, it would be easy to assign the worst of motives to the elderly woman. But even good people have flaws. The purest marble looks less pristine under a microscope. Amy squirmed in the pew. Jeff nudged her with his arm.

"Is Reverend Harbough getting to you?" he whispered. "I wouldn't think a sermon about the parable of the sheep and the goats would be a problem for you. You're one of the wooliest lambs I know."

"Quiet. It's something else I'm trying to sort out."

At the end of the sermon, the minister prayed for the congregation. Amy offered up one of her own. She desperately needed discernment on how to properly interpret what she'd seen and know what to do about it.

After the service, Natalie came over to her in the church parking lot and handed her a large envelope.

"Luke ran off color copies of the book illustrations for you. I'm not trying to be pushy, but have you had a chance to read it again?"

"No, but I will this afternoon. I need something light and happy to focus on."

"What's wrong?"

Amy glanced over her shoulder. Megan was out of hearing range with a group of her friends.

"More drama with Megan, but I think we're making progress with her." Amy paused. "But I saw something in a dream last night that's really troubling me."

"About your family?"

"No, it had to do with Mildred Burris."

"What?" Natalie's eyebrows shot up.

"I can't say, but I'd really appreciate it if you'd pray that I'd know what to do. It relates to a situation at the office."

"Is she in some kind of legal trouble?"

"Not yet, but this could have serious legal consequences for her. I hate to bring something up if it's not true, or if I'm not interpreting what I saw correctly."

"Shouldn't you talk to her first? That's what the Bible tells us to do."

Amy shook her head. "There's the Bible, and there's Mr. Phillips. And I don't have anything personal against Ms. Burris. It has to do with what she did to someone else. Anyway, please pray for me, even though I can't give you details."

"Sure."

The heaviness Amy felt about Ms. Burris was a weight on her soul as she climbed the steps to the writing room. It took every ounce of writer's discipline to push aside her anxiety and work on Natalie's idyllic summer tale. The story needed to reflect, not detract from, the beautiful watercolors. Two hours later she'd revised almost half the book. Amy laid out the new text beneath the applicable illustrations. The story now flowed, which gave her hope. She sent Natalie a brief, encouraging text message.

Going downstairs, Amy's thoughts returned to Ms. Burris and her dream.

Jeff was working on their lawn mower in the garage. "The grass will start growing in a few weeks," he said. "And I want to squeeze at least one more cutting season out of this old mower."

"I've been thinking about work, too," Amy said. "I'm going to run down to the office for a few minutes."

Jeff looked up in surprise.

"Did Mr. Phillips call you?"

"No."

"Is there something you have to finish typing before he comes in on Monday?"

"No, it has to do with what had me agitated in church. There's a file I need to look at."

"Have you made a mistake?"

"No. I wish I could tell you about it, but you know I can't."

Amy grabbed her purse from the kitchen. There was a chance one of the lawyers would be at the office if he had a trial or hearing scheduled for Monday morning. The legal profession didn't recognize a day of rest. However, when Amy pulled around to the back of the office, there weren't any cars in the parking area.

She went upstairs to the filing cabinets in the hallway outside Chris's office. The old floors of the second story creaked beneath her feet. The Dominick file already filled an entire drawer. Amy wasn't sure exactly what she was looking for. It took three trips to haul all the documents to a small conference room near Chris's office.

She found the folder that contained a copy of the will signed by Sanford Dominick shortly before his death. She'd read the will before but did so again in case something new jumped out at her. The document wasn't as detailed as the one Mr. Phillips drafted, but to her eye it met the basic requirements of a valid estate plan, assuming of course that Mr. Dominick was mentally competent and knew what he was doing when he signed it. There were three witnesses: a woman named Kathy Roberts, another named Thalia Botts, and a third signature that was illegible.

She flipped through several more folders but found nothing relevant to her search. She opened the file that included basic information filed with the clerk's office requesting probate of the will prepared by Mr. Phillips. One of the documents in the file was the death certificate. At the top, it set out Mr. Dominick's personal information. In the middle it listed the cause of death as "pneumonia," which Amy knew was a commonly stated reason. A dying person might have many illnesses, but the filling of the lungs with fluid was often the immediate cause of death. Beneath "pneumonia" was the typed name of the physician who signed the certificate. When she saw the name, Amy gasped.

It was Dr. Lawrence Kelly.

The doctor's signature on the death certificate looked similar to that of the unidentified witness on the will. Amy placed the will beside the death certificate. There was no doubt about the signatures. Dr. Kelly was a witness to the will.

Amy sat back in the chair. She'd come to the office to try to connect two dots. She'd ended up adding another one. She took the death certificate and the will to the upstairs copy room. She could always get the information from the filing cabinet, but she wanted to have copies at her desk. While she waited for the copy machine to warm up, she stared again at the death certificate. Sanford Dominick was a sick old man about to die. But the timing of his death needed to be in the hands of God, not another human being.

After making her copies, she returned everything to the filing cabinet and went downstairs to her office. It was a few minutes before she needed to go home and fix supper, and there was at least one piece of unfinished business she needed to attend to. Logging on to her computer, she accessed the personal information database and entered Lawrence Kelly along with his address and occupation. The doctor was a board-certified internist in his midthirties with a solo practice in a small town about twenty-five miles from Cross Plains. Nothing about his educational or professional training caught her eye as unusual, which wasn't surprising. He was married with two small children. The database didn't provide a clue why Dr. Kelly became involved in the care of Sanford Dominick. Amy printed off everything she found and placed it with her copy of the death certificate and will.

She was about to sign out of the database when she decided to check one more thing. She entered the information she had for Beverly Jackson, the nurse who cared for Mr. Dominick. She received her training at East Carolina medical school. Her employment history appeared on the second page of data. Halfway down the screen, Amy found an unexpected connection. Beverly Jackson formerly worked for Dr. Kelly.

She'd been a nurse in his office before going to work for Sanford Dominick. Ms. Burris could have connected both the nurse and the doctor with Mr. Dominick. Her dream was starting to make sense. Amy logged out of the program.

The following morning Amy was nervous as she drove to work. She'd lain in bed for more than an hour trying to decide what she should do. Her first dilemma was whether to talk to Mr. Phillips or Chris Lance. Going directly to the senior partner made sense from the standpoint of authority and ability to act, but they'd discussed her dreams in only one conversation, and she wasn't sure what he really thought about them. With Chris she had a credible, though rocky, track record. And if she was off base, it was much better to fail with Chris than in front of the senior partner. Shortly after she turned on her computer and before she made up her mind, she received a call on her cell phone. It was Bernie Masters.

"Most agents are still groping for the coffeepot at this time of the morning," he said when Amy answered. "But yours is working day and night to get you the best publishing contract in America."

"I appreciate that," Amy replied.

"I almost called this weekend, but I had to wait for a confirming e-mail that popped up on my computer a couple of minutes ago. It looks like we have an auction on our hands. Two New York publishers want to bid for your services. An acquisitions editor named Kate Heigel got back to me late last week and tripped over her toes apologizing for not letting me know that she's convinced you have a chance to be the next big thing. It seems she misplaced my query and didn't find it until her dog knocked a stack of papers off her desk. Once she read your synopsis and sample chapters for *Evil Deeds of Darkness,* she immediately downloaded your first novel and read it in one sitting."

"The title for the new novel is *Deeds of Darkness,* and unless the editor is a speed-reader, it would be impossible to finish *A Great and Precious Promise* so quickly."

"Right, but remember these people are pros. They can absorb a book like a sponge picks up water. And when the editor squeezed it out, she saw flecks of gold in it."

Even for Bernie it was a convoluted comparison.

"And you think she's serious about a contract?"

"Oh yeah. And when I told her who else was in the running, she tossed down the gauntlet. Believe me, when this lady wants something, she gets it. I don't know the limit of her authority, but it's probably in the low six figures before she has to go to a committee."

Bernie rattled off the names of several famous authors the editor had acquired over the years.

"And that doesn't include the rough-cut diamonds she's dug out of the mud."

"Is that what I'll be?"

"You bet, and I'll be proud to hold you up so anyone can see the facets of your genius waiting to be cut and polished by someone who really knows what they're doing."

"What happens next?"

"In the old days, you'd be getting on a plane to New York, but it's a new world order. Both of the editors want to interview you via video conference, and then we'll set a day for the bidding."

"Will you be on the phone calls?"

"Of course, and on the day of the auction, you and I will have a private line open so we can discuss the offers before responding. You're going to love it. It's one of my favorite things to do. You don't gamble, do you?"

"No."

"Well, for you this will be ten times the rush of splitting kings and doubling down at a high-stakes blackjack table in Vegas."

Amy wasn't sure what Bernie meant and didn't care to find out.

"What are they going to ask me in the interviews?"

"The usual stuff about your work habits, plot and character development, ideas for future projects."

"I don't have any ideas for future projects. I'm still at the beginning stages of *Deeds of Darkness.*"

"It doesn't really matter whether you toss out an idea that has a snowball's chance of ever being written or not. They just want to make sure you have a fertile imagination. Jot down a couple of three-sentence pitches. You know, boy and girl grow up together as friends in their small-town neighborhood, then secretly fall in love as teenagers but never tell each other because they think the other person would think it was weird. Later, their paths cross as adults, but they're already in relationships. The book is about getting a second chance to fall in love; however, they've changed so much as grown-ups the reader isn't sure it's going to work out, or should work out."

"That's not a bad idea."

"Yeah, another one of my clients is writing that book as we speak. She doesn't have your moral sensibilities, so it's not going to be next to your novels on the bookstore shelf. But you could take the same basic plotline, and by the time it came out the meat grinder of your imagination, no one would recognize it was from the same cut of meat."

Amy hesitated. "I wouldn't be comfortable doing that."

"Borrowing isn't the same thing as stealing, but it's not important," Bernie said, then paused. "Tell you what. I'll ask an editor buddy who doesn't work for either one of these companies to send me a list of sample questions that he'd ask so you can at least get a feel for what to expect."

"That would be great."

"You got it. Now, get to work so you can make it to quitting time at the law office and go home to your real job."

After the call ended Amy tried to let her

excitement at the interest from two big publishers in her writing overcome her fear of what lay ahead at the law office.

As soon as she organized everything for Mr. Phillips's arrival, she buzzed Janelle.

"Has Chris Lance come in yet?" she asked.

"He came by my desk two minutes ago on his way upstairs."

"Thanks."

Amy pressed her lips together for a few moments. She resolutely stepped into the hallway that led to the stairs.

Thirty-One

Chris wasn't in his office when Amy looked inside.

"What do you want?" a male voice immediately behind her asked in a commanding voice.

Amy jumped. It was Chris.

"Why do you keep sneaking up on me like that?" she asked.

"I wanted to make sure if you were about to steal something from my office I would catch you in the act." Chris grinned.

"You sure came into work in a good mood."

"Why shouldn't I be in a good mood?" Chris beamed. "I'm going to be a father!"

"Wow. Congratulations. Is Laura thrilled?"

"Over the top. She thought she might be pregnant when all the stuff happened with the Westside Lighting case. That made it even tougher on me."

"I'm sorry."

"Why do you want to see me? Did you see me holding a baby boy in a dream?"

"No, but I do want to talk to you about a dream."

They stepped into Chris's office. Amy pushed the door closed until it almost shut, then sat down.

"It has to do with the Dominick estate," she said.

Chris snapped his fingers. "Let me guess. Sanford Dominick isn't dead. He's living at Graceland where he and Elvis have started a garage band."

"No, Chris, this is serious."

"All right. I'm listening."

Amy took a deep breath.

"You need to find out if there is any connection between Mr. Dominick's death and the woman who was taking care of him at the time."

"The home health-care nurse?"

"Yes, Beverly Jackson." Amy paused. "And Dr. Lawrence Kelly, the doctor who signed the death certificate."

Chris sat up straighter in his chair.

"Are you accusing them of killing Dominick?"

"I'm not sure. I don't know."

Chris leaned forward. "Was anyone else in the dream?"

"Yes," Amy replied with a sigh. "Mildred Burris."

"What? Isn't she your spiritual guru?"

"I wouldn't use that term, but she's encouraged me in my faith."

"This is really crazy." Chris shook his head from side to side. "Start with the dream and tell me everything you remember, exactly as you saw it."

For a reason she didn't understand, Amy felt a serious check about providing Chris any details.

"I want to keep the dream part private, okay?" she said. "Its only purpose is to get you to investigate."

"I have to have a factual basis to accuse people of murder."

"I'm not saying it was murder."

"Then what are you saying?" Chris asked with obvious exasperation.

"That your job is to find ways to challenge the validity of the will that cuts Natasha Dominick out of most of the estate. Mr. Phillips mentioned that the treating neurologist will testify that Mr. Dominick wasn't mentally competent at the time —"

"Or maybe he won't. This is so strange that you bring this up. I interviewed Dr. Robinson on Friday, and he is a bit shaky on the key points. He says Dominick was in and out of lucidity up to the end. If someone caught him on a good day, Dominick might have the capacity to understand what he was doing. However, most of his days were bad, and he might not recognize someone he'd known for years."

"Which makes what I'm suggesting even more important. Look, I think Natasha is a gold digger, but that doesn't mean she should lose out based on a will that should not be accepted for probate."

"I'm tracking with you on that. But what in your dream made you think that isn't going to happen?"

Chris was circling back for another try. Amy licked her lips.

"Are you willing to ask Nurse Jackson and Dr. Kelly questions about the circumstances surrounding Mr. Dominick's death?"

"Of course, but if I don't have any idea what I'm trying to uncover, it's going to be a very short deposition."

Amy spoke slowly. "Do you know the cause of death listed on the death certificate?"

"Yeah, pneumonia."

"What if it should be asphyxiation?"

Now that she'd said the word, Amy felt worse, not better.

"You believe the nurse and the doctor smothered Dominick?"

"Maybe."

"And Ms. Burris was there, too?"

"In the dream they were in a room in Ms. Burris's house, and she was watching. Whether she was really there when it happened, I don't know. I can't believe she was."

Chris's eyes were wide open.

"What did they do? Put a pillow over his face?"

"No, it was something big and black and square. I'm not sure exactly. Mr. Dominick seemed to be struggling for a few seconds, and then he went completely still. At that point everyone in the room seemed happy about what had happened."

"That is incredibly creepy."

"Are you taking this seriously?"

"Yeah, but I feel like slapping myself to make sure I'm not dreaming right now." Chris popped himself on the cheek. "I'm awake."

Amy regretted saying anything to Chris, but she also knew having the same conversation with Mr. Phillips would have been even more awkward.

"That's it," she said, standing up. "I've got other work to do."

"Sure, and I'll try to figure out how to bring this up when I depose Nurse Jackson, Dr. Kelly, and Ms. Burris. Actually, Mr. Phillips told me if we depose Ms. Burris, he's going to handle it." Chris paused. "Is there anything you're not telling me?"

"No, that's all."

"Okay. If you remember anything else, let me know. I mean it." Chris tapped his fingers together in front of him as he thought. "But even if what you saw is true, getting someone to admit they smothered an old man is a long shot. That sort of thing only happens on low-budget TV shows."

"If you have to exhume the body because of other claims against the estate, maybe a forensic doctor could take a second look at the cause of death. That would give you reason to ask your questions."

"Yeah." Chris nodded, then looked at Amy. "Have you thought about putting something like this in one of your books? It might make for interesting reading."

Amy had heard enough. She turned toward the door and walked out.

"Hey, it's just a question," Chris called after her. "Thanks for stopping by."

Amy ignored him and continued toward the staircase. The verse about casting your pearls before swine came to her mind. But what else was she supposed to do? Based on her previous experiences, keeping quiet wasn't an option.

Chris's cavalier attitude made it tougher for Amy to know what to say about Dr. Ramsey, the geologist. In that situation, the only person she could talk to would be Mr. Phillips.

She left the office during her lunch break and drove to the park so she could eat a sandwich. To get her mind on something else, she took along Natalie's story. It was warm outside, and she sat on a bench at the edge of a grassy area where people brought their dogs for a walk. She took a bite of her sandwich. A man walked by with a forlorn-looking basset hound on a leash. The dog's face reflected Amy's mood.

Amy started at the beginning and read to the place where she'd stopped working. She made a few minor tweaks to what she'd already revised. With her sandwich in one hand and a red pen in the other, she continued with the story. The red pen got a good workout striking through entire sentences and shortening others considerably. Striving for maximum efficiency, she found her voice for the story. A crisper style would open up the narrative to younger readers, and simple elegance would appeal to older readers and grown-ups. During the twenty minutes she sat on the bench, she accomplished more than she would have thought possible. She slipped the pages and illustrations into a large envelope and returned to her car.

Back at the office, Chris had prepared notices to take the depositions of Beverly Jackson and Dr. Lawrence Kelly and laid them on her desk for mailing. On top, he'd left a Post-it note: *I did take you seriously. I'll ask Mr. Phillips to schedule Mildred Burris's deposition.*

The ball was now rolling. Amy wasn't glad about it, but in her heart she knew the circumstances of Mr. Dominick's death had to be confronted. Whether the truth would come out was beyond the scope of her dream. She knew God rarely showed the whole journey at once. Walking in the light was a one-step-at-a-time process.

The doctor's appointment for the removal of Ian's cast was scheduled for later in the afternoon. Amy wanted to get her concerns about Dr. Ramsey out in the open, but Mr. Phillips was out of the office. As she was leaving to pick up Ian from after-school care, her cell phone rang. It was Bernie.

"I know," Bernie said as soon as she pressed the Receive button. "You don't have to say it. Two phone calls from me in the same day is a record. But this news can't wait."

"What is it?"

"I've never seen acquisitions editors chomping at the bit like these two women in New York. You'd think they hadn't eaten in a week, and you were a big, juicy steak. They want to talk to you tomorrow. They couldn't agree on which one would go first, so I suggested that I flip a coin to decide. I didn't let them know I decided while the coin was in my pocket."

"What did you do?"

"Set the order the way I wanted to. Lynn Colville, the more aggressive editor, needs to go second. Knowing someone else has already had the chance to sway you will make her cut to the chase and put on the hard sell."

"But we won't be talking about money

tomorrow. This is the get-acquainted meeting."

"That's a delicate way to put it. By 'hard sell,' I mean each editor will try to convince you their company is the one to launch you into the bookselling stratosphere. They have big enough egos to believe what you think about them is important."

"It is, isn't it? I loved working with Cecilia."

"Then consider tomorrow a form of speed dating. However, the goal isn't to find true love."

Confused, Amy asked, "What is the goal?"

"Amy, publishers are like pawnshops. You don't pick a pawnshop based on the color of the shirt the guy behind the counter is wearing. You go with the one that offers you the best deal for what you have. This is the same. Both of these women are likely to pass you off to an associate editor for the nuts-and-bolts stuff of massaging a manuscript. Don't get me wrong. They'll keep an eye on the process. But their strength is recognizing talent and getting the horse into the company's stable."

Each phone call from Bernie was turning into an educational experience.

"Are you going to have time to send me potential questions from your editor friend?"

"Where are you now?"

"On the way to the doctor."

"You're not sick, are you?"

"No, Ian is getting the cast off his left arm. He broke it a few weeks ago riding a four-wheeler."

"Sometimes I forget you live out in the country."

To Bernie, Cross Plains was a rural area.

"The questions will be in your in-box as soon as you get home along with the schedule for the phone calls."

"I have to work tomorrow."

"Not from noon until three. Are you going to take the calls at the office or from home?"

"At the office, if it's okay with my boss. I had to leave early today for Ian's appointment. Mr. Phillips is going to question my priorities if I want to cut the middle out of my workday."

"He won't tell you no. The guy knows how good you are and won't do anything to upset you and rock the boat. We have to strike while the iron is hot. Bye."

Amy wondered how Bernie could be so sure of Mr. Phillips's response. She pulled into the parking lot for the after-school program.

Ian enthusiastically went through the procedure of getting his arm out of the cast.

"How long should we limit his activities?" Amy asked Dr. Fletchall.

"Normal use is fine. In fact, I encourage that. But I'm assuming Ian's definition of normal would be extreme in some dictionaries."

"Exactly."

"No jumping from the top of high buildings and no contact sports for another two to three weeks."

"It's okay, Mom," Ian replied. "Baseball practice won't start until next month. And baseball is safe."

"But they use a hard ball," Amy replied.

"He'll be fine by then. Just use a glove, not your arm to catch."

Ian kept rubbing his arm as they got in the car.

"It feels weird," he said.

"Does it hurt?"

"No, just kind of itchy."

The visit to the doctor's office had gone quicker than Amy expected. She glanced at her watch.

"Do you want to buy your dad's birthday present?" she asked Ian. "We have a few extra minutes."

"Is it this Saturday?"

"Yes."

"Has Megan already got him something?"

"No, but I can take you by yourself."

"What does he want? He likes that thing I gave him at Christmas for his truck."

"The AC/DC adapter. He uses it every day at work."

Amy backed out of the parking lot for the

doctor's office.

"He needs a new shirt," she said.

"Clothes?" Ian responded with disgust.

"Just because you don't like to get clothes as a present doesn't mean it's not a good gift for your father. He hates shopping so much that he appreciates someone doing it for him."

"Okay," Ian said.

There was a local men's clothing store where Amy shopped for Jeff when she wanted to buy him something special. It was in a storefront not far from the courthouse. Customer loyalty, low rent on the building, and an expert tailor who could handcraft suits for lawyers, bankers, and businessmen had kept the store in business. The front door chimed when they entered. A collection of expensive shoes lined one wall and the store smelled faintly of fine leather. A salesclerk came up to them.

"May I help you?" he asked.

Amy told him what they were looking for and Jeff's shirt size. Ian stood beside Amy shifting his weight from one foot to the other while she examined the shirts. She pulled one from the stack.

"What do you think of this blue one?" she asked Ian.

"It's okay, I guess." Ian paused. "But does it look kind of girly?"

"There's nothing girly about your dad. He

could wear pink and get away with it."

"I don't think he'd like that." Ian shook his head doubtfully.

"We'll take this one." Amy handed the shirt to the clerk.

On the way to the cash register they passed men's accessories. Amy saw the belts.

"My husband also needs a new brown belt," she said to the clerk.

The clerk led them over to a hanging display. "This particular brand is on sale this week. It's good quality and a reasonable price."

Amy found Jeff's size. On a counter beside the belts were other accessories. Amy saw several sets of cuff links. She picked up one.

"I saw an old set exactly like this one the other day," she said. "They belonged to the grandfather of one of my daughter's teachers."

"Then they weren't exactly like these," the clerk replied. "There are new cuff-link designs coming out all the time. We got these in last year. They've been a big seller."

"Huh," Amy grunted. She looked at the place where initials could be engraved on the cuff links. "My husband has never owned a monogrammed shirt. Ian, do you think your dad would like his initials monogrammed on his new shirt?"

"I guess so. His name is on his work shirts."

"This is different. How long would it take?"

Amy asked the clerk. "My husband's birthday is Saturday."

"No problem. I can have it ready by day after tomorrow."

"Let's do it."

Amy wrote Jeff's initials on a form the clerk pinned to the shirt. She paid for both items.

"Dad knows you buy the stuff I give him on his birthday and Christmas," Ian said. "But that doesn't make him appreciate it less."

Thirty-Two

Amy took a casserole from the freezer and put it in the oven before going upstairs to the writing room. Opening her e-mails, she found the information forwarded by Bernie. Most of the questions on the editor's list covered subjects Amy had thought about herself or discussed with Cecilia. Nevertheless, she typed short answers that she could use as reminders. Suddenly, she remembered that she'd not called Mr. Phillips to find out if he would let her block out the time from noon to three the following day. It was close to 6:00 p.m., and Janelle would have left the switch-board. Amy called the after-hours number for the office and entered Mr. Phillips's extension. If he didn't answer, she'd have to make another call to his cell phone and risk interrupting a golf game.

"This is Harold Phillips," the senior partner said.

"It's Amy. I'm sorry to call after hours."

She explained her situation to Mr. Phillips.

"And you want to do this from the office?" he asked.

"Yes, sir. The video and phone quality will be better if I use the equipment in one of the conference rooms."

Mr. Phillips was silent for a moment while Amy held her breath.

"What time can you come into the office tomorrow morning?" he asked.

"How early do you need me there?"

"Six o'clock. The reason I'm still here this evening is that I'm working on the Thompson Trust. I have information that I want to get out to the consulting firm in Houston no later than tomorrow afternoon. That means you'll need to have it in final form by noon."

Amy hesitated. She wanted to bring up her concerns about Claude Ramsey, but to do so now would make it look like she was trying to get out of doing the work.

"I'll be there," she said.

"All right. I'm going to stay as long as I have to tonight, so I may be a little late in the morning."

"Yes, sir. I'll see you when you come in."

The call ended. Amy sighed. If Mr. Phillips stayed into the night to work, the mountain of words she would face in the morning would reach into the stratosphere. She returned to the kitchen to finish preparing supper.

It was good seeing Ian able to use both

arms to eat. Megan seemed preoccupied, and Amy didn't try to draw her out during the meal. Instead, she told Jeff about her conversation with Bernie Masters.

"I have an idea what they're going to ask me, but I'm still going to be nervous," she said.

"Is it like you're trying to get a job?" Ian asked with his mouth full.

"Yes," Amy replied. "Except it goes both ways. I'm trying to figure out which one of the companies would be the best one to sell my books."

"That's easy," Ian replied. "Go with the biggest one."

"They're both big."

"But one of them has to be bigger," Ian insisted.

There was simple logic to Ian's response.

"And ask them for author references," Jeff said. "Then try to track down novelists who've been with each company and now write for someone else."

"That's a good idea," Amy said. "I can get their personal contact information from the database the firm uses."

Megan looked up from her plate.

"You can find out more stuff like that?" she asked.

"Yes. It's a little scary how many details about people's lives aren't private."

"Could you check someone out for me?"

Megan asked.

"I'm not supposed to use it for personal searches," Amy said. "If I want to use it for anything related to my books, I have to let Mr. Phillips know and get his okay. Who are you interested in?"

"A guy I met online. He seems nice enough, but I know there are all kinds of creepy old men out there pretending to be teenagers."

Amy and Jeff had just missed out on the full-fledged onslaught of the online dating scene. Amy knew it wasn't going away, but it made her uneasy.

"You know what we've told you about —" she began.

"And I'm following the rules," Megan interrupted. "Including talking to you. But it seems like this guy is almost in my head. He can read my moods and knows the perfect thing to say to me. None of the boys at school are like that at all."

"Where does he live?"

"Near Ocean Isle. He wants to meet me if we go down to the beach this summer."

Amy knew one of the features on the program at work would allow her to dig behind anonymous screen names and bogus social-networking entries and uncover real information about the people who used them.

"I can't help," she said. "But if you're still talking online to him this summer, maybe the two of you can meet when we go out as a family to play miniature golf."

"Yeah." Megan rolled her eyes. "That would be awesome."

"But thanks for bringing it up," Amy added quickly.

Later that evening Megan's door was cracked open when Amy walked by. She knocked and entered. Megan was on her computer and looked up.

"Here he is if you want to see him," she said before Amy spoke.

Amy looked over Megan's shoulder and saw a picture of a very clean-cut boy with dark hair and eyes. She quickly read his profile and saw the information available for viewing. Nothing seemed questionable.

"He looks nice," Amy said.

"If you and Dad would let me turn on the camera for my computer, I could find out if he's for real."

Amy was curious, which made her realize how strong the same feeling must be in Megan.

"Not yet," she said slowly.

"What if you were in the room but sitting someplace where he couldn't see you?"

It was an interesting idea, but Amy was still reluctant to open the floodgates.

"Did he suggest that to you?" she asked.

"No, I told him I had an ancient computer that didn't have a camera."

"That's not true."

"I know, and I felt bad about it as soon as I said it."

"If you're still talking to him this summer, we'll figure out a way for you to meet that's fun."

Megan looked up with a smile on her face.

Downstairs in the family room, Amy told Jeff what had happened. When she finished he shook his head.

"It sounds like your career as a romance writer has spilled over into your role as a mother," he said.

"You think so?"

"Yes. Who was the last boy you knew who lived at the beach and understood a young woman?"

"Uh, you."

"Yes, but we didn't meet in the ninth grade. Megan isn't ready for anything except a harmless imaginary romance."

"You're right," Amy admitted. "But now I'm going to have to manage her expectations."

"I'll step in if needed."

Amy went to bed earlier than normal. Jeff joined her, and she turned off the light. Within seconds he was fast asleep, leaving Amy staring at the ceiling. Jeff's ability to turn off his mental activity with a flick of the switch was a mystery. Amy lay in bed and methodically went down her prayer list until she finally drifted off. One of the last things she prayed was that she would take a trip to the living room. When the pressures of life piled up, she needed a divine intermission to rest and recuperate. Her alarm beeped shortly after 5:00 a.m. She turned over and crawled out of bed. She stared slightly bleary-eyed at herself in the bathroom mirror. There'd been no nighttime journey on her itinerary.

It was still dark when she arrived at the office. She made her way through the deserted mansion to her work area. In her purse were the answers she'd prepared and printed out for the interviews with the acquisitions editors later in the day. She placed the sheets in the top drawer of her desk and turned on her computer.

The dictation left by Mr. Phillips was extensive. Fortunately, his precise communication helped enormously. As she typed, Amy tried to push back the uneasiness she felt every time the senior partner mentioned Dr. Claude Ramsey. The bulk of the dictation was designed to supplement the hundreds of pages of information the consultant was going to have to analyze on behalf of the Thompson Trust. The Houston firm was going to be paid an initial retainer of $100,000 with an anticipated budget of $250,000. Included were funds for an investigative trip to Nigeria and what Amy took to be bribes for government officials. The bribes were described in the memo as "governmental fees to key personnel."

Amy was making steady progress as other people began to arrive at the office. Janelle came by to see her at 8:00 a.m.

"What time did you get here?" the receptionist asked.

"A little before six o'clock."

"Wow. What's going on?"

"I have to get out an important memo for Mr. Phillips on the Thompson Trust."

"Mr. Phillips was on a long conference call with some people about that yesterday afternoon."

"That's what I'm working on." Amy stretched her hands out in front of her. "Is there any coffee in the kitchen?"

"I started a pot a couple of minutes ago. Do you want me to get you a cup?"

"Thanks." Amy smiled. "But I need to stretch my legs."

While she was fixing her coffee, Chris came into the kitchen. He poured himself a cup.

"They're all set up," he said.

"What?"

"The depositions of Beverly Jackson, Dr. Kelly, and Mildred Burris. I talked to Mr. Phillips, and he agreed to push them to the front of the line."

"What did you tell him?"

"Don't worry. I didn't blow your cover. I simply pointed out that if we can quickly discredit the will signed a few days before Dominick's death, we can move on and focus on the claims of the illegitimate children. He thought it was a good strategy. Also, if Mildred Burris was involved in a murder or assisted suicide, it will drop her charity out of the running for a piece of the pie, too."

The casual way Chris tossed out the possibilities made Amy uneasy.

"You make it sound like a question on a law school exam," she said.

"You're right. I have to treat my cases with a certain amount of detachment to keep my thinking straight."

"Who told you to do that?"

"One of my law school professors. I don't remember much from the course, but he dropped several nuggets of practical advice that have stuck with me. That's one of them." Chris paused. "Besides, you're expending enough emotional energy in the Dominick case for both of us."

"Which is one reason I'd make a lousy lawyer."

"I don't know about that. Combine your intellect with your instincts, and you would be —"

"Don't go there," Amy cut in. "I'm already trying to juggle two careers and a family."

Before diving back into the dictation, Amy organized Mr. Phillips's desk for his arrival. She had returned to working on the lengthy memo when he arrived and came into her office.

"How's it going?" he asked.

"I'm on the last ten minutes," she said.

"Get it to me as soon as possible. I want to revise it before sending it out."

"Yes, sir. It will be on your desk shortly." Amy paused. "I have one question."

"What is it?"

Amy had to voice her concerns.

"I'm not sure that Dr. Ramsey is the right person to head up the analysis."

"I know you didn't recommend his company, but that decision has been made."

Now that she'd brought up the subject, Amy wasn't going to go away so easily. She spoke rapidly.

"While I was typing the memo, I wondered whether his previous connections in Nigeria were a good thing. He knows business and government people in the oil and mineral exploration area, but what if he has a conflict of interest or someone is paying him extra 'consultant fees' to buy his influence? There are people in Nigeria who will make a lot of money on this project even if it doesn't pan out. If Dr. Ramsey is working with them on other deals, he might recommend you go forward on this one to keep his friends happy. It's just a thought."

Amy stopped to take a breath. Mr. Phillips eyed her for a moment.

"Do any of your concerns come from your dreams?"

Amy swallowed. "Yes, sir."

"Tell me."

"It wasn't nearly as specific as with Michael Baldwin. I saw Dr. Ramsey's face the same night but didn't know who he was until his name came up the other day and I checked his firm website. I recognized him immediately."

"Did you see him with a big check, black hat, et cetera?"

"No, sir. But the way it happened makes me think he's not someone who should be trusted."

Mr. Phillips closed his eyes for a moment and rubbed his forehead.

"Amy, is this going to keep coming up? You're making something that is already complicated more difficult. I'm not prepared to practice law this way."

"What happens in the dreams is not something I can control, but if you tell me to keep quiet —"

"Let me think about it," Mr. Phillips interrupted.

The lawyer returned to his office, and Amy completed the memo. Mr. Phillips was right. He couldn't let her dreams dictate his professional decisions. Amy stopped typing and glanced up. But should he? When she took the memo into his office and put it on the corner of his desk he didn't look up.

The closer it got to noon, the more nervous Amy became. She'd received an e-mail from Bernie confirming everything. They were going to use their cell phones for any private communication they didn't want the acquisitions editors to hear. Amy hadn't eaten breakfast, and her stomach was growling at 11:30 a.m. She went back to the kitchen. Usually there was an unclaimed snack on the table for anyone to eat. Today the offerings included half a powdered donut, a tiny bag of airline pretzels, and a few pieces of freeze-dried apple. Amy was so hungry that her decision wasn't what to eat but the order to do so. Most people would have saved the donut for dessert, but Amy didn't. She guiltily ate the donut, followed by the pretzels, and then finished off the apples. As she put the last bite in her mouth, Janelle came into the kitchen carrying two large plastic containers.

"What am I going to do with this Cobb salad?" she asked. "Betsy ordered it, but then her husband came by to take her out for a surprise lunch."

Amy was chewing a piece of very dry, tasteless apple. She looked at the clock. She still had a few minutes before she needed to set up in the conference room.

"I'll take it," she said. "Who should I pay?"

"No one. Betsy told me to give it away."

The salad was simple and delicious, and even though she didn't have time to eat all of it, the meal and conversation with Janelle helped Amy's mood. While they ate, she told Janelle where to route the conference calls when they came into the office.

"That is so exciting," Janelle gushed.

"This is small compared to some of the other meetings you coordinate."

"Are you kidding me? There's no way a bunch of boring legal stuff can compare with this. Who knows, someday there may be a plaque on the outside of this building announcing that Amy Clarke the author worked here."

Amy laughed. She wished she could bottle Janelle's enthusiasm and take a drink every time she needed a pick-me-up.

At 11:57 a.m., Amy was set up in the conference room staring at a large screen where the caller's face would be projected. Behind her were wood-paneled walls, a couple of oil paintings, and a bookshelf. She didn't know where the editors would be sitting when they came on the line, but they couldn't be in a classier environment. Her cell phone vibrated. It was Bernie.

"Are we set?" he asked.

"Yes. The receptionist will route the call to this conference room."

"Do you look like a lawyer, a writer, or a secretary?"

Amy had tried to dress stylishly for the call. "I'm not high fashion, but there will be some color in the picture."

"Good. You'll be talking to Diana Carmichael. Diana is from India, and members of her family are some kind of local rulers in the southern part of the country. She went to school in England and sounds British. She came to New York when the new owners took over the company a couple of years ago."

"That's not the name you mentioned the other day. I spent some time researching Kate Heigel's background."

"They're on the same level. This is all about you, not them. Put some water and instant fertilizer on that little ego of yours so it can grow in a hurry."

The light on the phone connected to the video lit up, and Janelle's voice came through.

"Ms. Carmichael is on the line."

"Okay."

"She's holding on my end, too," Bernie said. "Activate the call."

In a couple of seconds a woman who appeared to be about Amy's age appeared. She had dark skin and was wearing glasses with modern frames. Bernie's face appeared in the top right-hand corner of the screen. He immediately started talking.

"Hey, Diana, thanks so much for setting this up. Is everyone connected?"

"Yes," Amy said. "Diana, it's nice meeting you."

"And you as well," the woman answered with a clipped British accent. She glanced sideways at a computer screen that was barely visible from the angle of the camera. "I'm sorry my assistant didn't get in touch with you earlier. Kate pitched your book to the committee this morning. I hate to be the bearer of bad news, but we decided it doesn't meet our needs at this time and won't be making an offer."

Amy felt her face go pale. She looked in desperation at Bernie, who spoke. "Kate and I had a lengthy conversation about Amy the other day, and all signs were full-speed ahead."

"Not now. Feel free to resubmit either a concept or a completed manuscript in the future. The writing is passable, but we're going in a different direction for this niche on our publishing calendar for the next twenty-four to thirty-six months."

"You've signed somebody else?" Bernie asked.

"Bernie, you know I can't answer that," Diana said in a patient tone of voice. "Listen, I really must be going. Best of luck to you both."

The screen went blank. Amy slowly picked up her cell phone.

"Bernie? Are you there?"

"That really ticks me off!" the agent exploded. "Kate Heigel owed me the decency of a direct call letting me know that we'd been kicked to the curb. Sending a second-string player to do it was an insult!"

"You said Diana and Kate were on the same level."

"Oh, they have the same title, but Kate is the queen bee. When I saw that Diana was going to handle the call, I assumed it was because Kate knew enough about you already and wanted Diana to pick up the scraps."

"Somebody knew enough to make a decision this morning."

"That's because another writer swooped in and scooped your spot. I've kept all this confidential, which means Kate has been playing me to get someone else to jump on board."

"What do you mean?"

"Kate told an agent who represented an author she wanted to sign that she was considering a hot, young, unknown writer in the character-driven romance genre, and if he didn't act fast, the door would hit his client's rear on the way out."

"So I was just a bargaining chip?"

"Yes." Bernie swore, then quickly apologized. "I know you don't say stuff like that, but sometimes it fits."

"What do we do now?"

"Talk to Lynn Colville at 1:30 p.m."

"Will you tell her what happened with Diana?"

"Are you kidding? I'll let her know I've talked to Kate, who told me she was very interested in signing you to a three-book deal, and we've just finished a conference call with Diana."

"That's not true."

"What part? Everything I said happened. I'm just leaving out the ending. When you tell someone about a book, do you tell them the whole story or just enough to make them want to read it?"

"It's not the same."

"Look, Kate was chomping at the bit the other day, and we both talked to Diana. The news from her wasn't what we wanted to hear, but Lynn doesn't have to know that. These editors are superparanoid about missing the chance to score the next big thing. It's professionally embarrassing for them to read about authors they rejected who then hit the jackpot for another company. That's the fear we have to play on."

"I'm not sure," Amy replied slowly.

"Just answer the writing questions. Leave the battle strategy to me."

Thirty-Three

Stuck with an additional hour of uncommitted time, Amy returned to her desk. Mr. Phillips was at lunch. She checked her inbox, and there was a message from Chris asking her to contact him about the depositions of Beverly Jackson and Dr. Lawrence Kelly. She picked up the phone and buzzed his office.

"What do you need?" she asked.

"Any more dreams would be nice. I've been fantasizing about asking Dr. Kelly a question that would reveal I had information about him that no one else in the world could know. Do you realize how much leverage that would give me with a witness? If a witness thinks I already know everything, he's much more likely to spill it all voluntarily."

"The dream puts him in the room under suspicious circumstances at the time of Mr. Dominick's death. What more could you want?"

"Something that will really shake him up if

he tries to deny having anything to do with it."

"I think the best approach is to bring out inconsistencies between his testimony and Beverly Jackson's. She won't be present when you depose him, will she?"

"No."

"I've told you everything."

"Okay, but maybe you'll get something else before next week. Is Mr. Phillips asking you to help him prepare for Ms. Burris's deposition?"

"He never does," Amy answered. "The only thing he asks me to do is run background checks."

"Will you do that for me with Kelly and Jackson?"

"I already did —"

"No, I mean everything. Run down every rabbit."

Amy was startled. For a second, Chris sounded like Bernie Masters.

"Okay," she said.

Not wanting to start a new project, she logged on to the system. It took only a few minutes to come to a dead end for additional information about Beverly Jackson. The nurse had lived a vanilla life. She'd been married to the same man for twenty years and had two children. She'd never been fired from a job and had one traffic ticket received in a town on the coast that was notorious for setting up speed traps for tourists.

Then Amy stumbled upon a new nugget of personal information. Jackson's younger child, a teenage boy, suffered from a severe case of cerebral palsy. Seeing a poignant picture of Jackson with her son made Amy wonder how the nurse could have justified her participation in Mr. Dominick's death. But as she stared at the picture for several moments, a possible rationale for Jackson's involvement with Mr. Dominick's death hit her.

Better than most people, the nurse would understand why a person might reach the point that continuing to live was an overwhelmingly negative prospect. Even in the last stages of life, Sanford Dominick may have retained the force of personality that could influence others to do what he wanted. If so, Jackson could have been a willing partner in helping the elderly man end his life on his own terms. Amy quickly sent the information gleaned from her research along with her own thoughts to Chris. He replied in less than a minute: *Yes! Keep digging.*

Further digging would have to wait until after her video call with Lynn Colville. Amy passed Janelle's desk on her way to the conference room.

"My second call should come in about five minutes," she said to the receptionist. "It will be from a woman named Lynn Colville."

"Okay. How did the first one go?"

"Short and disappointing," Amy replied bluntly. "But this is the one my agent thinks has promise."

"I hope so," Janelle replied. "Once someone spends five minutes with you, they can't help but see how smart you are."

"I'm not sure my daughter agrees." Amy shrugged. "And she's known me all of her fourteen years."

"That's different. I've always loved my mom, but it wasn't until I turned twenty that I really came to appreciate her."

"Megan will be fifteen in a few weeks. Maybe I can hold on to hope for five more years."

Amy went into the conference room, turned on the equipment, and called Bernie on her cell phone.

"Anything I need to know before this call gets started?" she asked.

"No worries. I confirmed with Lynn's office that she's good to go for a full hour to an hour and a half. There's nothing else on her calendar until three o'clock."

"Okay, but I don't want you to lie to her about anything."

Bernie was silent for a moment.

"Did you hear me?" Amy repeated.

"Yes, but you need to remember that Lynn is an acquisitions editor, not a priest. She'd think I was nuts if I didn't advocate for my client. I know where the lines lie. But you need to stick to the script and not offer any unsolicited mea culpa."

"What script?"

"Lynn's script, which means your job is to answer her questions. Don't editorialize or go off on tangents. Isn't that what the lawyers in your office tell witnesses who are going to testify in court?"

"Yes."

"Apply the same advice to yourself."

Amy could hear the tension in Bernie's voice. The light on the phone lit up, and Amy pushed it.

"Your call is on hold," Janelle said.

"She's on with me, too," Bernie said. "Take a deep breath, relax, and go with the flow."

"Send it through," Amy said to Janelle.

When she saw Lynn Colville's face, Amy was immediately reminded of her fourth-grade teacher, Ms. Edmondson. The similarity was so striking that Amy had to resist the urge to ask if they were somehow related. Like the teacher, Colville's auburn hair was cut short, and there were rimless glasses perched on the end of her slightly upturned nose. She had thick eyebrows that she didn't tame by plucking. After very brief preliminary pleasantries, Lynn launched into her questions, which were similar to the ones forwarded to Amy by Bernie. Amy had placed her cheat sheet on the shiny table in front of her.

"I like the concept of *Deeds of Darkness,*" Colville said after Amy had repeated her elevator pitch. "But tell me how you will make the transition from the heavy Christian influence in your other writing to a more literary romance novel with a strong dose of drama thrown in."

It was one of the questions Amy had anticipated, but hearing it from the lips of the New York editor made it sound more intimidating.

"It's my plan to avoid the stereotypical template used in most mainstream romance novels —"

"If I thought otherwise, we wouldn't be having this conversation," Colville cut in. "Talk to me about Christianity. We don't print books intended to proselytize."

Amy swallowed. "I'm writing a novel, not a sermon, so I won't be proselytizing in the traditional sense of the word. The Christian influence will still be there, but I'll introduce it in a way that's supported by the nature of the characters. And I'll use archetypal structure to give them texture and keep them from coming across as flat. For example, the protagonist is a damsel in distress even though she's married with a child."

"I see that." Colville wrinkled her brow in a way that again reminded Amy of Ms. Edmondson. "By spiritual, do you mean supernatural? I don't want to publish a book that relies on deus ex machina."

Amy was familiar with a writer's use of a contrived event, circumstance, or influence to solve a difficult plot point. The technique had been criticized since the days of Horace and Aristotle.

"Christianity is supernatural, but it can be a part of real life without creating an unsupported basis for resolution of issues in a story."

"I want a guarantee that you're not going to rely on God riding in on a white horse to save the day."

Amy recalled that was exactly what happens in the book of Revelation.

"What Amy is saying," Bernie cut in, "is that her writing has depth and doesn't need tricks."

"One writer's trick is another writer's stock-in-trade," Colville replied. "And before I take another step with the two of you, I need to know where the road is going."

"To big sales," Bernie said. "Amy hasn't started to tap into her potential for —"

"Save it, Bernie," Colville replied.

Bernie shut his mouth. Colville stared into the camera at Amy before speaking.

"Do I have a guarantee that you're not going to hijack a good story and turn it into religious pabulum?" Colville asked. "It's better to get this out on the table now rather than you waste six to nine months."

"I agree with you about that," Amy said. "But I want to tell the story the way I believe my heart and mind dictate."

"I've heard enough for today," Colville said. "Bernie, what's the status of discussions with other publishers?"

"We talked with Diana Carmichael earlier today."

Colville raised her eyebrows. "Where was Kate Heigel?"

"She asked Diana to handle the preliminaries," Bernie answered.

Amy squirmed in her chair.

"Because she didn't want to give you the bad news herself." Colville nodded knowingly. "That's how Kate operates. She's too nice for this business. She hates having to pull the plug. Am I right?"

"Yes," Bernie replied, glancing at Amy.

"Don't try to finesse me," Colville said. "My hand is holding the chain attached to the plug, too. Amy has real talent, but if I can't get comfortable with how she's going to corral her religious zeal, I'm going to pull it, too."

"It won't be a problem," Bernie said. "Amy is ready to step up to the plate for a big-league team."

"That's the question, isn't it?" Colville asked. "Should she play in the major leagues or a church league?"

"This isn't a problem; it's an opportunity," Bernie said. "When can we expect to hear from you?"

Colville glanced at her computer screen, then at Amy.

"Can you send me any more sample chapters?"

"Yes."

"Do it tomorrow, and I'll get back to you next week. Bernie has my contact information."

"Thanks, Lynn," Bernie replied. "You won't regret —"

The screen went blank as Colville abruptly ended the video call. Amy picked up her cell phone.

"Are you there?" she asked Bernie.

"Yes. That went well."

"Are you kidding?" Amy asked. "She thinks I'm a religious fanatic."

"And a talented writer. Lynn grilled you because that's what she's going to face from her bosses. If she didn't like your answers, she would have yanked the chain she mentioned and ended the call. She wouldn't waste her time reading more sample chapters if she didn't believe they would be good."

"I'm not so sure," Amy replied doubtfully. "You sound overly optimistic."

"You'd better hope I'm right," Bernie replied. "Because if I'm wrong, you're going to be an orphan writer without a place to lay her head."

Amy swallowed. Bernie had never sounded so harsh.

"I do," she said.

"I'll send you her e-mail address. Send the chapters to me, too."

After the call ended, Amy went to the kitchen, poured herself a rare cup of afternoon coffee, and resolved to dive into her office work. Her writing career might be teetering on the edge of a cliff, but she had skills that Mr. Phillips appreciated.

She logged on to the information database and entered specific information about Dr. Lawrence Kelly. She retraced her steps and reviewed the personal information she'd already found. The doctor was as squeaky clean as Nurse Jackson, without the added complication of a special-needs child. His two children attended a public elementary school, and his wife worked as a part-time teacher's aide at the school. That made Amy wonder if the doctor might be in some sort of financial difficulty. Student loans for college and medical school could be astronomical, and the amount of money a doctor could earn as an internist in a small town might not be that great. But unlike Beverly Jackson, there was no indication that Dr. Kelly was a beneficiary of Mr. Dominick's will. Amy paused.

Unless there was a secret side agreement between Jackson and Kelly.

If such an agreement existed, it would be virtually impossible to prove. It wouldn't be in writing, and Amy couldn't imagine either of them admitting such an arrangement in a deposition. Nevertheless, she entered her thoughts into the information she was going to send Chris.

Continuing her research, she saw a reference to a Lawrence Kelly with a California address. Beside Kelly's name was an icon indicating the presence of a criminal record. Even though there was a few months' difference in the dates of birth for the two men, Amy followed the link. When she did, she found a conviction for sexual battery against a minor, Internet child pornography, and a requirement that this Kelly register as a sex offender. The possibility that her Dr. Kelly was living a double life on opposite sides of the country was too remote to include in the memo for Chris. Asking a witness an inflammatory question with no basis in fact never served a valid purpose and made the lawyer look stupid.

Mr. Phillips didn't return to the office before Amy left for the day. She was glad for the time to be alone and allow her thoughts and feelings to settle down. When she pulled into the driveway, Jeff's truck was already there. Inside, she saw fresh flowers on the kitchen table. Jeff poked his head in from the family room.

"Check the oven. There's no need for you to fix supper. I brought a full meal home from LuAnn's Restaurant and put it in to keep it warm."

"Thanks, but what's the occasion?"

"Do I always need a reason?"

"No," Amy responded slowly. "And the flowers are beautiful."

"You deserve them."

Before Amy could spoil the moment by telling Jeff about the phone calls with the editors, Ian came bounding down the stairs.

Suddenly, there was a thud and a cry of "Ouch!"

"What's wrong?" Amy dashed out of the kitchen and found Ian holding his left arm.

"I missed the last step and landed on my arm."

He moved it back and forth gingerly. Jeff held the arm in his hands and pressed it gently.

"Does that hurt?"

Ian winced. "A little, but I can move it. When it broke it just hung there."

"Should we take him to the ER?" Amy asked Jeff.

"No," Ian responded emphatically. "I'm starving, and Dad made us wait to eat until you got home."

Amy looked at Jeff.

"Let's keep an eye on it during supper," Jeff said. "If it gets worse or starts to swell, we can go to the hospital."

Amy took Ian into the kitchen where he sat in his chair and rested his arm gingerly on the table. Jeff called upstairs for Megan to come down for supper.

"What's wrong with Ian?" she asked as soon as she came into the kitchen and saw his arm propped on the table.

"He tripped going down the stairs and landed on it."

Ian held up his arm and moved it back and forth.

"But it's feeling better now."

"Do you think he tripped because he's been using drugs?" Megan asked.

Amy was taking the baked chicken Jeff had brought home out of the oven.

"What a crazy thing to say," she replied.

"That's what you would have asked me if I'd tripped. Why should it be any different with Ian?"

Amy looked at Jeff and silently pleaded for help.

"Did you have a bad day at school?" he asked Megan.

"Not if you think it's good when your best friend stabs you in the back." Megan bit her lip. "And you find out that she's been planning it for weeks."

Amy put the chicken down and faced Megan.

"Bethany?" she asked.

Megan nodded, fighting back tears.

"Do you want to tell us about it?" Amy continued.

Megan motioned to Ian. "Not now."

Supper was a somber meal. The food was good, but it was eaten in silence. As soon as he finished, Ian carried his plate to the sink without being asked, rinsed it, and put it in the dishwasher.

"If it's okay, I'm going up to my room," he said. "I don't think I need to go to the hospital."

"Fine." Jeff nodded.

As soon as Ian's footsteps faded on the stairs, Amy and Jeff both turned to Megan.

"What happened with Bethany?" Amy asked.

"I don't want to talk about it."

"But you have to," Jeff responded. "We aren't going to let you suffer alone."

Megan looked at her father and a tear rolled down her cheek. Amy pulled a tissue from a box on the kitchen counter. Megan blew her nose.

"It all had to do with Mr. Ryan," she said. "Bethany was jealous of me because she knows I'm one of his favorite students. She started a rumor that I've been making fun of him behind his back. It got back to him, and I could see that it really hurt his feelings."

"You can tell him it's false," Amy said. "He'll believe you."

"No, he won't. Because part of it is true. Not that I meant it seriously, but Bethany and I were joking about him the other day, and I sent her a text message about how his hair is falling out, and he is getting a gut from eating too many french fries. She left her phone in his classroom with the text open, and he saw it."

"I hate text messaging," Jeff responded.

"I tried to talk to Mr. Ryan after class," Megan continued, "but he cut me off and asked me to leave." She buried her face in her hands. "How can I go back to school?"

Amy and Jeff exchanged a questioning look over the top of Megan's head.

"There's nothing you can do about it tonight," Amy said. "But Mr. Ryan is an adult who knows how silly students can act."

"He didn't think this was silly," Megan said without lifting her head. "I could see how much I hurt him when I looked in his eyes."

Amy pressed her lips together. She wasn't sure what else to say.

"Do you have any homework?" Jeff asked Megan.

"Yes, but how can I think about that?"

"At least try."

With a shrug Megan got up from the table and left the kitchen.

"What should we do?" Amy asked as soon as she was gone. "I could call Mr. Ryan."

"No." Jeff shook his head. "I'm going to

drive over to his townhome and talk to him. It may not be as bad as Megan thinks, but if it is, I'll try to see if I can help smooth things over."

Amy's gratitude for the meal and flowers couldn't compare with her appreciation for Jeff's willingness to help Megan. She leaned over and gave him a big kiss.

"What's that for?" he asked.

"Do I always need a reason?"

Thirty-Four

Jeff left, and Amy went upstairs to the writing room. Since sending her initial work to Bernie, she'd finished two more chapters of *Deeds of Darkness* and was close to completing a third one that introduced Roxanne's faith. As Amy reread it, she tried to view it through Lynn Colville's eyes. Nothing she'd written about the protagonist violated any known rule of writing, but there was no denying Roxanne's faith was the slender strand holding her life together. It didn't remove all doubt that she would prevail in the end — Amy had already made it clear in her synopsis that there would be equal scoops of tragedy mixed with triumph; however, she could see how Colville could easily criticize the chapter and argue that Roxanne's faith was a superfluous appendage that weakened the story because it gave her a crutch to lean on. To Colville, Roxanne probably should overcome the deeds of darkness with her own ingenuity and in her own strength.

Amy rewrote a paragraph to tone down the religious component, but it made the sentences seem to swirl in circles. She stopped. How could she plant a nugget of faith while concealing its true identity? Then she had an idea based not on religious theory but on her own Christian life. What if Roxanne was a dreamer? Dreams were a universal language inherently outside human control and could thus be both instructive and deceptive. Roxanne could be a lifelong dreamer who was only now beginning to connect what happened in the unconscious realm with the real world she inhabited. Amy's excitement grew. Anytime she wrote out of personal experience, she was able to bring a level of depth to her writing. She quickly rewrote several paragraphs and gave Roxanne an obscure yet vivid dream that foreshadowed her spiritual journey and provided information she would need later in the story. Amy really liked the flow of the new paragraphs.

She read them twice, then stopped.

Lynn Colville would fail to see the world of dreams as a mysterious cave filled with unknown discoveries. She would consider it a classic example of deus ex machina — the manipulation of plot and character by an unseen hand. Even if the information Amy introduced in the dreams created challenges for the main character, it wouldn't make any difference. The supernatural was taboo for the editor. Amy deleted her changes.

She didn't want to become an orphan so early in her writing career, but she couldn't write in a vacuum devoid of spiritual air. Before she could question herself any further, she put the chapters in a file and sent it to Bernie and Lynn Colville as an e-mail attachment.

Going downstairs, she found Jeff standing in the doorway of Megan's bedroom.

"Thanks, Dad," Megan said with a slightly teary smile. "That makes me feel tons better."

"What happened?" Amy asked.

"We'll talk downstairs," Jeff replied.

Jeff waited until they were in the family room to speak.

"Megan was right," he said in a soft voice. "Her text message really hurt the guy's feelings, which surprised me, but if your world revolves around your students, what they think and say about you is a big deal. At first he didn't want to talk to me, but he let me in when he saw I wasn't going to leave. I explained the situation from Megan's perspective and apologized on her behalf. I reminded him about the situation with Nate Drexel and told him this was a chance for Megan to say that she's sorry for something hurtful she's done to another person. That seemed to register with him. She's going to prepare an apology and give it to him tomorrow."

"Verbal or written?"

"I told her to do both. Maybe write a card and then say something when she gives it to him."

Amy was impressed with the way Jeff had managed the situation.

"That's good," she said.

"And to show her that there are no hard feelings, Mr. Ryan is going to invite Megan and a few of her friends over to his place for dinner next week near her birthday. He's not a chef and was glad to know how much she enjoys Chinese takeout."

"What is Amy going to do about Bethany?" Amy asked.

"I have no idea."

"Let me think about that one. She and Megan have been close ever since Megan went to public school. It's a relationship worth saving."

Jeff turned toward the computer.

"There's something else I need to talk to you about," Amy said, trying to sound strong. "Did you forget to ask about my phone calls with the two editors in New York?"

Jeff faced her with kindness in his eyes.

"No, and when I didn't hear from you after three o'clock, I called Bernie Masters. I figured Bernie would let me know without having to make you suffer through it. That's one reason for dinner and the flowers. I wanted you to know there are people in the world who love and appreciate you as you are. If you want to tell me about it now, I'll be glad to listen."

"What did Bernie say?" Amy sniffled slightly.

Jeff gave an accurate summary of the two phone calls. Bernie hadn't tried to sugarcoat it for him.

"That's about right," Amy sighed. "I sent them three more chapters of the new novel a few minutes ago. We'll see how Lynn Colville reacts."

Jeff held out his arms and wrapped them around her.

"Whatever happens, remember how this feels," he said.

Amy rested her head on Jeff's shoulder, and they held each other close.

"Thanks. I love you," she said as they parted.

"Better than the men in your books?"

"Yes. Your hugs are real."

Before she went to bed, Amy checked her e-mail. There was a simple message from Bernie:

> I like the new stuff. Very genuine. Your voice shines through.

The following day when Amy came home from work, Megan was cheerfully sitting at the kitchen table helping Ian with his homework.

"Good day at school?" Amy asked.

"Yep."

"Do you want to tell me about it?"

Megan shook her head and motioned to Ian.

"I know about your text message dissing Mr. Ryan," Ian responded without looking up from his book.

"How?" Amy and Megan asked at the same time.

"Mom, the walls in this house are made of paper."

Megan rolled her eyes. "I talked to Mr. Ryan before class, and we worked everything out. He's even going to throw a birthday party for me and a few friends next week. He said Dad already told him it was okay."

"That's right," Amy replied.

"Are you going to invite Bethany?" Ian asked.

Both Amy's and Megan's jaws dropped open.

"No," Megan said after a brief pause. "Mr. Ryan is upset with her for making me look bad. Is there anything else you want to tell us?"

"Huh-uh," Ian grunted. "I'm finished with my math. Can I go outside until supper?"

"Yes," Amy answered.

After Ian left, Amy turned to Megan.

"Now that you've worked things out with Mr. Ryan, what is your plan on restoring your relationship with Bethany?"

"None. She's furious that I've turned the tables on her. But that's her problem, not mine."

"She's been your best friend for almost four years. I don't think you should —"

"She wrecked our friendship in the time it took to leave her phone in a place where Mr. Ryan could see it," Megan interrupted.

"Did you talk to Mr. Ryan about her?"

"No, I wasn't even thinking about Bethany. This was all about Greg, I mean, Mr. Ryan and me."

Amy raised her eyebrows. "You don't call Mr. Ryan by his first name to his face, do you?"

Megan shifted in her chair. "It was a joke. I mean, he could be my older brother. Some of the seniors call him Greg outside class."

Amy remembered the mistake made by the girl at the pizza party who thought Amy was Greg Ryan's girlfriend.

"You shouldn't, even as a joke. He's not young enough to be your brother."

Amy didn't receive any feedback from Bernie or Lynn Colville all morning. She hoped no news was a sign the editor was taking a thoughtful look at the additional chapters Amy submitted.

Wednesday afternoon Chris came into her office with a stack of papers in his hand.

"I have something on Dr. Kelly and Nurse Jackson," he said.

"What is it?"

"Money transferred from Sanford Dominick's account to Beverly Jackson that was way more than she should have received for home health-care services."

"How much more?"

"Three payments of fifty thousand dollars each over a nine-month period, in addition to her regular fees for taking care of him."

"Okay, that looks bad." Amy nodded. "What did he pay Dr. Kelly?"

"Nothing except expenses not covered by Dominick's health insurance. But when I subpoenaed Jackson's financial records in advance of the depositions next week, I found a payment by her to Dr. Kelly for seventy-five thousand dollars shortly after she received her second installment from Dominick."

"Why would she do that?"

"Who knows for sure, but it looks like Kelly and Jackson *were* working together, and he used her as a buffer between himself and Dominick."

"If they'd convinced Mr. Dominick to voluntarily give them money, why would they want him to die?"

"I'm not sure. Maybe he refused to give

Jackson anything else. And don't forget, she's a beneficiary under the last will. If it holds up, she'll receive another two hundred thousand dollars. He was valuable to her dead or alive."

Amy shivered.

"There's no connection in the financial records with Ms. Burris, is there?" she asked.

"Yes, there is."

Amy's heart sank.

"Shortly after Natasha moved to Florida, Dominick paid a local construction company $225,000 to do some remodeling work. I was going over financial information with Natasha on the phone the other day and asked her about it. She didn't remember any work at their house here, so I got in touch with the construction company." Chris leaned in. "Get this. The work wasn't performed at Dominick's house; it was performed at Ms. Burris's house in Cross Plains. They only finished up a few months ago."

Amy now felt a sick feeling in her stomach. She'd seen and admired the work at the residence.

"My husband's company replaced the windows in the house," she said numbly.

"And got paid with Sanford Dominick's money. There's no legal reason Dominick couldn't help Ms. Burris out, especially if he was feeling guilty about ditching her. But it shows how all three of the people you saw in your dream benefited significantly from Dominick during a time when he was vulnerable and his health was going downhill."

"I don't think Ms. Burris would do that."

"Money talks louder than words." Chris shrugged.

"Does Mr. Phillips know about this?"

"Not yet, but he'll have everything he needs before he deposes her next week."

Shortly before the end of the day, Mr. Phillips buzzed Amy's phone and asked her to come into his office.

"I'm going to take your advice," the senior partner said as soon as she came close to his desk. "I'm not going to hire the Houston firm to advise the Thompson Trust on the Nigerian oil investment. Dr. Ramsey will not be giving us an opinion."

Instead of feeling vindicated, Amy suddenly felt insecure.

"Why?" she asked.

"Because I don't want to make a mistake about such an important decision. Ever since you told me about your reservations, I haven't been able to shake off the sense that you may be right. You proved to be a good judge of bad character with Michael Baldwin, and I don't want to repeat that mistake. We're going to go with the firm in Miami."

"Thanks for letting me know." Amy paused. "I only want what's best for the firm and its clients."

Driving home a few minutes later, Amy wasn't sure how to process what had happened with Mr. Phillips. She'd never been anything except a subordinate. To have her opinion given so much weight made her slightly light-headed. After supper that night, she told Jeff, in general terms, that Mr. Phillips had made an important decision for a client based on information she'd received in a dream.

"Wow, if that starts happening all the time, the practice of law will never be the same." Jeff paused. "But isn't it sometimes hard for you to figure out what your dreams mean?"

"Yes, it's nerve-racking to mention what I think. I'd hate to have to do it a lot."

"That may not be up to you."

"It's always up to me. The question is whether I'm willing to obey and what that obedience looks like."

As she listened to herself, Amy was reminded of Ms. Burris. She missed the older woman. Regardless of what Dr. Kelly and Beverly Jackson may have done to Sanford Dominick, Amy could not let herself believe Ms. Burris did anything wrong. Only if the elderly woman admitted it would Amy think it possible.

Later that evening she went up to the writing room to work on the next chapter in *Deeds of Darkness.* However, without any feedback from Lynn Colville, she didn't want to run the risk of wasting her time. She struggled for over an hour without writing a hundred words that made sense and finally turned off her computer.

That night she went to the living room.

It had been several weeks since she'd had a divine encounter, and given all the pressure she'd been under recently, Amy gladly yielded to the pull toward the place of peace. Enveloped by the breathing walls, the issues of life didn't disappear, but they receded into the background. The living room had never been a place where she tried to figure out the answers to her problems. Rather, it was a place where her problems shrank in the presence of the one who held the entire world in his hands. Refreshed, Amy could faintly hear the sounds of praise taking place beyond the walls. Her heart longed to join the throng where each instant revealed a new facet of the Lord that prompted a fresh response of worship.

As she felt herself being pulled away, a series of rapid images once again flashed before Amy's eyes. When she woke up, she looked at the clock. It was 1:30 a.m. Another hour passed before she drifted off to sleep once more.

The following morning one of the first items in her dictation queue was a letter from Mr. Phillips notifying Dr. Ramsey that the

Thompson Trust would not be retaining his group to assist in the evaluation of the Nigerian oil venture. Amy dutifully transcribed the letter. But instead of putting it in the stack for Mr. Phillips to review, she placed it to the side. Something didn't feel quite right about it. Shortly before noon, she received a text message from Bernie:

Heard from Lynn. Check your e-mail, then call me.

Amy's heart sank. Bernie would have called her immediately if he'd received good news from Colville. She logged on to her home account from her phone and quickly scrolled down to the message from the editor. She clicked it open:

> Received additional chapters. Will be in touch.
>
> Lynn Colville

The editor certainly wasn't wordy. It was time for Amy's lunch break, so she left the office, drove to the park, and called Bernie.

"What does this e-mail mean?" she asked as soon as the agent answered the phone. "Is it written code?"

"Yeah, the key is in the second sentence. Everybody in the publishing, entertainment, and music businesses knows the lingo. If someone in New York, Hollywood, or Nashville tells you they'll 'be in touch,' it means you'll never hear from them again. A friend of mine who represents musicians calls it a 'Nashville No.' "

"Are you sure? Colville seemed to pride herself on being honest and blunt. Remember how she criticized Kate Heigel for avoiding me and sending Diana Carmichael to turn me down?"

"Of course, but do people always do what they criticize other people of not doing?"

It took Amy a second to unravel Bernie's response.

"Not necessarily," she said.

"Exactly. Lynn let you down easy. Another key is what she wrote about the additional chapters. She received them but didn't read them. That tells me she'd made up her mind after our conversation the other day. It's how the dance is danced and the game is played. I'm sorry."

It was a weird way to be rejected.

"Would you call Colville and make sure?" Amy asked.

"Sure, but don't be disappointed if she doesn't return my call."

"What do we do next?"

Bernie was silent for a moment. "Let me mull that over, and I'll be in touch with you. Hey, I've got to jump on another call."

Amy had another question, but there wasn't anyone on the line to ask. Then she thought about Bernie's final comment that he would "be in touch."

"Uh-oh," she said softly to herself. "I think I just became a double orphan — no publisher, no agent."

She spent the remainder of the half hour sitting numbly in her car. She nibbled the edges of the sandwich she'd brought from home, but food had no taste. For some unknown reason her mouth was exceptionally dry, and she drank an entire bottle of water. Thoughts about her trip to the living room the previous evening helped a little bit, but nothing was going to remove the sting of double rejection. Returning to the office, she was greeted by a cheery Janelle.

"I hope you're having a great day," the receptionist said.

Amy hoped her plastic smile was enough to fool Janelle for the few seconds it took to pass her desk. She dutifully finished out the rest of the workday. Mr. Phillips signed a stack of letters and reviewed several documents without asking her about the letter to Claude Ramsey. Amy left it on her desk beneath a file in an unrelated matter. As she reached her car, her cell phone vibrated. It was a text message from Bernie:

Colville passed. Dead end.

That night during supper Amy kept looking at the kitchen clock for no apparent reason.

Time was passing, but it didn't mean anything. She knew she'd have to tell Jeff what happened later in the evening. He'd been so sweet after the conference calls that she hated having to give him really bad news.

"Bethany and I are friends again," Megan announced after putting a second helping of sweet potato casserole on her plate.

"How did that happen?" Jeff asked.

"Mr. Ryan did it. He talked to her one-on-one and then made us sit down with him after class today. He was really tough on Bethany, and she started to cry when she apologized to both of us. Seeing her that way made me willing to give her a second chance."

"A second chance?" Amy asked. "Does that mean you're going to keep score?"

"Come on, Mom," Megan said. "Be realistic. Are you saying if she tries to hurt me like that again, I'm supposed to ignore it?"

"No, but you have to forgive her if she's sorry."

"Yeah." Ian glanced up from a chicken leg that he'd picked almost totally clean. "It says in the Bible you have to forgive, like, 490 times."

"You used that up with me by the time you were three years old," Megan shot back at her brother.

"It also says not to borrow trouble from tomorrow for today," Jeff cut in. "I'm glad you and Bethany worked it out. Is she going to come to your birthday party next week?"

"Yes, both the one at Mr. Ryan's house and later here on my real birthday," Megan replied. "She'd already bought me a nice present before this blowup happened."

Amy hadn't started planning the spend-the-night party for Megan and four of her friends.

"And there's nothing for you to do," Megan said in anticipation of Amy's thoughts. "This isn't the third grade with the fairy princess theme."

For that party Amy had made a princess costume for Megan and put together elaborate gift bags for every girl who came.

"What are you going to do?" Amy asked.

"Just hang out. We may have some fun doing silly things with a new app Alecia found on her phone. It switches faces and puts them on other people's bodies."

"Bobby showed me that," Ian said. "It's funny."

"It's great that you and Bobby have something in common," Jeff replied.

"If we put Alecia's dog's head on Ian's body, nobody would be able to tell anything different," Megan said.

"Megan —" Amy started.

"It's okay, Mom," Ian cut in. "I forgive her. That's pretty good."

Amy stayed on the sidelines as the rest of the mealtime conversation went between Megan and Ian about goofy phone apps. She never would have guessed the two siblings would have discovered common ground. As soon as the children cleared out of the kitchen, Amy told Jeff about the e-mail from Lynn Colville, her conversation with Bernie, and the stake driven into the heart of her writing dreams.

"I'm sorry," she concluded. "I've tried to do my best."

"At least you went back to work at the law firm," Jeff replied soberly. "I thought it was a good idea at the time, but I had no idea how important it would turn out to be. Do you really think your chances of holding on to a job are good when Emily comes back from maternity leave?"

Amy was stunned that Jeff immediately went to the practical side of things.

"Well, I believe Mr. Phillips is pleased with my work, and he halfway promised me a permanent position the first day I reported back. Emily's baby is about a month old, so I should find out soon. But I'm devastated by what happened with the editor."

"And I know it will take time to get over it. I'm just thankful there seems a way forward for us as a family."

Amy didn't have the strength to convince Jeff he should have more sympathy for her. As soon as the dishes were put away, she fled upstairs to the writing room. She didn't necessarily want to be alone, but she couldn't mope on the couch while Jeff sat in front of the computer. She sat in her writing chair, her computer untouched. There was no use working on *Deeds of Darkness.* It had joined her in the orphanage.

Amy stared out the window at the familiar landscape. Spring had come during the past two weeks, and dusk was pixilated by pockets of daffodils and tulips. She wished there was color to brighten the darkness of her mood. Sighing deeply, Natalie's book popped into her thoughts.

She took out her copies of the lovely illustrations created by her friend. As she looked at each one, the slightest of smiles formed at the corners of her mouth. The paintings reflected the irrepressible joy of Natalie's life — a perfect antidote for melancholy. By the time Amy reached the last one, her imagination had left the attic room and was walking on warm beach sand, feeling a gentle breeze.

Turning on her computer, Amy returned to the spot where she'd stopped working on the text. A fresh idea popped into her head, and she started typing. An hour later she reread what she'd written. Regardless of anyone else's opinion, the words worked.

Amy was still a writer.

Thirty-Five

Before leaving the writing room, Amy called Natalie and told her what happened with the editors and Bernie. "I wish I was there to give you a huge hug," Natalie said when Amy finished.

"You helped me in a way you wouldn't guess." Amy told her about the positive effect of working on Natalie's story. "I know I'm going to struggle with my feelings, but this evening it kept me from sinking into the pit."

"I'm glad for that. When can we get together?"

"My schedule tomorrow is hectic, and Jeff's birthday is Saturday."

"We'll be out of town Saturday anyway. Would you be able to squeeze an hour out for lunch on Tuesday?"

That was the day Chris was going to depose Dr. Kelly and Nurse Jackson.

"Maybe. It depends on whether I have to help one of the young lawyers prepare for some depositions. I should know if I can get away by midmorning."

"Okay."

"Thanks for listening."

The following morning Amy finished organizing Mr. Phillips's mail and returned to her office. A few minutes later the senior partner buzzed and asked her to come into his office.

"Where is the letter I dictated to Dr. Ramsey?" the lawyer asked. "I don't recall signing it."

"On my desk," Amy replied without explanation. "I'll get it."

She retrieved the letter and placed it in front of Mr. Phillips, who signed it with a flourish.

Instead of leaving, Amy remained standing in front of his desk.

"What is it?" Mr. Phillips asked.

Amy cleared her throat.

"Do you remember Dr. Lawrence Kelly and Beverly Jackson, the doctor and nurse who helped take care of Mr. Dominick?"

"Of course."

"I had a dream about them." Amy paused. "And Mildred Burris. It was very specific. Would you like to hear it?"

Mr. Phillips gave Amy a frustrated look.

"I'm not trying to confuse things —"

"No, go ahead. I'll decide if this is relevant to anything."

Mr. Phillips's eyes opened wider as Amy

talked. At one point he started to take notes but stopped. Amy hesitated.

"Keep going," he said. "I'll wait until you finish."

"That's all I remember," Amy said. "Chris knows about this. That's why he moved up the depositions of Kelly and Jackson and obtained financial records from them. Do you know what he uncovered?"

"Not yet. We're scheduled to meet later today so he can brief me."

Amy told him about the money.

"That may or may not be significant. Sonny gave away lots of money over the years. He would go to Las Vegas and drop a ten-thousand-dollar tip on a showgirl or a bell-hop. And I remember one time he gave the man who cut his grass twenty thousand dollars as a Christmas gift. But he made money faster than he could give it away. He had a rare knack for being in the right place at the right time."

Perhaps remembering another instance of Mr. Dominick's random generosity, Mr. Phillips stared past Amy for a moment. The lawyer refocused and clapped his hands together.

"This changes one thing. What's my schedule look like next Tuesday when Chris is going to depose Kelly and Jackson?"

"Let's see. You're going to an executive board meeting for PKT, Inc."

"Bryce Pointer will have to move the meeting if he wants me there to hold his hand. I'm going to take these depositions myself."

After Chris met with Mr. Phillips, the younger lawyer buzzed Amy's phone.

"Can you come up to my office?" he asked.

"Now?"

"Yes."

"Okay."

As soon as Chris saw Amy, he motioned for her to come inside.

"You're really out of the closet, aren't you?" he asked.

"I hadn't thought of it in those terms, but I guess so."

"And you have Mr. Phillips wrapped around your finger." Chris smiled. "If you told him you had a dream in which he was handling contingency fee cases, he'd start chasing ambulances."

"Nobody has Mr. Phillips wrapped around their finger. Not even his wife. And ambulances get out of the way when they see his car coming."

Chris chuckled. "You've gotten my attention, too," he said, but then paused. "But not in exactly the same way as Mr. Phillips."

Amy gave him a puzzled look. Chris continued, "I love Laura, but as you probably know I've never really tracked with her on the religious stuff. Not that I've been antagonistic —"

Amy raised her eyebrows.

"Maybe a little bit," Chris corrected himself. "But I'm going to go home tonight and apologize for my attitude. You haven't met Laura, but she is awesome. I mean, she'd rather open the screen door and let a fly out than grab a swatter to smash it. She's always claimed it was her faith that made her that way, but I didn't buy it."

"The note she wrote me was very sweet."

"Yeah, and what I need from you is advice on how to talk to her the right way. I always catch myself treating her like a judge I'm trying to convince of my legal position."

"What exactly do you want to say to her?"

"That after living with her for the past two years and working with you for the past few months, I've realized there really might be a God."

"That's a good opening line."

"But she'll want more details."

"Of course she will. For a woman, the journey in a relationship is as important as the destination."

"Yeah, guys are all about the bottom line."

"I think I can help." Amy smiled. "But it's going to require some role play."

After a few minutes, Chris had refined his speech for Laura and cut out several disclaimers that Amy knew would have caused her to question his sincerity. Still, he wasn't quite getting it.

"You're not preparing a business contract designed to limit a company's liability down the road," Amy said. "Is your goal to show Laura that you want to learn more about God?"

"Yes, but not just facts." Chris pointed to his chest. "I want to know about it in here."

"Then make sure you say that."

Amy's conversation with Chris lifted her spirits in a way few things could have. The opportunity to actually see God using her in another person's life made her feel valuable. That evening she told Jeff about the young lawyer's openness to the Lord, and they prayed for him. Jeff ended his part of the prayer with a request that he would learn how to better communicate with Amy.

"Amen!" Amy said, a bit louder than necessary.

"Don't rub it in," Jeff replied, opening his eyes.

Jeff was showered with love on Saturday in the forms of family time, birthday gifts, and his favorite foods. Sunday evening Amy finished her revisions of Natalie's book. By cutting a third of the words, she'd maximized the effectiveness of the illustrations to release the reader's imagination. But it wasn't just deleting words that made the book better.

She'd restructured the entire narrative and given the children's point of view a unique voice that oozed innocence, the wonder of discovery, and the excitement that nature can bring to a fresh heart. Before she sent the revised text to Natalie, Amy took the book with illustrations downstairs to Jeff, who was sitting in front of the computer.

"What are you doing?" she asked.

"Uh, deciding how much money we need to have in our 401k by the time we retire. If the inflation rate averages less than five percent a year —"

"I have something more important for you to do than guess the rate of inflation," Amy interrupted. "I want you to read a children's book that Natalie and I wrote together. She painted the watercolor illustrations and wrote the first draft of the text, which I've changed and edited."

"You and Natalie have been working on a book? Why didn't you tell me?"

"I've not had it that long. She gave it to me a couple of weeks ago to tweak. I ended up making a lot of changes and want your unbiased opinion. You can read it in about fifteen minutes."

Jeff glanced back at the computer screen.

"Are you expecting the inflation rate to change significantly in the next fifteen minutes?" Amy asked.

"Okay," Jeff surrendered. "But I don't see

how what I think is going to matter. If you want to know what a child thinks about the book, you should show it to Ian."

"You're right, and he's the next person who will read it."

Jeff held out his hand. "Give it to me."

"Keep it in order. The pictures have to match up with the words."

"If I can read a blueprint, I can follow an illustrated children's book."

Amy put the sheets on the coffee table in front of the couch so Jeff would have plenty of room, then retreated to the kitchen. She poured herself a glass of water and leaned against the counter while she waited. After a couple of minutes, she heard Jeff chuckle. She suspected he'd reached the picture in which the children lure their father to the beach with the promise of buried treasure, which turns out to be his wife under a mound of sand with her head and brightly painted red toes sticking out. The minutes clicked by without any additional sounds from the family room. When fifteen minutes passed, Amy peeked through the door to make sure Jeff hadn't returned to the computer without telling her. But his head was still bowed over the coffee table. She saw him pick up another page and turn it over. Several minutes passed before he came into the kitchen.

"It's great," he said simply. "I finished it the first time and started over before realizing that you wanted an immediate answer."

Amy beamed. "I think it's good, too."

"I can tell you wrote it."

"Really?"

"Yeah. I'm no literary critic, but I can recognize what you've done. What do you call it?"

"Voice. But I tried to give the voice to the kids."

"You did, but the way the little girl talks reminds me of you."

"You didn't know me when I was six years old."

"But I've been around you when that's how old you acted."

Amy laughed.

"What about finding a publisher?" Jeff asked. "Are you going to ask Bernie to help?"

Even though she'd joked with Natalie about buying a beach house, Amy hadn't really considered whether the book was marketable.

"I don't think he works in the children's genre, and it's really up to Natalie. This book is her baby, not mine. She may be happy self-publishing a hundred copies and giving them away as Christmas presents. My next step is to let Ian read it. That will be the real test."

Amy took all the pages upstairs. Ian was on the floor of his room with his hand underneath his bed. He awkwardly turned his head as she entered.

"What are you doing?" Amy asked.

"Checking under my bed. I always find something I forgot I lost."

"Let me give you something else to look at."

Amy retreated to her bedroom while Ian read the book. Twenty minutes later he appeared in her doorway.

"What did you think?" Amy asked.

"You know I don't like to read too much, but it was okay." Ian laid the pages on the end of the bed. "I saw Mrs. Graham's name on the bottom of the pictures. She's a good artist."

"Yes."

"Did you write the story?"

"Mrs. Graham wrote the first draft, and then I changed it hoping to make it better."

Ian nodded. "You made the middle boy, Alfred, a lot like me."

"Did you like him?"

"Yeah. But don't you think his family should call him Al? Except maybe his mom when she's mad at him? Alfred sounds like an old man."

It was a legitimate question.

"I'll ask Mrs. Graham about that. We don't want anything to cause a reader the same age as the characters to think the story doesn't seem real."

"Oh, it seemed real to me. It made me want to go to the beach. Have you and Dad talked about where we can go this summer? I want it to be like the place in the book where there is tons of stuff to do and neat things to see."

Amy smiled. She'd received the feedback she needed.

"Yes, we'll try to find a good place."

Amy couldn't wait to contact Natalie. However, she couldn't reach her on either her house phone or her cell phone. Going upstairs to the writing room, she sent the revised text as an e-mail attachment along with a summary of the comments by Jeff and Ian.

Driving to work the following morning, Amy received a call. Glancing down at her phone on the passenger seat, she saw Natalie's face.

"I am so excited," Natalie began. "Luke read what you wrote and got a big grin on his face."

"You wrote it. I tweaked it."

"Be honest, Amy. You completely redid the text and connected the book to the illustrations so much better than I could. I wish I could give you a big hug."

"I can feel it through the phone."

"Are we still on for tomorrow?" Natalie asked.

"Probably, but I'll know later today. There is a lot going on at the office this week." Amy paused. "No surprise visits to Ms. Burris's house, okay?"

"I promise."

Early in the afternoon Mr. Phillips summoned Amy into his office. Chris was there, too. Seeing the young lawyer, Amy wondered how his talk with Laura had gone. Nothing in Chris's face gave her a clue.

"I was telling Chris that I'm going to cover the Kelly and Jackson depositions tomorrow," Mr. Phillips said. "He's given me his notes."

Amy glanced at Chris and picked up on his disappointment. She kicked herself for not considering that the young lawyer would want to seal the deal in the Dominick case. But arguing about it with Mr. Phillips would be fruitless.

"Yes, sir," she replied. "Is there anything you want me to do beforehand?"

"Organize Chris's information the way I like it. That shouldn't take too long."

"Yes, sir."

The young lawyer handed Amy a file folder.

"I've already marked the deposition exhibits," he said.

"Thanks," Amy replied.

She turned to leave.

"There's one more thing," Mr. Phillips said.

Amy faced him again.

"I want you to sit in on the deposition with me."

"Me? Wouldn't Chris be a better choice? He's done all the prep work."

"He's going to be working on another project with the time this will free up. My thought is that you might have" — Mr. Phillips paused as he searched for the right words — "other insights that need to be explored when I'm deposing the witnesses."

"I don't think that's likely," she responded as she felt her face flush.

"How can you know?" Mr. Phillips asked.

It was Amy's turn to try to find the correct words.

"Uh, I don't usually —" She stopped. "I mean —"

"That's what I suspected." Mr. Phillips nodded. "Plan on being there. We'll start at twelve thirty with Beverly Jackson, so eat lunch at your desk in case I have something for you to do at the last minute."

"Yes, sir."

Amy returned to her desk. Chris left Mr. Phillips's office a few minutes later and slipped around the corner to Amy's workstation.

"I'm in deep now, aren't I?" Amy said when she saw Chris standing in her doorway. "I wasn't trying to steal your opportunity to score a big win in the case. Once Mr. Phillips knew what was going on, there was no way I could control what he was going to do."

"I know, and it wouldn't have been right for me to claim credit for what you uncovered."

"I wish you could." Amy hung her head. "I'm not trying to draw attention to myself. I liked it better when I was an anonymous typist."

"Those days are gone."

"How was your talk with Laura?" Amy asked.

"You'd have to ask her, but I think I did a good job. She seemed happy, and I caught her smiling for no apparent reason a few times during the rest of the weekend. It could be because she's pregnant, but I'd like to believe she was thinking about me."

"Probably both." Amy brightened. "It's important to follow up so she knows you're serious —"

"I thought you wanted to shut up and be invisible."

Amy pointed toward the closed door to Mr. Phillips's office.

"Only with him."

After Chris left, Amy sent Natalie a text message telling her they wouldn't be able to meet for lunch.

The following morning Amy took extra care with her outfit and makeup. Jeff noticed.

"What's going on at work today?" he asked as they each poured coffee into a travel mug.

"I'm going to sit in with Mr. Phillips during a couple of depositions."

"Why does he need you? Is he afraid he'll forget to ask the right questions?"

"No, his mind is as sharp as ever, but if he

tells me to do something, it's never a debate."

Jeff kissed her on the cheek.

"Just like you and me," he said.

Amy was nervous and jumpy the entire morning. Mr. Phillips acted as if he didn't have a worry in the world. Discovery depositions were a way for lawyers to find out what the other side knew about the facts and circumstances of a case. For that reason, attorneys treated them more casually than courtroom testimony. Mistakes made by a lawyer during a deposition were corrected prior to trial. Mistakes made by witnesses, however, would be fodder for effective cross-examination in court. Amy knew Mr. Phillips's goals in deposing Dr. Kelly and Nurse Jackson were to obtain admissions and uncover inconsistencies. She had no idea how he was going to interject the information from her dream.

She sat at her desk and nibbled on an apple for lunch. Mr. Phillips didn't bring her any last-minute work, so she was left with nothing to do but fret about what lay ahead. Dr. Kelly and Beverly Jackson were the people who had done something wrong, but Amy was having trouble convincing herself that she wasn't the one on the hot seat. Five minutes before the depositions were scheduled to start, Mr. Phillips stuck his head into her office.

"Let's go. Beverly Jackson is here. Bring a legal pad for notes."

With a sigh, Amy got up from her desk and followed Mr. Phillips into the largest conference room on the main floor.

THIRTY-SIX

At one end of the shiny table sat a dark-haired court reporter with a recorder and stenomask in front of her. Beside her and wearing a dark blue outfit was a trim, middle-aged woman with green eyes and auburn hair. Mr. Phillips extended his hand, and the woman stood up.

"Mrs. Jackson, I'm Harold Phillips. I represent William McKay, the executor of Sanford Dominick's estate, and this is my legal assistant, Amy Clarke. She's going to join us today."

Nurse Jackson shook Mr. Phillips's hand, but her eyes went to Amy and opened wider.

"Are you the writer?" she asked.

"Uh, I'm a novelist."

"You wrote *A Great and Precious Promise,* right?"

"Yes." Amy glanced at Mr. Phillips, who looked caught off guard.

"Our book club read your book and loved it," Jackson continued. "I saw on your website the other day that a new book is coming out soon. Is it a sequel?"

"No, it's a stand-alone novel with new characters."

"I can't wait to read it. I wish I'd brought my copy of *A Great and Precious Promise* so you could sign it."

"We need to get started," Mr. Phillips interjected.

"What's the name of the new book?" Jackson asked as she sat down.

"*The Everlasting Arms,*" Amy replied.

"I can't wait to tell my friends that I met you."

Mr. Phillips cleared his throat. "Mrs. Jackson, you're here pursuant to a notice of deposition, and it's my understanding you've chosen not to have counsel present."

"You mean a lawyer?"

"Yes."

"I called your paralegal, and she told me you were going to ask me questions about Mr. Dominick. I'm not being sued, am I?"

"You're not currently named as a party in the litigation."

"Could that change?"

"Possibly."

"How could I be dragged into a lawsuit?" Jackson asked with a puzzled look on her face. "All I did was help take care of Mr. Dominick for the last two years of his life."

Amy knew Mr. Phillips hated dealing with

people who didn't have lawyers. He leaned forward and put his hands together on the table.

"Mrs. Jackson, I'm here to talk to you about Mr. Dominick, but I represent Mr. McKay, the executor, which means I can't give you any legal advice. I won't know what you're going to tell me until the court reporter swears you in and I ask you some questions. It's impossible for me to predict what could happen as a result of your testimony."

Jackson shifted in her seat. In spite of what she saw in her dream, Amy found herself wishing the nurse would tell Mr. Phillips that she wanted a lawyer to represent her. Jackson looked at Amy, who had no idea what message her face might reveal.

"I hate to spend the money to hire a lawyer," Jackson said slowly, then paused.

Amy held her breath. She saw Mr. Phillips get ready to speak again.

"Mr. Dominick was very kind to me," Jackson continued. "I'm sure you know he gave me $150,000 to help with expenses for my son who has cerebral palsy. It was an unbelievably kind thing to do, but after he met him, I think Kenny's struggles touched Mr. Dominick's heart. I don't have anything to hide, but —"

Mr. Phillips interrupted her. "Mrs. Jackson, we're here today to take your testimony, so please hold off for a minute. May I ask the court reporter to swear you in?"

Jackson looked again at Amy, who saw a silent plea for help in the woman's eyes. Amy felt her face flush.

"I want to have a lawyer with me," the nurse said.

"Are you sure?" Mr. Phillips asked.

"Yes."

Mr. Phillips pressed his lips together for a moment. "If you're not going to go forward with the deposition without legal representation, there's no use in continuing this conversation. I want to hear what you have to say, but it needs to be under oath."

"Okay." Jackson glanced at Amy again. "I guess you can't recommend a lawyer for me, can you?"

"No, we can't," Mr. Phillips replied. "How long do you think it will take you to retain counsel?"

"Uh, a couple of weeks, I guess."

Mr. Phillips turned to Amy. "Prepare a new notice for Mrs. Jackson and set it three weeks out."

"Please don't do it on a Wednesday," Jackson said. "Kenny is in treatment every Wednesday."

"Check my calendar and avoid Wednesday," Mr. Phillips said.

Amy left the conference room and walked rapidly toward her office. When she turned a corner past Janelle's desk, she almost ran into Chris.

"How's it going?" he asked.

"Nowhere. Beverly Jackson is going to hire a lawyer."

"Did he get anything out of her at all?"

"She was never sworn in." Amy looked over her shoulder at the conference room. She lowered her voice. "She read my novel."

"What are the chances of that? Do you think she was on the level?"

It hadn't occurred to Amy that someone would lie about reading her book.

"I hope so. Anyway, I have to get out a notice rescheduling the deposition."

"At least Dr. Kelly will have a lawyer sitting beside him. Mr. Phillips will find out something at three o'clock."

Amy continued to her office and quickly printed out a new notice for a Thursday morning in three weeks. She returned to the conference room with the original and two copies. Mr. Phillips signed them and slid one across the table to Beverly Jackson.

"Is that date satisfactory?" he asked.

The nurse took out her phone and checked her calendar.

"Yes, I can move a couple of things and be here."

"Then we're done for now," Mr. Phillips said, getting up from the table. "Please ask your attorney to contact me prior to the deposition."

Mr. Phillips turned toward the door. The court reporter started packing up her gear.

"I'll be back at three o'clock," she said to Mr. Phillips.

"Who was your favorite character in *A Great and Precious Promise*?" Amy asked Nurse Jackson.

"Of course everyone in the book club loved Jasmine, but her great-aunt Lilly stood out to me. When Lilly told Jasmine how she regretted never asking her husband's forgiveness before his death, I cried buckets."

In Amy's mind it was one of the top three scenes in the book.

"That scene moved me emotionally when I wrote it. I'm glad it touched you, too."

"Amy," Mr. Phillips said, his voice rising.

"Yes, sir."

"It was a thrill meeting you," Jackson said to Amy. "May I bring my book with me the next time I'm here so you can sign it?"

Amy glanced at Mr. Phillips, whose face was getting red.

"Sure."

Amy silently followed Mr. Phillips out of the conference room. When she prepared to go around the corner to her office, the senior partner spoke. "Come with me."

Amy swallowed.

"I had no idea —" she began before Mr. Phillips could speak.

"I know that," he snapped before she could continue. "But you took it a bit too far. Remember where you are and what you're doing here."

"Yes, sir."

"I wanted to set up Dr. Kelly by going first with Jackson," Mr. Phillips fumed. "Nailing down her testimony would have been a huge advantage."

"But you did the right thing notifying her of her right to have a lawyer."

"Of course I did, but you acted like you were ready to sit down and have a chat with her about your book."

"I was making sure she'd actually read it."

"Which had nothing to do with why she was here."

"No, it didn't," Amy admitted.

"At least we got an admission from her off the record about the $150,000 she received from Sonny. She claims he gave it to help her care for her son, but we know at least half of it went to Dr. Kelly."

In all the commotion in the conference room, Amy had missed the significance of Jackson's offhand comment. Mr. Phillips checked his watch.

"Since I don't have to be scrambling around organizing my questioning for Dr. Kelly based on information obtained from Nurse Jackson, I'm going out for a few minutes."

"Is there anything you want me to do while

you're gone?"

Mr. Phillips gave Amy a look that made her suspect he was about to give her a tongue-lashing.

"There are a few short pieces of dictation you should be able to transcribe," he said curtly. "That should help keep your mind on the office."

Relieved to be away from Mr. Phillips, Amy returned to her office and began working on the dictation. She finished three letters. While she watched the pages come out of the printer, she decided Mr. Phillips had overreacted to Beverly Jackson's familiarity with Amy as a writer. He'd taken out his frustration that the witness didn't want to answer questions without a lawyer present on Amy. With Harold Phillips, it was better to overlook an offense than try to address it.

She heard Mr. Phillips return. A few minutes later he buzzed her. His face was still a dark cloud. He reached over to the printer on his credenza and grabbed a sheet of paper and thrust it out to her.

"Read this."

Amy took the sheet. It was a short news article from the Internet. The subject was the consulting firm Mr. Phillips hired on Amy's recommendation.

"I'll save you a few minutes," Mr. Phillips said. "The consulting firm in Miami you recommended for the Thompson Trust is under investigation for illegal activity with foreign nations that are on the US government's do not trade list. The feds seized a bunch of their records as part of an ongoing investigation. There's no way we want to do business with them."

Amy's eyes widened. "I never saw anything about that in my dream."

"It would have been more helpful if you'd had insight into that instead of voicing some vague fears about Dr. Ramsey."

"As soon as we're done with Dr. Kelly, I'll call Ramsey and see if he'll take us back. I hope it's not too late to straighten out this mess."

Amy felt slightly dizzy.

"I'm sorry —"

"We'll talk later. It's time to face off with Dr. Kelly."

"Are you sure you need me?" Amy asked. "Or want me?"

Mr. Phillips clenched his jaw for a moment. "Let's go," he said.

"Yes, sir."

Amy stumbled after Mr. Phillips to the conference room. This time there were two men sitting on the other side of the table; one in his thirties, and the other looked to be around fifty-five. The older man, a lawyer named Ed Franconi, stood.

"Harold, good to see you."

"Ed."

The two lawyers shook hands.

"This is Dr. Kelly," his attorney said.

The man whose name had invaded Amy's dream with overwhelming negativity was slightly built with brown hair, brown eyes, and an intelligent face. His only unusual feature was a thin mustache on his upper lip. He stood up and shook Mr. Phillips's hand.

"This is my legal assistant, Amy Clarke," Mr. Phillips said.

"Mr. Franconi," Amy said. "We've talked several times on the phone over the years."

"Yes, it's nice to finally meet you."

Amy ignored Dr. Kelly. Thankfully, no one mentioned anything about her book. The court reporter swore in Dr. Kelly, and Mr. Phillips began.

Amy knew there was a rhythm to questioning a witness in a deposition. No attorney asked an important question in the first few minutes. Rather, the lawyer tried to establish a tempo of the witness answering routine questions so that when a disputed matter came up it took energy to break the pattern. Mr. Phillips began with questions about Dr. Kelly's educational and professional background. He spent much more time than actually necessary because he wanted to create a relaxed, cooperative atmosphere. Dr. Kelly was soft-spoken, and several times Mr. Phillips had to remind the witness to speak up.

"Tell me about your experience providing in-home care for elderly patients," Mr. Phillips said.

"Like most physicians, I rarely make house calls, but I've had several terminally ill patients whom I continued to follow at home after they couldn't come to the office."

"How did Sanford Dominick become your patient?"

Dr. Kelly didn't immediately answer but turned to his lawyer, who handed him a file. The doctor opened it.

"I was contacted by Beverly Jackson, a nurse who was providing home care for Mr. Dominick. She asked if I would be interested in providing general medical care. The patient had a number of medical conditions but needed a family practice doctor or internist to oversee his status. Mr. Dominick regularly saw a cardiologist and a neurologist, and he had the financial ability to pay for a doctor to come to his home. I agreed to accept him as a patient."

Amy expected Mr. Phillips to begin a line of questions about Dr. Kelly's connection with Beverly Jackson.

"Do you know Ms. Mildred Burris?" Mr. Phillips asked.

"Uh, yes." Dr. Kelly raised his eyebrows.

"How?"

"I first met her when I began seeing Mr. Dominick as a patient."

"What do you know about the nature of her relationship to Mr. Dominick?"

"He introduced her to me as a longtime friend who visited him on a regular basis."

"How many times did you see Mr. Dominick?"

"Do you want the specific dates?"

"Yes, and summarize what you did on each occasion."

The doctor opened his chart. Mr. Phillips already had copies of the medical records from Dr. Kelly and every other doctor who had seen Mr. Dominick, but Amy knew he'd still want to hear what the doctor said. As the doctor plowed through the data, Mr. Phillips interrupted several times with questions.

"Was Beverly Jackson always present at the time you examined Mr. Dominick?"

"I can't say for certain, but I don't recall a visit when she wasn't there. She usually scheduled the appointments."

"Were you present when Mr. Dominick died?"

Amy held her breath.

"Yes."

"Was Mrs. Jackson also present?"

"Yes, she'd called me a couple of hours earlier and informed me that it appeared the patient was close to death. It was about seven o'clock in the evening, and I came immediately."

"How did she know Mr. Dominick was

about to die?"

The doctor went through a list of telltale signs of impending death that made Amy's skin crawl.

"When I examined the patient, I concurred with Mrs. Jackson's assessment. I stayed with Mr. Dominick while Mrs. Jackson called Mrs. Dominick in Florida to give her an update."

"Did you speak with Mrs. Dominick?"

"Not until the next day when she arrived here."

"So she left Florida as soon as she knew her husband was about to die?"

"That was my understanding from Mrs. Jackson."

"Was Ms. Burris there when you arrived at the residence on the evening of Mr. Dominick's death?"

"Yes."

"Were the three of you in the same room with Mr. Dominick?"

A shiver went down Amy's spine.

"Yes, at various times during the course of the evening."

"Was Mr. Dominick conscious?"

"He was semiconscious and noncommunicative."

Mr. Phillips glanced down at his notes.

"We'll come back to that visit in a minute. You also saw Mr. Dominick fourteen days previously, and you described his condition then as 'stable with good vital signs.' Is that correct?"

"Yes."

"Who was present in the room at the time of that examination?" Mr. Phillips asked.

"Myself, Mrs. Jackson, and Ms. Burris."

"The same three people?" Mr. Phillips asked.

"Yes. That wasn't a regularly scheduled checkup. Ms. Burris asked me to come."

"She called you, not Mrs. Jackson?"

"Yes, although Mrs. Jackson knew about the request that I come."

"Tell me everything you remember about that visit, not just what's in your medical notes."

The witness smiled. To Amy it appeared Dr. Kelly was mocking Mr. Phillips — sending a signal that he was not going to be trapped by the cagey old lawyer.

"When I arrived, Mr. Dominick was sitting in a chair on the veranda adjacent to his bedroom. The veranda had several large windows that gave him a view of the pond at the rear of his property. Mr. Dominick liked to sit there, especially in the early morning."

"What time of day was it?"

"Around seven thirty in the morning. After leaving I went to the hospital for my rounds at nine thirty."

"How long were you at the Dominick residence?"

"An hour and a half, which was much

longer than usual. The medical examination only took about fifteen minutes."

"What did you do the rest of the time?"

Dr. Kelly paused and looked directly at Mr. Phillips.

"Watched and listened as Ms. Burris told Mr. Dominick how to become a Christian."

Mr. Phillips coughed into his hand. Amy's mouth dropped open.

"She did most of the talking," Dr. Kelly continued, "but Beverly Jackson contributed as well. I remember they read several passages of Scripture from a huge black Bible with beautiful illustrations and gold-leaf calligraphy. Mr. Dominick said he bought the Bible many years ago in England during World War II. It was a very rare edition. When they finished, Ms. Burris asked him if he wanted to pray, and he did. I considered it a divine opportunity, especially knowing what we do now."

"What is that?"

"That Mr. Dominick only had a short time to live. I'm a doctor, not a minister, but I talk to patients about spiritual matters if they want to do so. That was probably Mr. Dominick's last chance to hear and believe the gospel."

"Did you participate in this conversation?"

"No, Ms. Burris did a beautiful job."

Mr. Phillips shuffled through some of the papers on the table in front of him. Amy could tell he was trying to buy a moment's time to figure out what in the world to ask next.

"Was that the same day Mr. Dominick allegedly executed a new will essentially cutting his wife out of his estate?" Mr. Phillips regained some of his footing.

"No, that took place three days later. The attorney who prepared the will asked me to be present and determine if Mr. Dominick was mentally competent and knew the significance of his decisions."

Mr. Phillips glanced down at the sheets in front of him.

"Why isn't that visit in your medical notes?"

"It's on the back of the previous visit."

Mr. Phillips turned over a sheet of paper before launching into a series of questions about Dr. Kelly's evaluation of Mr. Dominick's mental status. Amy barely listened. Instead, in her mind's eye she stayed on the veranda where Ms. Burris led the man who had broken her heart sixty years earlier to the Lord. She'd reached out to Sanford Dominick, not because of his money, but in the love of God.

Thirty-Seven

When Amy refocused, Mr. Phillips was asking Dr. Kelly about the money Sanford Dominick gave Beverly Jackson.

"Yes, Mrs. Jackson told me about it and showed me the check."

"What was Mrs. Jackson's explanation for the payment?"

"Mr. Dominick wanted to help with expenses related to the long-term care of Mrs. Jackson's son, who has cerebral palsy. She was reluctant to accept it."

"But she cashed it, didn't she?"

"Yes, that is my understanding."

Mr. Phillips marked as an exhibit the check from Mrs. Jackson to Dr. Kelly written several weeks later.

"Did you receive this check for seventy-five thousand dollars from Mrs. Jackson?"

"Yes."

"Do you know the source of this money?"

"It was from Mr. Dominick's gift."

"Why did Mrs. Jackson give you half the

money instead of using it for the benefit of her son?"

"She didn't give me the money. The check was reimbursement for a handicapped van and several items of medical equipment. As a physician, I was able to obtain the items at a discount, which I passed along to her. Every penny of this money went to Kenny's care, just as Mr. Dominick intended."

Mr. Phillips turned to Amy with a questioning look in his eyes. She stared back, not sure if she should blink. Mr. Phillips returned to his prepared questions about Mr. Dominick's mental capacity at the time he signed the will a week or so before his death. Amy was impressed not by the lawyer's questions but by the doctor's responses.

"Before Mr. Dominick signed the papers, I administered the nine-point General Practitioner Assessment of Cognition," Dr. Kelly said. "The GPAOC assesses time orientation, numbering, placing hands correctly, awareness of current events, first name, last name, address, streets, and cities. Mr. Dominick scored seven out of nine, which was the same score he'd received several times over the past few months. He was confused about the day of the week and the name of the president. The validity of the test is enhanced by comparison of results over time."

"But did —"

"I'm not finished," the doctor interrupted.

"At the request of Mr. Valaoras, the attorney who prepared the will, I asked Mr. Dominick questions about his family members because it's my understanding he needed to know 'the natural objects of his affection' in order to be mentally competent to sign a will. Is that the correct terminology?"

"I'm asking the questions, Doctor," Mr. Phillips replied drily.

Dr. Kelly didn't change expression. "Mr. Dominick correctly named his wife and children, but when it came to his grandchildren, he committed three errors. He confused the names of the children of his daughters, Elizabeth and Leanne. Upon prompting, he acknowledged his mistakes and repeated the information correctly."

To Amy, Mr. Dominick's mental capacity sounded about the same as it was when he signed the will prepared by Mr. Phillips.

"Nevertheless, Mr. Dominick's initial responses on several questions were erroneous, weren't they?" Mr. Phillips asked.

"That's true."

"Are you aware that Dr. Robinson, the patient's neurologist, also evaluated Mr. Dominick's mental status around the same time?"

"No. I've not seen his report."

"Would it surprise you to learn that Dr. Robinson did not think Mr. Dominick was competent?"

"Not really. Given the patient's condition, I think he might respond differently to testing from day to day during the last months of his life. All I can testify about are my findings."

"And isn't it true that a board-certified neurologist would have more training and experience in this evaluating of mental competency than you would?"

"Yes."

Mr. Phillips grunted in satisfaction as he prepared to ask his next question.

"Are you aware it's a conflict of interest for you to testify regarding Mr. Dominick's mental competency while also being a witness to his signing of the will?"

Dr. Kelly turned to his lawyer and gave him a questioning look.

"Answer the question based on your knowledge and understanding," Mr. Franconi said.

"No, I did not know there was a problem. But I also thought it only took two witnesses to validate a will, and three of us signed, along with a notary public."

"Are you aware that Mrs. Jackson, as a beneficiary of the will, should not have signed as a witness?" Mr. Phillips countered.

"Objection, Harold," Mr. Franconi said. "I let you ask Dr. Kelly one legal question, but it's going to be up to the judge to determine the legitimacy of the witnesses to the will. Move on to something else."

While the lawyers argued, Amy scribbled a

note and slid it to Mr. Phillips — *Jackson didn't witness the will.* Mr. Phillips glanced down and grunted.

"Are you instructing him not to answer?" Mr. Phillips continued.

"Yes, and you're welcome to ask a judge to make him answer, if you want."

"I'll reserve my rights on that," Mr. Phillips said.

"I'm sure you will," Mr. Franconi responded evenly. "Is there anything else relevant to the purpose of this deposition that you want to ask Dr. Kelly?"

Mr. Phillips wasn't going to let the other lawyer cut him off and went over ground that he'd already plowed. Ten minutes later he closed his folder.

"That's all I have at this time subject to reconvening the deposition if other information should come to light or upon order of the court."

"No questions," Mr. Franconi said.

In less than a minute, Dr. Kelly and his lawyer packed up and left the conference room.

"I'll get back to work," Amy said to Mr. Phillips. "I have a couple of items left on the last batch of —"

"Meet me in my office," the senior partner said, cutting her off.

"Yes, sir." Amy swallowed.

Even though she'd had over an hour of

deposition testimony to try to figure out how she had misjudged Dr. Lawrence Kelly so completely, Amy had no idea what she was going to say to Mr. Phillips. She meekly followed him into his office. The lawyer dropped the file on his credenza and plopped down in his chair, leaving Amy standing before him. Several moments of silence passed.

"Well?" he asked.

"I'm not sure," Amy said slowly. "Looking back, I can see how I probably misinterpreted what I saw in the dream. I mean, Dr. Kelly, Beverly Jackson, and Ms. Burris were all in the room with Mr. Dominick, and there was a big black book, but I thought the book being placed over Mr. Dominick represented his being smothered, especially when he went limp, but I think that represented his making peace with God after a lifetime —"

"Stop it!" Mr. Phillips interrupted.

Amy shut her mouth. The senior partner rubbed his forehead with his hands.

"I can't practice law like this. Listening to you is like playing roulette in Vegas. You might hit it big or you might lose everything." Mr. Phillips paused. "Or maybe it's more like Russian roulette. There is a bullet in your gun that can blow the brains out of a case."

Amy felt herself trembling, and her voice shook when she spoke. "But Dr. Kelly was going to say what he did regardless of any dreams I had. It didn't really change anything."

"What about Claude Ramsey? What if I'd listened to you about him?"

Amy hesitated. "I'm still not comfortable —"

Mr. Phillips cut her off with a wave of his hand.

"Amy, I'm going to ask you a question, and I want a straightforward, truthful answer. Will you do that?"

"Yes, sir. I've always told you the truth."

"Can you keep what you see in your dreams to yourself or will you feel compelled to tell me, Chris Lance, or whomever else you think needs to hear about them?"

Amy knew the answer Mr. Phillips wanted to hear. And she wanted to give it to him. The living room was a holy, personal place where the world didn't intrude. She had no desire to take what she saw or heard there and expose it to unbelieving hearts and minds. If she kept quiet she could always pray. That would be the truly spiritual thing to do. For a split second, she saw herself saying, "Yes, sir," but the words couldn't make it past her lips.

"No, I can't," she replied with a sigh. "And it's not because I don't respect you. It's because I have to obey God. I may never have anything else to say —"

"But you can't guarantee it."

"No, sir. I can't."

Mr. Phillips looked at Amy for several seconds. His eyes didn't reveal what he was thinking. He pressed his lips together for a moment before he spoke.

"Clock out and go home," he said.

Amy swallowed. She had to know for sure what he meant.

"Do I come back in tomorrow?"

"Only to pick up your termination paperwork from Ms. Kirkpatrick. I'll send her a memo before I leave today."

Stunned, Amy turned away. She retrieved her purse from her office and stumbled past the reception desk.

"See you tomorrow," Janelle said brightly as she passed by.

Amy didn't respond. She got in her car and rested her forehead against the steering wheel. It was a day when Megan was taking care of Ian, so she didn't have to pick him up from the after-school program. Amy didn't want to go home. Her stomach knotted up at the thought of breaking the news of her firing to Jeff.

She started the car's motor and drove slowly out of the firm parking lot. When she reached a stop sign not far from the office, she turned left instead of right. Two blocks later she pulled into the driveway for Ms. Burris's house. Amy couldn't tell if the elderly woman was home and didn't know what she was going to say if she was. She parked her car and rang the front doorbell. No one answered. She waited and rang the bell again. Just as she was about to leave, the door opened. It was Ms. Burris. The older woman was wearing a peach-colored dress. As soon as she saw Amy, her face brightened.

"It's so good to see you," she said. "I was in the backyard and didn't hear the chime. Come in."

Amy followed her into the parlor where the Christmas tree had been. As she glanced around, Amy wondered how much of the work done on the house had been paid for by Mr. Dominick's money. They sat down.

"Do you know why I'm here?" Amy asked.

"No, except I can tell you're upset."

"Mr. Phillips fired me."

Ms. Burris's face fell.

Amy told her about the dream with the big black book. Ms. Burris leaned forward and asked her to repeat every word of it again.

"That's remarkable," she said.

"But I completely misinterpreted it. I can't believe I would consider the possibility that you —" Amy stopped. "I feel terrible."

"Mistakes happen. Spiritual discernment and human understanding rarely intersect."

"All I know is that I was one hundred percent wrong." Amy sighed. "The dream had nothing to do with the litigation over Mr. Dominick's estate. It all came to light this afternoon when Mr. Phillips deposed Dr. Kelly."

Without going into the questions Mr. Phillips asked about Sanford Dominick's mental capacity, Amy repeated what the doctor said about Ms. Burris's leading the elderly man to the Lord. Ms. Burris's eyes shone as she listened.

"Sometimes it takes decades for the fruit of forgiveness to come up," she said. "One of the hardest things I had to do was forgive Sonny for breaking my heart. I was at the church in my wedding gown when he sent one of the groomsmen to tell me he wasn't coming."

"But how could you have married him? You would have been unequally yoked."

"Sonny had a foxhole conversion during the war. At the time I believed it was real, but he turned away from God and me. What you witnessed in your dream was a homecoming."

"That's the reason —" Amy started.

"We were in my house in the dream. My father bought this place for Sonny and me as a wedding gift. This is where we were going to live."

Amy sat quietly for a moment with her hands in her lap.

"Why did I have this dream if what I saw had already happened?" she asked softly.

"Maybe it was for me." Ms. Burris smiled

slightly. "Listening to you has settled a big question that has weighed on my heart since the day at Sonny's house when he prayed. I desperately wanted him to believe, but it's so hard to be sure. Who can know the human heart? Your dream gives me a glimpse of what heaven saw the day we prayed together." There were now tears in Ms. Burris's eyes. "And nothing is more precious than that."

"You really loved him, didn't you?"

"And grieved for decades over the path he chose."

The enormous tragedy of Sanford Dominick's life hit Amy. The war hero received acclaim from many and made millions of dollars. But he died without experiencing the genuine love offered by the godly wife who would have been his perfect partner. Added to that was the anguish of Ms. Burris's heart for a life of singleness.

"I'm sorry," Amy said.

"My life has been full in many ways," Ms. Burris said. "But I can't deny there is an empty place that has never been filled."

Amy's job loss seemed small compared to what she'd just heard.

"I need to go home," she said, shifting in her seat. "And I dread telling Jeff that I've lost my job."

"He's a good man."

"Which doesn't make it easier."

Ms. Burris reached over and took Amy's

hand in hers.

"I'm here to help any way I can," she said.

The look in Ms. Burris's eyes told Amy she meant what she said.

Jeff pulled into the driveway immediately after Amy, and they parked beside each other in the garage. As soon as she got out of the car, Amy went over to him, gave him a long hug, and then told him what had happened. To her relief, he received the news calmly. They went into the house together. Megan and Ian were in the kitchen doing homework.

"We're going out to eat," Jeff said to them.

"But —" Amy started.

"My treat," Jeff interjected with a smile. "Because you deserve it."

"Why do I deserve a meal at a restaurant?"

"Mom, let Dad do what he wants to do," Ian cut in. "Bobby and his family almost never eat out. You have it good."

Amy looked gratefully at Jeff.

"Yes, I do."

Megan requested Chinese food, so they went to her favorite restaurant. Amy thought she wouldn't have much of an appetite but was surprised to find out how hungry she was. Losing a job was hard work. Afterward, they stopped off for frozen yogurt at a new place that had recently opened. Sitting at a round table in a shaded courtyard next to the yogurt shop, Amy told the children about getting fired. And she didn't stick to the basic facts. She told them the role her dreams played in Mr. Phillips's decision. Never before had she been so open with them about her trips to the living room and what happened there. Ian took the news in stride. Childlike faith was accepting and concrete. Megan seemed troubled.

"And it's because you wouldn't agree to keep quiet about your dreams?" she asked.

"Yes, and I can see Mr. Phillips's point. He doesn't want the distraction in his practice or for the other people at work. It's been very tough on me, especially when I don't correctly interpret what I'm seeing or hearing. That's happened twice recently and created a lot of confusion and drama."

"You mean you told Mr. Phillips something you thought was right but it wasn't?" Megan asked.

"Yes. And not just him. I've also talked with one of the associate attorneys."

"Wow, Mom. I'm not sure what I think about that. But you were right about the woman who visited the church and turned out to be pregnant."

"Yes."

Amy could see the wheels of Megan's mind turning but wasn't sure where her thoughts were going.

"I'm being open with you," Amy said after a few moments of silence, "but I'd appreciate it if you'd not discuss this with your friends."

"Not even Bethany and Alecia?" Megan asked.

"Yes, and if you have a question or thought, come to me. I may not have the answer, but it will make me feel better to know this stays in the family."

"It's part of protecting your mom," Jeff said. "Just like she's done for you ever since you were little."

"Sure." Ian took a final bite of peach yogurt topped with hot fudge sauce. "I think you're awesome."

THIRTY-EIGHT

That night Amy called Natalie with the news. Even over the phone, Amy could sense her friend's sympathy and shock.

"I have to go by the office for a few minutes in the morning to clean out my desk and see Ms. Kirkpatrick," Amy said, "but I'd really like to see you afterward if you have the time."

"Of course, when and where?"

They agreed to meet at the coffee shop at 10:00 a.m.

The following morning Amy mustered up as much courage as she could and marched through the front door of the law office. She'd dressed as if she were going to report for work.

"Good morning," Janelle said brightly.

Apparently news of her firing hadn't yet filtered down to the staff.

"Good morning," Amy replied as naturally as she could. "Is Ms. Kirkpatrick in her office?"

"I think so."

Amy went to the rear of the mansion. As soon as Ms. Kirkpatrick saw her, she motioned for her to come in, then closed the door.

"I just finished your paperwork," the administrator said crisply. "On my part, I want to thank you again for filling in. It took a load off my plate. Trying to provide a temp who can satisfy Mr. Phillips is impossible. You were a lifesaver."

Amy started to reach for the forms but pulled back her hand.

"Excuse me," she said.

Ms. Kirkpatrick continued, "I didn't know until late yesterday afternoon that Mr. Phillips talked with Emily and moved up her return-to-work date. She scrambled around and arranged day care for her baby so she can be here on Monday. We'd hoped there might be another position for you, but there are a couple of girls who aren't at full capacity. If a spot opens up in the future, do you want me to give you a call?"

Amy was flabbergasted but then quickly realized she shouldn't be. How could Mr. Phillips explain to Ms. Kirkpatrick his real reason for letting her go? It might even constitute religious discrimination, not that Amy wanted to file a lawsuit.

"That would be up to Mr. Phillips," she said noncommittally.

"It always is," Ms. Kirkpatrick replied with a shrug. She pointed to a line at the bottom of a form. "Sign here."

Amy cleaned out her desk. Mr. Phillips had an appointment out of the office, so they avoided another awkward encounter. By the time Amy reached the reception area, news of her departure had reached Janelle.

"I'm going to miss you terribly," the receptionist said with a sorrowful look on her face. "I feel like I've barely gotten to know you."

"Maybe we can still get together for lunch sometime," Amy replied. She glanced toward the stairwell to the second floor. "Is Chris here?"

"No, he had a motion hearing at nine thirty and told me not to expect him back before eleven."

"Okay."

"If we have lunch, maybe you can sign a copy of your new book for me. Mom still talks about how thrilled she was to receive the signed copy of *A Great and Precious Promise* for her birthday," Janelle said, brightening up slightly.

"That's good, and I'd be glad to sign a copy of my new book for you. It'll be on the shelves in a couple of weeks, or I could bring one to you when we get together."

"That would be way cooler. I'll buy you lunch."

Amy left and closed the front door of the

office behind her. Her forced departure was much different from the voluntary one twenty-four months before. That time there had been a small party in the kitchen with a signed "Best Wishes" card placed in the middle of a fancy fruit and cheese basket. She'd left the office feeling a mixture of freedom and excitement. This time, feeling numb and detached, she had her belongings jumbled together in a canvas tote bag.

Natalie was waiting for her at the coffee shop. As soon as Amy came through the door, her friend jumped up, ran over, and gave her a hug.

"I've felt sick about what happened ever since you called," Natalie said. "I want to barge into Mr. Phillips's office and tell him what I think of him."

The image of an enraged Natalie bursting in on the senior partner and chewing him out made Amy smile.

"You're the least likely person on the planet to do something like that," Amy said.

"You don't know what's burning in here." Natalie pointed to her chest.

"Douse it with a frothy cappuccino," Amy replied. "Let's get something to drink."

Sitting with Natalie and sipping a coffee brought a sense of normalcy back to Amy.

"The past few months have been a roller coaster," she said. "And I still don't know where I'll end up."

"How did Jeff react to the news?"

"Better than I could have written in a book. He's come a long way. But I can't leave him hanging. I'm going to have to figure out what to do that will bring in some income. And do it soon."

"Do you have any ideas?"

"Not yet. I'm going to call Bernie Masters and find out if he's really kicking me to the curb." Amy paused. "I don't want to look for another legal job, although I'm sure Ms. Kirkpatrick will give me a good reference. On the other hand, Mr. Phillips —" She stopped.

"Go ahead."

Amy told Natalie about her meeting with the office administrator. Natalie gritted her teeth.

"How cowardly! Mr. Phillips is supposed to be this super lawyer who intimidates everyone in court, but he's afraid to admit what he did to you."

Amy nudged Natalie's cup with her finger. "Quick, take another sip. I see flames behind your eyes."

Amy gently directed the conversation onto topics she and Natalie would have covered during a routine get-together.

"Oh, Luke is putting together a mock-up of our book with my illustrations and your text," Natalie said after they finished talking about their children.

"When can I see it?"

"In a few days. I'll call as soon as it's ready."

An hour later Amy arrived home to an empty house. For months she'd been living life at one hundred miles per hour, and the shock of slamming on the brakes made the house seem eerily quiet. She changed into casual clothes and went upstairs to the writing room. Before turning on her computer, she called Bernie. He didn't answer, so she left a message on his voice mail.

Amy stared out the window. Spring had arrived in full splendor in Cross Plains. In nature it was a time of new beginnings. What that meant for Amy was much less clear than for the flowers blooming in her neighbor's yard across the street. She turned on her computer and opened the file for her personal journal. It had been weeks since she'd written anything. There was a lot to add.

The next two days passed without a word from Bernie. He didn't even contact her when he received his portion of the modest advance for *The Everlasting Arms.* Thursday evening Amy presented the check to Jeff after cooking him one of his favorite suppers.

"I want you to put all of it in our account to pay bills," she said.

Jeff hesitated. "But you should use some of

it for yourself."

"No," Amy responded emphatically. "All of it in the joint account. How many months will this buy us?"

Jeff wrinkled his nose. "Uh, about three. Have you been down to the unemployment office to sign up for benefits?"

"I called today. It won't be much since I was out of work for a year and a half before going back, and there will be a penalty if the law firm files a response that I was discharged for cause."

"Ms. Kirkpatrick didn't —"

"Those sorts of things are discussed by the partners," Amy said. "I know because that's how it was handled in the past when someone was fired."

Amy was surprised how tired she was. The emotional strain of the past weeks and months had taken a toll. That night she fell asleep as soon as her head touched the pillow.

And she went to the living room.

Never before had she felt more like royalty. Nothing about the simple surroundings spoke of pomp and circumstance, but she was enveloped in a regal robe of affirmation. Unworthiness and reminders of failure shrank back. Amy's value was unshakable, minted in coin that couldn't be stolen and would never lose its luster.

She remembered again the verse from Song

of Songs that had been an anchor to her timid, teenage soul — *He brought me to the banqueting house, and his banner over me was love.* God's truth never changes; it isn't dependent on life's circumstances. Amy's seat at the table of the King had her name engraved on it.

When she woke up, Amy lay peacefully on her back, a seed of invisible faith for the future planted in her heart.

All day Friday Amy moved throughout the empty house with a song in her heart. She went to the grocery store and smiled at strangers. When she thought about Mr. Phillips or the law firm, the sting of hurt was gone. She was filled with an inexpressible joy. Ian noticed something was different shortly after she picked him up from school.

"Mom, you seem happy," he said.

"I am."

Ian seemed satisfied. A child's mind doesn't always require a reason for happiness. It can simply be a state of mind.

The party for Megan at Mr. Ryan's townhome was scheduled to begin at 7:00 p.m. Megan ate a light snack for supper.

"There's going to be food at Mr. Ryan's place," she said. "And I want to be able to try everything."

"Who's fixing it?" Amy asked.

"He is."

"What is he going to cook?" Jeff asked,

looking up from a plate of chicken divan with macaroni and cheese.

"He asked Bethany what I liked for dessert, and she told him."

"Brownies," Ian replied with his mouth full.

"Bethany told him I liked bananas Foster crepes."

"When did you eat one of those?" Amy asked.

"I haven't, but I think I'd love it."

"I hope he doesn't burn the house down."

"I didn't know bananas burn," Ian said.

"They do when you pour liquor on them," Jeff answered.

Ian's eyes widened. "You're going to let Megan drink?"

"No," Amy responded quickly. "The alcohol evaporates in the cooking process."

Ian looked skeptical.

"I'll find a video on the Internet after supper and show you how it works," Jeff said. "Then you can impress Bobby."

"Bobby loves starting fires."

Amy drove Megan to the party. To her relief, Megan was wearing blue jeans and a modest top.

"How many people are going to be there?" Amy asked.

"I'm not sure. That's part of my surprise. Everybody else gets there at seven thirty."

Amy parked in front of Mr. Ryan's townhome and waited until the teacher opened the door for Megan. He saw Amy and waved.

Leaving the parking lot for the complex, Amy remembered that she'd not cleaned out the bottom drawer of her desk at the office. The drawer was where Amy kept an extra makeup kit in case she needed to perform a touchup during the day.

The law firm parking lot was empty. Amy parked behind the office, entered the security code, and went inside. She felt no regrets as she made her way past the reception area and glanced into Mr. Phillips's office. Everything was neatly put away for the weekend. She wondered who'd done it.

Going into her office, she opened the bottom drawer of the desk. On top of her makeup kit was the ultrasound image of Emily's baby. Amy didn't feel any resentment against Emily. She had gladly prayed for her successful pregnancy and delivery of a healthy baby, which had come to pass. Maybe she needed the job more than Amy did.

On the edge of the desk was the information she printed out while researching Dr. Lawrence Kelly and Beverly Jackson. Amy flipped through the data. She had been so wrong, especially about the doctor. Why she had such a strong negative reaction to his name when she heard it in the living room would remain an unsolved mystery. She straightened the papers so she could feed them into the shredder in the copy room. On the bottom of the stack was the page she'd printed out about Lawrence Kelly, the criminal. Amy read it again and shuddered slightly; however, a nagging curiosity about the man lingered in the back of her mind.

She turned on her computer and waited for the CPU to boot up. At the password prompt, she hesitated, wondering if Ms. Kirkpatrick had already changed the password, a common procedure when an employee left the firm for any reason. Amy typed the combination of Jeff's middle name and Megan's birthday. It was accepted.

Glancing over her shoulder, she logged on to the personal database and entered the information she'd previously found about the other Lawrence Kelly. A new screen popped up. As she read the information, Amy shuddered again. If nothing else, she needed to pray that this man never hurt another person. A prompt directed her to a police mug shot. It took a few seconds for the photo to load. When it did and came into focus, Amy froze.

It was Greg Ryan.

The teacher was a few years younger, and his hair was dark, not blond. Her hands shaking, Amy pressed the Print button. She didn't want to make a mistake. The page snaked out of the machine, and she inspected it closely. There was no denying the eyes. And they revealed a depth of darkness previously hidden in all contact she'd had with him.

Amy dashed out of the office, knocking over a stack of files on the corner of her desk and tipping over a flower arrangement on a small table. She managed to get her phone out of her purse and desperately tried to call Jeff while pressing the handle for the front door. Instead of placing a call, she dropped her phone and the battery popped out. It took several agonizing seconds for her to reassemble the phone and call again. He answered as she ran around the side of the building.

"Jeff," she said, finding it hard to breathe. "Go get Megan! Now!"

"What?"

"Get her!" Amy screamed.

"What's happened?"

Amy took a couple of deep breaths and managed to tell him what she'd found.

"Are you sure?"

"Yes!"

"I'm on my way," Jeff said. "Call the police."

Amy dialed 911. A woman answered the phone.

"Police, fire, or medic?" she asked in an even cadence.

"Police!" Amy shouted.

"What seems to be the problem?"

Amy was in the midst of a full-blown panic attack and was unable to coherently communicate. The words and phrases she spit out only produced more questions from the operator. Her heart was pounding out of her chest.

"Where are you, ma'am?" the woman finally asked.

"Uh, uh," Amy stuttered, then gave the location of the townhome where Ryan lived.

"I'll ask a patrol car to check it out. Can I reach you at this number?"

"Yes."

Amy turned on the car's engine and gripped the steering wheel. She had to get to Megan. Forcing herself to breathe and concentrate, she retraced her route to the townhome. As soon as she turned into the complex, a pickup truck blew past her on the right. It was Jeff. Amy followed him to the rear unit where Ryan lived. When she got there, Jeff was out of his truck and heading up the sidewalk. Amy ran after him and reached him on the landing.

"The police are coming," Amy panted.

"I'm not waiting," Jeff said, his face set like flint.

He tried the knob. It was locked. He banged on the door with his fist. There was no answer. A couple of seconds passed. He banged harder.

"That's it," he said.

Jeff raised his thick leg in the air and slammed the full force of his work boot against the door beside the lock. The flimsy molding splintered. He kicked it again, and the door burst open.

THIRTY-NINE

Jeff charged into the townhome. From the landing Amy saw him collide with Ryan, who was coming around the corner from the hallway that led to his bedroom.

"Where is she?" Jeff roared.

"Are you crazy?" Ryan responded, pushing Jeff away.

"Lawrence Kelly!" Amy called out.

Ryan looked past Jeff and saw Amy.

"What are you talking about?" he asked.

Jeff grabbed Ryan by the shirt and shook him.

"Where's Megan?"

"I think she's in the kitchen." Ryan knocked away Jeff's hands.

Amy rushed past the two men, through the living area, and into the kitchen. Megan was sitting on the floor with her head leaning against a cabinet. She was wearing what she'd had on when she left the house. Her eyes were closed.

"Jeff!" Amy called out.

In a few seconds Jeff was beside her as Amy knelt on the floor in front of Megan. Her hands trembling, Amy held Megan's face.

"Megan, can you hear me?"

Megan's head flopped to the side.

"Call an ambulance!" Amy yelled at Jeff.

Before Jeff could make the call, they heard the sound of an approaching siren.

"It's the police," Amy said. "Get them. I'll stay here with her."

Jeff left, and Amy gently laid Megan's head in her lap. Megan groaned. It was one of the sweetest sounds Amy had ever heard. Amy stroked her cheek.

"I'm here," she said softly.

Jeff returned.

"Where is Ryan?" Amy asked.

"I don't know. He ran out of the house."

Seconds later a young police officer came into the room.

"We need an ambulance," Amy said to the officer. "She's been drugged."

The officer knelt on the floor and checked Megan's eyes. Her pupils were dilated. He grabbed his radio and called for an ambulance.

"What happened here?" the officer asked.

"You tell him," Amy said to Jeff. "I'm not leaving Megan. The information about Ryan is in my car."

Thirty minutes later Megan was lying on

clean sheets in the emergency room of the hospital. The nurse who took a blood sample from Megan's arm paged Dr. Simmons. Amy, wringing her hands, sat beside Megan, watching every twitch of her daughter's face. Jeff had not yet arrived at the hospital. Megan's eyes fluttered open.

"Wh-what?" she mumbled.

"Don't try to talk. Rest."

Jeff rushed into the room.

"How is she?" he asked.

"Starting to wake up."

"Has anyone examined her?"

"Just her vital signs, but I can't see anything physically wrong. Dr. Simmons is on his way."

"If he hurt her —" Jeff started, then stopped.

Amy looked up in her husband's face. "I'm going to believe we got there in time."

Jeff grabbed a chair and placed it beside Megan's head. He leaned over close to her face.

"Honey," he said softly. "It's me."

Megan's eyes fluttered open again as she tried to focus.

"Hey, Dad," she croaked.

A solitary tear escaped from the corner of Amy's right eye and rolled down her cheek.

It was midnight when Megan was released from the hospital. By that point, she'd had two bottles of water and a glass of orange juice. Amy and a nurse helped her get into a wheelchair.

"I don't know why I wanted orange juice," Megan said, licking her lips.

"It's what your body craved," Amy replied.

"Did it have something to do with what Mr. Ryan gave me?"

"I have no idea," Amy replied.

Amy rolled Megan to the ER exit where Jeff waited with his truck. They stopped as he pulled up closer. Amy stepped forward to help Megan out of the chair.

"I can do it," she said, standing up.

Amy kept her hand on Megan's elbow. Jeff opened the truck door. Megan turned to Amy.

"Thanks, Mom," she said.

Amy's lower lip trembled. She'd only shed one tear but knew there was a dam waiting to break at any moment. She nodded.

"And you, too, Dad." Megan looked at Jeff, who leaned over and wrapped her in a massive bear hug.

Megan sat in the middle as they drove home. Amy didn't like to ride in Jeff's truck because the suspension was too stiff. Tonight, with Megan safely between them, it was the best ride of her life.

The following morning there was an article on the bottom of the front page of the local newspaper about Greg Ryan/Lawrence Kelly. "Local Teacher Arrested" read the headline, and beneath it was the mug shot from California along with one taken at the local jail where Ryan was taken after the police found him hiding in the woods behind his townhome. Thankfully, there was no mention of Megan or the Clarke family. The article didn't provide a lot of details, simply stating the matter was "under investigation." Megan awoke feeling slightly groggy but perked up after eating the big breakfast Jeff prepared for the family. The house phone rang, and Amy answered. It was Dr. Simmons.

"Megan's blood work came back," he said. "She'd been given the drug Rohypnol, commonly called a roofie. Once it's out of her system, she should be okay."

"Was there any evidence of —" Amy paused, not wanting to finish the question.

"No sign of actual physical abuse," Dr. Simmons said. "I called a detective I know at the police department. Ryan denies he knows anything about Lawrence Kelly and asked for a lawyer. They took his fingerprints, of course, and should be able to confirm his identity by Monday or Tuesday. They found Rohypnol in Ryan's townhome and confiscated three computers."

Amy closed her eyes. She could only hope nothing about Megan would turn up on the Internet. She looked across the room at her daughter, who was watching her with wide-eyed innocence. Amy tried to give her a reassuring smile.

"I'm glad she's going to be okay," Amy said. "She just finished eating eggs, bacon, and toast for breakfast."

"And coffee," Ian added.

"That's good," the doctor said. "Schedule an appointment for her at my office later in the week. I want to keep a close eye on her for a while."

"I will. Thanks so much for calling."

Amy hung up the phone.

"Ian, go outside, please," she said.

"No," he replied. "I want to hear."

"Outside!" Jeff commanded in the voice that left no room for debate.

Ian grudgingly got up from the table and shuffled out of the room. Amy waited until she heard the door close before telling Jeff and Megan what Dr. Simmons said. Megan's eyes widened.

"Will I have to go to court or something?" she asked.

"Maybe. We'll have to wait and see."

Amy's cell phone vibrated. It was an unknown caller.

"I don't know who it is," she said.

"Take it," Jeff said. "I want to talk to Megan alone in the family room."

Amy answered the call.

"Amy, it's Chris Lance. I came to work this morning and went by your office looking for a file. It looks like a tornado hit in here."

"I was there last night."
"Just because you were fired doesn't give you the right to trash —"
"Have you seen the local paper?"
"No."
Amy told him what happened. When she mentioned Lawrence Kelly, he interrupted her.
"Wait. You're not talking about the doctor."
"No, no. This man was one of my daughter's teachers. I heard the name in a dream and thought it was Dr. Kelly. I was wrong."
Chris was silent for a moment.
"But you were also right," he said.
Tears suddenly flooded Amy's eyes.
"Yes, I was."
"Mr. Phillips needs to know about this," Chris continued. "He's made a huge mistake. Once he realizes what happened and how your dream —"
Tears rolled off Amy's cheeks onto the kitchen floor. She shook her head.
"Not now," she interrupted. "We'll talk later."
"Are you crying?"
"Yes."
"I'm sorry." Chris paused. "Is your daughter okay?"
More tears cascaded down Amy's face.
"Yes."
"Whew! I'm glad to hear that."
"Please don't say —"

"I won't," Chris responded immediately. "But is it okay if I tell Laura? She's super upset that you got fired."

The fact that a woman she'd never met cared about what had happened to her caused another wave of emotion to roll over Amy.

"Yeah, that would be fine," she said.

"Bye."

Amy sat at the kitchen table, put her head in her hands, and sobbed. Megan was going to be okay. A deeper tragedy that would have horribly scarred her daughter for the rest of her life had been avoided.

Because of a dream.

Amy dabbed her eyes with a handful of tissues and left the kitchen. Jeff and Megan were sitting on the green couch. Amy headed toward the stairs.

"Mom, what's wrong?" Megan asked.

"It — it hit me," Amy said, sniffling. "All at once."

She continued up the stairs, not stopping until she was in the writing room. She collapsed in her chair and buried her face in her hands. Time passed. Finally, she raised her eyes, her vision blurry. She wiped her eyes. Her chest stopped heaving. There was no more water behind the dam. The lake of anxiety and relief had been drained. A moment later she heard footsteps on the narrow stairway leading up to the attic. There was a gentle knock on the closed door.

"Come in," Amy responded.

The door slowly opened. It was Natalie.

"I should have called," she began. "But I couldn't wait to be with you."

"Good timing," Amy said. "I'm all cried out for now. We can sit and talk without a bucket nearby to catch my tears."

Amy was able to share the events of the past twenty-four hours. Natalie, whose dam still held a lot of water, listened, nodded, and cried.

"I know every disaster in life can't be avoided," Amy said when she finished. "Terrible things happen to good people every day. But what hit me after breakfast this morning was not how bad this was, but how good God was to keep it from being worse."

"Yeah, that probably happens more than any of us realize," Natalie said and smiled slightly. "You know, you sound like Ms. Burris."

"Oh." Amy's eyes brightened. "I went by to see her after I was fired. Let me tell you the rest of the story about her and Sonny Dominick."

Follow-up articles in the newspaper confirmed Greg Ryan as an alias used by Lawrence Kelly. Because of her age, Megan's name wasn't printed, but an ongoing investigation by the police confirmed that more girls were affected by the scandal. Molly Prichard and two girls in the eleventh grade came forward with stories consistent with being drugged by the teacher. Tragically, Kelly sold pictures of the girls that were posted in dark corners of the Internet. The photos would be evidence at Kelly's trial if he refused to plead guilty. The deeds of darkness would be brought to light.

Students and staff at the high school and people from the community rallied around the victims in an overwhelming outpouring of sympathy and support. When evil raised its head, good people rose up, too.

Chris Lance called Amy twice more to check on her. There was a tenderness in the young lawyer's voice that signaled a change in his heart.

"Oh, and it doesn't look good for Natasha in the Dominick case," Chris said toward the end of the second call. "The treating neurologist refused to completely disagree with Dr. Kelly, so Mr. Phillips is going to meet with the lawyers for Mr. Dominick's children and begin settlement negotiations. They may even toss a decent bone to the illegitimate children once paternity is established."

"You shouldn't be telling me about this. I no longer work at the firm."

"But you're still bound by the rules of confidentiality for what you do know." Chris paused. "And I thought maybe you could pray that it will work out. There's plenty of money for everyone."

"It's not always about winning."

"No, it's not."

Midweek Amy went to see Ms. Burris. They walked into the sunroom. The spring birds were thick around the multiple feeders in an explosion of color.

"Thanks for inviting me," Amy said as soon as they were seated.

"You're special," Ms. Burris replied. "To the Lord and to me."

The elderly woman's words made Amy think about the trip to the living room where she heard again about her place at God's banqueting table. She told Ms. Burris about it.

"The following day I was so happy. Then the situation with Megan blew up our world more than anything else could have."

She told Ms. Burris about the photographs, a fact left out of the newspaper articles. The older woman shook her head sadly.

"The timing of it all makes me wonder."

"Maybe you needed the dream before Megan's ordeal," Ms. Burris said, wiping her eyes with a tissue.

"Why?"

"So you could face it with strength and faith because of what you'd heard from the Lord."

"I don't think so," Amy said doubtfully. "I was in total panic mode."

"In your mind and emotions," Ms. Burris replied, then pointed to Amy's heart. "But not in there."

Amy started to object but stopped. Scenes from the law office and the hospital flashed through her mind. She'd not recognized it at the time, but within her spirit was a seed of confidence in God's goodness. Hidden, she'd not acknowledged it.

"You may be right," Amy admitted. "But I wish I'd known about it."

"Next time you will."

"Will there be a next time?"

"There always is, and we're going to start talking to the Lord about it in advance."

Ms. Burris bowed her head and began to pray.

Driving home from Ms. Burris's house, Amy felt encouraged. Her phone vibrated. It was Bernie Masters.

"Have you been praying for me?" the agent asked as soon as Amy answered.

"Uh, no. I've been receiving prayer myself."

"You should have included me, but I got through the operation okay without your help. A doctor who looked about sixteen years old put stents in a couple of places where some hot dogs with chili, onions, and mustard piled on them got stuck in my arteries. He wants me to give up hot dogs, but I can't do it. Instead, I'm going to cut back to mustard only."

"Maybe you should switch to tofu dogs. I didn't know you were sick."

"What? I told my niece to call all my clients. That's what you get when you don't pay someone who's working for you. Speaking of payment, did you get that monstrous check from the publisher for *The Everlasting Arms*?"

"Yes, and it came at a good time. I lost my job at the law firm."

"Don't tell me the details unless you need a shoulder to cry on," he said.

"I'm all cried out."

"Good, then get back to work as a writer. Dave Coley has been bumped up the ladder at the publishing company. They've given him one of those jobs with a fancy title, but all he'll do is go to meetings and listen to other people who are actually doing the work. Anyway, Cecilia called, and she wants to talk about the *Deeds of Deception* book."

"It's *Deeds of Darkness.*"

"Okay, but you know the title may change. The publishers like to control that stuff. Cecilia looked at your proposal and wants to know if you're willing to do something with the main character that shows how God can be with someone in the midst of a horrible tragedy. She thinks you're a fantastic talent and wants to keep on working with you. If you'll consider her suggestions, she thinks there's a shot they might want to exercise the option. Basically, she wants you to up the God factor a few notches."

"I can do that. I know exactly what surviving a tragedy feels like."

"Don't we all? Put something together and get it to me while the iron is in the fire. They haven't named Dave's replacement, which gives Cecilia a window of opportunity to do something on her own before another bean counter takes over."

"Will the end of the week be soon enough?"

"Tomorrow would be better, but if that's the best you can do, I'll have to take it."

Amy turned into her neighborhood. Natalie's street was on her left.

"Also, I've cowritten a children's book with a friend of mine who's an artist," she said. "Would you be interested in taking a look at it?"

"A kids' book? There's not much money in those unless you go heavy with the horror stuff. I don't know why, but kids like to be scared out of their heads right before they go to sleep. Or maybe it's the parents who —"

"This is about three children on a long summer vacation at the beach," Amy interrupted. "The watercolor illustrations are fantastic."

"Hmm," Bernie replied. "Sounds old-fashioned, but that can be a way to pitch it.

Send it along, and I'll take a look. I have a buddy who has a few contacts in that market. He'd split the agent fee with me, and I need the revenue. These heart doctors complain a lot, but they make tons of money."

"I'm glad you survived your surgery."

"Yeah, me, too. I still can't believe my niece dropped the ball. I'm going to have to call everyone I know. Bye."

Amy smiled as she placed the phone on the passenger seat of the car. She no longer felt like an orphan.

That evening she went upstairs from the family room later than usual and noticed that Megan's light was still on. It was a school night, and Megan should have already gone to sleep. Her door was closed, and Amy knocked.

"Come in."

Megan was sitting in the middle of her bed with her laptop beside her.

"What's going on?" Amy asked. "It's late."

"I met with Ms. Robbins today, and she suggested I start keeping a journal of my thoughts and feelings."

"That's a good idea."

"It's private," Megan added quickly.

"I understand. For years I've kept a journal that no one sees, not even your dad."

"Is it on your laptop in the writing room?"

"Yes, and you don't know my password."

"You always use something with my birthday in it and Dad or Ian's name."

"And I'm going to change the password tomorrow." Amy smiled.

"To Ian's birthday?"

"Or something so strange and bizarre that no one can guess it."

Megan looked down at her computer screen.

"Something strange happened to me," she said. "And I think I should talk to you about it."

Amy's heart sank. She had valiantly fought against the fear of darker disclosures but knew this moment might come. She grasped the seed of faith within her heart and sat down on the edge of Megan's bed.

"I'm listening."

Megan lowered the screen of the laptop.

"It's hard to describe," Megan said. "But I think you'll understand better than anybody in the world."

"I'll try," Amy said, hardly daring to breathe.

Megan looked up into Amy's eyes. But instead of a wound, Amy saw wonder. Megan spoke slowly and with deep conviction.

"Last night I had a dream that was different from any other dream I've had in my entire life. Mom, it was so real, more real than us sitting here. And in the dream, I went to a place . . ."

READING GROUP GUIDE

1. Why do you think Amy's mother didn't want her to tell anyone about her dreams? What effect did that have on Amy as she grew into the woman she is? How do you think Amy's life would have been different if her mother encouraged and supported her?
2. "If their dilemma had taken place in one of her books, they would have engaged in a heart-felt discussion about their unwavering love for each other and trust in God's faithfulness. But life doesn't always imitate art." Do you agree with what Amy thinks here after a hard discussion with Jeff about finances? How do our choices of what to read and watch influence our real lives and relationships?
3. Amy's life as an author isn't exactly what she was expecting, and the realities of life forced her back to her old job. Was there anything she could have done to maintain her freedom as a writer without a day job?

Have you ever struggled with the same dilemma: dream vs. reality?

4. When Amy told Natalie about the dream she had where Noah was injured on a field trip, she almost couldn't help herself from blurting out what she saw, then immediately wished she could take the words back. Have you ever had that same uncontrollable urge to say something to someone? How did it turn out for you and the recipient of your message? Why do you think Amy regretted speaking up? How would the course of the novel have changed had she kept her dream to herself?
5. Jeff says, "It's important for Megan to know her father cares about what she does, where she goes, and who she hangs out with." Describe the relationship between Jeff and Megan. How is it different from Amy's relationship with Megan? How do those relationships change over the course of the novel?
6. While Amy's visions from the living room inspired her first two novels, they hadn't really transferred to her everyday life until her vision about Noah. Why do you think they started changing and becoming more and more important?
7. After Amy shared the synopsis of *Deeds of Darkness* with Ms. Burris and Natalie, she felt deflated by their reaction. Why do you think they weren't enthusiastic about it?

Have you ever left a meeting with a friend feeling the same way? After time had passed, did your feelings change?

8. Amy received visions and warnings about her friend's family and clients at work, but when it came to her own family, she had no explicit warnings about the dangers facing them. Why do you think she didn't have visions about Ian's four-wheeler accident or Megan's ordeal?
9. When Megan started showing signs that something was wrong — sleeping so deeply that she didn't hear her parents knock — what did you think was the cause? Did you think Amy and Jeff responded well? How would you have reacted in their situation? Were you surprised by the cause of her strange behavior?
10. Did you learn something new about the life of an author or the publishing industry from reading *The Living Room*? What surprised you the most? Do you think all authors are like Amy and have similar experiences?

ACKNOWLEDGMENTS

Thanks to Allen Arnold and Natalie Hanemann for encouraging me to write about a novelist. Special appreciation to my wife, Kathy, for protecting my creative time. And thanks to Daisy Hutton, Ami McConnell, and Deborah Wiseman for shepherding this book to completion.

ABOUT THE AUTHOR

Robert Whitlow is the best-selling author of legal novels set in the South and winner of the Christy Award for Contemporary Fiction. He received his JD with honors from the University of Georgia School of Law where he served on the staff of the *Georgia Law Review.*

The employees of Thorndike Press hope you have enjoyed this Large Print book. All our Thorndike, Wheeler, and Kennebec Large Print titles are designed for easy reading, and all our books are made to last. Other Thorndike Press Large Print books are available at your library, through selected bookstores, or directly from us.

For information about titles, please call:
(800) 223-1244

or visit our Web site at:
http://gale.cengage.com/thorndike

To share your comments, please write:
Publisher
Thorndike Press
10 Water St., Suite 310
Waterville, ME 04901